BOOKS BY STANLEY STEWART

The Enclosed Garden
The Expanded Voice
The King James Version

THE
KING JAMES
VERSION

Stanley Stewart

THE KING JAMES VERSION

A Novel

Random House New York

Library of Congress Cataloging in Publication Data

Stewart, Stanley N
The King James version

I. Title
PZ4.S8533Ki [PS3569.T473] 813'.5'4 76–14194
ISBN 0–394–40042–9

Manufactured in the United States of America

First Edition

To Vahan

"He that is not a philosopher governs by guess, and will prove a dangerous statesman; for when uncontrolled affections meet with high fortune, they commonly begin tyranny and oppression."

—James I,
Proverbs and Aphorisms

THE
KING JAMES
VERSION

1

King James I of England farted. As always, he tried to stifle the sound; he was afflicted with an almost permanent flatulence, induced, he had no doubt, by his fondness for dark ale. Now he stretched luxuriously, and opened his eyes to regard his early visitors with slim enthusiasm. As if the effort required more than his present strength, he rolled over on his back and fixed an indifferent eye on the coffered ceiling of the royal bedchamber. He had only recently had his quarters redone, but the outcome of all the conferences and inconvenience he found increasingly depressing. He was not sure which was worse: the apparent disappearance from England of proper artistic sensibility, or the threatened collapse of the King's treasury.

"Someone must attend to these wretched murals," he said. "Is this any scene to greet a monarch's eye, straightaway, in the morning?"

The visitors soberly observed the ceiling panels: nymphs and satyrs prancing on a lawn, while others made love—rather awkwardly, it seemed—on a shaded but quite rocky hillside.

"Are there no artists left in England?" James said. "Either our Mr. Peake never learned to paint, or he's never tried to get a piece of mutton to stay put with a boulder between her shoulder blades."

The King's witticism was lost on no one; Sir George Peake was known as a man who would not be likely to know or care what to do with a naked woman under intimate circumstances on a hill or anyplace else.

James smiled; he was pleased with himself. He loved to exploit the gruffer side of his Scots background, especially when Prince Henry was around. James considered his older son plain stuffy, and now he watched him out of the corner of his eye for some response. On this particular occasion the joke at Mr. Peake's expense had a double edge, for James had heard, only the day before, that the Prince of Wales had retained Peake's services to do a large mural. The subject of the painting James thought singularly crude: Prince Henry, mounted on a horse, accompanied by his closest friend, Sir John Harington. They were to pose as if ready for the hunt. Passing curious, since Henry had little time for the hunt. The Puritans were growing restless with aristocratic pictorial matter, so the expense would not be likely to net the royal family any friends on that side. And besides, the choice of artists was just a bit shy of being an insult to James: not only was Peake something of the court hack portrait painter, but Henry had not even asked James for his advice in making the selection.

"And what, my Prince," the King said, "is your august opinion of this arcadian scene?"

"That would depend, sire," Henry said, "upon what use is to be made of these rooms. I mean, sire, that the work was done with the thought in mind of your relinquishing this apartment for larger quarters at St. James."

Hmmm. Well, that was true enough, but this morning he was in no mood to let the Prince off so easily. "Perhaps so, but are you advancing some low and practical philosophy of art? Or do you mean to criticize your pater's choice of artist?"

"Not in the least, sire. That is neither my intention nor my right."

"Oh, God," James said, "spare us from political philosophy before tea!"

Throwing back the satin quilt, he moved friskily from his canopied bed, taking pains to swat his Gentleman of the Bedchamber on the behind. The gesture was broad as a hurry-whore's, intended further to nettle the Prince of Wales. It was clear to James why Henry had come to see him, and though he felt cheerful this morning, it was true that he was slightly piqued at Henry's brashness. But there would be time to deal with that. Now he wanted to enjoy the crisp morning sun. The drapes had been drawn, and the light of a fine April day spilled into the room.

James's apartment in Whitehall overlooked the Thames, and was just above the wide terrace where curving stone stairs led to the barges. Already the watermen were hauling goods up from the wharf.

4

James found the scene especially attractive this morning: he watched the fishing boats scud along, midstream, toward Greenwich. The river shone like glass from the low, slant rays of the sun. It was so peaceful that for a moment James felt an urge to dress, to stroll down to the barges, to have his watermen row him down the Thames—perhaps to the Tower. On mornings like this, one's generosity could get the best of him. James knew a visit to the Tower was unthinkable at this time. The most unforgivable cruelty was to raise the hope of life in one so probably doomed. At the moment, too many questions needed to be answered as far as Arabella's fate was concerned. He knew that her life hung less on his warm feelings toward her than on the shape of political events which not even he could control.

Still, for a moment, his cousin's childlike, hauntingly innocent face floated before him, and he imagined himself arriving at the Tower, the people scurrying, the excitement, and then—yes, then to be able to tell her that her long wait was over. What a desperately insane world it was, that required the imprisonment of such a fragile woman.

"Tea," he rasped, turning from the window. There was no point in pondering the imponderable. He couldn't control events. If he had learned anything in his experience, it was this fact. Even kings—perhaps especially kings—were the victims, not the makers, of events. "And a finger of rum in it to soothe the ruffled edges," he added.

Ordinarily, James resisted the temptation to drink in the morning. To him, it seemed like giving up. And the day seemed so bright! But there was Henry, his lips sternly pursed, waiting to quarrel with him. And already, beyond the door of his bedchamber, twenty or more men were waiting, strung out through the court, men whom he must see today. Each required something of him; each wanted something. They all had needs. Above them all in his mind there was always the unspoken, haunting request—from Arabella—for the simplest gift of all. The most awful power was that to take life.

He had kept his son, proud Henry Stuart, waiting long enough. After his first sip of tea, laced with the dark and heady rum that he loved, he spoke abruptly.

"I am aware of your disappointment, Henry, but to a single post even a king may appoint but one man at a time."

That was all he said. He let the words ring in silence. It was Henry's turn to speak.

"Sire," Henry said finally, "I cannot overstate how much this appointment means to me. And to the Queen."

So, that was to be his tack. He would simply ignore James's implied statement that the matter had been decided. And was the pointed remark about the Queen meant as a threat? James had no illusions on this point. Anne had her own interests. She was a beautiful woman, but a shrewd one withal, not only in this matter but in general. At court, she had worked her way into a position of power by playing the Howard faction off against the Pembrokes. A clever woman, no doubt about it. James sipped his tea and waited.

"Sire," Henry said, "mine is a modest request. It is, I believe, not a great position of state, by any means. And I have never presumed to ask a favor of this kind before . . ."

This was true enough. But so what? To a king like James, Henry's tack was entirely wrong-headed. He didn't keep track of his benevolences with a mind toward evening everything out. What sense did it make to treat people equally? They differed in power and influence, and intelligent royal patronage mirrored those differences. To the weak, James dispensed charm and kindly advice. On the inconsequential but beautiful, he showered kingly affection. To the rich and powerful, well, to them he gave whatever he could not avoid giving.

James's theory was simply this: Give to the demanding, and let the self-sufficient and reticent take care of themselves. Ask and you shall receive, especially if you have the means to insist. A proper king simply couldn't ignore the repeated and loud request. When confronted by indignant demands, the court gave undue attention to them, looking, perhaps, askance at the Crown. In this instance, the king responded generously, and also loudly so that everyone would know the source of benefit. Machiavelli, one of the few thinkers of any value since antiquity, had convinced him on this point. It made absolutely no sense to do someone an anonymous favor. And if it happened that in his benevolence the king must deprive a subject of something he valued, then he must get someone else to appear the cause of that denial. Thus: Be generous with the other man's goods (unless it is clear that his impoverishment somehow weakens the Crown), and let all your acts of generosity be public ones. In this single axiom lay the basic principles of domestic statecraft, which was, after all, just that: a craft, an art, which is to say that its practice could be bungled.

He had made an exception to his own hard-and-fast principle by appointing Robert Carr as his Gentleman of the Bedchamber. But

Carr was, in his mind, merely that exception that proved the rule. When the king is forced to give, when he is under pressure from powerful and persistent factions contending for the same goal, then he has no choice but to avoid giving to any visible group or person. In such a case, he must give with absolute abandon to a party not even in contention—or, better still, to one with no possible claim upon the benefice.

Henry seemed to think his independence from his father should lend special weight to his request in the matter of this appointment. To act according to Henry's expectations, James must quite literally reverse his point of view. For if Henry, who found it hard to accept anything from James, could make a gift sound like an affront, what possible value could accrue to the giver?

Henry's tone had always implied that the King was not (as James had always insisted he was) the fountain of all benefits in the state. This was the problem. Obviously, it had philosophical as well as political implications. Henry did not detail his needs before the King, and thus disallowed him the opportunity to lavish his older son with public signs of favor, as any father longs to do. Henry did not even appear to enjoy the King's company (and this bothered James immensely). When the Prince of Wales said he had never asked such a favor before, his honesty came close to being rude.

"To say that you ask little," James said, "is to let go an understatement. Indeed, you ask nothing, either of your king or your father."

"Why then," Henry said with just an edge in his voice, "do you deny me this little I do ask?"

James laughed, but he was not at all sure that he had concealed his pique. Actually, he was more irritated with himself than with Henry. He had been silly to drop that little jibe; he had merely provided the Prince with an acceptable opening. What was more, he had let his own hurt feelings show, and this was a mistake. He had always found his older son prickly to talk to—not just distant but prickly. Henry seemed to dislike him, or, as seemed more accurate to James, to treat him with disdain, to make a show of his close relationship with his mother. But what bothered James most was that he knew he favored his younger son, Charles. He had tried to be fair, a good and just parent, but it was possible Henry's disdain was no more than a means of lashing out at a father who had, he felt, turned his back on him.

The two brothers could not have been more different. Henry was taller, of course, but not just because he was older. He had been long and thin at birth, and it seemed to James that he had always had a sickly, pinched look about him. Doctors were always fussing with him, whispering together and framing theories at the slightest touch of ague. When asked directly if there was anything wrong with Henry, and if so, what precisely, the doctors would fall silent, or protest that they were just considering all the possibilities of his symptoms. At court, Henry tended to hang back and let others do the talking; he often disappeared with one or two close friends to consume a few pints together in one of the seamier taverns near the Haymarket. James didn't know what to think of the rumors that Henry had been known to end occasional evenings by himself, demanding bed and breakfast at the well-stocked brothel in Knightsbridge. As for the long discussions over pints in Charing Cross, though the lad was often seen in the company of Inigo Jones, James couldn't imagine what Henry knew that was worth talking about. And—no doubt about it—this nettled the King, because Henry was possessed of an admirable self-assurance.

Perhaps others dismissed Henry's carriage as the easy accomplishment of one who, born to greatness, need merely exercise the simple virtue of staying alive. James knew better. Being heir to a throne was his life's story. And yet all his life he had felt a nagging sense of foreboding in him, deep down, a feeling of disquiet that he had never quite defined. He knew that others sensed this uneasiness in him. The court had grown used to his dependence on close advisers. Wiser heads around Whitehall were aware that he used these people for other than political purposes. James liked to have young, good-looking people around, especially young men. They provided emotional fuel, to keep him young, or at least feeling so, to make him cheerful, to assuage that dull but persistent unease.

The most powerful men at court knew James to be, in politics, shrewdly independent to the point of being secretive and unpredictable. Hence, he was dangerous to his friends as well as his foes. As for his enemies, he kept them few in number. If they became political liabilities, even his friends seemed to fall victims to misfortune, apt to die suddenly of undiagnosed ills. When news of a soaring fever in a friend reached his ears, James would rush his personal physicians to take charge. But even the best of medicine has its limits; royal physicians would watch helplessly as a recently healthy friend of the throne heaved up his insides in purple bile. Applying clysters and letting blood proved ineffective against the unswerving course of what was a virulent (and some suspected contagious, political) disease. While the silly cultivated James, playing on his pretended sentimentality, the wise hedged their bets, trimmed, and made their plans.

The wisest of these—canniest of the canny, slyest of the sly, virtually prescient with his network of spies—was Henry Howard, the Earl of Northampton. James tried never to underestimate this man; unsentimental himself, he seemed never to impute strong sentiments to the King. Not only did Northampton hedge and trim, he cultivated alliances and stockpiled weapons. (James was not without his own informants; spies, he had learned while still in Scotland, were not above receiving pay from more than one source.)

James felt a surge of anger at the thought of Northampton. He was the quiet, strong center of the Howard faction, whose money and power placed them beyond—almost beyond—the reach of the Crown. As long as the Howard faction flourished, the threat to Arabella was starkly real. She was, as his mother had been, a Catholic. And then there was the threat to his own neck. History had long insisted that having royalty in the Tower was a two-edged sword. His own mother had helped write the last bloody chapter to that homily on public order. Beware when someone in line to the succession can be seen as a religious figure for those out of power to rally round: heads may roll in any direction.

With all this obvious to James, and to most people at court, here was the Prince of Wales stupidly arguing for the preferment of yet another member of the Howard faction. If he made Harington his Gentleman of the Bedchamber, either Arabella would have to part with her head, or he himself would have to give up sleeping! This was nothing against Harington, who was a young man of good character. James liked him, and had, in fact, rewarded him well for his sometime custodianship (after the Gunpowder Plot) of Princess Elizabeth. In the last several years, however, he had fastened himself too closely to her, and therefore too closely to the Suffolk-Howard-Catholic party. Though perhaps harmless himself, he *was* Catholic; Arabella still lived, quickening hopes that she might replace James with a sovereign more friendly to Rome. The stakes in England were high; key men in the realm were prepared to gamble heavily. They awaited only the opportunity and a convenient tool. The latter need not be a willing one, just available: Harington was out.

"You must come let me teach you politics," James said sardonically, adding, "Without sound principles of government, how do you plan to keep your head so neatly on your shoulders? Not to mention my own dislike of the poniard in the ribs . . ."

Henry flushed very red. Clearly, he had seen the remark as a reflection on Harington's religious connections. James was sorry he had made it; soon the Queen would hear of it, and, of course, that meant long interviews with the Spanish Ambassador, and probably with Northampton. The tongue-clucking would start all over again. When would he learn to let others do the talking? He was angry with himself, but there was little he could do without making the innuendo even more pronounced.

"Sire," Henry was saying, "I know not what political advantage you can imagine you gain by denying me this appointment."

This was surely a direct insult. James was watching Henry closely now.

"You do but antagonize certain of your own court by advancing a . . ."

The Prince looked coolly at Robert Carr, who was moving about the room, doing his best, James thought, to ignore the references to him. Henry seemed at that moment on the verge of uttering one of his fatuously inflated threats: perhaps even to challenge the commoner to a duel. How impractical Henry was, and how much he had to learn before his head could ever fit a crown. How unlike his kinsman and predecessor, old Henry VIII, one of the greediest, most effective collectors of power since Julius Caesar.

Henry was impatient for recognition, perhaps even justifiably so. He wanted some evidence of his growing importance at court, and he had chosen—unwisely, as it happened—the issue of the present appointment as a test of wills with his father. Unfortunately for him, all the factions at court regarded the appointment as a sensitive one, critical to their own causes. A steady stream of advocates for one or another young man had visited the King. The Spanish party had made a case for the elevation of young Essex, then abroad, who had married Thomas Howard's second daughter, the fetching Frances (with whom James planned to become better acquainted). They made their case calmly, despite the fact the Essex had made himself a laughingstock. James bore witness that young Devereux survived his wedding night a virgin. Much embarrassed, the Howards packed him off with the army to France while trying to decide what to do about him. He was a tryingly dull young man, but as a tool of Suffolk and Northampton, he might prove useful to the Catholics. For who was better equipped to spy at court than one routinely admitted to the King's bedchamber? Nevertheless, James had the feeling that the Essex gambit was not taken seriously, even by Northampton.

As expected, the Pembroke-Bedford entourage had, with their usual aplomb, fielded a candidate. William Herbert, the Third Earl of Pembroke, the nephew of Sir Philip Sidney, was a generous patron of the arts. Rumor held that he shared more than his wealth with Will Shakespeare; the myserious "bad angel" of the *Sonnets* was, apparently, Mary Fitton, Herbert's attractive mistress (whom James himself had coveted). Lucy Russell, Countess of Bedford, joined with Pembroke to urge the appointment of the poet John Donne, who was becoming anxious for a place at court.

The idea appealed to James. Donne had remained curiously apolitical, and his selection might help mellow tough old Thomas Egerton, Lord Ellesmere; England's Lord Chancellor had always been fond of Donne. On the other hand, regardless of his attempts to disguise his Catholic background, Donne's family attachments were suspect. But at James's bidding, Donne had shown that his heart was in the right place by writing a scurrilous attack on St. Ignatius. Anyone who could put self-interest before conscience must be accounted promising by a thoughtful king. James toyed with the idea, thinking he might allay certain of Northampton's apprehensions without really increasing his power. But, at the last, James had decided that Donne was too valuable to waste in such a position. The right opportunity would come, and James would settle the matter of Donne's future.

Although the Howard faction put forward a name, Robert Howard, Suffolk's younger son, James felt that he was but a stalking horse for Harington, the Queen's candidate. The Haringtons were beholden to the Howards for several financial dealings that James knew about, and if Harington proved to be available to the Howards, even as an informer, well, that would do much to restrict the King's movements. Besides, almost any choice among the more visible parties would be strenuously scrutinized for its political implications. In choosing Robert Carr—this "newcomer," as the Prince called him—James had merely followed his instincts of self-preservation, which seemed to grow stronger hour by hour.

The court was in a tense mood. James sensed a new restlessness beneath the surface of things. The great show of gaiety: court masques, plays, the almost perpetual banquets and celebrations—ever since the Gunpowder Plot, the tone had changed, becoming almost too gay. The banquets were becoming drunken affairs, lasting sometimes for days. But, elsewhere, different symptoms showed another side of the same people. Thievery was rampant, especially on the outskirts of London. But even in the city, thieves and mountebanks preyed on the people with means, who in turn bled those with none. The English were suing each other in wildly increasing numbers, as if they enjoyed the prospect of each new court battle. Sometimes their king wondered if, soon, they would not require a barrister present every time an Englishman signed his name. It was clear to him, if not to anyone else: people were scared.

By a neutral appointment, James meant to damp things down. He would not turn over the realm to any ranting Anabaptist, nor would he return the Crown to Rome, but such were the fears of many. So, many were watching him closely, as if they expected him suddenly to hand away what he was trying with all his energies to hang on to: power. They were fanatics, of course. Religious fanatics, pure and simple. He knew he must deal with them, and deal with them shrewdly. They were everywhere. He had hoped that, after the Powder Plot, the tides of suspicion and intrigue would retreat, but that had been a futile hope. Not a week passed, now, without a denunciation of one of his magistrates; not a month went by without publication of some foul pamphlet, without a beating, or a stabbing, or a shooting. First a Catholic, then a Puritan. And so it went. And, always, everybody with God and righteousness on his side. Duels were fought on an almost regular basis, and James, for one, was surprised that no one thought to schedule them with a mind to selling tickets.

The best he could do was to encourage a permissive emphasis on the most responsible and apolitical of all vices: lust. He had Inigo Jones design gowns to show off bare bosoms, for around Whitehall plenty of opportunity was at hand for sexual explorations. James wanted it that way. It took people's minds off their suspicions and worries. But the religious fanatics seemed only to grow louder in their rantings, to see in this licentiousness one more reason for alarm.

Surely, in all this furor, someone had thought of doing away with him. *He* had thought of it. A knife in his ribs, and son Henry—or, more likely, the lovely Arabella—would ascend the throne, with the blessings of Rome. That would make the Catholics happy, and the Dissenters would experience no slighter portion of bliss, for it would confirm their suspicions while doing nothing to frustrate their yearnings for martyrdom.

"We must discuss art," James said abruptly.

Henry nodded.

"Have you strong opinions?"

"Of what matters, sire?" Henry said uneasily.

"Of murals," James said. "We must have your Mr. Peake's opinion of these ceiling panels. Will he consider recantation?"

Henry shifted uncomfortably. James suggested he bring his painter with them on the occasion of their next interview, which he hoped would be soon. He felt a tug of compassion as he caught Henry's look of frustration—angry, proud, yet still hurt. Sir John might be an ass, but Prince Henry fancied him and that made him important. A sad young man, Henry. If only there were some way to reach him, to get to know him.

When the door had closed behind Henry and his men, James noticed that Carr was immediately ill at ease. The King rather enjoyed such moments, and he regarded Carr unmercifully, eyes fixed in an attentive stare as if he expected his subject to deliver a momentous line. Although by no means an accomplished courtier, Carr had the good sense to remain silent. Staring down at the newly laid floor, he seemed to have acquired a sudden interest in the grain of its oaken squares.

"So you see," James said in his soft, rolling, theatrical tones, "part of your charge must be to protect my person from all unpleasantness before breakfast."

"Excuse me, Your Majesty," Carr fumbled, "but I . . ." He caught himself before protesting that he was but a commoner. "The Prince . . ."

"The Prince of Wales be damned," James said. "I must have my breakfast—and a spot of sherry afterwards—in peace. As for this

. . . timidity of yours, that can be a blessing or a blight. Take, for example, your egregious and unprecedented affront to Sir Ralph yesterday."

Carr was patently amazed that James had heard of the episode, and he seemed even more astonished at the King's jaunty attitude. "Your Majesty," he said, "I had thought not to mention that matter."

James laughed. "You astound me! You shall speak of that matter because I ask it! You are about the King's business when you put off such as Sir Ralph, who would see me." With a grand flourish, he strode forward and planted a deliberately wet kiss on Carr's cheek.

"Sire, I would have been pleased to admit him, as my Lord Cecil instructed. But Sir Ralph Winwood, I much regret, would offer me . . ."

James was amused. "You would accuse poor old Sir Ralph of trying to bribe you?"

"Sire, it does seem preposterous."

"Robert Carr," James said, "Robert, Robert. We must do something about your name. And your rank is embarrassing. We must do something about that, too. It depresses my Henry. So, you would vex the King with stolid honesty, as you stun his court with your charms." He draped himself into a chair and, after calling for his breakfast, continued in a tone of bemusement. "Sir Robert. I like it not. Too formal! What were you called as a sprout?"

Carr did not answer.

"Shyness," James persisted, "is a virtue to be admired in commoners. As for my close associates, they are all of them uncommonly immodest men. Moreover, they are generous for practical reasons. Why would you affront good old Sir Ralph, who only wanted to pack your empty purse with a few pounds? Next time someone offers you a . . . token of his appreciation for the benefits afforded him by the Crown, oblige him, or you'll die poor."

Carr nodded.

"Why d'you suppose Prince Henry wanted Sir John i' your place?" James let his rich Scottish burr come through. "Too much honesty, milad, would throw the court into bedlam. People must be allowed to expect ordinary behavior from men in office. Unless each person operates with a normal amount of greed, the state cannot function. You must let people be nice to you. By being nice to you, they are trying to express their love for me, which should be encouraged.

Furthermore, they feel sorry for me, since Parliament gives me no money. Such as Sir Ralph would share God's blessings with us, which shows him as good a Christian as an Englishman. Besides, he seeks release of lands held by the Crown as a result of his father's complicity in the Powder Treason."

Originally, James knew, Carr had thought of his appointment only as a chance to see the court from the inside, to listen and to learn the ways of the great. But James could almost see it dawning on Carr that he himself had power, that he was no longer the inconsequential Scottish page he once was. His appointment—even his acquaintance with the King—had come about by accident, as had so many other promising events in his life. But be that as it may, this latest turn of events had left him exposed in an entirely new way; he was simply not prepared to deal with titled people. To say no to his betters . . . well. James chuckled to himself. Carr had spent three years with the son of Lord Hay (presumably to improve his Latin, but actually to remove him from the clutches of the infamous, infuriating Thomas Overbury), but he had returned to England with precious few academic blandishments. James knew that Carr was learning how good fortune had delivered to him what a mastery of Latin might well have denied.

He kissed Carr again. "Does that offend you?" he said lightly. Clearly, it did. "Good," he said. "The King loves all his subjects, especially the pretty ones. And, philosophically, by loving his subjects, the King expresses his love of himself in his subjects: in me, you live and move and have your social being."

Carr looked thoughtful.

"Like you metaphysics?" James asked.

"I have little knowledge of it, sire."

"It is the purest science. And yet, at my universities, they shunt it off as archaic."

On this subject, Carr had overheard a learned opinion, which he admired. "Sire, if I may speak boldly, touching this matter . . ."

James nodded, only partially aware that Carr had said very little during what he considered the conversation.

"I have heard that the doctors at the universities ignore the statutes providing the studies deemed legal, and teach illegally, in violation of law."

"Yes?" said James, amused.

"Pardon, sire, but my father called me 'Robin' . . ."

For a moment James seemed to lose the thread of the conversation.

"Ay, Your Majesty," Carr explained, "Robin . . . my name as a sprout. I know not why, but I know that my father's opinion in such matters be just. He loved Elizabeth, the Queen, amighty. England can have but one monarch at a time, he would say, and so said until the matter of the Queen's sister—and your dear mother, no doubt, Your Majesty, and no offense, with your permission, sire." He broke off, apparently aware that he had acquired the all-too-critical-on-occasion close attention of his monarch.

James could see the perspiration suddenly appear through Carr's neatly trimmed mustache. After a thoughtful pause, he spoke. "I grasp your point. You urge me to deal firmly with these ragamuffin doctors and weaselly chancellors. But," he drawled, "if I do that, they but become more truculent and outrageous in their treason and Puritanism."

Now it was Carr's turn to look thoughtful; he remained silent.

"Robin," James said, shifting his tone, "I like it. Indeed, my impressions of you from the first are borne out. You have a mind for politics. We must read Polybius together. But not this morning. Polybius can wait. This morning, have the groom fetch us horses, and we'll ride upriver to Chelsea." Pleased with the morning's prospects, he ogled his new favorite with theatrical clownishness.

When Carr had left the room, James smiled to himself. He was more than satisfied with his handling of the appointment. Henry and the Queen would be in a fret about it, but, after all, of late that was their usual state of mind. And besides, he liked Carr. He liked seeing that heady mixture of exhilaration and dread shine out of Carr's handsome, eager face, and he liked watching others react to him. Upstart that he was, Carr drew out the jealousy in established courtiers that more sophisticated competition did not. He seemed to be the special child of Fortune, beloved of the gods. For a young man of such modest parentage to ride out as companion to the King was a social achievement of giddy proportions.

At the window again, James gave play to his imagination, sure that he knew precisely what was running through young Carr's head. The King would, as he had hinted, give him a title. In which case, why shouldn't the King ride out with him? This was human nature: today's gift is merely tomorrow's due. As for the Winwoods of this world, he would have to reevaluate the possibilities of his office. If the King

. . . But why call him the King? Say James. Or why be so formal? Soon it must be Jamie. If old Jamie wanted him to take fees for his services, why, then he must oblige by taking as many fees as were offered. For that matter, he might consider insinuating rewards to those who proffered the larger amounts; he could imply that he would speak a word in favor of their request when he was alone with the King. And he could be reticent, even slow, in admitting the tight-fisted to the King's presence.

Such thoughts would only be normal. Carr could become rich and powerful. He could, at last, join the worthies at occasions of state; attend the illustrious weddings and masques at the Banqueting House at Whitehall; have his name spoken in awe; be recognized like Raleigh and Essex; see the admiring faces of the younger men (envying him, of course, instead of the other way round). But most of all, if James was any judge, Carr desired access to the beautiful women of the court. James had observed him closely, hungering after the most glorious (and unobtainable) jewel among the panoply, the tasteful, intelligent, gracious, incredibly lovely Countess of Bedford.

At every recent masque or play, Carr's eyes had been drawn to her: ever surrounded, her glittering smile and green eyes heaping love and charm on everyone near her. Carr—who could hide his feelings from no one, much less from James—had come to hate John Donne, whose wit the Countess seemed to admire without limit. Donne was always around her, admitted to her presence; always whispering to her, laughing, touching her, sending her poems; doing the very things that Carr longed to do. Now, James knew, Carr would try to penetrate that charmed circle, not with poetry but with himself. The Pembrokes, the Herberts, even the Howards could not ignore him.

At that moment, the King's Cupbearer arrived with breakfast, and, as Carr admitted him to the bedchamber, James was sure he caught just a glimpse of a proprietary smile.

FRANCES HOWARD DEVEREUX held the mirror closer, tipping it to catch the fading afternoon rays of the sun, and peered at the reflected, smooth curve of her cheekbone, the delicately arched eyebrows. She smiled, and turned her head first one way, then the other, admiring the slant of the eyes, the heart-shaped mouth with lips hinting ever so slightly of a pout. She was beautiful and the world was in front of her, as it seemed to be in front of everyone who was young and beautiful and from just the right family. How many like her were there? To be young, beautiful, and a Howard, all at once. Sometimes she remembered that, as well as being a Howard, she was also a Devereux, and that line of thought always brought with it a less happy sense.

The sun was setting, and she went to the window and stood for a moment, only half-dressed, letting her eyes run across the long, gleaming slopes of lawn leading from the house to the gently curving row of trees and flowers where the river bent, marking the western perimeter of the Audley End estate. At least the part of it that she knew about or thought about. Tenant farms occupied the land beyond the river, and she had never passed that way except in a carriage, with a proper footman and attendants, on her way to London. Occasionally she rode north—toward Cambridge—with her sister, climbing the hills, the horse's hooves beating on the soft earth below her. But more than anything in the surrounding area, she loved Audley End itself. Even as the house grew, wing upon new wing, her love only increased, for it seemed merely to become more like the place she had loved ever since childhood. Lawns sloping to disappear in lily ponds, swans gliding. She could remember chasing bullfrogs near the water, and though the lily pads seemed smaller to her now, she still looked forward to warm days in summer, with the sunlight playing on the water, and the smells of earth and lawn strong in her nostrils. It was true that sometimes, when she looked in the mirror, and remembered who she was, everything seemed to have changed. But just as surely, Audley End seemed to be an unchanging child's paradise, walled up from harm's way and from the passage of time.

She responded to a knock on the door by turning back to her mirror. She was late, she knew, but she was not ready to go downstairs. Without being aware of it, she slipped a hand inside her loose undergarment and fondled a breast. At that moment, she thought of her great-uncle, the Earl of Northampton, who never failed to admire her spectacular—if precocious—development as a woman. What a pleasure it gave her to see his eyes, twinkling, fall across her with exaggerated interest. "By all the angels and saints," he would say, "this young Howard is the handsomest of the lot!" His voice was always very deep, like a rumble, and yet soft. Frances liked his neatly trimmed beard and mustache; it made it hard for her to tell if he was smiling, or teasing, or what. He was interesting. At times, she thought he knew all about her, and, to tell the truth, this bothered her a bit. Did he truly know her secret thoughts? Her secrets? She even wondered if he knew of pleasures taken, at night, alone, the moon lacing the room with soft shadows, when her body seemed to fall in love with her own smooth fingers. Of course, she always told Father Arrowsmith, but that was different.

Frances stood before the perfect, full-length mirror. She cupped a large, firm breast in each hand, and her mood suddenly changed. Though young, she was also not getting younger. She was being forced to wait. To wait. That was what her life was at that moment. That was what it had always been: waiting and more waiting. Delay. The promise of the future, but nothing today. Waiting to get married. And now, married, waiting to get divorced, so that she could wait to get married again. And, since she was a Catholic, her situation was not promising.

At six, she had been engaged to Robert Devereux, son of the Earl of Essex. Seven years later, when she was thirteen, they were married in a ceremony that brought together most of the important people in England. By that time, Robert's father had gone to the block for his misdeeds, and Frances' husband was the new, young Earl of Essex. No one had expected the marriage to be consummated at that time, but she could still remember the dreary jests, the coarse laughter and embarrassment as her husband muled about, shrugging his shoulders and grinning as if he knew what was going on, which might have been the case but she didn't think so.

As far as Frances was concerned, none of it had done any good. Three years ago, the two families had agreed that it was time for Essex to come back to England and take charge of her. None of Frances' memories of Essex had ever been exactly warm, but if the truth were told, she nourished definite hopes in the form of sexual fantasies that he would be the kind of husband a blossoming and beautiful sixteen-year-old bride requires. He wasn't.

Son of one of the greatest lovers in England, her husband stumbled about, gaping at her and spilling tea, when he wasn't trying to prove that he had conquered the new fad of smoking tobacco. He was a simpleton, a twit, a monstrous, tragic mistake. So she waited. She had known from the start that it wouldn't be easy. The Devereux family was proud, and the Howard faction didn't want to rock the boat. But in her veins flowed the rich and turbulent blood of the greatest family in England: the blood of martyrs and of men who had made the history of England, the same blood, even, of Anne Boleyn herself. The portrait of Anne, hanging in the South Wing library, left no doubt about the resemblance. Except that Frances was yet more splendid. And she would be smarter, too. She could have all she wanted, but it would take time and planning. She had withstood every assault on her one claim to annulment. She clung desperately to the one thing she most longed to lose: her virginity.

Frances was not stupid. She listened to her great-uncle, who knew more than anyone except, perhaps, a Jesuit. In her virginity lay her best chance for—not divorce, really—but "nullity." The difference was important. "It would be as if the marriage never took place," Northampton had said. He hadn't said it to her, exactly; she had overheard the conversation. Nor had he been making a serious point. He was merely indicating an interesting technicality in the law to her parents, and several other family members present. But the meaning was there all the same: it was possible for her to be free and still Catholic. A "nullity" action was not legally a divorce; if Father Arrowsmith went along with it (and he would, she knew he would), it could be accomplished to the satisfaction of all, including the Church. How Frances adored Father Arrowsmith! And how she missed him! He hadn't come by for months. No priest had visited Audley End since—could it be?—last fall! How could the King—how could anyone—be so cruel?

As she stood before the mirror, Frances twisted to show the curve of her hip, the stunningly slim waist, the imponderably large and firm breasts, and then, facing the mirror and spreading her legs, the lovely triangle of soft blond hair. This region of longing and pleasure must remain untapped at all costs, or she would be tied to Essex for eternity. Her sister Catherine was well married to the son of the Earl of Salisbury, Robert Cecil, whose father's name he bore: William. Frances the beautiful and Catherine the good. It was better to be beautiful. She was more than satisfied. Catherine (named after her mother) was her mother's favorite, and, truth to tell, her father liked her better, too. Catherine was a very nice young lady. But her great-uncle knew the true Howard when he saw her, and Frances was his favorite grandniece.

Fastening her undergarments, she called for help in dressing, then went swiftly downstairs, where she took up station at the entrance to the dining room in the South Wing. Motioning her attendant away, she fell to listening. Frances had been an eavesdropper from the time she was the merest child. She had found eavesdropping not only a reliable source of information, but one of power as well. Catherine had been almost wholly in her power for years because of a certain meeting in the summerhouse. Now Frances understood, of course, but at the time she had enjoyed a power she did not fathom. She knew only that Catherine—for once not so dutiful and good—had wanted to keep secret the meeting with her French tutor: a skinny runt of a man, but he had conducted his lesson without clothes, kissing and embracing Catherine, or so it had appeared to an awe-struck eight-year-old Frances hidden behind the hedgerow.

Now Frances caught a deep breath and listened intently. Northampton was talking. It was the usual subject of politics, which Frances found boring. The King. Parliament. The Howard position. (She had come to think of these three topics as identical.) Northampton seemed to know more about politics than anyone in the family, but that was not why Frances liked him.

"The Howards must take a position," he was saying. "The Catherine gambit has failed utterly."

Frances took a note of that, and decided that she must investigate its meaning. What had happened to Catherine?

"With Northumberland in the Tower for his supposed role in the Powder Plot," her great-uncle continued, "and the Countess of Shrewsbury also there for the Arabella-Seymour folly, we must be assertive as ever, lest it appear that we were dependent on the one or diffident of the other."

Frances could not hear all that was said in response; the voices seemed to fall, but it was clear that her father was not inclined to agree with Northampton's reasoning.

"Face facts, Nephew," Northampton said. "If we do not exercise power, you may be sure that others will. James will decide, either way. But that sly old bastard knows his decision will decide the balance of power at court."

"To hell with it," the Earl of Suffolk hurled back; he had had too much to drink. "Let that Carr simpleton run things. He rises on Mercury's winged feet—no, like a rocket over the Thames—proclaimed Viscount ere he knew the meaning 'Baron'! What matter? If our taxes will not rise, what care? Have we not the Exchequer? Has James not given us more telling station?"

The King had placed both Howard men on the new Commission, which was supposed to oversee the Exchequer.

"You do not intend to abdicate on the basis of that, do you?" Northampton said.

Frances could not hear Suffolk's answer, and found herself leaning nearer and nearer the open door.

"To do as you suggest," Suffolk said, "would mean the end of us. We just beat the Spanish in the war. How do you justify aligning ourselves with them at court?"

"I advocate active participation at court, not commitment to the Spanish party. We must use *them,* not be used by them. The struggle is over Rochester, not the Spanish, don't you see?"

"The fight is over the Spaniards and the Pope!" Suffolk said. "Like it or not, we are on our way out."

Frances could see that her father and Northampton were on the brink of a quarrel, and she chose that moment to enter, uninvited.

"Uncle," she said, with a slight curtsy.

Northampton gave Frances a reassuring smile. "Well, well," he rumbled. "Niece Frances . . ."

She was pleased that he chose to greet her first as a Howard.

"And my Lady Essex!"

Frances felt a pulse of anger well in her. There was a single let to her perfect enjoyment, one source of all her frustrations. She, the most beautiful woman in England, now only nineteen, and married to an impossible oaf. And though married, a virgin. And worse, married at the age of thirteen to perhaps the only man in England to whom she would not surrender her virginity. (Verily, she had tried to give it up to him once to no avail, and would never risk surrendering it again to so little purpose, to so hopeless a man.)

"My lord," she said, looking boldly into her great-uncle's laughing grey eyes, "I am overjoyed to see you at Audley End. Was your trip from London pleasant?"

Northampton roared. "Pleasant! A trip to anywhere from London at any time is awful! Truly awful! The roads are quagmires, full of drunken louts and thieves and Puritan preachers predicting the end of the world. A Protestant needs at least three armed men to travel in England. And a Howard needs ten."

Northampton was fond of identifying the Howard family with the Catholic cause. This was partly for the benefit of the Earl of Suffolk, who looked very unhappy. It was a capital offense to deliver a Catholic Mass in England. Only a month ago, a Jesuit priest had been captured, tried, and sent to the block—all for mere possession of the bread and wine. It was said that he suffered on the rack for thirty hours, but that he never once denounced either the saints or his Holy Mother, the Church.

"Henry," her father said firmly, "you must have done with this loose talk. It is dangerous, and you know it."

"I do but jest," Northampton said.

Although he was clearly the leader of the Howard clan, Northampton respected Suffolk, and he tried not to antagonize him. The fact was that, although Northampton dangerously flaunted his Catholicism, Suffolk was guarded in all matters of state, especially those of religion. He had often said that, if men did not take care, religion would hurl England into her bloodiest war.

Frances was unsure of her father's practice, if not of his sympathies. The Howard family had sent too many of its young men to the block as martyrs to the cause of the Holy Church for them to embrace Protestantism with any cheer. Of the Howard martyrs, Frances loved Henry Howard, the Earl of Surrey, best. His poetry had first been read to her by her own French tutor, who was neither skinny nor a runt. "In your own language," he had said, "in your own family, is poetry the equal of Homer and Pindar."

On long summer afternoons, beneath the arbors near the summerhouse, with the scent of rosemary in the air, this handsome young man —convinced that Frances would never speak French—read to her the love sonnets of Surrey. The feelings aroused may have been more than he had hoped for. These poems had been written by her great-grandfather, and so intense was their impact that Frances had all but offered the tutor her virginity. (In the years since, of course, she did not regret the young man's apprehensive decline of that opportunity.)

After the tutor left Audley End, she had continued to read Surrey: here was a Howard who understood love in all its delicious intensity. He would have sympathized with her longings. He would know that, although she had not found anyone with whom to share it, her love yearned to be set free, to be heaped upon a worthy someone, smothering his worthiness with the delights of her body. All she had to remember was a comic night following the wedding to the fourteen-year-old Earl of Essex, with knacks and japes and bubbles on all sides: drinking, singing, epithalamia; the entrance, nude, to the bedchamber. Now she tried to erase that picture from her mind. The inanity of it. Surely, God would spare her the fulfillment of her marital duty. He intended marriage as a sacrament; it was holy, a gift, meant for the satisfactions of honest love. Thus her marriage, legal though it might be, could not be binding. It was made without her consent, and without love. And in that union—regardless of what anyone said—God could have played no part. Was he not a god of love? Would he single out a defenseless girl of thirteen to doom for a lifetime? On this question, Frances had no doubts whatsoever. She would be free of that marriage.

And now Northampton seemed determined to bring up for discussion the entire unpleasant affair.

"You see," he was saying, "the Essex matter cannot be separated from the ongoing life of the court. Our women are absent, which gives full reign to such as the Countess of Bedford, the Countess of Rutland, and the like. They gather their literary minions about them: Jonson, Donne, Drummond, Campion, and soon—God save us—that upstart Overbury." Northampton's tone changed abruptly, and now he almost shouted, as if at once both challenging and pleading: "Who in blazes is Overbury? Who is he that we must deal with him? My God, his nails! One moment you think you have this thing worked out, and up pops another intellectual, fawning over someone you have either never heard of, or were sure you could ignore. And then we have the large, moon eyes of our King, and his adoring looks. We cannot afford to remain on our haunches while men like Overbury write their silly, obnoxious books. We must make a show of ourselves this spring." He seemed suddenly tired. "Don't you agree, my Lady Frances?"

"Spring *is* the best time in London," she said.

"And for the fairest blossom on the Howard tree," Northampton said, "we must not lose the initiative."

Frances looked at her father and saw tears on his cheeks. She turned to her mother, standing tall and untrammeled before the fireplace. "Why does Father weep?" she said.

"You shall, I fear, know much too soon," the Countess said, with no display of emotion.

Suffolk pushed from the table, sending a goblet of wine bouncing across the marble floor. "I like it not," he said. "I like it not." He stood before his shorter uncle. "This will bring no good to the Howards. Fanny is a wedded woman. No matter about the difficulty with Essex, she is a properly wedded woman. As for Essex, he is about the proper business of England. When he returns, he will consummate his marriage. Then Fanny will go to court."

So that was the issue! Something had happened to Catherine, and now no Howard women remained at court.

Northampton poured another goblet of wine and offered it to Suffolk. "You are a good man," he said.

Suffolk took the drink and studied his wife.

"I am deeply troubled about Catherine," Northampton was saying. "I know your suffering, for it is no different from my own."

"Henry," Suffolk said, "you are no father."

"And you are no mother," said the Countess.

"Nor is any of you a daughter," Frances said.

At this point, Northampton offered himself as peacemaker. "No need to quarrel," he said. "I am a bachelor, true. But this makes me the greater lover of my greater family, which is you. Nephew, I love your Frances as if she were my own." He gave Frances that look of pleasure in her physical appearance that she so liked. "Why, she is as my own, aren't you, Fanny?"

Frances could see that he was turning things her way. How she loved him. She was sure he understood her longing for court, her loneliness. True, she loved Audley End. But after her marriage, she had been more or less imprisoned there. And she had changed. Her body had changed, and she had changed with it. She needed new clothing. She wanted to have dresses such as those worn by the most fashionable women, those designed originally for masques and pageants. And she wanted to meet eligible men. Yes, she considered *herself* eligible. She had the same rights as other women, to seek and to expect love, and to give her love willingly, not under constraint of law. She could no longer bear the monstrous burden of her marital virginity. It was a blasphemy against her God-given beauty.

"Yes, Uncle," she said, offering him a quite impudent kiss on the mouth. "I am truly yours, and have always been."

"Fanny," her father said, "you do not understand your great-uncle's drift. He means well. But he would use you as he used Catherine, and with the same—"

"Silence," said the Countess. "I have listened to your whimpering long enough. You will not shame my daughter with the rankest gossip of court fools. She has returned to Audley End because that is her wish. That is all. And I shall not hear one word more of it, except as passes between the two of us."

Suffolk faced his wife as if startled, and then it was clear that he was angry. "You have seen the Bard's play of late, *Macbeth*?"

The Countess observed her husband icily. "Do not play at riddles with me," she said. "I pray you rather say when and where were the Howards bereft of their loved Thomas? Scourge of Cádiz and the Azores! Dread conqueror of the Armada! Will such a *man* add nothing more to Audley End than gaping stairwells and clamorous clocks?"

Finality filled her voice. Frances had never heard her mother talk like that. Never before had she seen her in any way question her husband. She had supposed that Suffolk ruled his family in much the same way as James ruled England: by divine right—and, should the need arise, by brute force. The idea that her mother might influence the family, or even in some measure control it, both depressed and intrigued her. And though the look in her father's eyes hurt her deeply, she must, for her own good, increase his pain. He wished to keep her walled up at Audley End, for God knows how long. At nineteen, was she to chase the bullfrogs through the ponds of another summer? Not if she could go to London. Not if she could take in the theatre season, and go shopping for clothes on the South Bank. She had changed too much to be satisfied with her country existence, pleasant and carefree though it was.

"My lord," she said, "I know the play *Macbeth,* which I might like to see but have only read, as we have some few miserable volumes of recent plays in our library." She made her voice sound soft and reassuring, if petulant and beguiling. She put her arms around her father's neck, and kissed him. " 'Twas at the Globe last year, when I had to remain at Audley End. This wretched woman does murder to help her Scottish husband—a churl—fetch the Crown. Surely," she added slyly, "Mother does no murder, or even wrong, to see me at court in the spring."

It had to work, and it would, since Frances had cleverly provided a way for Suffolk to withdraw the insult to his wife. The Countess stood tall and unyielding, exactly as she had stood throughout this—

to Frances—excruciatingly long exchange. Northampton, pretending nonchalance, poured himself a goblet of sherry. She could see from his composure that they had won. A final touch was needed, then. Frances strode slowly and deliberately to her mother and, with her most lavish smile, kissed her on the cheek.

"Mother," she said, "you are truly understanding. You would set the weary bird free of its tiny cage."

At that, Frances left the three of them to settle details. She hurried from the room, almost as if she feared her presence might change her new prospects for the spring. For a young Howard beauty, what prospect could exceed the vision of London, emerging from the cold and mists of winter into the greenness and bustle and brilliance of May?

THE TRIP ACROSS THE CHANNEL had not been pleasant. A strong northwesterly wind had nearly driven the ship off course, and it had certainly played havoc with his insides. Overbury never thought of himself as much of a seaman; he liked travel on the water, so long as it was either in Venice or, properly conducted, on the Thames. He was glad when the ship put into port; impatient after his long journey, he several times braced the porters, who trundled luggage with the proximate speed of a regal progress. No one was at the pier to meet him; he had expected no one. He had gotten quite used to traveling alone. Well, not alone, really. He had his man, Gibbs, of course, though even that situation seemed precarious now. In any case, he had hardly expected the King's Guard to meet the ship. He wasn't even sure that his family had gotten the letters telling of his return. The decision to come home had been made abruptly.

Gibbs had slipped past the crowd and hired a carriage. It had all gone quite well, and, since he had much work to do, Overbury was pleased. They made no stops on the way to his apartment in Fleet Street (Gibbs could go right back out to the vintners), and, once home, Overbury went directly to the library. He used a small wooden stool to fetch a book from the top shelf of his rather large collection, and from the book he took a small brass key. Climbing down, he crossed the room to a glazed cabinet, which he unlocked. The case was filled with books, but without hesitation Overbury withdrew one in particular, a heavy, leather-bound ledger. He seated himself, then rose to light a candle; though it was still daylight, the room was too dark for reading. Then he fell to close study of the ledger.

Within a short time Gibbs returned, followed by a young boy; they were loaded down with groceries and—more important—with wine and spirits.

"I assume our credit is still good," Overbury observed through the doorway.

But Gibbs didn't answer. Unusual man, that Gibbs. He wasn't really a servant in the ordinary sense. The two had met in Italy; Gibbs, though a commoner, had managed a year or two at Brasenose, and had struck out on his own to see Europe. He had run out of money soon after his departure, and had simply and naturally attached himself to his new friend, seeing to his clothing, performing little errands, suggesting places to dine, arguing with innkeepers. It had been fine at first. But, as time went on, Overbury realized that he had committed himself, at least implicitly. He really must have a talk with Gibbs. Thus far, he had only once broached the subject. "You know," he had said, "my father is very ill, and will likely die. The news is that the estate is not all that was expected . . ." But Gibbs had only reminded him that it was he, Gibbs, who had taken on the responsibility of corresponding with the family, and that he understood the situation quite well. And he probably did, too. The truth was that Overbury and Gibbs were now bound together in an unspoken way, totally immune to the legal processes which someone trained in law, as Overbury was, had thought governed all human relationships.

He closed the ledger, retrieved papers from the desk, and scrutinized them with rapt attention. It was becoming clear to him that either he had been away too long or he had come back just in time. Gibbs brought him a sherry and took a seat, watching him without speaking.

"I'm not good at this sort of thing," Overbury said finally, indicating the pile of papers. "I understand the general drift, but that's all."

Gibbs still said nothing.

"It's all perfectly legal. I'll have to look into it. I can't say. I simply don't know." He scribbled a note. "I must go out before everything closes. By nine o'clock, I'll be at the Serpentine. A man's luck can't all be bad. Take this note to my brother. If anyone calls for me, say that I'll be at the Serpentine—after nine, but not before."

That was one of the good things about Gibbs. He understood

without detailed explanations. And even though, unlike servants, he had the right to ask questions, he never exercised it. He made it his job to handle all matters of minor physical conveniences with his left hand. The rest of his time he spent handling the enormous emotional task of running Overbury's personal affairs. And Overbury was getting more and more edgy about not paying Gibbs. This was one of the many matters that needed to be settled.

Though it was getting well on toward evening, and the shops were beginning to close, Overbury left his apartment and walked the short distance to Humphrey Mitford's office. Mitford was surprised to see him, but if he was disappointed he didn't show it. He remained quite cool, as a matter of fact, when Overbury demanded every farthing that was owed him. Mitford stated flatly that Overbury had already received everything that was owed, down to the last tuppence.

"Indeed," Overbury said. "How extraordinary! If memory serves, I was told, while still in Rome, that my book was in its third printing."

"Quite true," Mitford said, "and we are now running off the fourth. But we've not begun to sell them yet. The book has been in good demand, but as you are aware, costs of printing have shot up. A master printer now draws half a dozen shillings for a single day's work! More, depending on the kind of shop a man runs . . ."

"I fail to see how that concerns me," Overbury said flatly. "My fees were agreed upon in advance."

Mitford's eyebrows arched above the metal rims of his glasses, and he seemed undecided whether to speak. Then he slowly unfolded a leather pouch, scavenged a brier pipe from among the galley proofs and papers scattered across his desk, loaded the pipe deliberately, and settled back with a heavy draw.

"I wonder if you'd be good enough to let me have a look at your ledgers," Overbury said. "Only as they apply to my account, of course."

Mitford shook his head firmly, and for a moment Overbury pondered the situation.

"Must I have a solicitor to look at the accounts ledger?"

"Mr. Overbury," Mitford said with a distinct edge in his voice, "I am aware that you have certain doubts about the way we have handled your book. Now you threaten me with a legal suit. Do you have any idea what would happen to printers if all of their authors sued them for . . . for even a sixpence a copy? We'd have to close up shop!

29

Half the time I'm in there, working right along with the others, setting type, working the chases. And for a small—the smallest—of profits! Mr. Overbury, I made no unusual or illegal profit on your book. However, if you wish, I will—even now—withdraw your book from the press, and you can have another printer bring out the new edition. I would have to charge, of course, for the setting of the pages already done. Even so, I would do it at cost, if that would make you happy. But I will not tolerate these insinuations!"

"My good man, I insinuate nothing! You have cheated me!"

"I repeat," Mitford said, quietly but firmly, "you received payment in full—"

"At a half-shilling per copy?"

"Correct."

"That is just my point," Overbury said. "I received no such amount. Forget the fourth printing. In three printings, my share should be roughly a hundred and twenty-five pounds, a good piece of coin in any realm!" And, he thought, much more to him now than it would have been three years ago, when he had written his *Brief Description of the Low Countries,* more or less as a jest. Who would have thought, then, that in the end it would be the money that counted? "Yet you have paid me just forty-five and six."

"I can only tell you circumstances," Mitford said. "I can only repeat myself. I had to pay to have the proofreading done. You were abroad, so I had to pay an apprentice. It is slow and expensive work."

"Surely," Overbury said, "it could not have cost more than two or three pounds. Even if your apprentice had to work for a fortnight, without sleep."

Mitford relit his pipe; he could see that he was getting nowhere. He pushed back from the desk, drew on his pipe in short, loud puffs, and said gruffly, "Correct. A trivial service. Cost you only a guinea." He turned to face Overbury, but paused and once again seemed undecided.

"We have a disparity of over fifty pounds. Please go on!"

But Mitford was fussing with his pipe, pressing the tobacco down with the head of a nail. Overbury could see that he was not prepared to say anything else on the subject. Was he hiding something? Or was it simply that he was unable to explain the disappearance of such a large sum of money? Overbury headed for the door, stopping only to tell Mitford to go on with the new printing. All said and done, he had come out better than expected.

An odd man, this Mitford. And even more odd was Overbury's own response to him. The man was a thief, no doubt about that, yet Overbury found it impossible to be angry. Something about that great hulk, with the hamlike arms hanging out from behind the massive, leather apron. Or the beguilingly broad smile (a tooth missing right in front), or just the hint of a durableness that had always seemed to Overbury peculiar to the English lower classes. But he had no time to think about that now. He had too much else on his mind. The coachman was turning north from the Strand, and Overbury took his first real look at London since his return. Once the city had struck him as a sprawling, turbulent giant. But no longer. Though new buildings had sprung up along Charing Cross, and more people were about, the streets seemed quite provincial.

Three years ago, the biggest, most spectacular gaming house in London was the Serpentine. It still was. A good twenty-minute ride from the Strand, on the London side of the River Tyburn, the redecorated inn was filled with all the right sort of people: emissaries who had ridden up from St. James to carry on the really important business of state; wealthy entrepreneurs, spreading their new-found riches around; gorgeous courtesans, the very best in England. Overbury felt the same old excitement. There was nothing quite like this in Rome.

He went immediately to the dice table.

Overbury was accustomed to attracting attention. He was physically very impressive: quite tall, very firm of build. His dark hair and neatly trimmed beard made his sharp blue eyes and strong, high cheekbones all the more striking. The turned heads were expected, and he paid little attention to them but pushed right up to the table. No matter how crowded a gaming house was, he knew one could always find a niche if one were serious about placing a wager.

A very nervous man had the dice. Overbury looked him over quickly, then glanced questioningly at the croupier, who indicated that any wager would be excepted. Overbury had £60 with him. He bet £60 against the dice.

The dice lost, and the man left the table. Overbury switched his bet; the dice were now held by a very composed young man who looked to be a student on leave from one of the universities. It was quite a spell before Overbury's turn came. He had more than £200 in front of him, and he knew it was his time to win. The year, especially the past six months, had gone very badly with him, very badly indeed. Loss: the business with the printer was infinitesimal to what the Overbury family had lost. The season was due to change; one good night at the Serpentine (he had had many such good nights in the past), and the whole disastrous downward spiral would be brought to a halt.

He was pleased to see that his hand showed not the slightest tremor as he threw the dice. £400. His luck had declared itself. He bet the entire amount, won again, and was prepared to follow the upward swing of his fate when an attendant asked him to step away from the table. Overbury was decidedly irritated by such an untimely interruption, and though the attendant persisted, he had no intention of withdrawing.

Out of the corner of his eye, he saw the young man—the one who had held on so well earlier—shift his bet away from the dice. Overbury smiled to himself: so he thinks I'm to lose, eh? Right then, he would have bet all he owned (and, in point of fact, he was almost doing just that) on his holding the dice another round. This would give him nearly £800—enough for many Englishmen to live well on for a lifetime, but for him little more than sufficient till he could get settled. For one thing, his wardrobe was no longer the best. If things didn't change, he would soon be threadbare, and for a man with his ambition this could be disastrous: it was one thing to be down on your luck, but to look that way was another, totally unacceptable condition.

Overbury threw the dice, knowing that he would win, and watched the look on the young man's face (he, too, had bet heavily) turn from apprehension to delight.

Astonished, he saw the young man scrape his winnings to him, and then all the sounds of the people around him—people he had been unaware of before—swept over him. He turned away from the table, chagrined by a dull ache newly sprung in the pit of his stomach. Nothing left to bet; nothing, even, for transportation home. He'd have to persuade a coachman to drive him back to London on the promise of payment, and hope that Gibbs, who never had money, would find means of settling up.

He slipped away from the table, trying to draw as little attention to himself as possible. He thought he had detected a promising glance from an obviously wealthy and quite attractive woman, and now he looked her way till she again turned her head. She was wearing an immense silver wig, hair piled high in spectacular swirls, the color and sheen meant to highlight her lovely green eyes. Overbury nodded ever so slightly, and she looked away only after letting her eyes play on his for just the appropriate moment longer. He edged his way toward her. Not that he expected to introduce himself, or to speak to her at all. Only an oaf would be so callow. Women came, unescorted, to the Serpentine because it was one of the few public places in England where they were allowed admittance. But women of quality—and she was one such without doubt—only showed up when they knew that a friend of the family would be there, too. The woman was accompanied by an enormous man, fat beyond decency, to whom she now paid totally undue and rapt attention. For my benefit, Overbury thought. She wants to punish me before we've even met.

He hoped to get close enough to find out who owned those beautiful eyes, but he had only moved a few steps when he bumped into the attendant who had approached him at the table.

"Mr. Overbury, sir? Will you follow me, please?" As if reluctant to allow for a response, he started to press off through the crowd, explaining as he went. "My master sends his compliments, and requests your presence."

I haven't lost *that* much money, Overbury thought. He had heard that heavy losers were sometimes invited into one of the second-floor suites, where they were allowed to recover their dignity overnight, and were treated with every courtesy the house had to offer—including accompanied or unaccompanied bed and breakfast. But then he realized that the Serpentine's owner did not know him, so how could he ask for him by name?

He followed the attendant toward the wide stairway, which led upward to a terrace where many of the regular patrons were being entertained with drinks and conversation, in some cases waited upon by professional hostesses. Then he was led to the second landing, which came to a sumptuously decorated foyer. A closer glance drew a slight smile from Overbury: the artwork here belonged to the school which he had come to call "Italian whorehouse": lovers forever bent in ridiculous postures that would soon exhaust the most ardent passion. Overbury was still waiting for the inevitable expression of that artistic mentality, which had to exist somewhere: a statue of lovers, rapturously transported while standing on their heads.

The attendant ushered him into the first room off the wide but empty hallway. By now, he had begun to think of meeting the proprietor as an opportunity to inquire about the handsome woman in the silver wig. He was nursing the hope that she belonged to that most blessed group of all upper-class women, the group who had done the most for and meant the most to him over the past three years: widows. The fat man was obviously not her husband; no one ever brought his wife here. Well-to-do widows often came two or three together, as a safely scandalous expression of their modernity. And though they seldom conversed with anyone but each other, or gentlemen of close acquaintance, they loved to think they were under the same roof with dangerous highwaymen.

The attendant left without a word, and Overbury examined the room. He was especially interested in a large, ebony-finished writing table, the upright portion of which was fashioned as a nymph. The candelabra on each side were legs parted at an angle of close to a hundred and eighty degrees. The nymph was leaning forward, presumably on her elbows, with her head tilted slightly but not so much as to restrain her open-mouthed smile, directed impertinently at the viewer. Here, Overbury thought, is the mentality responsible for the decorations in the foyer.

At that moment, the far door opened and a man entered. He looked at first glance to be in his late fifties, but a closer inspection indicated that his superficial appearance deceived. He was rather short, but his dark coloring and sharp features—the beard especially, which was more keenly manicured, even, than his own—gave one the sense of great strength, drawing attention from the skin, which, laced with fine lines where the brows of less fortunate men were plowed by adversity, was nonetheless aglow with the sheen of many pampered years: threescore would be close. He was dressed elegantly, and Overbury thought he smiled as if aware that his finery had been found impressive. Then, before he had so much as introduced himself, he smoothly worked the lid of a gold snuffbox and drew his right thumb and index finger ever so easily past his nostrils.

Overbury had the feeling that he knew this man, and he found himself ransacking his brain for the setting that went with the face.

"Good evening," he said. "You seem to be as busy as a friar in a convent tonight."

"I'm afraid it's always like this," the man said.

"May I ask, before I forget, who the woman in the silver wig happens to be? Something familiar about her . . ."

"Striking woman!" the man said. "I know just who you mean. That elegant creature, my good sir, is Diana, Countess of Rutland."

"Yes," Overbury said, "I thought I recognized her husband. He appears to have put on weight since last I saw him . . ."

"Not her husband," the man said. "Actually, her husband was taken by the plague, only this past summer it was . . ."

"Poor man," Overbury said. "I've been away a while. As the proprietor of such an establishment, you must—"

"I'm not the proprietor!" the man said with an animated gesture. "Not at all. I seldom even come here. Indeed, I only came tonight to see you."

Overbury, though seldom at a loss for words, chose not to speak. He watched carefully as the man fixed himself a drink—dark rum and mineral water, it appeared—and settled comfortably into the soft cushions of a couch by the writing table.

"Ordinarily I don't like to fetch my own drinks," the man said. "But I've asked that we be left alone until our business has been completed."

"I confess that I know of no business between us," Overbury said. "That is, unless you are Mr. Humphrey Mitford's solicitor . . ."

The man shrugged; obviously, he had never heard of Mitford.

"Then I cannot imagine what it would be like to transact business with someone who—you'll pardon me—will not so much as introduce himself . . ."

The man sniffed tolerantly. "I quite understand. It's odd, perhaps. But I'm afraid it would be better for the moment if we avoided . . . personalities . . ."

Longing (but determined not) to request a drop of sack, Overbury had all but decided that the evening was not turning out well for him.

"I do not wish to be either mysterious or obtuse," the man said. "I am here to make a generous offer, and, frankly, I am under the impression that you would be more apt to take the offer on its own merits than you would if you knew me. Simply a matter of your own prejudices, you understand."

Overbury allowed some interest to show.

"You and your family are in serious financial trouble," the man said. "I know this, and of course I assure you that reason and experience have taught me the value of discretion." He dipped at the snuff-box. "Mr. Overbury, I've done a good bit of checking on you, and I am prepared to assure your future at this time."

In spite of himself, Overbury could not restrain a volley of laughter at this point. "I'm sorry," he said. "Do go on!"

The man smiled good-naturedly. "I am pleased that I amuse you. That is a sign that you and I will get on well. And since it is clear that you'd much prefer proper introductions, I shall alter my approach. You may remember me, as I remember you, from a function that we both attended in Edinburgh. I happened to be visiting the court; it was shortly before James came to London. You were present—"

"Yes, yes, at a dinner. As the least person to coax a place at table, to be sure."

"You were, as I recall, slightly out of the way. But I surely remember your face." He extended his hand. "I am Henry Howard. How do you do?"

It was a disarming ploy to be sure, but now Overbury understood. Henry Howard, the bloody Earl of Northampton! No wonder he had prolonged introducing himself. Had Overbury been in his place, he would have existed permanently incognito.

Northampton was surely one of the two or three most powerful men in England, and, for that matter (since the two were the same), in the world. To give the devil his due, Overbury admired him for that. But he was among those who were unconvinced that Northampton was not involved in the Gunpowder Plot. He *had* to be involved in it, and Overbury had said so at the time. He was not impressed by James's apparent credulity on this point. The fact was that no Catholic initiative of such magnitude could have gone so far without Northampton's complicity, surely not without his knowledge. How else could so many men have conspired over the span of nearly a year's time to survive, to dig a mine next to the House of Lords, to abandon that project when it proved feasible to hire a vault beneath that place, to lug in thirty-six barrels full of gunpowder, to shield it carefully with metal staves for increase of explosive power, to cover the whole of this devilish magazine with coal and firewood, and then to alert every Catholic gentleman in England to expect a wonderful event on November 5, 1605, which would return England to her old faith? The bombs were to explode ("for God and man—nay, Jesuits! —hath concurred to punish the wickedness of this time") as King James, accompanied by the Royal Family, read his first address to the Parliament.

The only difference between Northampton and Northumberland was that Northumberland got caught. They were traitors alike. Nor were the rest of the Howard clan much better. Had they not, after all, been the virtual sole cause of Wyatt's rebellion?

"I am prepared to offer you," Northampton was saying, "a lucrative position at court."

Overbury made to speak, but Northampton raised his hand.

"Hear me out. I know your situation. You owe no less than five thousand pounds more than either you or your family can raise. You have not paid your rent in four years. You filled your cupboard today on—shall we say—the civility of your neighbors."

Overbury was becoming annoyed. It wasn't that Northampton had as much as a single fact wrong (which he did: Overbury figured his debt at closer to £7,500; he was truly in desperate need of money). It was that he couldn't stand the surpassing arrogance of this man, supposing that he would place himself in the debt of a total stranger. And to be beholden to a traitor! And, by hook or by crook, Northampton seemed to know of Overbury's violently partisan views in politics. Overbury hated everything Northampton stood for, and of course this meant that he hated English Catholics. Not Catholics, mind you, but English Catholics. To him the distinction mattered. In Italy, he had grown to love the ceremony, the color, the marvelous earthiness of the people. To be a Catholic in Italy was not only acceptable, but, to Overbury, a requirement of loyal citizenship. He considered his hatred of Northampton to be totally impersonal, and not religious but political.

Even so, it made no immediate sense to declare what would have been obvious to the dullest of wits (which Northampton was most certainly not): that any alliance between the two of them was impossible. Something lay behind the visit, and that something pointed to an end of Overbury's economic woes, with or without Northampton, who was much too wise ever to do anyone a favor.

"Doubtless you have reason for wishing to retain me, my lord," he said. "And I would be less than generous if I failed to appreciate your offer—though, to be sure, I am not at all clear on what employment you had in mind. But I must decline, in any case. Personal reasons, my lord."

"I shall be quite direct," Northampton said, after a pause. "I do not fancy losing. And we Howards have sustained more than a single loss of late. I am aware of your religious views, sir, and I respect them. But I have means to help you, and there are services which I require of you. I propose to supplement your earnings from the position at court with a monthly fee for—let us say—advice. Twenty pounds per month, over and above your salary, tenure in which I personally guarantee. In addition, I shall immediately and without fanfare settle all your personal and family debts. This, in itself, is no small undertaking. And I shall further see you newly appointed with a wardrobe of your own choosing—which alone will doubtless make some tailor at the New Exchange a man of means. I put it to you that this is a most handsome offer."

"My lord, it is more than generous; it is magnanimous beyond reason, which some would tell us is but good sense. For myself, I am reminded of the proverb 'Beware the Greeks bearing gifts.' "

Northampton smiled. "Again, sir, I do not take your political opinions personally. Nor do your barbs touch me in the least. My intentions in this matter, as in others, are honorable in that they are based on self-interest—as, I assume, are yours, and all men's. This, in my experience, is the one principle of politics which allows of no exception."

Overbury nodded, letting the remark pass unanswered, and for a moment the room was silent. Then, placing his goblet on the desk as if to signal his impending departure, Northampton spoke with finality.

"You are an intelligent man whom chance has made important. Within days, you will know what I know now. The young man whom you tutored in Edinburgh—Robert Carr, by name—has gained the attentions of the King. He has been given a title, an estate, and an income. This fact is indicative of the monstrous irrationality that governs events. His talents, as you know perhaps better than anyone else, are pathetically slim. Be that as it may, he cannot fail to emerge as a man to reckon with. Nor, sir, is he so dense as to think himself equal to the task that goes with his good fortune. He has conducted surprisingly thorough inquiries into your whereabouts, which fact makes his intentions perfectly clear to me. He will make you his personal secretary. A portable brain, so to speak."

Overbury stirred, though he tried to cover his surprise. He could almost feel the penetration of Northampton's gaze.

"The nature of your relationship to this young man"—Northampton's tone was professionally neutral—"is also clear to me. As no doubt it is to James, who will probably accede to Carr's wishes in the matter, but without relish. I doubt that James will like you, incidentally: he seems to dislike everyone to whom Carr takes a fancy. My own interest is not in the least personal, for I neither like nor dislike Carr, whom you may now think of as Viscount Rochester. Rather, I resent his intrusion on the political scene, which was complicated enough before his unfortunate ascent from the practices, whatever they are these days, of Scottish pages. My interest, plainly, is to gain access to proper intelligence, given this sudden, unforeseen development. And my offer is to supplement your stipend—"

Here Overbury interrupted sharply. "For the rather obvious purpose of making me a spy."

"You are an intelligent but insolent young man," Northampton said harshly. "It is said that Overbury's worst enemy is a loose tongue; best learn to keep it from wagging to no profit. I had thought to help you on the enlightened basis of mutual service. I cannot function— no man of state can—without information. I cannot properly discharge my duties, represent the interests of my family. But I see that your prejudice forbids any cooperation. Please accept my best wishes on your return to England." He nodded curtly and left the room.

Overbury gazed at Northampton's empty crystal goblet. Perhaps he could have handled his refusal with more tact, at least without turning it into an insult. The gratuitous insult is never forgiven, but clangs in the memory more loudly than it sounds when first delivered. Stupid! he thought to himself. Stupid. Perhaps he'd best think about this rumor concerning his loose tongue. Perhaps these days in England it could be dangerous to speak one's mind too openly. The court was, very likely, if not dominated by its Catholic queen, at least mindful of her presence.

Actually, the night had been good to him after all, and he was glad he had come to the Serpentine. True, he had lost the £800, and he no longer had the £60 that was in his pocket when he left the Strand. But he had received a great windfall of information worth much, much more. Yes, he could sleep tonight knowing that he would not have to struggle merely to survive. Gibbs would be taken care of; Gibbs could remain with him.

If he felt uneasy, it was perhaps because he had treated Northampton badly. One thing was clear: not only was Northampton a clever man, but he was an unnervingly honest one. And he was obviously prepared to fight hard to protect his interests at court. And perhaps some uneasiness would be natural, knowing that the instrument of his arrival at court would be Robin Carr. Astonishing. The art of life was based on the soundest principle of irony.

At his lowest ebb, Overbury had gone to Edinburgh as tutor to several minor figures in the Scottish court. Of these, the most minor —and the least promising by far—was a young Scot, a page at court, whom everyone called Robin. One could hardly look at him without recalling the tale of Narcissus: he was truly beautiful, and he drew the admiring glances of men as well as women.

But Robin Carr's beauty was, as they say, only as deep as anyone could see: he lacked the slightest inclination for any of the seven arts, and seemed even more impervious to instruction in the social graces. He stumbled rather than fenced, fell against the beat rather than danced, stuttered rather than conversed; when on horseback, he survived rather than rode. Overbury had the feeling that, without his good looks, Robin would be at a loss in this cruel world. But people did rather like him. And his one virtue, his beauty, had taken him far. Overbury adopted his first axiom of politics: one cannot argue with success. Northampton's immediate response to Robin's new status was proof enough.

As Overbury reached the terrace on his way to the main floor, he caught sight of the gorgeous creature whom he now knew to be the Countess of Rutland: her head tossed back in gay and glittering laughter, she was heaping her attentions on none other than the Earl of Northampton. The Countess turned toward Overbury, who could see that Northampton was trying to point him out among the throng. Then Northampton caught his eye and, with a broad and friendly smile (as if their interview of only moments ago had never happened), beckoned him to join them.

For a moment, Overbury didn't move; he was tired, and it was not an invitation he could have expected. But Northampton was providing him with a twofold opportunity: not only could he soften the edges of his insult, but he could meet the Countess, too. He made his way toward where they stood.

During the introduction, Overbury watched for signs of uneasiness in the Countess, but these were not forthcoming. In fact, the conversation was light—and agreeable, in that it soon turned to himself.

"I have read of your travels in the Netherlands, Mr. Overbury, and, though I am by no means a critic, you are most surely an author of remarkable wit."

She seemed to overflow, even to the point of gushing, but her warmth rang true. No wonder people crowded around her. Although it did not encourage him to think so, he was certain she was like this with everybody. Could it be that God made some people to live outside the terrible onslaughts—those deadly thrusts and parries— that dominate the lives of most of his creatures? Overbury, who had been pursued by many women, was enthralled.

"My lady," he said, "without a measure of wit no Englishman would easily survive the tedium of a visit to the Low Countries. I am most humbly grateful for your kind words. It is good to know that someone of your reputation for literary taste has taken pains to read my modest book of travels."

He soon learned that Northampton had read his book, too, which somehow came as a surprise. He hadn't thought of Northampton as a man who would waste time with what was obviously not intended as very taxing intellectual fare. Northampton was saying that he liked those "Netherlandish louts" even less after reading the book than before, if that were possible. Actually, the conversation was becoming animated and quite pleasant. Northampton motioned inconspicuously, and without so much as an interruption they were seated on the terrace, with brandwine in front of them. The Countess had sent her friend off to the tables to place a small wager for her, and the three were enjoying themselves as Overbury would not have thought possible.

"Most awful dullards going," Northampton said. "Miserable Anabaptists, the lot of them. Cities crawling with heretics and hermits shouting to high heaven that the world is coming to an end. They should garrotte the lot of them!"

Overbury laughed; on this he could agree even with Northampton. If there was anything he hated worse than a Catholic, it was a Puritan.

Traitors, all of them. And the fuel of Anabaptism, which meant the fuel of dissent and schism in the main emanated from the Netherlands.

"Have the tables been good to you?" the Countess inquired.

"Only one has had a shot at me so far." Overbury grimaced.

They decided on one last visit to the dice table. Overbury could see no harm in accepting a loan of £50 from Northampton, which transaction drew no attention at all (and now there could be no problem of repayment). Beneath the warmth of the Countess's shining green eyes, he spent the next two hours at the most crowded table. Then, with over £1,000, and after paying back an amused Northampton, he hired a carriage and left the Serpentine.

He had forgotten for a moment his discomfort in Northampton's presence. For all his sinister political connections, Northampton was a man worthy of respect. He was intelligent. Subtle. Like himself, really, he thought now, with a half-chuckle. The two were not so different: bachelors, attorneys, men of decided convictions. Neither had ever been faulted for his sentimentality. Northampton would make a formidable enemy, but then so would Overbury. Perhaps the excitement of his return, and the fatigue of this long, damp night, suggested these absurd fancies of conflict. Perhaps the Earl's harsh words—and his own—would be forgotten. Perhaps he'd see no more of Northampton.

Except for the pleasant fact that in Northampton he had found an entrée to the Countess of Rutland! Now Overbury eased back into the leather seat of his coach. He was very tired, but he felt content—even happy—to be home.

EARLIER THAT NIGHT, an hour or so before Overbury set out for the printer's shop, a young woman left her small apartment over the Blue Boar on the South Bank, bound for a destination near Blackfriar's. She walked swiftly, as was her habit, and lingered only by the tiny shops on the Bridge, where she examined buttons and considered fabrics.

As she approached Thames Street, she momentarily enjoyed an admiring glance from a man in a passing carriage. She was not beautiful, but men found her attractive. Her face was framed by a stunning shock of blond hair, and she had large, luminous blue eyes, which possessed a strangely brooding, haunted look. She bore the mien and coloring of her Viking ancestors, but she lacked their sturdy frame, and her slender limbs and wide eyes gave her more the appearance of a startled fawn. She would never come to know the man in the carriage, but their destinies from that night on would be irrevocably intertwined. By a complicated web of circumstances, the destinies of Thomas Overbury and Ann Turner would involve the most powerful men in England in a deadly struggle for survival.

Now she continued toward Blackfriar's, trundling a large portfolio and a few lengths of fabric that she had purchased on the Bridge. At Blackfriar's, she turned toward the river again, hurrying, as it was starting to rain. As she stepped to the door of a house near the wharves, she found herself shivering, and gathered about her a fine shawl which she had woven herself from Shetland wool. She couldn't tell if the house was occupied; it was one of a row of tenements whose backs opened on the wharves. Obviously, some of the houses were used for processing fish unloaded on the docks below.

She worked the brass knocker on the door, then waited a moment, looking back along the darkening street, where the last of the fruiterers and fishmongers were closing down their barrows. Again she knocked and waited. When several minutes had passed, she turned to see the last vendors leaving, and thought of making her own departure.

It seemed she was on a fool's errand. She had no notion of whether she was expected, or even of whether anyone was in the building to which she had been sent. She studied the exterior of the house: it was very old and ramshackled, two stories high. Most of the houses in this section, hard by the river, had been built a long time ago. The windows of this one, she noticed, were all enclosed by iron grillwork.

By now it was raining, and she was anxious to retrace her steps to Thames Street, where there were always people no matter what the weather. She had never liked to stay anyplace alone. It didn't matter whom she was with, particularly, but she didn't like to stay alone. This was why she rather liked the place of her work, if not the work itself. Trembling in the cold, she imagined herself, knees drawn to chin, before the massive stone fireplace at the Blue Boar.

She had taken a step down from the landing when the door to the house opened with a lurch. Then whoever was on the other side just as suddenly returned it nearly to its stop. Peering through the small opening, she finally made out a woman, bedraggled, perhaps in her late forties or early fifties, but with a sad face that made her appear much older. The woman scowled and stepped aside without a word.

"I am—"

"Mrs. Turner," the woman said. "He is expecting you." She indicated a long, dark hallway that led to the back of what looked to be an exceptionally large apartment.

Ann found herself trying to breathe shallowly in order to avoid a most sickening odor. The back of the house must rest on the riverbank, she reasoned, and perhaps the lower floors were used to prepare fish for sale. But that didn't make sense, since she had always liked the pungent smell of freshly cut fish. Often, when she was up early, she would drift down along the embankment to watch the fishermen unload their boats and the fishmongers cut and stack the morning's catch. No, the smell could not be only fish, and it wasn't a fresh smell at all; she sensed another ingredient, powerfully and sickeningly sweet —a mixture that made her dread a full-bodied whiff of the place.

She made her way along the hallway, past almost totally darkened rooms, her free arm stretched out in front of her, and was startled when her hand touched something smooth and very cold. Apparently, the hallway led to a window which she hadn't been able to see. Leaning close to the glass, she could make out the outline of the old shops stacked on London Bridge. Light from a few windows was visible through the gathering mist and drizzle. A few barges were still about. Ann shivered in response to what seemed at the moment a cold and desolate scene.

Why had the woman left her to find Dr. Forman on her own? If she were Forman's wife, that might explain her inhospitality, but Franklin hadn't mentioned Forman's being married. But then Franklin was an important, busy man, with much on his mind of greater consequence than her problems. It was known to all at the Blue Boar that Franklin had gone to the University, and that, before his banishment, he had spent two years there, just like any gentleman's son.

At that moment, to her left, a door clanked; someone was working the lock from the inside. The door came ajar and the meager light from inside the room now revealed the large head and upper frame of a man whom she took to be Dr. Forman. Smiling, he stepped to the side, allowing her to enter the room without introduction. Then he relocked the door with the same gusto employed in opening it, with a great clamor, and, obviously, with difficulty.

"Good evening. I've been expecting you," he said. "I am Dr. Forman."

He was much taller and heavier set than she had imagined. Somehow she thought of doctors as less physical-looking. This one was unusually wide of shoulder, and had thick, dark hair, with not much grey in it. Very bushy brows gave his eyes an intense look.

Although she had never thought of herself in a position to worry about such matters, she was pleased to notice that he was, all in all, quite good-looking. Not that this was any kind of requirement, but it did make things less disagreeable. She had disciplined herself to respond to all men in pretty much the same way, with a look on the verge of hunger. No matter how old or ugly a man was, he preferred to think of himself as a Greek god. It was best to recognize this about men, to oblige them, and so to hurt no one. The more misguided a man was about her feelings toward him, the more money he would part with gladly. Who would invest solid coin in the same truth he could obtain, without cost, from a glance in a mirror?

"My lord," she answered at last. She was not sure how to address him. She had little to do with doctors of any sort. She was afraid of them. Besides, according to Franklin, the College of Physicians had brought Dr. Forman before the King's Bench, declaring him no doctor at all. Yet that was, for her, a nicety of issue she neither understood nor cared about. "He can do for you," Franklin had said, "what no other man on earth can." That was what mattered.

She required the services of a magician, and was happy to have been able to contact one. They were not easy to lay hold of; it seemed almost weekly they were losing their heads to the executioner's ax. But even Franklin, who was an educated man, and could almost read Latin, had said that at one time or another every man jack in England could do with the services of a magician. "It depends on the problem!" he had said. Only a magician could bring the "unusual" to bear on certain kinds of problems.

If natural devices failed (and they had, hadn't they?), well, then one had to seek supernatural ones, or admit defeat. And at twenty-two years old she could not believe that her life would go on as hopelessly as it always had.

"Please," Dr. Forman was saying, "consider me a friend. Do not fret about titles. Think of me as your father."

She shrank only slightly as he removed her shawl, and then she returned his steady gaze with her usual look of almost disembodied composure: eyes wide, lips slightly parted.

"You see," he said, "that is what I am—a father—to those who need me."

Think of me as your father! What good was a father to her now? She needed most unusual help, and at that moment it seemed far from forthcoming. It appeared, in fact, that she would owe her new failure to her faith in Franklin, whose word, no matter how many times it proved false, was one of the few things she trusted. As so often before, she had listened to him, even when something inside her protested that he was mad. She must be crazy, too: that was the only possible explanation for the way she followed his advice.

Take the time he had convinced her to place a sign in the window of his shop. Franklin was an apothecary, who, she had to admit, catered to many of the wealthiest women in London. Actually, as a chemist, he was really quite successful, and she had toyed with the idea of marrying him. He was famous for his clysters, which he prescribed for all maladies alike, whether a patient was sounding a death rattle or merely dripping phlegm from the nose.

Once she herself, to her woe, had fallen into his professional clutches. He had missed her at the Blue Boar, and upon learning that she was ill—and before her symptoms could be decently described— had arrived at his diagnosis and treatment: "A clyster. She must have a clyster at once."

Ann learned of her deliverance when her son, then only seven, tiptoed to her bed with the news, apologetically told, that an insistent visitor was at the door. Soon the boy himself was ushered out, and Franklin, who had fetched his powders and tools, was pouring and mixing like a maniac. She was quite fevered at the time, and even in the best of spirits knew little of medical science. Certainly, she had no warning when, without preamble, Franklin threw back her thin blanket, wrenched her most uncomfortably about, pulled her to her knees and, ignoring her screams, pushed what felt like a small pine tree up her rear end.

"The treatment was a success," Franklin later put about at the Blue Boar, and crowed, "The best clyster I ever concocted." And truly the fever disappeared almost at once. But in its place came far worse distractions: all in all, the worst day and night of Ann's life. Had she not been a Christian, and known better, she would have prayed for death. In truth, in her humiliation, she longed for it.

As soon as the treatment was finished, she filled the bed most violently, which fact left Franklin overjoyed. Afterward, hour upon hour, she dragged herself from bed to chamberpot, but could seldom position herself in time. Finally, effort exhausted her. She lay, trembling, in bed, helpless to deal with the irresistible powers of Franklin's mixture.

For one with an acute sense of smell, recuperation led to even greater woe. Her own room became unbearable. Even her son—and a more loyal boy could not be found in England—excused himself often from her company, and when he was about he smiled bravely in a homeric pretense that all was well. Ann was too weak to cope, and though Davy did his best to clean up the place, science had worked its wonders in such a way that not only the bed and floor, but somehow (by her own efforts to tidy up, no doubt) the walls and window casings were spotted. The lad worked like a Trojan in short spurts, rubbing and washing and rinsing. In addition, he carried water to his mother, who seemed to guzzle it by the gallon. And then, inevitably, he would hasten away for a breath of fresh air.

Two days later, Franklin returned to his patient, insisting that follow-up treatment was required. In a twinkling, he had his tools spread about, and was measuring out powders and quoting authorities. Ann could only dissuade him from a second purge by using every remaining ounce of her own energy and art to shift his attention. Finally, she distracted him to the point where he put down his jars and clambered on top of her. Falling back with a gasp, she wanly indicated the unlatched door. (This was a nicety that she insisted upon, even in her present extremity; it wouldn't do to have little Davy as a witness to such chores.)

Franklin tended to the door, still citing authorities—"Paracelcides the wise and . . . ah . . . Maimonidorus the Good . . ."—and announced that the remedy could be delayed, under specified circumstances, for as long as a fortnight. Then he dropped his Venetians and leaped upon her in his usual, graceless manner. But on this occasion Ann thanked merciful God that she had been spared the worse fate of a second visitation from science.

As crazy as that night was, this one seemed to make no more sense. Even so, she now smiled at Dr. Forman, let him take the

---

47

portfolio from her, and thanked him for overlooking the matter of his title.

"Titles mean so little," she said. "It's what a person really is . . ."

"And," Dr. Forman said, smiling, "if my informant is correct, that is why you need a father. You wish to assume a new title, so to speak, a new professional name, one more nearly like what you think you are."

Although his tone was friendly enough, he seemed somehow to be laughing at her. She decided to be quite direct with him.

"I am here, sir, because I know of no other way to help my-self . . ."

"Precisely," he said, still smiling.

"I have tried every way I know. But unless one designs costumes already, one's not asked to design them. I can have nothing. I mean not just money."

"No," he said, as if that went without saying.

"I am poor, but I don't want to be rich."

"Of course not!"

"I mean I must help my boy. Davy. It's different with a man. He'll be lost unless I do better, get on . . ."

Dr. Forman had slumped to the floor, where he sat stolidly, no longer looking at her.

"Hmmm," he said.

"As I said, sir," Ann continued, "I have tried others. I have made clothes without pay, and advertised to give them away, where proper folk will see them. I put a sign in Franklin's 'pothecary shop to give the gowns away. But even the few who took them never returned." (Another of Franklin's ideas that hadn't worked out.) "So I am left," she finished, "to go on hopelessly, stupidly, in a life of no interest to me. Of no use to myself or Davy."

Dr. Forman looked grave. "What of God?" he said suddenly and loudly. "My dear child, what of the eternal?"

This seemed like a silly question, coming from a magician, but Ann decided to tell him the truth. "I am Catholic," she said quietly, as if she might be overheard.

Dr. Forman shook his head ever so slightly, and pursed his lips.

"To such as me," she went on, "of poor Catholic parents . . . They died, leaving only memories of hatred, and stories of their wonderful lives under Queen Mary. What can God do for me? I'm not allowed to see a priest. I cannot confess my wretchedness and sins. I've seen no priest since my unfortunate marriage, which was done secretly, with great danger. In the years since . . ."

She hadn't meant to talk about herself; the men about the Blue Boar never asked, and it was not her way. Until now. And the more she talked, the less she could control herself. She wept, then sobbed, dabbing at her eyes with her fine, wool shawl.

For a while, Dr. Forman gave no hint of a response. Then he spoke sharply. "No need to feel sorry for yourself," he said. "I've seen worse cases, by far. Worse failures."

The sod! She covered her face now, and little by little regained her composure. She could see Dr. Forman out of the corner of her eye.

"Truly," he said, "blessèd art thou among women."

Ann looked up, startled. "You blaspheme, sir," she said quickly and coldly.

"Not at all," Dr. Forman said, rising, and with great nonchalance he opened the portfolio she had brought with her. He went through the sketches slowly. "I do not believe that blasphemy is possible," he mused. "Or, to put it more precisely, all blasphemy affirms what it purports to deny. Blasphemy is, therefore, a form of worship. When I tell you to call me 'father,' I mean it in the sense of spiritual adviser, guide, sustainer, priest."

"You are no priest," Ann said, "but a magician. Likely, you have signed your name in blood, and sold your soul to the devil. But I care not. You can help me because you *are* a magician. Or so I was told . . ."

Finally, he turned from the drawings. "You did these?" When she affirmed that she had, he went over them again, even more slowly.

The room was very cold, and Ann rubbed her hands together, walking back and forth in front of the unlit fireplace, stopping casually to stare at the pile of wood, ready for lighting. Dr. Forman appeared not to notice. She broadened her gestures to show how cold she was, but he was absorbed with the drawings.

"Why did you come here?" he said without looking up.

"It was Franklin's doing," she said.

"Hmm, Franklin, yes . . . A good enough sort, I suppose. A bit limited in . . . the range of his vision, I should say. But not a bad sort at all."

Ann looked at him curiously, wondering if his words meant that he, too, had once been the recipient of Franklin's ministrations.

"Yes, quite," he said, as though she had answered his question directly. But then he stood up and took her by the shoulders. "Now, I must know precisely—precisely, now—what it is you wish from me. Precisely. Precisely what it is you wish from me."

"I wish . . ." Actually, it was not easy to put into words. "It is very simple . . ."

Dr. Forman raised his eyebrows and smiled; he seemed to know it wasn't simple at all, but he said nothing to help.

"I mean . . . I want . . . I must work . . . with Master Jones. I must!" Now the words literally flooded out, as before. "I have seen many of his settings, and they are marvelous, and I think that he is the most magnificent person, and even . . . even . . ."

"That you could help him?"

"Yes. How did you know? That I could help him. I spent every hour when he was redecorating the Banqueting House at Whitehall, just watching. I nettled people to get them to take me out there. It is . . . how can I say it? . . . I know so little of words . . ."

"You are wrong, my dear," he said. "You are most eloquent. But you speak in a different language." He indicated the drawings. "It is a language of gay colors and lace and pleats and ruffs, and I confess I know nothing of it. But you love beauty, my child, and yours is a gift to create beauty. You admire yourself in Inigo Jones, who is a fraud, which you are not—"

"Sir," Ann interrupted, "he is—"

"A fraud, but no matter. Ignore the remark. The man is also a genius. Though a genius is merely a man who is clever in selecting whom to steal from. He has plundered the ruins of a dead civilization, and for this they turn him into a living God . . . But I can see that I only alarm you, and to no purpose. The question is still how can I help you? I begin to grasp the situation, even if you do not."

"I want to design costumes for Inigo Jones. I know nothing of history or ruins. I cannot even—" She caught herself.

"Read?"

"Or write my name."

"But your eye, my child! You have the eye and hand that Master Jones should envy. Why do you not simply present yourself to him? Take him these sketches?"

"I have tried."

"Ah," Dr. Forman said. "Then try another."

"No," she answered in a tone that sent Dr. Forman's great eyebrows up. "I am determined to design for Master Jones. It is what I must do, to amount to something. His are the greatest, gayest productions. The finest people, and the gayest masques. This is what I must do."

Dr. Forman nodded his head, very slowly, studying her.

"Franklin told me that you have means to manage such things," she said. "You are a magician, and can make people do things, they know not even why themselves."

"Yes," he said in a low voice, matter-of-factly. "Yes, I have means. And, if you wish, shall use them. But you must understand your situation in this, and mine. I require it. That you understand the cost perfectly."

Ann reached inside her blouse and withdrew a small bundle. Franklin had told her about this detail, at least. Even a magician has to eat. Though she rather suspected that Dr. Forman had quite down-to-earth means of making people do his bidding. It was true that he healed people, but then so did Franklin. Perhaps Dr. Forman had secret medicines and machines which he would tell no one about, lest they then have power over him. The most important thing was that he might change her life. She handed him the money.

"It must be all you have," he said (just as Franklin had said he would). "I have no way of knowing if you are telling the truth, and, truth to tell, I don't care. It is you who must care."

True, she had taken the liberty of spending a few shillings that day on the Bridge, but in the bundle now was all the money she possessed. Which was not much, at that.

"Now we must move on," he said. "We do have means, and you shall learn them."

He stationed a couch in front of the fireplace, and Ann seated herself comfortably. Then he lit the wood, and as the blaze grew, the room took on a strange glow. The flames leaped higher, and the figures on the fire screen brightened.

There seemed to be bodies moving within the landscape.

The fire screen was about four feet high, and perhaps twice as long in width. In the candlelight, Ann had noticed nothing unusual about it. But now the needlework details stood out brilliantly. Fascinated, she could scarcely believe what she saw. There *were* people . . . naked

. . . all sorts of them . . . young, mostly . . . men, women . . . and yes, children.

Her attention was drawn from the screen by a pleasant aroma—a very sweet smell, perhaps the ingredient that, when mixed with the stench of rotting flesh on the floor below, had made her almost ill. A heady aroma, and at once both strange and familiar. She turned to see Dr. Forman brewing a pot of tea. Near the fireplace was an ebony-covered casket, partitioned into sections, from which he now selected leaves to add to the tea that was already steeping.

"Just the thing for a chilly night," he said.

He brought the tea, sat down beside her; and then they both fell to drinking. Dr. Forman had neglected to add sugar or cream, but Ann was glad of it, glad to savor the full aroma and taste—which was very different from the breakfast variety to which she was accustomed. She reckoned that this must be an almost priceless delicacy, fetched from the Far East, perhaps, like the strange, Oriental-looking fire screen.

She was pleased, too, that Dr. Forman filled her cup as soon as she emptied it. Another cup of hot tea before leaving would brace her against the walk home. She was feeling a bit drowsy, but light-hearted, too; in fact, she almost laughed out loud, but restrained herself: she would look silly, laughing for no reason. She even felt warm toward Dr. Forman,

"You seem quite happy with yourself," he said when she turned to look at him. "Or do I appear funny to you?"

"Not in the least," she said, draining her cup again. "You're not funny at all. I'm funny. The fire screen is funny."

"Yes, the fire screen . . ." He poured more tea. "I'd drink this perhaps more slowly, though, if I were you. Savor it. Like the fire screen, it has come too far to give ordinary satisfaction."

"A fancy, expensive tea, no doubt," Ann said. "One must fetch it in the better shops."

"Not really so expensive," he said. "But rare, indeed. And you'd not likely find it in even the grandest shop in Piccadilly."

Impressed, she sipped more slowly. She felt warm and contented, and let her head sink back into the couch. The fire screen was changing colors in the most marvelous way, becoming even brighter, and the naked figures moved across it. She caught her breath as a sudden stab of longing took her in the pit of the stomach. It was as if the figures were real and not real at the same time: beautiful, as in art, and yet her in it, moving with them. Above, in a lavender sky, a great golden moon shone, sending off rays like galaxies of tiny stars. The people were gathered in a circle around what appeared to be the only ugly thing in the world: a monstrous, grinning boar. She saw now that they were not dancing, but copulating—making love in all sorts of ways, some of which she recognized at once, others of which were foreign to her.

She felt another wave of longing, to be alive, to be touched, to hold them, to be held by them. Suddenly, they shifted, changed partners, seemed to expect her to join in. She tried to shout, but it was too late. A man with his head shaven had already severed his penis with a gleaming blade, which now dripped with blood. He seemed to be deliriously happy. Ann was terrified, and—*God help me!* she thought —excited.

Another man was lost in ecstasy, a child no more than ten years old, kneeling, her young mouth caressing the end of his huge instrument. Ann felt herself moving toward the man (or was it toward the girl?), wanting to cry out because the pain—warm and deep and unbelievably delicious—seemed to be tearing her insides apart.

"And now," a voice was saying, a voice from far away, "we must render thanksgiving."

Ann was grudgingly aware of Dr. Forman. He had crossed the room, and was moving a heavy figurine from an oak cabinet to a desk near the couch. Its main form was that of a lion with the neck of a serpent. Astride its back . . . no, growing out of its back . . . was the torso and thick head of a man with pointed ears, his mouth open as if to devour something large. From his shoulders grew two more heads, one of a bull, the other of a goat. The eyes in the human head appeared to glow.

"You are in the presence of Ashmodeus," Dr. Forman said in a voice sounding far removed. "Open yourself to him. Give and he will repay you eternally. Obey. Be compliant. Place your money—all that you possess, yourself—before him, and he will grant you complete sovereignty over your life. Obey immediately."

She watched him rustle about with her bundle of coins.

"Daughter," he intoned, "with your eyes fixed only upon Ashmodeus, brother of Astoreth, remove every stitch of your clothing."

Ann had begun to comply almost before the request, but now she glanced about uncertainly.

"Do not turn your head!" Dr. Forman said sternly. "Do as Ashmodeus wills."

"My lord," Ann said as she removed the rest of her clothing, "this is blasphemous. And unlawful."

Somewhere a new voice was saying, "King James is an ass. He writes books, pays men to affirm the existence of Ashmodeus and his brothers, and then he passes laws against them. He is a fool. He claims that, with his sword, he will deny you sovereignty over your life, which I give to you and to you only. You have affirmed your own will in this matter, and let that be the end of it. Turn your eyes to the fire screen and join in, for this is my desire."

Now it seemed that the entire world—all the people and the strange animal in the center of the circle—was dancing, singing. The sky was suddenly soft blue, and the signs of the Zodiac emerged in brilliant gold.

Dr. Forman's voice came softly from behind her. "You have said that you will to design clothing, to work for a great master of the theatre, and already it is done. This station is yours by right, and it shall be yours, in fact, before the week is out."

She felt his strong hands upon her, but his voice was soothing.

"Beloved Ashmodeus, god of the eternal ebb and flow of creation and destruction, true god of friendship, brother of Astoreth, allow your creature domain over her own will, and over that substance which thou hast promised shall be hers. She has given you her all; she will give her all this moment, as a fair token of her gratitude in that you release her from the oppression of herself. Loose her from all bondage, and grant her peace."

He removed his hands.

"Dear child," he said, "stand alone before your father, Ashmodeus, and let him feast his sapphire eyes on you."

She stood, without shivering, before the fire screen. Dr. Forman touched her breasts. "You are magnificent," he said, in a voice that seemed to echo. "Surely no man can afford such splendors. Oh, and to believe that I, an old man, have been chosen by Ashmodeus, in whose eyes we live and move and have our being . . ."

She started to speak, but he hushed her.

"Quiet, now. Ingratitude is a sin, in any religion. And I among all men owe thanks. To have thought . . . Yes, I have known many women. But above all of them, you . . . surely, you are sought after by the greatest of the realm . . ."

He embraced her and she felt warmth, from the bone marrow outward.

"Now," he said, "in my person, you shall be visited by Prince Ashmodeus himself."

She felt herself being pushed down onto the fur rug by the fireplace, with Dr. Forman slowly descending on her, and Mother of God, it all seemed so different: emotional, confusing. He had not bothered to remove his coat, and Ann clutched at the rough tweed. It was not a fabric she had ever liked, but now she clutched at it, felt the wool on her legs and arms, and even the fur beneath her felt warm and woolly and rough. The rhythm of his thrusts made her feel that she was being pushed into the fabric of the rug. Her lower body seemed to envelop him, and the room, and then she wanted to cry out, but could not. She saw herself in the fire screen, an incredibly handsome blond youth astride her: a warm, liquid wave descended over her, and it seemed now that she was weeping after all.

"No, no," she cried, but the rhythm increased. "Please," she insisted, pushing, pushing him back. "I must. You must."

She guided him backwards until they had changed places on the rug. He had the biggest leather-stretcher she'd ever seen; now she took it tenderly, rubbed her soft cheek against it, moist with herself. Then, ever so slowly, with a burning she had never felt before, she came down upon that throbbing flesh with a mouth as soft and warm and experienced as she could make it. But with a difference, too. She administered her art fully, gently, warmly, but also ravenously, until not a trace of loneliness remained in her. And above her, two brightly shining emerald eyes looked down, imparting reassurance, understanding, love.

11

By May-day the overcast had lifted. The day dawned, bright and warm, with only a few white clouds scudding high in thin waves. The festival would fill the better part of a week, and preparations had been under way about St. James for almost twice that long: apartments overflowing with visitors, London all a-bustle, cooks and servants scurrying about, their faces fastened to looks of determination. Workers were still raising the tents and pavilions on the green that would serve to house displays.

Queen Anne had maintained high spirits during these days of preparation, appearing often to check on decorations, asking questions, and showing herself amused. The reason for her excitement was obvious to James, and probably to everyone else who knew the schedule of events. The festival would open in early afternoon today with a well-planned tilting contest, in which Prince Henry would be the most celebrated entrant (and all but certain victor). James knew that the whole idea of having London's traditional May festival centered at Whitehall rather than on the embankment, as usual, was Henry's. The lion's share of the work for the occasion had fallen to one of his cronies, a commoner named Inigo Jones. And what a commoner Jones was!

James had only recently appointed Master Jones to be the Surveyor of Public Projects (a post James himself had invented) in an effort to soften his denial of Henry's request for Harington's advancement. In the King's mind, this post as Surveyor of Public Projects was intended to be far less exalted than its sound (its total annual stipend would be a modest £30).

Henry had shown himself so delighted by James's gesture that, for a moment, the King had entertained second thoughts about its wisdom. Almost before the ink was dry on the document, Master Jones and Prince Henry had fallen to nightly conferences at the Mermaid, a tavern known as the haunt of many of Henry's untitled friends, but never before, according to reliable sources of information, of Henry himself. The story had come to James that when Henry arrived at the Mermaid, Inigo Jones, summoned from the private dining room, would take a corner table with the Prince, where they would talk rapidly and often simultaneously, rattling large sheets of paper— obviously, plans for the festival.

It was hard to describe this group: it was not, in the usual sense of commonality, a formal group at all. No one was ever initiated into it. Who were they, then, and how did they fit together? Many were from the theatre, but all were dining companions moving between the Mermaid and the Mitre for almost nightly dinners and conversations. Many were lawyers, and several were poets; Lionel Cranfield, whose vigor in the field of making money had come to the King's attention, was an almost constant participant, and yet some people doubted that he had ever even read a book.

Neither could one discern among its members a single religious or political aim of the group. James had people inquiring into this aspect of the society. Not that these men were secretive or sinister: it was well known that they sought each other's society, and they were always in evidence, conducting their apparently continual social, literary and economic affairs as public events. And many of the most promising young men in the realm belonged to this group: John Donne, Egerton's brilliant protégé, an attorney; Ben Jonson, the poet and playwright; Christopher Brooke, Sir Henry Goodyere, Henry Wotton; and the apparently brilliant Master Inigo Jones himself.

James had noticed, however, how pointedly the most important intellectual in England—Francis Bacon (the King's own Solicitor General)—deprived himself of the company of this precocious group. Perhaps they told themselves that Sir Francis could not tear himself away from his state duties, but it was not likely that any difference in rank could stick as a persuasive reason for his absence. Sir Henry

Goodyere bore a title, and Donne, though a commoner, had been close to Essex and, even now, owned the energetic and emotional patronage of Thomas Egerton, the elegant Lord Ellesmere (Chancellor of England). Beyond that, even James was impressed by the way in which Donne captivated the best-trained minds in his court, namely, those associated with Southampton, the Pembrokes and the Countess of Bedford.

The May festival would begin with the tilting match and end three days later, at midnight, with a masque (the last of three), written by Ben Jonson. It was to be the major social event of the year, and included a dance to which virtually every estimable person in England had been invited. Not only would it celebrate the coming of spring in its most ecstatic manifestations, it would also announce the official opening of the new theatre season. And of course the hand of Inigo Jones in all this was hardly coincidental. He was preeminently the best and the most successful (were the two not the same?) theatrical designer and entrepreneur in all of England, and by awarding him an office under the Crown, James had merely made official what was already obvious: his own love of the stage.

Now he strolled across the Green toward the Banqueting House, which he had ordered built shortly after his succession. The original structure, erected by Elizabeth, must have cost practically nothing! It was a rambling, leaning monstrosity made of old timbers, canvas-covered walls and nearly three hundred panes of rippling glass. It was wondrous that the roof had not caved in long before James had the building pulled down. The walls and ceiling were covered with every conceivable manner of flower, vine or fruit, save in those spots where coats of arms were peeling away.

Simon Basil, the King's first Surveyor of Public Works, was responsible for the construction, but James knew that Tobie Samways, a lowly clerk in Basil's office, sketched the actual design for ten shillings and a hogshead of canary. Because he knew that his own masques would often be presented there, Inigo Jones volunteered—indeed, insisted on—his help with the crenellated balustrade atop the building on the east (toward the tilt-yard) and west (in the direction of the wine cellar and the King's old apartments at York House). It was Jones's fault that the whole of it looked suspiciously like St. Peter's Basilica. (It was Jones, not Simon Basil, who had spent a year in Italy, gazing at ruins and church walls.)

The interior was even worse.

"I don't like it," James had said. "A myriad of blazing windows may displease, but seven makes a cave: slim light and less symmetry. Why must we have pillars set before windows in support of thin air?"

But he wasn't truly angry: Basil and James had learned their lesson; besides, this structure was more suited than the old to masques and entertainments. And it was built by a Stuart, not a Tudor.

James let his chest fill with the balmy scent of the first May morning of the year, then coughed with unsavory phlegm. Rheum, unfortunately: the last dismal token of the English winter. He chanced another deep breath, and felt good. He liked all the activity about him. He liked the sun that had found his face through the leaves of the big tree by the water. This morning he was happy.

Squadrons of ducks were playing in the water. A young man, displaying unusual get-up-and-go even for spring, was already out in a small boat with a daintily dressed young lady. James fingered his thin beard and out of the corner of his eye watched the couple, leaning together in the middle of the boat that scarcely moved. Then he strolled over to watch the workers constructing the viewing stands. He could see Inigo Jones moving about, giving directions, and now he could not resist looking to see if Henry was nearby, too. He wasn't.

James had mixed feelings about this afternoon's tilt. Henry had not asked his advice about participating. In fact, no one had consulted him about it. But to raise objections seemed ill-advised, especially since the Queen had taken such an obvious public role as sponsor.

They had the course arranged aslant between the Banqueting House and St. James Palace, roughly parallel to the long pond. The tilt-yard had no precise dimensions, but was always set up in the same general location. This time it appeared that the men would send their horses at each other on a course much narrower than usual—twenty yards across, it appeared—and would thus be much closer to the viewers: the unmistakable theatrical hand, again, of Inigo Jones. If someone fell, he might well land right in the stands. And one had to remember that horses fell, too.

Atop the stands were pennants—this was a nice touch!—with the lion of Scotland marked magnificently in black on purple. Inigo Jones intended a fine compliment to the House of Stuart. From a theatrical point of view, the effect promised to be stunning. And after all, James reminded himself, most often men were not injured in these events.

The modern tilt was nothing like its medieval antecedent. Then, men hurtled at each other with the intent of unseating the opponent. And when a man fell from his horse, especially in armor, bones were easily broken. Sad cases were on record of breaks so severe, and of bruises swelling so quickly, that the injured man could not be extricated from his metal suit without the excruciating and lengthy application of the workman's chisel. Nowadays, if a participant fell, it was by accident. Indeed, if one did in fact unseat his opponent, the rules of competition declared him a loser by default.

The one rule accepted in every tilting match was that no contact be made between the lance and one's adversary: the optimum result was deftly to remove the "favor" loosely tied to his left arm, and if this could be done without so much as tapping his armor, one would then be the likely winner. But this almost never happened. In fact, James had never heard of a favor ever having fallen except by the accident of wind or of faulty tying. Nobody really aimed at the favor, out of risk of hitting the opponent (or, worse still, of unseating himself). It was extraordinarily difficult to maneuver the tip of a heavy lance, which loomed many feet beyond the unsteady, hooded head of one's hurtling mount; one must rely on muscles that were seldom used.

And beyond this, the audience was a source of apprehension: hundreds of spectators, many of them worthies whose respect one desired. To fall, or even to look awkward, meant embarrassment. Tempers often flared, and more than one duel had been fought over a disputed match.

The tilting was judged by a panel designated by the sponsors of the event. The Lord Mayor of London was a fixture on panels in or near London. Beyond such ceremonial appointees, the membership usually comprised men known for their high equestrian standards or scholars versed in the ancient practices of jousting. The winner would be the entrant whose performance most fit the panel's collective notion of what knights should be like. Inigo Jones obviously grasped this aspect of the tilt, for what James saw in front of him now was something like the preparation for an elaborate masque, the theatrical form which he had all but made synonymous with his name.

Just then he became aware of a flurry behind him. A horseman was making his way along the pond, as if oblivious of the crowds in his path. Soon he was near enough to identify: it was Robin, claiming important business with the King.

"Here I am, Robin," James said good-naturedly, though he was annoyed that his pleasant morning stroll, his enjoyment in watching the preparations for the festival, was over. "What is it that puts the lives of my subjects in jeopardy and upsets your sovereign's ducks on the pond?"

"Your Majesty," Robin said, bowing stiffly, "it is urgent that I speak to you alone."

Hmmm. There he went: a statement of fact rather than a request. Rather baldly, his Gentleman of the Bedchamber, his aid and adviser but nonetheless his subject, had, under pretense of serving, tendered his sovereign a thinly veiled directive that he attend to him immediately and in private. And this effrontery from a man who only weeks ago could scarcely speak without a stammer or walk without stumbling in the King's presence. Ah, well.

James led him closer to the pond, where now the young couple in the boat regarded them uncertainly, having lost the focus of their concentration.

"Now, Robin," he said, "you have interrupted my walk, and my reflections on the demise of the institution of trial by combat, for what I take to be high purpose . . ."

Carr smiled intimately, and James admired his teeth, which were straight, and whiter by far than those of most Scots—than his own, for instance. He had often wondered what made one man's teeth whiter than another's. Dr. Edwards (Mayerne was of no opinion) insisted that the distribution of the humors in the body determined the color and strength of one's bones. Here again was the weakness of medicine, which often could do no more than provide as an answer a different way of putting your question.

"I have news, James."

"I had suspicions . . ." the King murmured.

"Thomas Overbury suggested that you ought to be told at once."

Robin always seemed to know when and how to make matters worse. James hadn't minded Carr's appointing Overbury as his aide (God knew he needed one), but it seemed that he was forever either deferring to Overbury or blaming him, one or the other, and James could not decide which was worse. An aide was just that. And he was Robin's aide, not James's.

"Spare me the personal opinions of Mr. Overbury, please," James said. "He is a man who should take care to be less certain of his King's wishes for him."

Robin looked quizzically at him, but appeared unruffled by the remark. "Now that we are on that subject, James, that is, of your wishes for Overbury, perhaps we could arrange some elevation of his . . ."

"Perhaps," James said, "but not this morning. It goes without saying that not even Mr. Overbury would be so presumptuous as to send you on an errand to interrupt my walk, all a-flutter, merely to urge his own advancement."

"No. Quite right," Robin said crisply, missing the point again but smiling broadly.

He was surely a marvelously handsome young Scot. If there was jealousy of him at court, at least it was of a Scot, and that pleased James.

"The news is," he continued, "and you have shown great interest in the subject, which is why I took the liberty . . ." He seemed to respond, now, to James's tight grimace. "In Newcastle, James, nine of your subjects have been hung!"

"Hanged," James said.

"Precisely," Carr said, imitating Overbury (and missing the point all at once). "Nine people, five women and four men, condemned as witches, in Newcastle."

"This is interesting news, Robin," James said, "but it would have been just as interesting an hour from now."

"But that isn't all. Two more witches are still to be tried. I knew that you would wish to go . . ."

James looked at Carr with an exaggerated stare of incredulity. "My sweet Robin! To Newcastle? On May-day?"

"But you have always said . . . taken such an . . ."

"Are you suggesting, Robin, that you might like to go to Newcastle with me? That you might consider missing the festivities? If we went that far north, perhaps a little visit to Edinburgh?"

Carr smiled, but seemed taken aback by the tone of anger that met him.

"I have no intention of leaving Whitehall now. You—and Overbury, too, I have no doubt—know that everybody is here, that Prince Henry will be—"

"Yes, in the tilt, I know."

"And then we have a week of revelry, masquing, dancing, drinking
. . . Why give this up for a dreary pilgrimage to Newcastle?"

James knew the answer, but he was not sure that Carr did. Overbury wanted to get James away from London, away from every claimant to the King's attention but Carr.

"Tell Mr. Overbury," he said, "that I commission him to fetch the
principals in this case for me."

"To bring them to London?" Carr said weakly.

James nodded. "You say it is a serious matter, and it is. Nine of
my subjects hanged, and two others face the same rope? On whose
witness? Who is judge of this assize? What is the evidence? Why was
I not informed? Who is more knowledgeable of the black art than I?"

Carr shrugged innocently. "Precisely," he said, smiling blandly.
"You should have been informed. And I shall look into the matter
right away."

"Let Overbury look into it," James said. "Contact Bacon.
You must prepare for the weekend. For the tilts, the masques, the
women . . ." He looked at Robin, whose bright blue eyes shone
innocently. "You do plan to attend?"

BY THIS TIME in her life, Ann Turner was burdened by few illusions
about herself, having surrendered the greater part of them years ago,
when her husband left her and Davy for the New World rather than
face imprisonment for nonpayment of a scrivener's loan. She knew
there was little she could do to change her life without changing her
address. Though tolerant of her problems, Master Inigo Jones would
not see her established in her new situation while carrying her old
acquaintances around for baggage, especially considering the quality
of the friends she had collected. Franklin, for instance: even at the
Blue Boar (no stranger to the patronage of commoners), the rudest
churls avoided his persistent company.

She had expected her separation from the Boar to be difficult. Once
men had you, regardless how you felt about them, whether you
wished to see them or not, they were hard to get rid of. They pretended not to notice when you avoided their glance. Or they sulked
and stood about, as if patiently awaiting your return to good sense.
Men were stubborn. And there was always money to think about,
always Davy, always tomorrow.

So she had stolen away from her old lodgings over the Boar, leaving not even a whisper of goodbye behind her. That night she had coaxed old Franklin off down the steps, staggering with fatigue and satisfaction, urging him not to awaken the boy. When he was out of sight, she had quietly stirred Davy herself and, taking practically nothing with her (which was almost all she had), had slipped off to the small shop which Master Jones had announced would be her own. Here she would make dresses, design costumes and discuss sketches with Master Jones or one of his assistants.

Across from the Bear Garden, and so near the Globe, the shop was in a most favorable location for them both, Master Jones had said. It appeared that he had owned the building for some time, but Ann was too shy to inquire into details. She had no inclination whatever to ask Master Jones about his connection with Dr. Forman. Far from it: she was relieved that he had put no questions to her about her own acquaintance with the magician.

And she was happy with the results of that strange, brief meeting in those waterfront quarters. Her dreams and her new world were one and the same. The days passed in a lazy, dreamlike haze as she sketched designs for her patrons—who were apt to be ladies of rank, cultivating Master Jones's newest protégé—and for her employer. He used her ideas in making costumes for court entertainments. She liked it when he dropped by the shop: he swept in with such flare, such grace, and such clothes. He seemed attired as if to step onstage in one of his own masques.

But most of all she liked to spend time with her ladies. Invariably, they made a fuss about her work, which they found "modish." And though she was shy when the discussion turned to her, she did take pleasure when the ladies admired her looks. She had long since grown weary of the awkward, repetitious admiration of men, but a compliment from a lady, especially one of worth, was true and gratifying for being made without self-interest.

In response to their praise, Ann strove mightily to make each gown —worried each detail—fit the lady for whom it was designed in every way: fabric, color, neckline, needlework, lace, overlay, ornamentation. Everything perfect, but only for the one lady. She would sit quietly, watching the one client, while the others talked. She would pretend to listen to their opinions on what the gown required, but in truth she never really heard. Ann knew that she and she alone could design the most beautiful dress possible for the lady who had come to her.

So the long days of work passed: drawing, cutting, sewing, fitting, running down to the Bridge for supplies. Sometimes, when no one was around, she would stand in the shop, smiling, or perhaps she would move an article of clothing in the small showcase facing the street. Spring was in the air. Davy seemed happy, now that she didn't have to spend her nights at the Boar, now that she had time for him.

And then Franklin found her.

"Bankside is crowded," he crowed when Ann inquired about his discovery of her new shop, "but not so crowded by half as to let a gem like you slip from sight."

"But I left no word," she said.

"None," he said, "not one. It was Davy, you see, a comer, that one. Dropped by the place one day, set for some spice-candy of the sort I use as remedy for the rheum."

How appalling he was with his green and twisted gap-toothed smile. Now she wondered how she had ever managed to be near him. She simply had to get rid of him, not just for Davy, no longer even primarily for him. If she could remove Franklin from the scene, Ann would face entirely new prospects—for greater pleasure in her work, yes, but also for satisfaction of her most secret desires for herself.

She had met a man.

Sir Ralph Winwood was his name.

He had important friends and a very nice voice. Though she had only dreamed of such things, though good sense argued the foolishness of such hopes, Ann could tell that this man of importance was keen for her. Any woman could have seen it, and in such matters Ann was not just any woman. She had not even used her usual ploy of appearing totally distracted, of letting her large eyes gaze vacantly in the direction of her prospect; indeed, she had not tried to tempt a man since that night with Dr. Forman.

Sir Ralph had entered the shop one day after standing by the showcase, as if admiring her display. He immediately claimed interest in Ann's latest creation, a green velvet gown with a white lace overlay, but he appeared unperturbed when she told him it was not for sale.

"I am most awfully sorry, my lord," she said, "but I placed it in the window only for show. It belongs to—I have only just finished it —the Countess of Essex."

"Hmmm," he said in a low, pleasant voice.

"She is to wear it," Ann, not usually talkative, volunteered, "for the May festival."

Sir Ralph did not answer; nor did he leave, but, after introducing himself with considerable formality, proceeded to relax about the place, examine fabrics, look over her drawing table. "Hmmm," he said often.

And he remained when patrons entered; one, an extraordinarily beautiful woman, had come for a fitting. Even with her back to him, Ann knew that he was watching, not the grand and lovely lady, but her, that he was fascinated by *her*. The women took no notice, and, when they stepped into the dressing room, Sir Ralph whispered to her.

"My dear, you have come to the attention of the Countess of Rutland. I am impressed."

Ann didn't know who the Countess of Rutland was (the beautiful one, she assumed), but she smiled her most luscious smile, and enjoyed the way Sir Ralph appeared to melt. She suspected that men found her looks haunting, and partly sad. But when her full mouth widened in one of her infrequent smiles, the transformation seemed to startle them. And on Sir Ralph it seemed to work more than its usual effect. Ann enjoyed seeing that such a man desired her.

He wasn't particularly handsome, but he knew how to dress, how to stand, how to talk. And what mattered most was a man's composure. Franklin was such an idiot by comparison, rattling on and on in his wild, scratchy voice, even while making love. Sir Ralph could stand for a long time without saying anything, making her wonder what he would say next, or whether he would speak at all. Ann found him exciting.

The Countess and her woman returned, settled on the appointments of the gown Ann was to make up, and left. Sir Ralph strode toward her confidently.

"Convenient location," he said.

Ann said nothing.

"The shop, I mean. Hard to miss it, whether one is on his way to the theatre or to the bear-baiting pit."

"Yes," she said quietly. "People are forever walking by . . ."

She wanted to tell him how much pleasure she took just watching them go by, especially near twilight, with the clouds drifting red and fast behind the Globe, and the smell of the pastures beyond pungent in her nostrils, mixed with the familiar, bracing scent of the Thames. To be free of the old life (except for Franklin), to be free to work all day, and into the night, too, and to see others moving free and happy —she wanted to tell him this.

Now she loved everything and everybody. She was not one to bear grudges, and if Franklin would but go away, she would love him, too. She even had a good feeling about Dr. Forman: after all, she had done nothing with him than she hadn't done with many others; perhaps she had enjoyed it more, but she had not gone back to see him. If she found herself imagining how things would be with Sir Ralph, and if she thought of that night with Dr. Forman for comparison, what of that? She was trying this moment to think only of Sir Ralph.

Sir Ralph helped out: "So! You design for various ladies?"

"For anyone who wishes, my lord," she answered. "But I am on regular commission for Master Inigo Jones."

She tried to make this last come out softly, without fanfare, but she could see from the twinkle in Sir Ralph's eyes that he had caught her excitement.

"Hmmm," he said. "The Countesses of Rutland and Essex. His Majesty's Master Surveyor. And, I expect, your achievements for Inigo Jones are to dazzle the court on May-day?"

She nodded.

"And you?" he asked. "Where will you be when the torches are set ablaze in Whitehall?"

Ann smiled radiantly.

"Buried in the recesses of St. James, no doubt," he said.

"I must be there to help my ladies," she said.

"Well then," said Sir Ralph, "we must find some way of persuading your ladies to help you—ah, to help me." He touched her lightly on the cheek and left the shop.

Ann pondered the meaning of that parting remark. Then, almost as soon as the door closed behind Sir Ralph, Franklin arrived with Davy in tow.

"Spotted this rascal near the Bridge," he said, as if he had earned his night's bed and board.

God's wounds, this creature was annoying, but she refused to let him bother her tonight. Sir Ralph would surely be back, and meanwhile she must not let Franklin mar the joy inside her. Within an hour, she had poured sufficient ale into him that she was able to send him off without so much as a plaintive sigh.

She put Davy to bed, and then sat watching him long after he had fallen asleep. He was growing fast, and yet, with his shock of blond hair tousled across his forehead, almost covering his eyes, and not a trace of frown anywhere, he looked so young, so innocent, so vulnerable, that she kissed him hard, and felt the tears burn down her cheeks as she squeezed him to her.

Blessed Mother, was it all real? Was the nightmare of her life coming to a close? Could it be, with her ruined marriage, the endless nights at the Blue Boar, that she might really begin again?

For a time she walked slowly around the shop, half-heartedly straightening materials and tools for tomorrow's work. She opened the door and stepped outside. Above, the clouds were hurtling beneath a full moon. The smell of May was in the air, and she had much work left to do before the festival. But that was good. She needed her work, not only for money, but for the work itself. With the breeze off the Thames in her nostrils, and the clear stillness of the darkened houses around her, she felt welling within her a deep sense of peace. She stood quietly, listening as, just then, the bellman cried in the distance:

> *Midnight calls your bellman to his task,*
> *To see your doors and windows are all fast.*
> *And that no villainy or murder may be done,*
> *Before we bid good morrow to the sun.*

IN THE PERPETUAL TRUMP GAME of intrigue dealt in the court of St. James, Overbury had overplayed his hand. Possessing the kind of intelligence lending to flexibility in only small matters, he recognized that he must either "trim" or take the consequences. The latter course looked unpromising: poor food, worse company, a cramped journey by coach to Yorkshire—a place populated almost solely by Yorkshiremen, who spoke in a brogue thicker than the dullest Scot's. So Overbury quietly dispatched a message under the King's seal to the Judge

of the Assize, ordering him to fetch the remaining witches to Whitehall for the King's examination.

All in all, given his original miscalculation, the matter had turned
out about as well as could be expected. Overbury was suspicious of
state-sponsored festivals, events which seemed advantageous to the
interests of his adversaries. On the other hand, he was encouraged on
this occasion by the prospect of seeing the Countess of Rutland again.
Though during the past month he had penned several impertinently
ardent letters to her, and though she had not seen fit to answer even
one, he had exacted from the Countess a near-promise that he might
escort her to the feted event of the week, the Inigo Jones production
of the new Daniel masque, *The Queen's Wake.* The Queen, Princess
Elizabeth and young Prince Charles were to be in the cast. Overbury
felt that, once he appeared at the Banquet Hall with the Countess, he
would surely be knighted, perhaps made a baron. Why not? James
would not permit a man to appear in polite company with the most
eminent, most beautiful woman in Britain without so much as the
blandishment of a title.

Overbury's social position was a definite embarrassment. He had to
sign letters carrying the most august authority with no more than his
bare name. "Don't you see?" he often said to Carr. "This remains a
serious threat to your own aspirations."

Carr was a serious courtier. He moved about, overhearing conversations whose wisdom he passed off, in the King's presence, as his
own. This was a common enough practice; in the indolent, it was
virtually the only alternative to a vow of perpetual silence. Robin's
trouble was that he abused court practice by getting things consis-
tently mixed up. Nor could he distinguish when a remark was meant
seriously or merely passed off in jest. No one had ever been able to
explain to him the wonders of irony. And after taking it upon himself
to instruct Carr in Latin, James had soon found time for more and
more infrequent lessons, before quietly suspending them entirely.

Everyone knew that Overbury did Carr's job. He advised Carr, who
advised James on all matters, foreign and domestic; he handled all of
Carr's correspondence, which included briefing the Privy Council of
developments in both areas; he prepared the Star Chamber for its
advising sessions with the King. In this way, though possessing no
state title or official position, Overbury had in a few weeks become one

of the most influential men in England. But his power was indirect, worked through Carr, and therefore subject to counter-influences of the court. Everyone who mattered—Cecil, Suffolk, Northampton, the Spanish Party and all their minions—knew that Carr had little mind of his own. They constantly importuned Robin with ideas, opinions, rumors, arguments, bribes, until it was more than he could possibly absorb. And sometimes they suggested he follow a course of action to which they were irrevocably opposed, hoping that, by confusing things entirely, he might bring about their desired end.

Whether or no his power was limited, Overbury sensed that he had reached the apex of his career. He suspected that James was not fond of him; perhaps the King resented his earlier attachment to Robin. On the other hand, James didn't totally dislike him, either. The two would likely keep their distance from each other, which meant that Overbury could not expect such gratuities of money and estates as James now heaped upon his favorite (to the outcry of both houses of Parliament). No, his true enemy was the lovely, willowy, elusive Queen Anne, whose well-known hatred of Carr had no convenient outlet until Overbury came along.

No single incident stood out in his mind as evidence of her dislike, but she fairly bristled when he was around. And although he did his best to avoid her, Robin had nonetheless several times inquired what he had done to give the Queen displeasure. "Thomas," he had said only days ago, "the Queen thinks you are insolent."

Carr might lack grace, but he had no lack of candor. At that moment, both the Pembroke and Howard factions were sponsoring the view that Overbury was arrogant and unworthy of trust. The former accusation was patently unfair. But even Overbury's few friends—even Overbury himself—preferred to ignore the social impact of his notable self-confidence. Overbury realized that it put some people off, but he suspected, too, that others (the Countess of Rutland, for example) found his arch manner attractive. Still, he took Robin's warning to heart. It was one thing to enjoy the luxury of rejecting Northampton's patronage, but quite another to cultivate Queen Anne as an adversary.

So it was not without reason that Overbury found an unforeseen encounter in the courtyard of St. James faintly disquieting. Moments before the tilting events in Green Park were scheduled to begin, he caught sight of Carr, struggling from the palace basement replete in a new suit of armor. He seemed to have trouble breathing, and he looked miserable. The armor, he explained, had been fashioned to a version of himself a year earlier and one stone lighter.

"Such minor discomforts go with high station," Overbury said, chuckling.

The situation became all the funnier as Carr, struggling to breathe, fought against his impulse to laugh. At just that moment, several ladies approached swiftly, and had almost passed before Overbury realized they were in the presence of Queen Anne, accompanied by Princess Elizabeth and the very fetching, youngest Howard girl, Lady Essex.

Giving no pause to her step, the Queen spoke: "There go Carr and his keeper."

Having caught the madness of the season (and having stopped at one of the booths in the Green Park for a tankard), Overbury was altogether ready to enjoy the Queen's wit. Seeing Carr standing there, arms out stiffly, looking sadly like an ape, he guffawed so loudly that he surprised even himself by the sudden volume.

It was not until the ladies had passed that he realized the meaning of the Queen's observation. She had intended, not a jest, but a rebuke. She had meant merely to insult both him and Carr in one brief sentence: Carr and keeper, Carr and governor. It was a most withering remark, belittling to Carr, but devastatingly perceptive with respect to their relationship in all its courtly implications. Surely she would regard Overbury's full-bodied guffaw as, at best, a sign of rudeness, or, at worst, evidence of contempt.

Robin's mind was elsewhere, fixed on the more immediate problem of staying astride his horse.

"This is how I broke my leg," he said earnestly.

"And how you became rich," Overbury added, as they made their way toward the tilt-yard.

The story was well-known. Carr, once a page to James in Edinburgh, had been dispatched by the Queen for his rude manners. She had not cared for him even then, and had sent him to France, where he would study in the service of Lord Hay. She had all but forgotten him when, during a progress of Hay's entourage upon his return to England, Carr tumbled from his mount directly in front of the King's stand in the tilt-yard.

James himself had gone to help him up. And what he saw when he reached the fallen rider was a face, though twisted in agony, more beautiful than any at court. James had the man sent to a house close by in Charing Cross Road, and placed him in the care of Sir Theodore Mayerne, his most celebrated physician. During the weeks of his convalescence, Carr was visited often by the King, who brought him gifts of fruit and sweets, and who was delighted to find that this gorgeous young man was not only a Scot but had once been a member of his own household.

"You and horses," Overbury said now, "are made for each other. If you catch a kingdom by falling, imagine what will happen if you stay astride."

Carr seemed pleased with himself. "Thomas, today is our day," he announced. "I have persuaded Jamie to give you a title."

This was perfect. And Overbury had not yet marched grandly into the Banqueting House with the Countess of Rutland on his arm. Whatever apprehensions he had entertained dissolved in the excitement of this news. But what title? There were so many in England. An earldom was out of the question; Carr himself was only a viscount. He would be glad of a modest barony.

"You are to be knighted," Carr said.

Ah well, no barony, but at least knighthood. It was preferable to having no title at all. Ordinarily, no considerations accompanied so humble an elevation, but then no statute barred James from parting with custom. Another stipend—£500 a year—would not attract too much attention in Parliament. Besides, Overbury was a Protestant, and the Commons was up in arms about the Catholic leanings of James's court. He would be Sir Thomas Overbury: not a bad beginning, after only six weeks of his return to England.

"And you are to be the new Server to the King," Carr said.

This made it even better: an official position in the King's house: nothing overwhelming, but one must be tactful. "What precisely . . ."

"Is a Server?" Carr said. "A new post! Just as Jamie invented the post of Master Surveyor for Simon Basil, and now Master Jones, he has made this title for you. You'll be with the King, privately, just as I am. Serving. A server. No, the Server, just as I am His Majesty's Gentleman of the Bedchamber."

Overbury waited for word of the perquisites of his new office.

"Although my status," Carr said evenly, "will be changing, too."

Overbury feigned sudden interest in the stableboys' efforts to settle the first two competitors in their saddles.

"The Raleigh estate in Sherbourne," Carr said. "It will be mine. And I shall be appointed permanent member of the Privy Council."

This was indeed an auspicious day. For a moment, Overbury thought of dashing out to the Serpentine for a spell at the tables, to make the most of this windfall hour. But he must soon call on the Countess. Besides, the trumpets had already sounded, and the crowd was settling into the grandstands. Robin left for the staging area, where stableboys were still eying with suspicion their armored masters, who tottered uncertainly on grandly festooned stallions.

At that moment, from the courtyard of St. James Palace, the royal procession emerged. In front of a double line of equestrians came a resplendently arrayed elephant, carrying an elaborate golden coach upon its back from which, to the enthusiastic shouts of onlookers, lovely young women waved, fluttering the loose gossamer of their Inigo Jones creations.

Overbury smiled: river nymphs. Under the guise of good theatre, this master craftsman, Jones, had maneuvered the noblest families in England—the Royal Family itself, for there was young Elizabeth!— to appear half-nude before the London rabble.

And at the head of the procession proper, astride his favorite white stallion, nodding and smiling with pursed lips, rode King James. At his left, riding a small white mare, Queen Anne of Denmark beamed at the cheering crowd.

Overbury took in a bountiful draught of that May afternoon air. To be a part of all that splendor, and yet removed from it! On that bright day, with the sun and the King's face shining on him, it seemed he was within sight of his highest goals. Yes, and it was time to fetch the Countess of Rutland, time to start enjoying this, one of England's few remaining pagan holidays.

FROM ATOP THE ELEPHANT Frances could see the man with whom she had only moments ago fallen in love. The coach pitched and rolled beneath her like a ship in the Channel, but she could still see that this gentleman was no rider. She imagined herself instructing him on morning gallops from Audley End to the marketplace in Saffron Walden. Carr would come for a stay in the summer, standing like a stick in his stirrups, and when he left he would be riding like one of the Queen's Guards.

The elephant swung along in a mercifully slow, steady gait. The young ladies with her looked a touch seasick, all gripping at the coach rail, their faces frozen in identically unconvincing smiles: it was a long way down. Princess Elizabeth was frantic, claiming that they were being pitched about because the girth straps were not attached sufficiently tight: in fact, she thought the coach was slipping from the animal's back.

Queen Anne would play the title figure, Tethys, in the Daniel masque—Neptune's wife, and so Queen of the Ocean—and the countesses were all nymphs, representing the rivers closest to their country estates: Arundel was Arun; Dorset, Ayr; Montgomery, the Severn. Frances, Countess of Essex, was the nymph of the River Lee. Her Grace, Lady Elizabeth, would play the spirit of the Thames. At Inigo Jones's insistence, the young ladies were being introduced to the crowd in their costumes.

Now the beast's African guide brought the elephant to kneel in front of the stands. Two pages came forward with portable stairs; as the ladies stepped down from the coach, the throng gave a great show of enthusiasm for the revealing garments. Even Frances, blessed by all circumstances of birth and training, was awed that such splendor could be fashioned of mere fabric and thread. Though in the masque itself, except for the sheerest film of gossamer, the gowns would leave the ladies' breasts exposed, Queen Anne had persuaded Master Jones that this display was fit only for the suffused lighting of the performance. For the present occasion, Master Jones had acceded to a second layer of similar but darker material draped over the shoulders, but as the crowd indicated, in the sun's glare the added fabric fell short of meeting the Queen's purpose.

The nymphs curtsied toward the King and took their place in the stands with the others from the troupe, including young Prince Charles, attired as Zephyrus, in a green satin robe with embroidery of golden flowers. (His silver wings were to be wired to him just before the performance.)

Inigo Jones, dressed as the president of a medieval tournament, strode to the center of the tilt-yard, and his very presence and carriage brought a hush to the stands. "These barriers," he said, turning grandly as Prince Henry appeared from behind the tent, "for our beloved Henry Stuart." Then, after the briefest pause, he added in a voice much louder, "This day declared the Prince of Wales!"

It had been Frances' impression that Londoners were not keen on Henry's elevation to Prince of Wales, fearing his sentiments were too close to Rome for an English king. But the crowd roared its hearty approval. Even King James was on his feet, cheering.

"We commemorate," Master Jones said, "with acid on steel, His Majesty's Ascension Day . . ."

"What does he mean?" Frances asked of no one in particular, but it was Lady Elizabeth who answered.

"Henry's armor—wonderful curious—etched with the genealogy of our family."

"We are a fortnight tardy," Master Jones declared, "but so all London might bear witness on May-day as father and son ascend on the same day." At the sound of the heralds' trumpets, he turned toward the staging area.

Two men advanced, carrying flatswords, to do combat. One wore the Stuart tartan; the other, dressed like an Italian coxcomb, drew chuckles from the crowd. Both men were skilled with their weapons, and Frances applauded with the crowd when Inigo Jones signaled the match at an end. No one was surprised when, grinning widely, Inigo Jones raised the hand of the Scot as winner; the match had been set up with Scotland as Britain against the inherited weaknesses of the Mediterranean. A jape.

The tilt began. Three rushes from the first pair produced no decision. The second pair were not well matched; the obviously better horseman made his opponent look foolish by feinting a thrust on the first pass, and then laughing out loud when the other man fair leapt from his saddle.

Frances awaited the third match, and at last Master Jones's clear voice rang out.

"Riding northward, in the livery of Buckinghamshire, Georges Villiers, Knight of Buckingham. Riding southward, newly attired in the livery of Sherbourne House, Robert Carr, Viscount Rochester."

At just that moment, a man burst from the stands and appeared to hurl curses at the royal party. Scuffles broke out, and for a time Frances was afraid that the Cockneys were in their cups and spoiling for a fight. Ruffians spilled onto the tilt-yard, a few breaking in the direction of the King's entourage. Lady Elizabeth had fastened hold of Frances' costume, and even Catherine, who seldom showed emotion these days, betrayed alarm.

"Tyrant!" one of the men cried out. "Reprobate traitor!"

Guards ran toward him, but, whether intentionally or no, the scuffling impeded their advance.

"God a'mercy!" the man shouted. "That Englishmen should be turned out of their own houses for bloody Scots!"

Finally a soldier succeeded in koshing him on the pate with the flat of his broadsword; the crowd fell silent as the man was dragged away.

Now bored by the distraction, Frances gently helped the Princess release the grip on her dress, and was pleased as Carr rode out from the barrier.

The pair charged, and it took no one long to recognize Villiers as the better rider. Yet Frances thought his attempt to embarrass Carr churlish. Besides, Carr did not budge at Villiers' feint, but clung doggedly to his mount.

The second charge was like the first, with Villiers making a stab at the token tied to Carr's arm. As everyone could see, aiming the lance was far beyond Carr's ability; for the moment, he seemed satisfied to prop his lance against thigh and saddle. Handsome he was, but uncommon awkward.

On the third and last charge, Carr, quickening his pace, bent over his mount, as if he was determined to aim his lance. The crowd showed interest in this, for Carr was aiming—or pretending to aim —at his opponent's body. The riders closed, and though it was hard to tell precisely what happened in what sequence, two things occurred.

Carr flailed the tip of his lance toward Villiers' arm. Villiers fell from his mount, bounced, and sent his lance sailing upward, but with his opponent's blue token wedged fast to the tip of it.

Arguments flared in the stands. Inigo Jones, looking crestfallen at this turn of events, consulted with the official judges of the event.

By this time, Carr had riddent back and Prince Henry was helping Villiers to his feet. Thomas Overbury ran to Carr, who was in a fret, casting forlorn glances at King James.

The judges declared Villiers the victor.

"But he fell from his mount!" someone shouted.

"The rusty Scot won it!"

The crowd was becoming boisterous, and Inigo Jones began to

worry about his cast. The days were already getting long, and the masque, with its torchlight and fireworks, required full darkness. Though it meant a long wait for his players, he sent word that they be removed at once to the Banqueting House across the way.

As twilight finally descended, Frances lingered over a goblet of Spanish sherry and watched the lengthening shadows of the statuary on the terrace. Master Jones had arranged a supper for the cast, but the roast cony stuffed with almond dressing, usually to her liking, had little appeal. She longed instead for the intimate company of a man she had not met, but whose lover she was determined she would soon become.

Master Jones had a clever plan for their entrance, which would take place only after all the guests had been seated. Accordingly, he directed the cast, excepting Queen Anne and Prince Charles, down the marble stairway leading from the terrace to the pier, where a boat was waiting. When all were aboard, he waved them off and the watermen rowed into the gathering darkness, downstream. By and bye, they turned the boat around and, lighting torches which they handed to the ladies, headed back to the pier. The ladies doffed their shoulder wraps, leaving their bosoms clad only by the sheer gossamer. To the sound of lutes and recorders, the masquers climbed the broad stairway, crossed the terrace, and entered the darkened Banqueting House by the appointed southeast French door.

As they crossed behind the curtain, their torches made the hangings appear to be sky, with dark clouds surrounded by bright stars. They placed the lamps, and several hid behind the temporary partition between the south wall and the stage; others, along with Frances, hurried to pavilions east and west of the performing area, which with the partition made a U around the stage. The curtain opened, revealing two gigantic statues—Neptune and Nereus—on pedestals of solid gold. Pilasters at the back of the stage supported friezes representing clouds, nymphs and nude putti holding draperies which unfolded in such a way as to make the demarcation between curtain and action unclear.

The three scenes of the masque presented an allegory of love in the Royal Family, in verse, song and dance. It began with little Prince Charles, Duke of York, stepping out between the huge statues. At the same time, a seaport came into view behind him, with many ships at anchor, which setting fit the song of gifts brought from far by the

Queen for her sovereign spouse. Prince Charles, as Zephyrus, blood of James's blood, bore these many gifts to his father, Neptune, seated in the audience. The Nereids danced, and then as the music changed so did the setting.

The heavens opened and the Queen descended in a circle of silver light. Everything in her throne room looked undersea. The room itself was supported by two gold columns, which also upheld a frieze of two dolphins wreathed together, sending out shoots of what appeared to be water but was really no more than an illusion of light and shadow. The entire room seemed filled with shining jewels refracted through pale green water.

Now the Queen presented her river nymphs. Of course, Her Grace, Lady Elizabeth, went first, followed by Trent and Arun and Derwent. Then Frances stepped onstage, drifting in turns to imitate a river's twisting shores, as the Queen spoke: "The beauteous nymph of crystal-streaming Lee."

Frances' headpiece was of shells and coral; from its crest, fashioned like a shell, streamed a pale green veil. Sky-blue lengths of taffeta, embroidered to look like seaweed and wound about her body to suggest the Lee's meanders, were of sedge and gold. Her shoulders were spangled with cypress ruffs; even her shoes suggested the glittering stones of a clear stream. Above all, highlighted by a silver weave about her neck and shoulder, was the palest of pale green transparent veil, wrapped about the fullest Howard bosom anyone could remember.

This Carr could not help looking at her now.

To the choral accompaniment of twelve singers offstage, she joined the other nymphs in a slow dance intended to represent the harmony of the English countryside. As they retired, the scene changed, and so did the song. Frances hoped that Carr would grasp its meaning:

> Pleasures only shadows be
> Cast by bodies we conceive,
> And are made the things we deem
> In those figures which they seem.
> But these pleasures vanish fast;
> Pleasures are not if they last.
> Feed apace, then, greedy eyes,

On the wonder you behold;
Take it sudden as it flies,
Though you take it not to hold.

Frances loved this song. She was in no position to think of permanence with Carr; she wanted only to grasp hold of the present week, before the festival—this time, this place, this man—was beyond enjoyment. Had Carr any sense at all, he must be thinking the same.

The music widened a last time; the scene shifted to a garden, and the Queen advanced, carrying a sword which was said to be worth £20,000. She presented the sword to Prince Charles, who gave it to his brother, and the audience stood to applaud. As the torches around the Hall were set ablaze, music for dancing burst forth.

Catherine complained of feeling unwell; she thought she might return to Suffolk House to settle in for the night. But Frances knew that her sister feared an encounter with her husband, young William Cecil, Viscount Clapthorne.

Frances had gathered the threads of the story into a simple narrative of infidelity. While in London last winter, shopping at Britain's Burse, Catherine had met her old French tutor, who, it seems, was passing through the city on his way to an estate in Cambridgeshire where he had gained employment. The shock of the meeting must have upset her, for it seemed that she lost her composure—forgot herself completely, in fact—and literally fell into her old lover's arms. The tutor unwisely extended his stay in London, and 'hen his employers made clamorous inquiries as to his whereabouts, discovery of his companion's identity was at once gossip's windfall.

Since then, young William had not contacted his wife in any way, and except for occasional diplomatic assignments for James, occupied himself with frequenting stews, often drinking and wenching to excess.

Frances tactfully bid her sister good night.

Since no suitable place could be sectioned off in the overcrowded Banqueting House for the ladies to change from their costumes, Master Jones had arranged for a caravan of closed carriages to transport them back through Green Park to St. James, where basement suites had been set up as dressing rooms. Frances had given Katherine Fine, her favorite personal servant, leave to visit her family during the festival, so she chose Ann Turner to help her change. Ann had worked right along with the Queen's chief embroiderer, Christopher Shaw, on the costumes for the masque, and she and Frances had become friends. From the beginning, Frances felt easy in Ann's company, and the commoner seemed relaxed around her as well. Not that Ann was disrespectful; on the contrary, she seemed oblivious to Frances' station, concerned only with her work on the gown for the masque. She would touch Frances in such a way as to suggest she stand absolutely still, and with her large, blue eyes wide, she would study every contour of Frances' body—touching, smoothing, almost caressing with what seemed like love. To Frances, this sylphlike, quiet women was very appealing. She attributed her own atypical friendliness to this commoner to the fact that Ann was, on the one hand, already a widely admired dress designer, and, on the other, a Catholic.

Soon Frances was properly dressed for the night's revels. Eager to meet Carr, she hurried back to the Banqueting House. At last, their eyes met—just as she entered, in fact—and at that moment she hated him intensely: he was dancing with the Countess of Bedford, smiling, ingratiating himself. She began to wonder if she had indeed caught his eye. And when the dance ended, he remained with the usual company surrounding the Countess, a gaggle of authors, attorneys and other commoners who fawned upon her in a disgusting hope of patronage.

Samuel Daniel, author of the festival's first masque, *The Queen's Wake,* was with her, and Ben Jonson. William Drummond, a dismal creature and more hopeless verser, stood about, grinning. Most repugnant of all was this upstart, Thomas Overbury, flaunting his acquaintance with the Countess of Rutland, talking much overloud and gesturing in such a way as to make clear to all that he was drunk. Frances did like John Donne, who was also there. Her father had once invited him to Audley End to discuss his possible employment as Secretary to himself, Commissioner of the Exchequer and Lord Chamberlain of the King's Household, but nothing had come of it.

Frances was mystified that she and the Howards (was not her great-grandfather one of the most celebrated poets in the annals of English literature?) were barred from this elite group. It made no sense that the Countess of Bedford, at her best a plain woman, and not she, Frances Howard, was the focus of such adoration. Intelligent men were forever pining after her. Even now, with music playing for the dance, they ignored everyone but her; Carr seemed all but oblivious to Frances' furtive contrived-to-be-discovered glances.

In a manuscript in the library at Audley End was a poem in which John Donne described this silly Lucy as a saint. Frances suspected that Northampton had purchased the artifact from a thief. Her great-uncle routinely acquired such items when entertaining requests for employment. And the blasphemy was all the greater given the fact that the Countess of Bedford was a married woman.

Until she had met (or almost met) Carr, Frances had often expressed sympathy for the Countess. Over five years ago, the Earl of Bedford had fallen from his horse while taking a jump during the hunt. He had caught one foot on the stone wall, and come down most devilishly hard, taking the full brunt of it in his privates. His miserably broken legs never healed properly, but it was said the Earl would gladly have traded his arms as well to have landed on his rump.

From that day on, the Countess left her crippled, seething husband in their western county seat when she came to London for the social season. "The old earl," her great-uncle once said, "has more horns than a brass choir."

And here was Carr, who must have seen the interest in Frances' eyes, bent on joining the band of flatterers around her. It was clear to Frances that she would have to lay plans, that Carr was beyond reach for the moment. She must solicit the aid of her great-uncle; he knew the workings of such things. He could persuade her father to invite Carr and—why not?—even that Overbury to Audley End. It was no good leaving the matter, as it was now, to chance.

She lost no time finding Northampton; she asked that he join her at the balustrade of the terrace, where she did not have to wait for him long.

"My dear Frances," he said, "you must relax. You fret within yourself when you should be happy. You have made a fine impression on the court, and, I believe, on the King."

"I cannot know this, Uncle," she said. "I have been with Catherine and Lady Elizabeth."

"And does not this bode well?" he asked.

Frances regarded him, wondering if she could trust him without reservation. "I do not think so," she said evenly. "It appears I do not enjoy the grace that I had been led to believe I possessed. Others, one in special, appear more attractive in the very eyes I struggle most to please . . ."

"If your father is angry with you, that is a small matter. I shall take care of it."

Piqued, Frances told him all, exactly what she wished settled—Carr's invitation to Audley End—before the festival ended.

"So it's the King's man, is it?" Northampton smiled. "You do have the Howard blood in you. We are not ones to be taken lightly."

"Perhaps not," Frances said, "but neither Rochester nor this Lucy creature from Bedford seems to know this."

Northampton appeared to stop listening, and Frances regretted speaking to him. Favorite grandniece or otherwise, she had put him in difficult straits; he could not openly countenance her planned adultery, which surely a man as clever as he could see this was the issue.

But then he took notice of her again, smiling. "My dear Frances," he said lightly, yet with a note of authority peculiar to him, "you pose an interesting notion. However, a serious let to its realization exists in the estimable person of Thomas Overbury. Do you know him?"

"He affects the Countess of Rutland," Frances said.

Northampton nodded.

"And the Queen does not like him."

"The Queen," Northampton said firmly, "is one of us, and you must remember that. Her support is public, and therefore of limited value. Worse than that, it may hurt us, for being expected. Overbury has no reason . . . but then perhaps he could be made to have reason . . . to support an attachment between the two of you . . ."

He seemed reluctant to say more, but Frances pressed him for details.

"I have heard a rumor," he said, "which we may be able to turn to your advantage. My associates tell me your young man, and the King's favorite, plans to wed your friend Lucy, Countess of Bedford."

Frances felt a burning hollowness in the pit of her. *This* was a rumor to be turned to her advantage?

"You are upset," Northampton said. "You are a beauty, and a Howard, but unsettled in the devious ways of the court. Trust me. Overbury may hate all Howards and all Catholics, but he will be of no mind to see Carr married into the Bedford lot."

"But she is already married," Frances said, exasperated.

"Attorneys in Lincoln's Inn have settled that, since her husband cannot lawfully beget children, he cannot satisfy the wife's lawful demand. The marriage will be annulled."

"Annulled?" Frances said.

Northampton smiled, for his grandniece had spoken loudly enough to attract an audience. "Yes, and to your benefit," he said quietly. "You don't want Carr off in Bedford, do you? And neither will Overbury, when he thinks of old Jonson, Herbert of Cherbury, and the others surrounding his only access to the King."

"But you said he hates all Catholics."

"Yes, and what do you think Jonson is? And Lucy herself, for that matter? Anabaptists?"

Frances was beginning to see the drift of his thinking.

"For Overbury," he continued, "it will be a Hobson's choice, all right. But he'll have to decide it our way or surrender his own hopes of preferment."

Frances kissed him.

"I must help circulate this rumor," he said. "Perhaps have a word with Overbury."

Suddenly the torches in the hall went out. Angry, the revelers poured onto the terrace, demanding to know on whose authority the festivities, set for many days, had been called off in one night. A man had just staggered over the balustrade when a huge explosion ripped the night. And then another and another. The sky burst into light: thousands of shooting stars—blue, white and red. Presumably, Inigo Jones had instructed that the hall be darkened while the watermen, who had rowed back out on the Thames, set off fireworks.

After the display, Frances reentered the hall. Accompanied by musicians, a countertenor sang a popular song about a lad who comes upon Bessy, sleeping in her bower. As he becomes amorous, she pretends to be asleep:

> *First a soft kiss he doth take,*
> *She lay still and would not wake;*
> *Then his hands learnéd to woo,*
> *She dreamt not what he would do,*

But still slept, while he smiled
To see love by sleep beguiled.
Jamy then began to play,
Bessy as one buried lay,
Gladly still through this sleight
Deceived in her own deceit.
And since this trance begoon
She sleeps every afternoon.

Drunken laughter followed, and laudatory remarks about Campion's wit. Frances thought the song clever enough, and when sung by a minstrel in the hush of Audley End's Great Hall, even faintly exciting. But now she found herself in the middle of the Bedford party. Ben Jonson was much in his cups.

"By His nails," he shouted, "Donne is the cleverest poet by half on any subject—save politics, of which I am the acknowledged master!"

Frances looked about for Carr, but just then a woman screamed. A man was apparently clawing at her breast.

"Got the little pest!" the man said, handing the lady something on the end of his finger.

This sent the intellectuals into fits of laughter, and Frances was quite put off by their reaction. It was only a flea: everybody had them, so why was it funny?

"Drummond first," Jonson was shouting in imitation of Inigo Jones's effeminate, clear voice. "Proceeding eastward from his Bread Street brothel, in the livery of Orpheus . . . that is, after his calamity . . . he challenges all comers while writing without a head."

The revelers caught the spirit of "flighting," now in parody of the tilt, and pressed in as if cheering their champion. Drummond, looking a touch unsure of himself, drained his tankard in one prolonged draught, then inquired as to the subject of the competition.

"Why, what but a flea?" Jonson said. "You must listen and remember. Great poetry requires great memories, lest one steal his lines from inferior authors."

Drummond dutifully pretended to fish out another flea from the woman's bodice, and to hold it aloft:

How happier is that flea
Which in thy breast doth play

Than that pied butterfly
Which courts the flame, and in the same doth die?

His audience found this disagreeable, and all but drowned out the next
lines:

That hath a light delight,
Poor fool, contented only with a sight,
When this doth sport and swell with dearest food,
And if he die, he—knightlike!—dies in blood.

Someone in the crowd handed him another tankard.
"Terrible," Jonson said, shaking his head.
"Embarrassing," Donne said.
"You must try again," commanded the Countess of Bedford.
Drummond handed the imaginary flea back to the same woman,
and continued:

Poor flea, then thou didst die,
Yet by so fair a hand
That thus to die was destine to command;
Thou die didst, yet didst try
A lover's last delight,
To vault on virgin plains, her kiss, and bite;
Thou diedst, yet hast thy tomb
Between those paps, oh dear and stately room!
Flea, happier far, more blest,
Than Phoenix burning in his spicy nest.

This try was met by more derision than the first.
"Die didst?" Jonson asked.
"Didst die?" Christopher Brooke said.
"The flea was not between anyone's paps, but on one only!" some-
one cried. "Let another champion enter the lists."
Jonson called Donne forward: "Proceeding southward, in sage
black, from Lincoln's Inn for impecunious lawyers, the best poet in
some things, including fleas . . ."
Donne smiled easily, and drawing a young lady from the crowd,
addressed her:

Mark but this flea, and mark in this,
How little that which thou deniest me is;
It sucked me first, and now sucks thee,
And in this flea our two bloods mingled be.
Thou knowest this cannot be said
A sin, nor shame, nor . . . loss of maidenhead.
Yet this enjoys before it woo,
And—pampered—swells with one blood made of two,
And this, alas, is more than we would do.

Donne's wit pleased everybody, and even Frances smiled. The audience called for more, and Donne went on without apparent effort, grasping the lady's hand:

Oh stay, three lives in one flea spare!
Where we almost—yes—more than married are.
This flea is you and I, and this
Our marriage bed and marriage temple is;
Though parents grudge, and you, we're met,
And cloistered in these living walls of jet.
Though use make you apt to kill me
Let not to that self-murder added be,
And sacrilege—three sins in killing three.
Ah—cruel and sudden, hast thou since
Purpled thy nail in blood of innocence?
Wherein could this flea guilty be
Except in that drop which it sucked from thee?
Yet thou triumph'st, and say'st that thou
Find'st not thyself nor me the weaker now.
Tis true, then learn how false fears be:
Just so much honor, when thou yield'st to me,
Will waste, as this flea's death took life from thee.

With that, as the crowd cheered, Donne kissed the young lady, whom he had obviously not met before.

Frances moved on, hoping to find someone with whom she might not feel awkward and alone. She was accustomed to being with Catherine on such occasions, and now even her mother seemed to have left the Hall. She was drifting toward the stage, where a lute and recorder ensemble was playing as if oblivious to the tumult in the Hall, when trumpets announced the arrival of the King.

James appeared to be as drunk as his guests. He embraced Carr —who, it seemed to Frances, materialized from nowhere—and kissed him on the mouth. Overbury was there, too, smiling broadly. Behind the King, and appearing rather worn, was her father. She was glad to see him, or at least thought she was: the news he brought when they met a moment later was shocking, though he spoke firmly, quietly.

"The Earl of Essex has been recalled from France, and is already on his way home."

"Oh no!" Frances cried. "Please, not now!"

Suffolk made as if to speak, but already his daughter was gathering her skirt to rush away.

Across the terrace she went. Revelers were everywhere, but she circled the Banqueting House and crossed to the tilt-yard. She ran into Green Park, where the fresh air made the tears feel cool on her hot cheeks. All of her plans lay in ruin, all of her hopes in getting away from Audley End. She maneuvered to avoid the couples scattered on the Green and hurried to the basement chambers of the palace, where she slumped into a chair and wept.

"My lady, may I help?"

She recognized Ann's soft, husky voice.

Oh, if only she—or anyone—could help her. Frances took the handkerchief Ann offered and wept quietly into it. After a time she felt better; she was grateful that Ann had stayed so late, grateful for her presence.

"I wish you could help me," Frances said. Soon she was rattling on about her troubles, taking comfort in the thoughtful cast of Ann's luminous blue eyes.

"Oh, my lady," Ann said when it appeared that Frances had finished. "Someone can help you. You'll find a way."

"But once this husband of mine beds me," Frances cried, "I shall be married to him forever! Save he take lessons from the Earl of Bedford in how to fall from his horse."

"You must not permit him to bed you," Ann said matter-of-factly.

This remark seemed strange. "What am I to do, fight him off with a chamberpot?"

Ann appeared deep in thought. Frances took new interest in what she might say. Her own contacts with the stableboys at Audley End taught her not to underestimate the canniness of commoners. They often possessed practical knowledge inaccessible to the likes of Howards (though her great-uncle seemed an exception to this).

"Is there any way to help me that you know yourself?" Frances said.

"Yes," Ann said. "It is in potions. Potions may be given to render a man unable to bed a woman."

This was remarkable. Frances knew from her afternoon in the garden blinds by the summerhouse that men were able to bed women. But she had thought that, like this wan French tutor, all men were perpetually eager and able to do so. She knew nothing of remedies, by powder or draught, to what she thought man's nature.

She shook her head slowly. "Such strong medicine must be most awfully difficult to manufacture or obtain."

"I do not know," Ann said.

"Well then?" Frances said, nettled.

"An apothecary of my acquaintance knows much of powders, potions and clysters. He is acclaimed, my lady, for his clysters."

"I do not see," Frances said icily, "how an enema will restrain my silly husband from consummating his marriage. I do not even know how one persuades a husband to submit to such indignity."

Ann laughed, and Frances realized that her own remark was the cause of the commoner's amusement.

"This apothecary," Frances said, "is he discreet?"

"Not at all," Ann said. "But I am so, and such a lady as you need not suffer his acquaintance. For though you have seen him at my shop, you have not yet noticed him. Truly, he is unworthy of your attention."

"You would do all this for me?" Frances said.

Ann smiled and, by way of answer, took a comb to Frances' hair. "Because," she said, "we are friends. And because I was like you— not in being a lady of worth, but married, I mean—to a man without choice."

Frances kissed Ann warmly. "We are friends," she said. "And I do need a true friend."

For a while the two sat talking, deciding the means of delivery and of administering the potion. Since the plan required only that Frances show up at the shop in Southwark, place the draught in a parcel of clothing and remove it thence to Audley End, or, if need be, to Essex' place, she was encouraged to add one last embellishment to their design.

"Such a draught must be much in demand?"

"It is used much by young ladies of quality," Ann said, "married to elder earls and marquises."

"And what of its opposite?" Frances asked innocently.

Ann seemed not to grasp her meaning.

"A potion of equal but opposite capacity," Frances said, "such as renders man, not incapable, but the contrary."

"Ah," Ann said thoughtfully, "my friend says such may be had, but it costs considerable."

Frances assured Ann that money was available in large amounts, if necessary: "My father spends ten thousand pounds a year on improvements at Audley End, and I have jewelry of my own."

She had to make clear the importance of this last consideration; this source of money could, if necessary, warrant perfect secrecy.

"My great-uncle," she continued, "will arrange this visit. It is all to be done for this one man, who is as oblivious of my existence as I of your apothecary's. He pines away for the aging Countess of Bedford—whose plainness makes me wonder if she has prior access to this potion. I must have it. For, now that you know my heart, tell me what good the one is to me without the other?"

As she left the fitting room, Frances smiled at her own cleverness. The plan was perfectly symmetrical. A draught to lose one husband (for what difference how a man comes by his incapacity, so long as he be incapable?), another to replace him with her choice. If the Countess of Bedford could get her marriage annulled, why then, so could Frances. Should Essex fail with her (she must contrive to have witnesses to her husband's incapacity), she would be free of him by law, free to marry Carr, who would soon be frantic to wed her.

She set off across the park again. The night rang with the ebullience of love satisfied. She could hear them—lovers—dallying on the lawns beneath the trees. Her mind raced. She stood at the edge of the mirror-black pond and breathed deeply, letting one finger play across the hardness of her right nipple, while the trembling, warm fingers of her other hand searched beneath her undergarments to satisfy her longing.

III

Had the outbreak of violence at the festival been merely a matter of high spirits, James would have given it no mind. Fighting, like hunting and whoring, was a disguised service to the state; it let men vent their spleens, calmed the tempest within, and made them tractable. But the incident on May-day had more to it than good fun; it bore an ominous political undercurrent. Though these men were drunk, right enough, and though every year the revelers tore down the tents and grandstands in ceremonial acceptance of the fact that the week's celebration was at an end, this time they took no pleasure in it. They had even set fire to the tents, which would now have to be replaced. Guards on the scene testified to the ugliness of their mood:

"Bedlam mad."

"It was the Scots they was after."

"Some had lost soap charters."

"Dissenters, they was."

From the beginning of his reign, James had moved fast to secure union between Scotland and England. He had given much (exclusive rights to mine alum, import wine and make soap, for instance) to his Scottish friends, Carr in particular. And he had ruthlessly enforced ecclesiastical uniformity ("No bishop, no king," he had said before walking out of the Convocation at Hampton Court). As for the soap charters, the Crown had to get money where it could. Why give the charters away? (And how did leaving them, without levy, in their inherited hands differ from a witless gift?) James had also returned to the medieval practice of taking commissions on customs at seaports, which included London, though Sir Edward Coke had warned him that this move was only tenuously legal, and politically dangerous. But what sovereign had not taken risks? The trouble was that Englishmen were as clannish as Highland Scots. And now their resentments seemed alarmingly to surface all at once.

James had not called a meeting of the Privy Council for several months, this because he considered his most pressing problems to be economic rather than political. Soon he must address Parliament with his semiannual request for more money. Unhappily, Parliament—the Commons in particular—seemed ill-disposed toward his financial needs. Instead of dreaming up new taxes, they gave increasing attention to dissenting speeches against his present customs policy. Legal or otherwise, Elizabeth had not resorted to such tactics for raising money without consulting Parliament, and therefore neither should their Scottish king. Unpromising situation.

The Council met in the old York House, whose rich appointments had been set by Cardinal Wolsey at a time when meddling commoners would have lost their heads for complaining in Parliament about such expense. At Overbury's suggestion, relayed by Carr, Sir Nicholas Bacon was on hand to do a sketch of the dignitaries at the meeting, from which he would later execute a large oil on canvas for presentation to Suffolk on the occasion of James's intended visit to Audley End. James quite liked the members of his Privy Council, the reason for his selecting them in the first place. Even when they disagreed separately (frequently Northampton and Arundel had at each other), their minor divisions did little more than spice up the meeting. Indeed, Arundel, flushed with rage, papers piled high in front of him, was now signaling that he planned to speak on his usual subject, the Pope and the Earl of Northampton. James had heard that, in order to avoid trouble, the two men had agreed to alternate in their attendance, but Northampton moved smoothly into the room just before the meeting began.

Arundel's presentation had to wait for those of the Secretary of State and the Treasury Commissioner. James had indicated his preference that Cecil proceed first, thus preparing the ground for Suffolk's report from the Exchequer.

Robert Cecil, Earl of Salisbury, had risen from a sickbed to attend the meeting. This great old man, with his thick swatch of grey hair standing higher than many a youth's, spoke succinctly, his huge, gravelly voice measured by his characteristic restraint—awesome despite his sadly hunched back and twisted neck.

Everyone respected him; he had spent over thirty years in the Crown's service, first as Elizabeth's most trusted adviser, then as the only important holdover following James's succession. Once James was securely on the throne, he had sent the other eminent figure from Elizabeth's inner circle, Sir Walter Raleigh, to the Tower. James liked Raleigh, found him fascinating, in fact. But he had to imprison him or consent to endless harassment from a man whose true sentiments were for perpetual war against practically everybody: Spain, France, the Netherlands, Germany. Not that James was opposed to the use of force: sometimes the Crown had to rely on guns and ships; had he not himself recently dispatched an army to the Low Countries? The question was one of priorities. It was better to spend money on festivals and masques than on an endless struggle against Continental powers. Cecil recognized this wisdom, or at least acceded to it.

Respect showed in the attentiveness of the Council members, even though Cecil intoned a litany of foreign woes. Sir Nicholas stopped his drawing to listen, and Thomas Overbury, whom James had permitted to assist Carr during the meeting, appeared uncharacteristically enthralled.

"Our Continental policy is in shambles," Cecil was saying. "We try to act the peacemaker between Spain and the Dutch republic, but are drawn instead to commit troops to the republic lest Spain attack by sea. We make concessions to France to block Spain's movement to the Low Countires by land. And yet we have not paid the soldiers we have sent under arms to the Dutch.

"This peace on the Continent that only England seems to desire is costly.

"To show that we are even-handed in our appease—ah, peacemaking, we offer Prince Henry's hand in marriage to the daughter of Philip of Spain, which promise, promulgated in scurrilous tracts and broadsides within days, has produced an apoplexy peculiar only to the Puritans of our island.

"My own concern is foreign relations, which increase in danger to us. Another war for which we are not prepared may soon drag us to the Continent. The succession in Germany is in doubt. This very day our troops leave the Dutch republic they were sent to protect to attack the Archduke Leopold, of whose existence most Englishmen are as yet unaware. We seek to free the imprisoned Juliers, who is a Protestant, and therefore the rightful ruler. I have no doubt that the English infantry will prevail, even without pay. But I must admit to grave doubts of any peace there. Protestants in the area are already fighting amongst themselves. And when we shift our support, as I expect we shall, to more settled Catholic influences, dissenters in the Commons and in the streets at home will react angrily."

Salisbury had not raised his voice, had not so much as altered his inflection for emphasis, and now he concluded matter-of-factly. It was a ruthlessly fair account, and everyone knew it. James would willingly have applauded the performance, but he could not ignore what was obvious to all, namely, that Cecil—a far cry from the daring Raleigh though he might be—nonetheless did not fully approve of James's policy of accommodation. Somewhere within him lay the vestige of a marauder's spirit whose audacity inhered in the very fabric of Elizabeth's reign, which provoked, and then proceeded to win, the battle with the Spanish Armada. No matter: Cecil did not approve, but he did support Crown policy abroad, which was all that James required of him.

Out of deference to the old warhorse, James asked for tea to be served before Suffolk went on with his report. Suffolk knew he was no match for Cecil. Cecil had once been Lord Treasurer himself, but as James loaded him with more and more titles, finally naming him Secretary of State, Salisbury had asked to be relieved of the Exchequer. Cecil favored Thomas Howard as his successor; James inclined toward Northampton. Rather than decide at once, James was letting the matter slide, with both Howards on the Governing Commission.

Cecil appeared to like Suffolk well enough, but he kept him at a distance, even after his older son, William, had married Suffolk's eldest daughter, Catherine. James had heard that Salisbury remained majestically aloof from all gossip surrounding the Howard girl's unfortunate, widely trumpeted indiscretion with a penniless tutor who happened through London on his way north from France, forbidding his own son from ever speaking ill in his presence of his daughter-in-law. James decided that it must be about time to have a word with the young man, as a gesture of kindness to his father.

A good time might be prior to his Royal Progress to Audley End, which was to begin shortly after his address to Parliament.

Suffolk's report was accurate but dismal, at once diffuse and brief.

But the Council understood his meaning well enough. The Crown had little left but its own jewels.

Arundel petitioned to be heard. He was simple-mindedly patriotic, and therefore more anti-Catholic than an Anabaptist Tom o' Bedlam. James let him speak. He started in a roundabout way by pointing out what everyone knew, that most of the members of the Privy Council also sat with the Star Chamber. It followed that, should the occasion require it, matters belonging before the Star Chamber could be brought up presently. Northampton had opened a golden snuffbox from which he dipped with exaggerated movements, succeeding in Arundel's distraction.

Nobody particularly liked Arundel. They braced themselves for the familiar attack on Northampton, which Arundel apparently had never considered varying.

"Men in high places," he said, "gather to themselves sufficient weapons to equip an army. They employ legions of spies, some in the households of fellow members of this very Council . . ."

James caught the suggestion of a smile on Northampton's handsomely bearded face.

Lennox interrupted. "Permit me, my lord," he said without standing. "I pray you tell us the general scope of this disquisition. It would be helpful to know who amongst us possesses secrets worth spying upon. Who has the time and energy to do me in? I can save him trouble. Let him but introduce me to the services of but one more attorney, and both I and my progeny shall sue for the peace of penury —done in, the lot of us."

His remark drew chuckles. Lennox seldom had much to say, but he was good to have around. His world-weariness could cloy, but it was less embarrassing than Arundel's misguided loyalty.

"I am speaking," Arundel said, "of the Whore of Babylon, and well you know it."

James felt alarm, not because of Arundel's predictable charge, but because Carr seemed ready to speak. Overbury was remonstrating with him, but with no success.

"My lords," Carr said, speaking for his first time before the Council. "If it be so that the Pope has paid agents hired here, as my Lord Arundel says, and I for one believe him, then it is our duty to find out who he is, which will settle this thing once and for all. In the Book of Revelations—"

Overbury quieted Carr, who, as all were aware, had no idea of the Book of Revelations, nor of what he was talking about. It was Northampton with whom Carr had been amiably chatting at tea. A helpless creature, that one. If the Queen had no use for Overbury, God knew that Robin did.

James insisted that Arundel get on with it.

"We have discussed this matter before," Arundel said, "at which time Your Majesty generously declined to prefer action to Sir Edward on the grounds that evidence was not sufficient to warrant prosecution before the King's Bench."

"To put words in the King's mouth," James said, only half in jest, "is not the wisest of pastimes."

"Beg pardon, Your Majesty," Arundel said, bowing, "but I was led to believe that you . . . Surely you would not . . ."

"Led by whom?" James said more sternly. "My good man, do not instruct me on what I would or would not do. A king *would* do exactly as he in fact *does*. Now, some months ago you made a charge which I said, if substantiated, would be serious. We discussed this matter, but in no case do I recall saying anything prejudicial regarding it. My judgment in such matters must be based on facts. Sir Edward Coke will, I assure you, undertake to prosecute all violations of law. Now, we grow weary of pettifoggery. I grow weary of it. Deliver yourself of your accusation forthwith."

"Thank you, Your Majesty," Arundel said, subdued. "I have evidence, my lords, that there are papists dwelling in the environs— or, to be more precise, on the estate—of Audley End, the residence of—"

"Your Grace," Northampton interrupted easily, "I find myself several times embarrassed by the reference to Audley End, not because it is known to be the estate of my honorable nephew, Lord Chamberlain of the Royal Household, but because of the implication one might possibly construe from it. Though a sometime student of law myself, I do not recall that an Englishman may be brought to the bar for *being* anything, but only for doing crimes proscribed by the Crown. Whether we sit as members of the Star Chamber or Privy Council, it is our duty to attend to evidence of any unlawful acts. Let us overlook the imputations about his Majesty's wisdom in making appointments . . ."

This was a masterful shot. Arundel looked sheepishly over at James, who sought to look expressionless.

"Perhaps my lord has forgotten," Northampton continued, "that it was not he, but the Earl of Suffolk, who discovered thirty-six barrels of gunpowder beneath Parliament. Yes, yes, if you insist I suppose we can say that this information came to him through spies, but is it not more to the point—we were all to be there when the bombs went off —that the information came in time?"

James pursed his lips in a smile. This was a devilishly clever ruse, Northampton pretending that it was his nephew and not he whom Arundel was after. James liked Northampton, admired him, too; he had thought he would not underestimate so formidable a man, but even James was surprised at what followed.

"I have said that I am several times embarrassed," Northampton said, "and you must know why. Before these innuendos about the Howards fornicating with the Babylonian Whore, I was about to present to this honorable body a resolve of my own, aimed partly at providing sufficient opportunity for all to show their duty to the Crown. And my thoughts are also pertinent to certain stresses ably pointed out by my Lord Salisbury. Perhaps I shall make my proposal in any case.

"The suspicions of our Catholic clients on the Continent might be assuaged without our pressing this issue of marriage between Prince Henry and the Infanta, should we but give some proper thought to the final disposition of the remains of His Majesty's revered mother, high if not highest claimant to the throne of England, Mary Stuart, Queen of Scotland."

Archbishop Abbot, struggling to conceal rage, spoke sardonically.

"My lord, you presuppose—indeed, you suggest rather than merely presuppose—that her burial and her 'final disposition' are not one and the same thing."

Northampton ignored the challenge, waiting now for someone else to speak. It was an interesting concept. Northampton knew, because James himself had told him, that the King had no strong feelings for his mother. From James's point of view, she had spent most of her life running away from him. And when she left Scotland, she did nothing to secure his life amidst the waves of conflicting political interests. But that was all behind him now, and Northampton's notion would not cost him so much as a shilling.

Publicly, of course, James pined for his mother. He had written several letters to Elizabeth, asking Mary's release, but Elizabeth had understood their true intent. She was shrewd and reliable. He knew she would not put him to the test of his feelings for Mary, so long as he did not put her to the same test. She had answered his letters with oblique and idle commonplaces, and she had not, for two decades, released his mother. Yes, both James and Elizabeth understood that the only serious issue was whether he would invade England. And she guessed James's sentiment exactly. What if Elizabeth *had* freed the Queen of Scots? What would have happened to his own claim to the Scottish throne? And if he had tried and failed in a military venture, what of his aspirations to the English throne? English law forbade a foreigner from ascending the throne, so without Elizabeth's help, how could he be named her successor? If he was not even allowed to own property in England, how could he hope to assume the substantial holdings that went with the Crown?

These questions made it easy for him to see that, while Elizabeth lived, he depended upon her for his future, and, as when the barons had sought to do him in, even for his life.

As for Northampton, his feelings for Mary Stuart were a mystery. Years ago, Elizabeth had clapped him in the Tower when her spies intercepted letters he had sent to Mary while yet, in the early days of her captivity, she was at Bolton Castle. Rumor had more than once connected their names; both were Catholics, and the Howard name was one of the greatest in England. For a time, hope of that union became a rallying point for the beleaguered Roman minority, who dreamt of Mary's ascent to the throne occupied by a bastard and a heretic.

Elizabeth, who had no heart for a direct attack on the eminent Howard family, and who thought the letters reflected no more than the eager ambitions of a young man, let Henry Howard go within months. Northampton helped to hasten her decision by pinning the blame on his older brother, the Duke of Norfolk (who, for his romantic obsession with Mary Stuart, took leave of his head). Whether or not Northampton seriously entertained the idea of a liaison with Mary, after that time, so far as James could discover, he never let word pass his lips. Nor had he openly or covertly sponsored the frequent moves by Catholics to free Mary from captivity. More than once he spurned suggestions by dissenters that a league between themselves and Catholics be formed to wrest power from Elizabeth and (later) James with a mind to establish full religious toleration in England.

The Howard family had amazing recuperative powers. Northampton remained unmarried, turning his attention from his brother to his promising nephew, who had distinguished himself in the struggle against Spain. The move was auspicious, for James elevated Thomas Howard to the newly created Earldom of Suffolk. Furthermore, to his nephew's daughters he took a special fancy. He adopted their country retreat to be his own, pouring some of his own funds into its redecoration. If not quite like his father, after whom he was named, Henry Howard, Earl of Northampton, was one of the most intelligent men at court. If no poet (English schoolboys still read his father's verse), he nevertheless had a sharp tongue, as Arundel and the Archbishop were finding out.

"After we indecently excavate the body," Abbot said, "where shall we bury this daughter of Rome? Beneath the altar at St. Paul's?"

Northampton toyed with his snuffbox, unperturbed. "Why," he said blandly, "I had thought . . . Let me put it this way: Where do we normally inter those of royal blood?"

"Sir," Abbot said, "you go too far."

If Northampton caught the emphasis on "Sir," decidedly not the correct salutation for an earl, he gave no sign. Instead, with obvious enjoyment, his voice resonating just above a whisper, he answered slowly. "From a political point of view, which is the only proper concern of this Council, the idea has merit. Were Mary Stuart not His Majesty's mother, it would not change the fact that she was treated abominably. To show respect now can hurt no one. And it may provide His Majesty with an opportunity to reconsider the Spanish marriage . . ."

It was a brilliant ploy. Now, should Arundel or Abbot speak, it would appear that they encouraged increased commitment through marriage to Spain.

When Salisbury spoke, his voice bore the authentic ring of disinterested wisdom. "Mary Stuart is past our help now. But the indecent disposition of her remains is a shame on this kingdom. To this day, her grave is not so much as marked by a headstone. Even the Pope

—especially the Pope—deserves a headstone."

The tension in the room seemed to disappear in a sprinkling of laughter.

"Is it any wonder," Salisbury went on, "that the ignorant and superstitious venerate bits of kerchief supposed dipped in her blood?"

This was true. Mary was executed in the basement of Brockington Castle. She died gracefully, with much courage and, many present insisted, with signs from heaven at her passing of her special grace. After her head was severed from her body, her lips were seen unmistakably to frame these words: "Sweet Jesus." The faithful rushed forward to dip their handkerchiefs in her blood. And now they prayed to her in this land—in which the giving of the sacraments after the Roman Rite was a capital offense.

Northampton nodded. "We created a martyr," he said. "And, if our conduct remains sufficiently craven, perhaps a saint."

At this, James snorted: his mother, the passionate and willful Queen of Scots, a saint! Northampton was refreshing almost to a fault. Perhaps he once imagined himself the husband of Mary Stuart, with a grip, however tenuous, on the throne. This would have made him James's stepfather. Northampton was amusing because he possessed no illusions about Mary, about those who worshiped her, or about anyone, including himself. He was that invaluable man a king needs to have about, who refuses to deceive himself. Unlike the Jesuits and the Dissenters, who earnestly held to every article of their faith, Northampton was unwedded to any principle. Not once had James ever heard him appeal to principle.

Experience had taught James that men of principle were not to be trusted. They used principle to justify their actions, which grew conveniently from the very principle in question. Such men were hard to deal with. Take Henry Barrow, for instance, or John Greenwood: men of principle—Brownist principle—arguing with the King's law, inveighing against everything except their own conscience, down to the moment they were hanged. Principle, Brownism, Anabaptism, servietism and papism, were all of them expressions of the same thing: Pride (obstinacy), a deadly sin before God, and a nuisance to the state.

On the other hand, one could trust men like Northampton because their actions made sense. One need but locate their interests, and he could predict, within moderate limits, their next move. This predictability was a great convenience to sovereigns. Men of good sense supported stability, for only in stable circumstances could anyone—and a wise man is by nature self-interested—flourish and enjoy himself. So James expected Northampton to support the Crown, not in principle, but in fact. With his support in fact, what need did James have of Northampton's support in principle? And if no need, what interest?

James recognized two kinds of men in government: the self-seekers and the foot-shufflers. Take the earliest incident of his reign. Right from the beginning, the foot-shufflers had plagued him. James was in York on his way with his entourage to London to his Coronation. Men in the crowd had captured a cut-purse in the very act of lifting a man's purse. Naturally, James ordered the man dealt with on the spot. Was it only a Scot would ask, Why waste time and money?

"Hang the lout," he had said, and when the men delayed, and the crowd fell silent, he had the added problem of not wanting to seem wishy-washy in his first act as sovereign. "I said hang the bastard, and I mean at once—there, from that tree."

They had hanged him without too much grumbling. But afterwards the foot-shufflers beset James. Had it been necessary? What of the local magistrates? What of witnesses? What of the need for a trial of facts? What were the facts? Speeches were made against James in Parliament, all of them by churls who valued—above all things, apparently—the passage of time between an act of knavery and its punishment. One outdoor (and therefore unlawful) preacher had suggested that James, and not the cut-purse, be brought to the bar for reviling Queen Elizabeth: he took James's reference to the thief as a "bastard" to be a fiendishly clever aside against England's Virgin Queen.

These were the men who, when they entered the King's presence, shifted about, looking at their feet, delivering themselves of a half-dozen "ahems" and "Your Majesty's" before coming to the point. They were, to politics, what *coitus interruptus* was to sex. They could not see for the life of them that they were the true enemies of both law and sense. They desired, but lacked the courage to recognize it, that government be replaced by an eternal debate, something like the papists' idea of Purgatory, filled with talk.

Northampton was at the far pole from such men. Neither Arundel nor Abbot had expected so bold a stroke by someone already under attack as a partisan of Rome: to disinter Mary Stuart's body, to bring it to London, to have it solemnly buried in Westminster Abbey. Abbot and Arundel were agitated, gesturing messages of make-do strategy to each other in a most unseemly way. And now Northampton met their imputations forcefully:

"Having defended my nephew, I see that I must speak also for myself. At the risk of sounding both repetitious and immodest, may I remind my Lord Archbishop that it was not he, but I, who acted —voluntarily, for Lord Bacon and Sir Edward were formally in charge—as prosecutor to Father Garnet in the Powder Treason. We are back to this same legal fiction. Garnet was not charged for being a Catholic. My Lord Archbishop, what is the Church of England's creed if not Catholic? Neither was Father Garnet tried as a papist, as you call it, but as a traitor—for conspiracy to commit murder and treason. Do you remember the drift of that trial? The sentence, and its execution?"

James remembered, and Abbot, from the stricken look on his face, probably remembered too well. Just when it seemed that Suffolk's role in the discovery of the Plot had been forgotten, and feeling against Catholics was at a high pitch, with the Howard family the unfortunate focus of much wrath, Northampton had volunteered to prosecute Father Garnet for his part in the conspiracy to blow up Parliament at the moment when King James was to deliver his first address. Francis Bacon had willingly stepped far enough aside (for, in fact, Northampton was a member of the King's Commission, and had a right to cross-examine) to let him prosecute.

As for the defendant, nobody claimed that Father Garnet had taken part in the Plot itself. He was charged with refusing to inform authorities of the conspiracy, knowledge of which had come to him during confessions of three active participants: Catesby, Greenwell and Guy Fawkes.

"Suppose," Northampton had said to Father Garnet, who was already weary from almost eight hours in the dock, "that today I tell you in confession that I plan to kill the King and all the Royal Family with a dagger. Do you seriously argue, as an English subject, that you would conceal that knowledge?"

This was the question that cut to the heart of the King's case. Garnet's voice trembled. "Yes, my lord. Whatever my personal feelings of revulsion, I should have to conceal it."

Here, Sir Edward Coke, who had prosecuted Fawkes and the others, broke in. "Is confession not followed by contrition and absolution?"

It was.

"Then," Coke stormed, "I demand to know if you absolved this murdering heathen, Greenwell, or no!"

"Yes, my lord."

"In that case," Coke said, "pray tell me, what did Greenwell do for contrition? Was he sorry?"

"He was, my lord. And said that he would do better."

At that, Coke leapt to his feet as if physically to attack Father Garnet. "Better, indeed! So you absolved him, did you? But how could you absolve him? Right after seeing he joined Catesby and Fawkes to set about with bombs, to do murder! So! Either what you knew was not from the confession, and requires no secrecy, or, if it was in the confessional, Greenwell offered no penitence, and therefore you could not absolve him."

"My lord," Father Garnet said, wavering. "I wish to God I had never heard of the Powder Plot."

"Nonsense!" came Northampton's thundering, impatient voice. "Your wishes in this matter at this date are beside the point. You knew of the Plot and you concealed it. This Commission has patiently watched you dissemble and equivocate: you were definitely not here on that date, you are very sure of it, though your own confederates swear that you were. The conspiracy was told you not before, not after, but only during the act of confession. You must think us all fools!

"During Elizabeth's reign—to our woe—two infamous bulls emanating from the Pope in Rome entered our land, giving instructions that no sin fell upon the head of our sovereign's murderer. What make you of this? Why, marry! It is so simple: these instructions to do murder were intended for very few!

"You tell us that you committed these bulls to the flames. So be it. But let the proof be what it will, I look to the root. I wonder, Mr. Garnet, what Apostle warrants you in undertaking wicked plots, neglecting all laws, especially the laws of England? To letters applauding these base assassins, you answer that you were only commending the men, not their plot. As if these worthies were drawn together for any purpose other than the plot itself.

"Mr. Garnet, a man that is religious in any kind, but morally honest in his own kind, would expect a priest, upon hearing this rash disclosure, to have behaved differently.

"Catesby came to you, vexed with worry about the innocents—the five Roman Catholics in Parliament—who must die with the guilty —the lot of us—when the bombs exploded. I have stood longer on this point to let you see how, the more you strive to get out of the wood, having lost the right way, the further you creep in. For the wisdom of men is folly before God. And impossible it is, Mr. Garnet, that any counsel or proceeding in this *world* shall come to good proof in *this* world or the *next,* not covered with blood, or pursued with tyranny.

"If, as you say, there be no other way to heaven than by destroying God's anointed, why then, Mr. Garnet, set up a ladder for yourself, and climb to heaven by yourself. We'll not go with you.

"The worst I wish you as you stand there—convicted out of your own mouth!—is remorse and repentance, which is more than you urged upon Catesby, Greenwell and Fawkes."

Even in his fatigue and depression, Garnet had the strength left to be shaken by Northampton's speech. If anyone present might have held out hope of mercy, it was Henry Howard, whose family's loyalty to the faith had lasted through the terrible times of Henry VIII. When necessary, they had faced the martyr's flames. They poured money into preserving remnants of Rome in England: private Masses were still held, if no longer at Audley End, at least on Howard estates lying farther from London. But Northampton had brushed aside Garnet's legal defense, namely, that he held his information, not as a subject of the Crown, but as a sworn member of a privileged audience.

Salisbury, who presided over the hearing, gave him a chance to answer without further cross-examination, but Garnet replied that he could say nothing without sentencing others who had trusted him. The jury was gone from the courtroom for only fifteen minutes before returning with their verdict of guilty. Garnet could think of no reason why his sentence should be delayed.

"No, my lord," he said, stifling a sob, "but I most humbly desire your lordships all to commend my life to the King's Majesty, for I am as willing to die, or do him service."

It was a sentence given him by his attorney, but Salisbury had, in fact, come to James about the sentence. Salisbury, not Northampton.

Old Cecil spoke about Catholic unrest in the country, about the general virtue of mercy, the new Dutch tariffs, the fact that Father Garnet had not actually participated in the Plot. But he had fallen short of actually pleading for Garnet's life. James had waited for Northampton to come to him, which he finally did, but he, unlike Salisbury, did not so much as mention Garnet's name.The King knew that Northampton considered his request for a formal audience to be sufficient sign of his concern; he was hoping James would raise the subject himself, which, when it was clear that Northampton was ready to take his departure, he finally did.

"Stay a moment," James said. "You omit mention of the priest."

Northampton stopped, turned, but said nothing.

"Salisbury came to see me about it."

Now Northampton had his opening. "Your Majesty," he said, "in truth, my niece plagues me about him. I was doubtful about troubling you with the matter."

"Then he must hang?" James said.

"That was his sentence," Northampton said.

James wrinkled his nose, picked at his beard and sidled toward Northampton good-naturedly. "Awful way to go . . ."

Northampton nodded. "Treason, you see. The usual sentence. With all these scruffy Anabaptists about, we must set an example."

"Then you make no representation of his cause?"

"I made my representation before the bar. I cannot deny that Father Garnet moved me . . ."

This news had reached the King, and now he wondered if Northampton had spies watching his spies. Northampton had covered for himself, even in this showing of emotion. Was his audience simply a tactical move to convey that? Merely to convince James that he held allegiance to no one but himself?

"I don't want to see him hang, Your Majesty," Northampton said coolly. "But the law is firm on this, and the law cannot be firmer than the determination of those who uphold it. I do not say Father Garnet is malicious. Your Majesty knows the Howard predilections in religion. But he is dangerous. He has done treason, and there can be but one end to it."

Hmmm. This was not precisely how James had planned the interview. The truth was that hanging Fawkes and the others presented no problem, but, with Anne forever pleading for Garnet's life, James found that he had no stomach for this particular execution. He delayed in sending the final orders.

Weeks passed, a month, two months, until further delay seemed impossible. Only Queen Anne spoke for Garnet, who had no way of knowing of her intercession. Her pleas were pathetic, full of tears and loud cries, totally unpunctuated by the slightest familiarity with English law or customs. The Danes, if she gave much evidence, must be good-hearted people. James was moved, but he knew her appeals to be completely irrelevant.

If he were to extend mercy, someone besides the Queen must take the blame. The virtue of kingly mercy was lost upon a Protestant nation when extended to a Catholic. Sad. But neither Salisbury nor Northampton nor Suffolk nor anybody would speak up, permitting James a chance to accede to their impassioned pleas. With only Anne's unsophisticated entreaties to consider, he had no choice. He waited until he could wait no longer; it appeared that Father Garnet did not have one friend in all of England.

James asked Northampton to join him on the site when the sentence was carried out in front of St. Paul's Church. In their disguises they were able to get quite close to the scaffold. They were only a few yards away when the cart with Father Garnet, the Recorder and the Executioner, Derrick, arrived. James was sure that no man had ever faced the rope with greater fear than was etched on Father Garnet's young face that day. When asked to confess his guilt on this, his last opportunity, he was at first too weak to make himself heard. Then he repeated his claim that he knew only the general aim of the Plot, and that specific knowledge came from the confession, which priestly vows barred him from revealing.

"Good countrymen," he said in a voice that trembled, "I am come hither this blessed day of the Invention of the Holy Cross to end all the crosses of my life."

James wondered who was responsible for this idiocy. They execute a candidate for martyrdom without bothering to check the Roman calendar of holy days!

As Garnet rehearsed the narrative of his woes, James felt himself pushed forward; shouting went up, and a fight broke out in front of the tavern across the street.

"Hang all the bloody papists!" someone cried.

James heard a crash and the tinkling of glass, saw the large window of the tavern give way, and men flinging desperate blows inside and outside the building. "Someone ought to stop them," he said to no one in particular, but sensing that the fight was mean-hearted and spreading.

"Why? Kill the rotters!" an old woman shouted. "Let them kill each other!"

"Be more room in the pesthouse this summer!"

"They've got a papist over there!" a man cried.

Now they were fighting with clubs and knives.

"Where are the constables?"

"In bed with the King, likely."

This was beginning to sound like a bloodthirsty mob.

Derrick was placing the rope around Garnet's neck, but James had the mad notion that only he knew it. A body came partway through the splintered tavern window, coming to rest on a jagged pane. Two men carried a man to the steps of St. Paul's, where they tried to fend off others who seemed determined to wrest the body from them.

And then, all at once, they seemed to notice that Derrick was ready. It had been someone's clever idea to build the gallows on a platform, lofty like a stage, so that many could see. (At Tyburn, there was the inconvenience of the Triple Tree, which stood in the middle of the road, plainly visible only when not in use.) The crowd surged forward, and James felt himself pushed ever closer to the platform. Garnet was now praying loudly, in English; he opened his eyes, blinked, and closed them again. The recorder, distressed at this, spoke scathingly:

"Do not deceive yourself. You may pray and pray, but you came to this place to die. If you know anything that might be of danger to His Majesty, or England, speak now. Otherwise, pray quickly."

"I commend me," Father Garnet said, "to all good Catholics. I pray God preserve His Majesty, the Queen, and all their posterity . . . And my lords of the Privy Council, whom I am most heartily sorry to have deceived . . ."

"You didn't deceive nobody, you bloody traitor!" a man shouted.

"I did not know they had such proof against me until it was shown me. When it was shown, I thought it most honor to confess. As for brother Greenwell, I regret charging him, but I thought he was safely landed in Spain. I pray God that Catholics may not fare worse in England because of me. I warn them not to enter into any treasons, plots, rebellions or insurrections against the King . . .."

Amen, thought James.

Then three things happened at once. Garnet began to pray loudly in Latin, crossing himself, and his executioner, apparently thinking his prayers at an end (or being deficient in Latin) dispatched him prematurely. Father Garnet dropped with stunning speed. (Here was another nicety of the high scaffold—he must look into extending the principle.)

James, who had never seen a hanging up close (the cut-purse had been virtually out of sight), watched Garnet swing slowly to and fro. All at once, he felt ill. A woman stepped from behind him and spat. His eyes followed as the spittle made its way down the left arm of Father Garnet's shirt (they had not allowed him to wear his cassock). Oddly, he felt rage, and was tempted to strike the woman. But already others were spitting on Garnet. James looked about for Northampton, and found him leaning against the casement of the tavern window.

He was smiling; James had the distinct impression that Northampton had been watching him, and not the execution, all along.

"We had better get out of here," James said. "These Bow-bell Cockney churls are in an ugly mood."

Northampton still smiled. He seemed to be enjoying himself. "Nothing unusual," he said. "Their natural state, I should say."

HURRIEDLY, ANN LOCKED the door to the shop and set off west on Southwark. It was Sunday afternoon, so more than likely she could find Franklin at the Bear Garden, especially given the rumor she had heard that the Pit and all the theatres would soon be closed and not reopened until the plague subsided. Franklin was fanatically loyal to dog-fights and bear-baiting. On most Sunday afternoons he was able to gorge himself completely, for the two events were usually featured together; on rare occasions, depending on what animals were in fair supply, a bull-bait was thrown in for good measure. Ann hated violence, but she could hardly resent the crowds thronging past her shop: ever so often, one or two wandered back during the week to ask about her services, and in this way she had acquired several regular clients.

As she made her way into the Bear Garden, Ann was surprised to see how many Londoners defied the plague for the cruel diversion of bear-baiting. They looked casual enough now, but she knew that the event worked a change in them. Until recently, Franklin had stopped by the shop when the fights were over, and she found his flushed, glassy-eyed appearance of excitement especially repulsive.

And yet she knew that the taste for blood was not unusual.

Today the King himself was on hand; royal banners were spread across the front barrier of the most favorable seating. Black-and-purple insignia of the House of Stuarts hung from halberds at the rear of the arena.

Ann edged her way around the stands but failed to locate Franklin until after the dog-fight had begun. He was not pleased to see her; in fact, until one dog was borne away, leaving the apparent victor drenched in blood, unmoving except for the twitch of his hind legs, he would not let her speak. James's presence obviously delighted him. "Look there," he said, "the King and Prince Henry. Old James loves to see good dogs have a go at each other."

His excitement grew as the next event unfolded. It seemed the customary rules would not obtain: one of the King's Guard gave the bear's keeper, who had chained his animal to a thick post in the center of the circular arena, His Majesty's instructions. Ordinarily, once the bear was staked, a pack of dogs was set upon him. Now Ann watched the King settle back as the bear-handler made his announcement:

"Your Majesty, honored guests of King James, loyal patrons of the Garden, it is a singular honor to pronounce this notable change in our program. At His Majesty's expense, we offer for your pleasure great mastiffs shipped lately from Muscovy. Admirable ferocious beasts, they come upon the largest bear in captivity today, not, as is their wont, by a pack in number, but assaulting selfishly, one by one."

This novelty caused a mixed response among the spectators. Franklin, arguing with a nearby acquaintance, claimed that this technique was common—preferred, in fact—in Wales. Even the King's party seemed divided on the virtues of sending dogs singly; Prince Henry stood and appeared to motion angrily at the handler. But if his aim was to delay the fight, he was too late.

The mastiff dashed to the bear, barking, growling, looking for a hold on the bear's vulnerable hindquarter. The bear squealed as the dog, circling quickly, ripped at one of its joints. In an effort to get loose of its chains, the bear shook itself, then flayed at the air, trying to rake the dog with its claws.

"What kind of bear is it?" Ann asked, attempting friendliness.

"Who knows?" Franklin said. "What difference does it make? It may be female for all I know; a female fights as good or better than a male, you know. And many's the handler who's lost a nose for his pains to learn a bear's gender."

Having claimed that his bear was the largest in captivity, the handler now seemed displeased with its performance. The bear appeared rather to defend itself than attack the dog. Having the dog pulled back, the handler mashed a bowl of pepper into the bear's muzzle. The beast howled and sneezed mightily, wiping at its nose and eyes.

Franklin shrieked with glee, but though he sat right next to Ann, she could scarcely hear him above the cries of the delighted spectators. When he saw that Ann was upset by the peppering, his entertainment seemed, if anything, to increase.

Set loose, the mastiff moved in more confidently, snapping at the angry gash in the bear's hind parts. To protect itself, the bear tried to sit on the wound. Then, in a blindingly quick move, it caught hold of the mastiff with its great paw and proceeded to chew at the dog's neck till the fiendish cry ceased.

The handler looked up at King James, and another mastiff was released, only to meet with a hasty end. A third came, then a fourth; the bear had learned how to deal with the dogs.

"I must talk to you," Ann said. "How many dogs will there be?"

Franklin was in a disagreeable mood. "His Majesty does not consult with me in such matters. He may have brought a dozen dogs from Muscovy. Look at that one! He's tore the bear's nose!"

As the bear howled, its keeper mashed more pepper in its bloodied muzzle. Enraged, the bear swept the mastiff loose of one ear. Swinging in the other direction, its right paw opened the dog's underbelly. As the dog lay twitching, the bear roared, rubbing at its nose and eyes.

"It's the pepper!" Franklin squealed. "That pepper is what gets him. He'll tear the next dog apart, sure, when he's well-peppered."

"I must—please!—talk to you," Ann said.

Franklin did not hear—or pretended not to. He was observing the activity near the barrier, where the handler was talking to one of the King's Guard. Finally the handler shook his head and strode to the center of the arena.

"Let it please His Majesty that the remainder of the dogs scheduled to engage the largest bear in captivity be . . ."

His announcement was lost in the angry shouts of the crowd; oranges and orange peels rained down on the arena. While the bear-handler dodged the falling fruit, trying to recapture the dignity of his address, the bear, having stopped sneezing, settled down with an orange.

Franklin was so furious one would think his own snout had been mashed in a pepper-pot.

Little by little the information got through: the bear-bait was over for that Sunday afternoon; Prince Henry had specially petitioned to his father to spare the remaining mastiffs, of which he had grown fond. Unhappily, that was not all: this would likely be the last bear-bait for some time. Until further notice, the Bear Garden would schedule no events.

As they left the Bear Garden with a noticeably subdued crowd, Ann was relieved that Franklin directed his displeasure at Prince Henry rather than at her.

"Effeminate coward," he fumed. "Little Charlie has more spunk. A mastiff's only a beast. No use moaning for him, fretting over him. Next thing, they'll want to stop the pit dogs from being pit dogs! Madness! The Lord Mayor belongs in Bedlam."

Silently, Ann turned up the lane, and without protest Franklin followed, past the Globe to the pasture, then along the Thames.

"It must be nice to be able to escape to the country," Ann said as they strolled along the bank, "with the heat and plague gettin' worse."

Franklin agreed half-heartedly. "Wouldn't be so bad if the Lord Mayor would leave the Garden open. Give men an interest, during the heat, them as can't resort to Northumberland. Take their minds off the plague-bill, I say."

Easily spoken! Take their minds off the plague-bill! What a churl! What a despicable man. The lists tacked up on every city block of those taken by the plague were already long and swiftly lengthening.

"Mmmm," she said.

They had walked far enough.

"You must help me," Ann said.

Franklin said nothing, which came as no surprise.

"You did not bring the potion," she said. "My lady must have it."

"I explained, love . . ."

"Yes, but my lady must have it now. She was forced to leave London without it. I had promised it."

"No fault of yours," he answered. "Old Forman is firm on this. If she requires this service, she must see him."

Ann tried to hide her irritation. "But she cannot do this. Surely you know why. Dr. Forman is not for such a great lady."

Franklin laughed. "Perhaps not, but many are for him. And there's not a one that doesn't come back with the King's sickness or anything requiring the skill of their beloved Dr. Forman. He's a marvel, that one. She'll see him and be glad of it."

Ann began to suspect that she had set out on a fool's errand; perhaps it had been a mistake ever to mention this love potion. Only a few weeks ago, her life had taken a change for the better. While the festival was in swing, she had experienced a sense of pride in herself; she received much attention for her new technique of stiffening ladies' ruffs with yellow starch (Franklin had shown her how to make the mixture). For the first time in her life, she felt loved: Sir Ralph came to see her often in the basement of St. James, and Frances treated her warmly, as a friend.

Things seemed different now. Clients had left London, and with the imminent closing of the theatres, her services to Inigo Jones would not likely prosper until autumn. Most of her ladies were well ensconced in the countryside, prepared if necessary to wait out the plague until Harvest Home. Then, as the days grew shorter, and when the hay was cut and stacked in the fields of their country manors, their thoughts would return to the city. But for the time being, Ann had little to do. Sir Ralph had spoken of a summer sojourn to the Lake Country, of taking her and Davy along with him. She had heard about but never seen the clear lakes surrounded by tangled forests. From his description, the summer there would be cool and serene, far removed from the horrors of the plague.

Except for dissenters and members of Parliament, most of those who could afford to had already left London. As was often the case during a plague summer, the city was half empty. It was said that King James and the Royal Family would leave as soon as he addressed the Parliament, and that after his departure the few people of quality still in London would not be far behind. Only those with no means of escape would remain.

Ann suspected that, even without the plague, she would feel uneasy.

When Frances had taken leave of her only a day ago, she had done so in anger.

"You said I should have this potion! Now I must leave London without it." The tone of her voice was not friendly.

"You shall have it," Ann had answered.

"Shall? When? When Carr has left Audley End for the sweet embraces of the Countess of Bedford?"

Ann had tried to reassure her. "No. Soon."

"But I cannot return to London for many months."

"I shall bring it to you."

"How?"

"That will not be difficult . . ."

"When?"

"Soon, my lady. In a week or so."

"It must be by Midsummer," Frances had said. "The King's party arrives soon after Midsummer, and no one can say how long they will stay."

"By Midsummer," Ann had promised, without the slightest notion of how she could arrange to get away.

She did not like the idea of her friend being unhappy with her, and doubtful of her promise to bring the potion. And yet she knew she must disappoint Frances again. She must go to Audley End to tell her that she, one of the grandest ladies in the realm, must humble herself before the most notorious lecher and mountebank in England.

Though it was unlike her, Ann stopped walking, turned and looked Franklin squarely in the eyes. "You trifle with me!" she said, trying to sound threatening.

"Not at all, love," he said, laughing. "With her. What is she to you?"

"The business must be privy between us. I promised."

"I have not. It is impossible."

Ann made as if to protest, but Franklin went on with finality.

"Impossible. It is not for me to change it. And if I could, why should I? Your mysterious lady of quality is nothing to me, nothing more to me than . . ."

He paused, and Ann realized as he measured her with wide eyes how terribly hurt and angry he was.

". . . than your gentleman of quality, who makes so grand a show about your shop these days!"

She did not know how to answer. Perhaps Franklin thought she preferred Sir Ralph for his money, which was far from true. He did have means, and, she gathered, only recently his stipend from the Crown had been increased because of added responsibilities. His job was to check prison ledgers for liabilities in individual accounts; many prisoners, it had been discovered, were released after paying only part or even none of the cost of housing and feeding them. ("Outrageous indulgence—total abdication," he had said. "As if the victims should help support their assailants!") Ann herself had spent several months in Newgate Prison on a false charge of pinching a customer's purse, and had gone free without giving them a guinea, but she said nothing of this. Sir Ralph would not likely understand, though he was a good man for all that, kind to Davy, and more considerate of her than any lover she had known. He was gentle: he made love slowly, as if trying not to hurt her, or make noise. Though she preferred more lengthy and strenuous witness of his affections, he didn't know that; he was probably trying to be nice to her, to show respect.

Not a word of marriage had crossed Sir Ralph's lips, but then Ann did not fault him for this. She had not expected such thoughts to enter his mind; she was as far beneath him in quality as he was, say, beneath the Countess of Essex. Besides, had the question of marriage arisen, Ann would perforce have to give thought to her marital status from a legal point of view. Her husband had been gone for many years, but she had no certainty (or even suspicion) that he was dead. Nullity might be a realistic goal for such as Frances, but with Davy around it would not be likely that the magistrates would entertain a similar claim on Ann's part.

As things stood now, Ann was content—no, genuinely happy—to have the love of two such superior beings as Sir Ralph and Lady Essex; she would have done anything in the world to repay their graciousness in caring for her.

She could hardly blame Franklin for the obvious delight he now took in tormenting her. Cruelly, she had left him virtually alone; she had not meant to cause him pain, but she knew the effect was the same.

"Doubtless," he was saying, "tonight you keep company with one or another of your friends of quality . . ."

They had gone far upstream, and were within sight of Lambeth

Palace; Franklin's tone signaled his wish to turn back. The sun was sinking behind Old Church in Chelsea.

"Yes," she lied, knowing that Sir Ralph's work would keep him from her tonight. "And I must get back to look after Davy . . ."

Without much conversation they walked back downstream, back through the sheep pasture, past the Globe, into the lenthening twilight. Ann sensed that, at last, Franklin had struggled free of her. He made no protest, no plea. He seemed almost relieved when they reached her shop.

"It must be nice to be rich," he said, almost as she had hours earlier. "To be able to escape from this dismal place in the summer."

She knew what he meant: it would be good to be rid of her completely, to be free of his loneliness and futility. She knew that she must not turn to him for help again, that she must let him get on with his life without her. And yet he was her link with the past, which seemed to hold out her only means of helping Frances.

Though she dreaded the trip, she had to go to Audley End; she must tell Frances the truth. But who would take care of Davy? She had no alternative: she must ask Sir Ralph for this favor. Yet even if he agreed, Davy would be alone during those hours that Sir Ralph's work called him away. And what if he was unable to stay with Davy? A warm flash of despair swept over her; her gown felt hot and moist. She could not take Davy, but neither could she leave him in the shop alone. The plague was spreading, and he was only a child. He needed her, but Frances needed her, too.

She considered sending the bad news by letter. Yes, it would be best to hide the truth in a brief message posted to Audley End: Davy was ill (how could she know different?), and therefore Ann was unable to bring word herself. After much trouble, Ann had discovered this love potion to be a hoax, a jest on Franklin's part which she (how silly it seemed now!) had taken seriously.

But that meant asking Franklin to write it, which meant exposing Frances' identity. No, Ann would go to Audley End, if only for a few days. Rather than deceive her friend, she would give her warning: for a lady of quality, the cost of Dr. Forman's aid and friendship was too high.

As Ann unlocked the door and called to Davy, a cart rumbled past, heading toward the Bridge. She turned just in time to see in the wagon-bottom the bodies of two women.

"I'm here," Davy called out, running toward her.

Ann watched as the cart slowly rolled to the first turn on Southwark. It would fill up fast on the other side of the river, and the driver would proceed north to Highgate Cemetery to bury his dead. Somewhere behind him—perhaps nearby—another driver readied another cart to follow the same route.

Davy was tugging at her.

"Did you stay inside?" she asked.

"Yes, Mother," he said, "and I cleaned the back room."

She squeezed him. "You must obey," she said earnestly.

But he hadn't heard her. "Come," he said, skipping away, "Sir Ralph is helping me. He's here!"

It seemed too good to be true. She had not expected to see him, and wanted to be with him so badly. She ran to the back room and threw herself into Sir Ralph's arms, pressing her face into the smooth velvet of his tippet. Then, when she felt his fingertips beneath her chin, she let his lips find hers. She was so glad to be with him, to be there in his arms, that she scarcely caught the tone of his greeting.

"Dear Ann," he said, smiling and shaking his head.

"I'm so happy you're here," she said. "It's been so hot, so terrible, today. And I went to the Bear Garden, and it was just awful, and—"

"What on earth for?" he said. "I mean, why would you want to go there? Dreadful place, a resort of thieves and unworthy people . . ."

"I had to carry a message to a friend," she said, sorry that she had raised the subject. She returned to the topic of the weather. "It would be so nice to get into the country, to where it's cool and peaceful . . ."

Sir Ralph appeared to welcome the chance to speak of the summer holiday. "Yes," he said. "I hear it's especially nice in the north—lakes leaping with large fish, woods teeming with deer anxious to be sliced for meat. Wish I could be going with you this year. Perhaps next time. My own schedule will not permit it, I fear."

He must have seen her disappointment; he took her in his arms.

"I'll likely not be going, either," she said.

"We can go!" Davy shouted.

"By all means, go," Sir Ralph said. "Don't not go on my account."

"Not at all," Ann lied. "I've much to do here, once I get back from Audley End."

"When are you going?" he asked.

"I must be there by Midsummer, within a fortnight, in fact . . ."

He appeared to ponder her answer, and Ann hoped he would ask about Davy and thus relieve her of raising yet another burdensome problem.

"Yes," he said, "a fine estate. You'll enjoy it there."

Apparently she had no choice. "I'm most awfully sorry to put myself on you this way," she said, moving away from him and trying to find the right words, "but I really can't take Davy with me. I'll only be gone a few days. Would you mind awfully staying here with him, just staying the nights here, and looking after him?"

"Oh," he said even before Davy had landed from his first leap of joy, and Ann knew what his answer would be. "I'd love to do it, but you see I must leave London myself, on business. Shan't be back for a month at least."

"Where are you going?" she asked.

"To Holland. Amsterdam, actually."

"Ah. I've heard much good of the Dutch. British soldiers like it there. Clean."

"Place is full of heretics," he observed, "but they are industrious fanatics."

After a brief silence, she asked quietly, "When are you leaving?"

"In the morning, betimes," he said. "That's why I dropped by, to tell you, so you'd not worry."

Though he spent the night with her, Ann knew that, without intending to, she had made him feel uncomfortable. He had not actually promised to take her and Davy to the Lake Country; he had only mentioned the possibility. She had behaved foolishly—she, who had always been so good at hiding her feelings, had behaved like a petulant child. She tried to make it up to him. As they lay together, with the curtains drawn and the moonlight playing through the clouds, she waited for a very long time without moving. She wanted him to enjoy himself, to feel relaxed, unhurried. She wanted him to know that he owed her nothing, that he need not worry about her. She and Davy loved him, but he needn't regard them as a burden. Now, he embraced her, his mouth clinging to hers. She felt the lump of his groin pressing at her belly, and she knew that his embarrassment had passed.

IV

June had started badly and was getting worse, with moist, enervating, unmerciful heat. They said that fishermen returned before the day was half gone, complaining of poor catches, most of which they threw overboard before their boats were as far upstream as Greenwich. The air in poorly ventilated St. James was appalling to breathe; pages spent most of their time—but to little avail—emptying chamberpots. With the stench and heat together, James was discouraged from eating all but the lightest foods; even the taste of beer had lost its verve. The Lord Mayor had closed the theatres, and though the summer had just begun, already the narrow streets winding behind Cheapside were posted with names of souls lost to the plague.

Depressing. And lately it seemed that every man's ambition was to vent his spleen on the King, whose own temper was also growing short; minor cavils from Henry, Robin and even Salisbury had escalated into quarrels. James felt ingratitude and betrayal on all sides. Henry's churlishness about the dogs at the Bear Garden had been embarrassing, and his holier-than-thou attitude had only increased the sting of his public rebuke. Anne nagged at him about Overbury, whom she was determined to see dismissed. (Unable to suppress his annoyance longer, about a week ago James had promised to have his Server hanged.) The heat seemed to have propagated the hopes of foreign governments, whose emissaries were noticeably more aggressive with complaints and importunities.

And Parliament, which had been in session for an unconscionable length of time without accomplishing anything, hadn't provided James with a cent. Over two years had passed since he had taken his problems in a speech to both houses: at that time, the Crown was £ 1,500,000 in debt. Even then, the Puritans had sat with their dour, sad, clean-shaven faces, refusing to remove their prosaic hats; they had sent word that the King must jettison the extravagance of masques and revels, which the country could not afford. Old Salisbury had gone to work on the problem, and had succeeded in lowering, but by no means eliminating, the deficit. Only in desperation had James revived the medieval technique of taking "ship money." Coke had argued against the practice; the Puritans, and even members who were far from Puritans, had stubbornly opposed both the principle and the practice. This was to be one of the central points of James's imminent speech: Parliament had not denied Elizabeth's needs, and yet James, who had not one but three courts to support (his, Anne's and Henry's), went begging.

Just the other day, Cecil had presented him with a long document sent by the Commons, entitled "A Petition of Right"; the text included a raft of "grievances," and a request that James appear to answer a variety of questions, one of which concerned the Crown's response to a recent book, *The Interpreter,* written by one John Cowell. The Puritans had, in effect, issued him a summons!

"Tell them I've not read the silly book!" James said. "And if I have, what of it? The King summons Parliament, not the other way round!" Another point for him to stress, should he decide, after the effrontery of Commons, to go through with the speech.

Cecil favored immediate proroguing of Parliament. "The Commons is in an ugly mood," he said. "Every day we have new charges and initiatives. Yesterday they voted to keep record of their proceeding, which I like not. It is uncivilized; these people are becoming impossible to deal with. Prorogue the session until after this heat and spleen have passed."

Cecil was looking unusually pinched and tiny these days; his great grey mane looked thin. Forty years of service to the Crown was showing badly. The tumor in his stomach was now too big to allow much food to stay down. He had scurvy; anyone could see that. He had always stood crookedly, as if some invisible weight were pulling him to one side; he had bad curvature of the spine, which now in sickness and age twisted him into ever more dreadful postures. Once a powerful speaker, now more often than not his voice trembled with fatigue.

James told him he could not possibly prorogue Parliament; he needed money.

As for Cowell, in the presence of Cecil, Coke, Carr and Overbury, James examined the lawyer himself. He had already glanced at the book, which was nothing more than a dictionary of legal definitions, and was surprised that so many had even noticed it—much less found it a cause for concern. According to Cowell, since the King's "Prerogative" derived from inheritance rather than from Parliament, it differed in kind from all other legal authority, existing above both Civil and Common Law. The King, like the Roman Emperor, was subject to God only.

Salisbury said the Commons didn't care a damn for Justinian or precedent, even less for Roman emperors, and would as soon see the world aborn tomorrow. He wanted to know if Cowell was aware that his book was taken as an outline of Crown policy on impositions and port customs, and had seriously exacerbated already difficult relations between the King and Parliament.

"The customs are legal," Cowell said flatly.

"And the anger in the Commons?" Salisbury said. "Is it illegal?"

Cowell looked subdued.

"How would you explain your view of unlimited monarchy to a Parliament that holds your purse-strings?" Salisbury said.

Sir Edward Coke interrupted: "Your views on ship money aside— and incidentally, I disagree with them—what would you advise for the conduct of your own defense? What prerogative would obtain in your trial?"

"Before whose bench?" Cowell said. "On what charge?"

"Treason," Coke said lightly. "With various members of Parliament as complainants. Before them! There is precedent for this; they might charge a commission to examine you. Several have already approached me about procedures."

Cowell was no longer merely subdued; he appeared to grasp the meaning of Coke's words. He was no problem: James could throw a word or two about him into his speech, and see to it that, after all his books were burnt, he was quietly released from the Tower.

But these were more dangerous times than even James had thought.

While Coke regarded Cowell closely, the King looked as searchingly at Coke. Did Coke mean that Parliament, which after all had summoned him and not Cowell to answer questions on *The Interpreter,* was considering an attack upon his customs policy along adversary lines, but in Parliament rather than in court? Coke was no liar, nor was he prone to exaggerate. James would have given much to know how the Lord Chief Justice had answered those zealots in the Commons who—whether implicitly or explicitly, he could not tell—had broached the technical question of how one deals with both of the King's two bodies at the same time.

These self-righteous Puritans annoyed him. He hated their monklike way of dressing, their constant spouting of scripture, even their integrity. Mostly, he despised their hatred and spite toward him. Elizabeth had managed to hold their loyalty, but she had relied on foreign wars and expeditions. James admired—envied—her audacity, but would never himself pursue such a course. The war was over. And yet when Englishmen fought others they had no time to fight amongst themselves; they stopped worrying about their rights when the British troops were exposed abroad, when the likes of Raleigh and Drake enjoyed romantic, profitable adventures at sea or in strange lands. Except for the present skirmish over the successor to John Williams (and had not the Puritans themselves pushed him into this defense of Protestantism?), James had steered the country clear of military conflicts. He had settled the all-important differences with Spain and taken a Catholic wife, and when the time was right he would marry off his older son to the Spanish Infanta.

Their "Petition of Right" proved what he had never doubted: that Puritans were an ungrateful, niggardly lot who cared nothing for peace or justice.

When the day came, and passed, for his address to Parliament, James heard, in fact, that the only part they liked was a frivolous passage he had thrown in for fun: a suggestion that the laws on poaching be changed.

"The present law," he had said, "provides a discourse against stealing deer and conies, but provides punishment only for poachers that steal the game at night, thus giving great encouragement to thieving while the sun shines. Our present law lets every man, no matter how poor a farmer he may be, hunt pheasant and partridge in his own land. I ask you, how can we breed and preserve fowl when, as soon as they fly over the hedge and light in a poor farmer's close, they are killed? Shall I cast a roof over all of Windsor, or brand every partridge with the royal coat of arms?"

A ripple of laughter had coursed through the Great Chamber, but only for this small part, meant half in jest to provide transition between more important matters. Beyond being self-righteous in the extreme, Puritans were stubborn, and no admirers of the art of oratory.

The June speech was better than either of his earlier addresses to Parliament, and a good deal longer as well. James had decided to quit himself of the polite cadences of Cicero in favor of the trenchancy of gutter English—"I must speak frankly to you" . . . "Let me speak bluntly to the Lower House . . ." This simpler style more eloquently fit the central theme to which he set himself:

"The monarchy is the supremest thing upon earth. Kings, and don't forget it, are God's Lieutenants on earth, and sit on God's throne, not yours. By God himself they are called Gods; they create, destroy, give life and death, judge, and are accountable to no man. Therefore, just as it is blasphemy to dispute with God, so is it sedition to dispute with a King in the height of his power."

The last sentence perhaps owed something to Cicero, but the overall impact of the passage was English of the tavern variety.

The speech, which James had written with the help of Cecil, Carr and Overbury, stressed three closely related points. The first was the simplest: James—and James only—called Parliament into session, and for the single purpose of gaining the necessary support of his government. Second: Parliament required guidance on the nature and function of "grievances," and on the proper procedures in putting them forward to the King. One did not simply haul grievances over to St. James in a great sack. The third point was more complicated: the confusion in Parliament about Crown policy on law. Although he was born under a different system of Civil Law, it did not follow, as some believed, that James planned to jettison the Common Law. "I place the Common Law," he had said, "above the Law of Moses! But, on the other hand, I know that nobody understands it except lawyers."

James had taxed the Commons not to try his patience with a second "Petition of Right." It was dangerous to regard any law as a grievance in and of itself, especially if the body itself has the power—indeed, the duty—to change such laws. Then James had chastised some members for the disgusting vigor with which they sought out grievances:

"I have heard," he said, investing his voice with scorn, "that when someone mentioned the word 'grievances,' everybody set about to make a great muster of them. By their own spleen they multiplied grievances, dashing from one public house to another to fetch apprentices who might have complaints to match their own. I tell you, if you noise these grievances about, all things in government seem out of joint.

"I give fair warning," he continued darkly, pausing to watch those stolid Puritans peer out from under the rims of their silly hats, "do not meddle with government, which is my craft."

That was the most telling line in the speech, and James had written it himself. Then, after reminding the Parliament of the British armies in Ireland and the Dutch Republic, of rising costs, and of their own traditional generosity toward the Crown, he asked them for money:

"Freeness in giving graces the gift," he concluded. "Pay no attention to those few churls amongst you who say I give too liberally to Scottishmen. You would not accept a King who dealt niggardly with old retainers."

So much for the meddling remonstrances about the great wealth in Edinburgh and among the retinue of Scots at St. James. Only recently, James had made Carr a gift of another £10,000, and sent another windfall of approximately the same size to Sir James Hay. Not only was James grateful for Hay's years of loyalty to him, but Hay's almost prescient taste was responsible for the King's good luck in meeting Carr.

James awaited the outcome of the speech. He had said what had to be said. The dolts in the Commons, whether they had heard the speech themselves or listened to a zealot's garbled version of it afterwards, had little choice now but to accede to his request, for he had issued it in his sovereign role as a demand. Yes, he had threatened Parliament, at least those members who trifled with his needs: "I warn you" . . . "Take care in future that your satires and railings bear no jot of treason or scandal against me or my posterity." The words had rung true—blunt, perhaps, but just what those scurvy cowards deserved. The broadsides and pamphlets of these Puritan jackals—attacking his pleasures, his choice of friends, his spendthrift ways, his drinking, his morals, the monarchy, the Church of England—were almost without exception published anonymously, which made their sedition more treacherous.

Had the situation been otherwise, James would have ordered Cecil to his sickbed (he looked terrible). Instead he sent him the next day to Whitehall to inquire about responses to the speech. He wanted the matter of finances settled before taking his leave for Audley End. He wanted to enjoy the summer holiday.

Throughout the day James was restless, anxious to hear from Salisbury, unable to concentrate on the last-minute press of other state business. Gondomar, the Spanish Ambassador, called on him with greetings from Philip; James, in turn, assured him that plans for Henry's marriage to the Infanta were proceeding well.

"We move slowly," James said, "so as not to stumble." (He remembered only afterward that he had enlightened the Ambassador with the same wisdom at their last meeting.)

He paid little attention when Carr and Overbury briefed him on arrangements for the King's Progress north. Anne came to see him under the guise of wishing him well on negotiations with Parliament, but actually to register her feelings (no secret) about Overbury.

He sent word asking his physician, the learned and eminent Sir Theodore Turquet de Mayerne, to come to St. James as soon as possible, which proved to be within hours.

"Old Salisbury," James said to him. "You told me he had but a small growth in his stomach. But the little beagle looks ghastly. Even that gravelly, gruff voice is waning. Take a look at him again, and let me know your opinion."

Late in the afternoon, Northampton squeezed in (he had, apparently, taken up with Carr of late, and so had no difficulty getting in to see James). The Spanish Marriage, he claimed, if consummated soon, could now produce new and favorable trade conditions. Northampton's spies, whom James suspected were none other than domestics in his sister-in-law's employ (Lady Suffolk was in almost constant touch with the Spanish Party), had learned that Spain would, if the wedding took place before winter, guarantee removal of all tariffs on imports and exports in the Spanish Netherlands, and in her holdings in the New World. Naturally, such an agreement would entail reciprocal treatment, but even so, it would provide England with immediate prospects of expanded trade.

James was pleased, but he would not commit himself to an exact time. So irreversible a connection with the world's major Catholic power must be handled delicately, especially given the drift of sentiment in the Commons. Much depended on what Cecil had to say on his return, but James omitted mention of this to Northampton. He did ask Northampton's opinion of the speech, and was met by the bright smile characteristic of the Howards:

"Interesting," he said. "Risky, but interesting."

James was not inclined to pursue the remark; his instincts told him that Cecil was waiting outside, and so he was. As Northampton left, Carr showed Salisbury in. When it was clear that Carr intended to stay, old Salisbury bent his shriveled neck and regarded him in a manner intended to show his displeasure. Just then, with the tilt of his lean head, his eyes appearing overlarge and his spindly twisted neck imperiously set against his enormous mink collar, Salisbury looked faintly like an angry bird: a tiny bantam cock too old and scrawny to fight. James had heard that Salisbury and Carr had exchanged harsh words on more than one occasion, but he chose now to take no notice of their rift.

Salisbury persisted. "Your Majesty, I have words for your ears alone. Certain members of the Commons required my word on this."

"I do not see how they will know the difference," Carr said, with an arch inflection reminiscent of his tutor, Overbury.

Salisbury could not have shown more surprise than James felt at this forceful and clever outburst. Yet in deference to Salisbury, James assured Carr that he would shortly confer with him on the matter. Resentfully, Carr withdrew.

Unfortunately, the secret news was all bad, the very worst by far of this deadly June. The Commons remained adamant on all fronts: impositions, tenures, monopolies, ship money.

"They offer this," Salisbury said, "that the King surrender all claims to revenue by anciently derived Crown sources. In response, Parliament will guarantee the King an income of two hundred thousand pounds per annum."

"For what?" James spat. "It costs more than that to stable my horses."

"For your personal expenses," Salisbury said evenly.

"For the management of three courts?" James said angrily.

Salisbury nodded.

"It is not nearly enough," James said.

"So I have told them, many times over."

"I spent more than that sum on the May Festival," James said, as if he were, in his amazement, now musing to himself.

"Your Majesty," Salisbury said, "the Speaker of the Lower House thought it well to say that many members would bar such festivals, and—"

"They would bar everything," James interrupted, "fucking as well as festivals. They oppose all pleasure, and hate to see me spend money. Do they want the Queen to look like a milkmaid? Those whoreson fruitmongers! Who do they think they are? I shall have twenty festivals a season if I wish. An orgy a week. I'll throw those craven bastards all in Newgate Prison, by His nails! By God's blood and nails, I am going to do them in!"

Salisbury was now tiredly studying the grain of the floor; despite his fury, James knew that Cecil, God bless him, had had more than enough for one day.

"Tell them we'll consider—no, that we'll try it, if they'll make the figure higher, one million pounds, which is still far less than I need."

"Do you mean that you accept the principle of their offer?" Salisbury said, suddenly alert. "You would surrender all Crown claims to gathering revenue outside of Parliament?"

Old, tired and sick as he was, the little pygmy leapt on the issue; for the moment his voice deepened and crackled with power. "Are you mindful of the consequences here? Suppose the figure is one million pounds, or even twice that. The agreement would mean that you concede, in perpetuity, the 'right' of the Crown to obtain funds by selling Crown land or granting charters or taking of ship money. Do you grant the legal consequences, and charge me to fashion such a contract?"

"Yes," James said in exasperation. "I grant them and I charge you —at least for July. Find out what it would mean to my heirs. What are the true consequences. Get what you can now, and work out details. I must have rest. When I get back from Audley End, I shall settle the contract permanently. Let it be a temporary settlement, for July, so we can have a month of peace."

"Yes, Your Majesty," Salisbury said. "We are all tired. When I complete negotiations on the contract, I myself shall go to Hatfield for some fresh air."

Salisbury may not have gotten from James all that he came for, but he knew the interview was over, and now he collapsed into a chair. James felt moved by the soul-weariness he saw in the decrepit old man. Cecil was trying to smile, but his face was pinched in a taut grimace. Great beads of sweat coursed down his forehead and nose, and into his eyes and beard. There would not soon be another like him.

"Will you join me for a sherry?" James asked.

Salisbury now managed a smile, nodding as if to say, Will I have to drink with your friend Rochester? James filled two silver goblets; he shrugged to indicate that Carr was well off outside.

"Philip sent me this—a hogshead of the driest sherry that ever he tasted. Do you like it?"

"Yes," Salisbury said, but James could see him struggle to keep the swallow down.

They sat looking at each other. James, whose eyes often watered involuntarily (Mayerne had never explained why), hoped that Salisbury would not distinguish tears in his sovereign's eyes.

"So you'll go to Hatfield," James said.

The house had once belonged to James. Cecil acquired it during a wild weekend at his own awesome country house, Theobald's. James was on hand for the revels, accompanied by his brother-in-law, King Philip of Denmark. The hunting and riding in the area were so superb, and in fact James took so great a fancy to the place, that he insisted Cecil make the trade: Theobald's for the much less valuable Hatfield House. Cecil, unerring servant to the Crown, had not shown the slightest flicker of resentment, then or since.

Now James knew that he might not see this old warrior again.

"You've done marvelous things to Hatfield, I hear," he said.

"Yes," Salisbury said.

"It stood in need of it."

James laughed, and then Salisbury could not restrain himself from joining in.

"I leave for Audley End in the morning," James said.

"Yes," Salisbury said. "Have a good trip. Bring me back a pheasant."

"Yes," James said. "We plan to do some hunting." As Salisbury seemed to be able to keep down the wine, he poured again. "Will your son be joining you at Hatfield?"

"No."

"Has he ever sorted out his differences with his wife?"

"No. I think not."

"Silly."

"Yes."

"The young can be most awfully silly. The Howards are not a bad lot. His wife is beautiful. I must speak to him."

Damn. It was sad. Hot, frustrating, miserable weather. He would be leaving London without a shilling in his satchel. And if Cecil died, what then? Who would deal with Parliament then?

The two men drank silently.

IT WASN'T THAT Frances took no pride in her celebrated great-grandfather's poetry; she had memorized many of his sonnets, and better-known passages from his longer poems. She simply had no notion until now what they meant. She thought poetry was like archery or dancing, one more token of polite activity, further evidence of how nobility spent time, of how different were aristocratic interests from those of common folk. She knew that many poems celebrated the glorious moments of love, and these she took to be reasonable and accurate portents of the marvels that lay in store for her. Other possibilities in verse form she merely overlooked, or thought to be inferior poetry. Until she met Carr. Since her return to Audley End, lines that she had memorized years ago came back—but with a shock of understanding:

> *This creeping fire my cold limbs so oppressed,*
> *That in the heart that harbored freedom late,*
> *Endless despair long thraldom hath impressed.*
> *One eke so cold in frozen snow is found*
> *Whose chilling venom of repugnant kind*
> *The fervent heat doth quench of Cupid's wound*
> *And with the spot of change infects the mind.*

These lines which she, like all loyal Howards, had put to memory for recitation at family gatherings now for the first time made a terrible sense. Lovers were helpless victims, torn by contraries: cold fire, warm snow. Her love could hardly be separated from despair. Though she was determined to capture Carr's affections, she doubted the likelihood of her success. She was, though a great lady by most standards, a slave, subject to involuntary visions of her beloved's smiling face. At last she understood that when Cupid's arrow strikes a victim—man or woman—the pain is real.

Love had done much more than elevate Frances' understanding of poetry. She, who had always taken doctors, like grooms and smithies, for granted, began to worry about the substance of medical science. The jars and powders and quiet efficiency of apothecaries now much distracted her. She yearned to believe the claims of medicine, which before, whether she had rheum or ague, she had never doubted. For more urgent than any fever she had ever had was the imminent test of her marital status. Through Ann Turner she had acquired a great store of powder—a kind of salt, Ann had said, much used in the making of gunpowder. Frances depended wholly, if not confidently, on the effectiveness of this invention to restrain the ardor of Robert Devereux, Lord Essex, who had returned to England eager to assume the duties and privileges of a husband.

Love was mad; it infected the mind, yes: *"And with the spot of change infects the mind."* Fickleness, change, despair, were all symptoms—except that in the mad world of Frances' passion only fickleness and change could remedy her lovesickness. She had to rid herself of Essex to obtain Carr. Thus all lovers were slaves, victims, powerless to help themselves. Essex—she wasn't blind—was a victim, too, silly creature that he was, pining and sighing about. He had a noxious habit of arching his eyebrows when in her presence, as if waiting for her to say something. The effect was to give his flat face a concave appearance, which, with his lank, dark hair covering his brow, made him look uncommon vapid. Had Frances never seen Carr she would not have fancied her husband's looks; the comparison rendered him repulsive.

Though no one, much less Essex, had openly rebuked her, Frances knew that sympathy at Audley End was shifting to her husband. He had been given the state suite with the reasonable expectation—keenest on his part, perhaps, but shared by all—that Frances would join him, if not at once, then in a day or two. Soon a week had passed, and Essex, who was nervous and high-strung by nature, was showing considerable embarrassment. Frances felt a bit sorry for him, but she had no intention of giving up her own rooms overlooking the stables and the wilderness area; they would be useful during the King's Progress. Still, though she was chary about the final test of Franklin's powder, she knew that she must soon allow her husband to bed her. She would have to depend on the potency of this innocent-looking white powder.

"It is most powerful," Ann had said. "Franklin uses it to make *aguis forta.*"

"*Aqua fortis,*" Frances had said. "I have heard of this strong water. I hope it be sufficient strong to render one man weak."

"It is. Just one small spoonful a day will do it."

At the time, Ann's directions had presented no problem; the doubts stirred after Frances was back at Audley End. Had she understood correctly: just one spoonful? That seemed a harmless dose. One spoonful regardless of how many meals or services of tea lent proper opportunities? Or had Ann prescribed a single portion per serving? The difference was considerable, and Frances was annoyed with herself for not sorting the matter out when she had the chance. Then too, suppose Ann had said a spoonful a day, but was in fact herself mistaken? Perhaps Franklin's directions had been garbled, or given in haste. With no convenient way of quickly contacting Ann, Frances was forced to act on her own.

Working through Katherine, her youngest and cleverest servant, she had no trouble lacing her husband's tea with powder. Some care was required, for when the powder first met liquid it roiled angrily and gave off smoke; one couldn't just drop it in with Essex standing about. Frances decided upon a full day's measure (should she have heard correctly) to every pot, and Essex was a prodigious drinker of tea, finishing off several pots with breakfast alone.

It was Frances' good fortune to be well-liked and trusted amongst the large kitchen staff. She learned that Essex was fond of venison pasties, several of which he consumed a day, and each of which received a heaping spoonful of powder. And in the evening, when Essex presented himself to Frances in her dressing room, she would hand him a cordial—he had acquired the taste for brandwine while in France—to which she had added a pinch or two for good measure.

At first, results were not promising; Essex looked more ardent than ever, hanging on her every glance, his eyebrows arched over bovine eyes, conveying sad impatience.

Within days, her mother came to see her: the situation was becoming a scandal; Essex had waited for years to claim what her mother called his "due."

"So you did not wish to move into the state rooms," her mother said. "No matter. The King is coming, and we must ready them for His Majesty in any case. But you, Lady Essex, Frances Howard, must permit your husband to share your bed. We are an honorable family. He has been patient. You are not a child. It is his God-given right."

His "due," Frances thought, nodding compliance.

After dinner that evening, she returned to her room; it was filled with her husband's things. She asked Katherine to wait on the two of them throughout the night, to sleep in the adjacent room and, for an indefinite period, to stay close.

Essex had spent the day in Saffron Walden with her father, and it was late when he came to her room. Though Midsummer was only days away, the last of dusk had departed, and the candles were burning.

"Madam," he said truculently. "I have waited long enough. Too long."

"Yes, my lord," Frances said.

Essex looked surprised; he staggered into the room and threw off his jerkin.

"Where is your valet?" Frances said.

"I don't need a valet to take off my kettledrums," he said.

"Here," she said, "let me." She helped him off with his buskins. "I'll be right back," she added sweetly, handing him his cordial. "Settle in with this!"

When she left, he was grinning like a maniac.

Katherine helped Frances into her nightgown, and now, as she reentered the bedroom, she left the door to the dressing room open. Essex looked apprehensive.

Frances laughed. "She's only a commoner," she said. "I may have need of her tonight, and I don't plan to get out of bed."

Essex extracted the intended encouragement from this; leering vilely, he took Frances in his arms.

"Have you finished your brandy?" she asked softly.

"And another," he answered.

"May I have a drop?" she said as he coaxed her into bed.

Trembling, he brought her brandy and, after a vain attempt to let the bed curtain down, pulled her nightgown from her. Frances offered

131

no resistance; she knew the wisdom of her mother's words. Appearing encouraged, even passionate, Essex dispensed with his own gown.

Frances could not restrain a swift, downward glance at the target of all her strenuous efforts: absolute success. Though inexperienced in these matters (except as an observer), she saw that her husband's passion was, for all practical purposes, feigned.

She gladly offered no resistance as Essex threw himself on top of her.

"You are beautiful," he breathed. "Beautiful."

He began to move as if making love. He stopped, kissed Frances on the mouth, kissed each breast, paused, manipulated her breasts, kissed her again (this time working his tongue between her lips), then embraced her vigorously before slumping clumsily with his full weight upon her, his head next to hers on the pillow.

"My lord?" she said when moments had passed. "Is anything wrong?"

"I don't know," he said. "I don't understand. I have dreamt of this."

"Yes," she said. "And I too, my lord."

"Robert," he said. "Or husband."

"Yes, my lord. Robert."

There was silence again before Essex began slowly to remove himself from her. Franklin's "strong water" had worked wonders, for Essex rolled away from her with no more capacity than a babe: minuscule, soft, wrinkled, cuddly. She could have kissed it but, since the powder might weaken under such stimulation, dared not.

"I don't understand," Essex repeated. "I must have had too much to drink."

Frances suppressed an urge to laugh.

"Or the heat," he continued. *Mon Dieu,* it is hot . . ."

"Yes," she said.

Her answer seemed to irritate Essex. "Is that all you can say?" he said, leaping into his nightgown. "You think that mere heat and a few tankards would hinder me?" He paused, and then added pointedly, "Have ever hindered me?"

The sod! What value or what pain did he think this vulgar boast would be to her? Seeing Katherine at the door, Frances decided to turn the situation to some benefit: she moved toward her husband, naked, arms outstretched, as if imploring him to consummate their marriage.

"Why no, my lord. I think nothing of heat or ale, but of you only . . ."

Now Essex held her from him. Good.

"Something is wrong!" he said loudly.

"With me, my lord?"

Now he stood as if transfixed by the perfection of her body: open, available, his for the taking. Ever so slowly, he shook his head. "No, my love, not with you. I don't know. By tomorrow night I warrant I'll make you my wife."

As Frances put on her nightgown, she smiled gaily. "Don't worry," she said, climbing into bed. "You are distraught and and fatigued. Travel and change are difficult. You need sleep."

Her plan was working.

"Put out the candles," she called to Katherine. "We are going to sleep."

Essex appeared to believe that a night's rest would help him; in the morning, he seemed to look forward to day's end—which, when it came, left her a maid. As Frances now expected, so did the next. And the next. Drunk or sober, early or late, with or without the door ajar, before or after a brisk ride through the meadow (one attempt in the meadow itself)—nothing worked for him. Never had a more ardent lover been more thoroughly reduced. And he, the son of England's most heralded and handsome lover, the Earl of Essex who had found romantic favor in the adoring eyes of Elizabeth herself, took his condition badly.

"I feel bilious," he said. He complained often that everything, even the air he breathed, tasted salty.

Frances felt no sympathy for him, though he was soon unable to conceal his embarrassment. She had brought the apothecary's art into play in order to enjoy the same passion—the same love—that Essex, if left unhindered, would take in possessing her. She wanted Carr as much as Essex wanted her.

Even though her design had worked thus far, she knew that much remained to be done. With Essex now lodging in her rooms, it was easier to control his intake of powder, and she no longer feared his capacity to bed her. But she had still to prepare for the King's Progress, and for the appearance at Audley End of Robert Carr. And yet she had no potion to attract this beautiful man.

As Frances had suspected, Essex refused to suffer the humiliation of remaining at Audley End for the royal visit. He knew that the news of his unwanted celibacy would be no secret long. Within a week, he announced that he would, prior to the King's arrival, leave to ready Essex House for his wife. She was to stay with her family during the King's Progress; then she must come to him, where, in more settled, familiar surroundings, he would make her his wife in fact as she was in name. Frances happily agreed. The matter was settled; Essex would take Katherine with him to help adjust the household to the ways of its new mistress, whose tastes Katherine knew better than anyone.

With the problem of Essex under control, Frances could turn her thoughts to Carr. She was anxious for Ann Turner's arrival. Though she had managed to obtain the powder for her husband, she had yet to receive the love-philter which Ann had promised to deliver to Audley End under the guise of coming to help her with preparations for the King's visit.

Happily, the day before Midsummer, Ann arrived as arranged, to take the northernmost rooms on the second floor of the stables. The rooms were spacious, well-appointed, and almost exactly opposite the windows in Frances' bedroom.

"Did you bring it?" Frances said the moment they were alone.

She had not. "I bring troublesome news," she said. "It is a most curious potion, involving many people. I dread to say what Franklin told me."

Frances insisted on a full account.

"Attraction," Ann said, "is more difficult than rendering unable. It requires your presence, which I like not. You must not go to London . . ."

"To see this Franklin?"

"No, dear Frances. To see Dr. Forman, who instructs Franklin of these mixtures."

"But why must I go, and not you?"

"I don't know," Ann said earnestly. "I offered to go, and fear your going. The plague is spreading, and I can only stay here a few days. I must get back to Davy. I had to leave him with Franklin. The shop is closed. The stores and theatres are closed, and the Bear Garden. I am afraid for Davy, and you . . ."

Frances showed her irritation. "Why did you not bring him?"

"My lady," Ann said, slipping back into formal address, "you did not . . ."

"Oh," Frances said, "how stupid of me! I did not think of it."

"But at the time there was no plague," Ann said. "And now there are riots in the streets . . . apprentices . . ."

Politics—a dreary subject at any time—struck Frances on this occasion as an annoying distraction. "If I must go," she said, "but not see Franklin, how shall I find this Dr. Forman?"

From beneath her farthingale, Ann fetched a slip of paper, which, Frances discovered, bore a waterfront address.

"But this is right in the worst plague area," Frances said. "I am to go here?"

"Do not go," Ann said.

Frances truly wanted to be Ann's friend, without the usual let of social standing, but this flat imperative distressed her. "Excuse me," she said, "but I understood you to say that I must go, or have none of this curious mixture."

"Then have none," Ann said. "This doctor—"

"Yes," Frances interrupted, "insists that I visit him in person. So I shall."

"Dear Frances, this doctor is a . . ."

"Yes?"

"A sorcerer."

"And what of it? What else was Queen Elizabeth's John Dee but a notorious magician? Do you think I have not heard of your Dr. Forman? Last year he came through Saffron Walden, healing people of the King's sickness."

"I have heard of such things," Ann said. "But he will ask more of you than he did of them. He will demand of you all that you have to give him."

Frances found this remark as naïve as it was impertinent. She could well afford this doctor's services, whatever the cost. Had not Ann herself been able to afford his help? And had she not herself admitted how wonderfully he had changed her life for the better? Besides, given his success with *aqua fortis,* Frances was keen to meet Forman, and to obtain his philter, plague or no.

So the plan required an unforeseen risk. Given her choice, Frances would have avoided London at this time. But the risk of plague could not be great: her uncle was still in London, and so was the Royal Family. No, though she resented the change in plans, and the inconvenience of the trip, she would not let fear keep her from obtaining this love-elixir.

The change in plan did present one difficulty. Her husband and her mother demanded an explanation of her sudden departure. She told them that in her haste Ann Turner had left much behind in London, and pointed out that her stay would be brief—which seemed important to Essex but left her mother unimpressed.

"This is a bad plague summer," Lady Suffolk persisted.

"But Uncle Henry is still in London," Frances said. "And the King's visit is no ordinary one," she added craftily. "It's no use not getting it right."

She had echoed one of her mother's most oft-used expressions, but it met with cold-eyed skepticism. "And what of your husband? I thought he was leaving for Essex House."

"Yes," Frances said smoothly. "He returns to Essex House to make ready for my stay, once the King has passed."

Frances was sure that her mother would see through so implausible a story, but if she did she gave no sign. Lady Suffolk must have had much on her mind: Audley End was in a tumult of activity; workmen were frantically rushing to finish the many redecorations begun in early spring. The most ambitious of these, a magnificent curved stairway which would provide access from the Great Hall to the Picture Gallery, was taking longer than expected. Its unique marble balusters were carved to spell out the motto of the Order of the Garter: HONI SOIT QUI MAL Y PENSE (Shame on him who thinks ill of it). Her father, who had recently been named to the Order, had poured enormous sums into the redecorations, but it seemed that not enough time remained before the King's arrival to complete work on the staircase, and a similarly ambitious alteration of the main entrance was also unfinished.

The next day, Frances set off with Ann for London. When they reached the city, Frances found her uncle distracted by political and and other family problems, but he promised to spend an evening with her before she returned to Audley End.

"I'll go back with you," he said. "You'll not want for company."

Northampton warned her not to walk abroad in London, which was experiencing its worst epidemic of plague in a decade. Wherever one turned, the doors of houses read, "God have mercy on us." Streets were posted with lengthening bills of the dead. And the inevitable wagons rumbled through the city, from twilight to dawn, with their loads for burial.

Frances was of no mind to promenade. After a night's rest, she traveled to Southwark, telling the coachman to return for her before dusk. He seemed unconcerned by her request, and appeared not to notice the fact that the dress shop to which he had delivered her was, like most places of business in the area, closed.

After greeting Frances with a kiss, Ann went to fetch a hackney-coach. ("He'll cost the earth," she had said, "but I know one who will wait for you until you return.") She had agreed to handle all arrangements; she would pay the coachman after Frances' return, and he was not to know the identity of his passenger.

The sun was shining on the Thames when Frances arrived at Forman's place. The street was far from crowded, but scattered carts were about, and on the river a few boats were moving, evidence that the plague had not yet brought commerce to a halt.

The coachman insisted that he knock for her admittance before helping Frances from the carriage.

The house had a foul odor. The shutters and blinds were drawn: one of the means, Frances imagined, by which the large man who introduced himself as Dr. Forman intimidated less noteworthy visitors.

They entered what appeared to be Forman's studio. It had a large fireplace, a huge desk, several large couches of foreign design and—strewn all about—books on shelves, the floor, the darkened window casements.

"Welcome," Forman said (without nodding, much less bowing), indicating that he wished her to sit.

Frances took a place on the couch facing him.

"My friend told me to expect you," Forman said, but he didn't say which friend that was—Franklin or Ann Turner.

Forman was a strangely attractive man. Frances' eyes, which had become accustomed to the darkness, fixed him with a steady gaze.

"You are welcome," he was saying. "It is early, but never too early to receive an interesting visitor. Nor for a pot of specially brewed tea."

Chirpily, though they were in the depth of summer, he knelt to light the fireplace: he meant to prepare tea right there in the room. His servants must have deserted him in fear of the plague.

"I have heard," Frances said, "that if a servant is a born Londoner, and leaves his master to avoid plague, he will return by August end."

Forman smiled cheerfully. "Perhaps. I have heard the same opinion. I have never had servants myself. Wouldn't have them. Wrong, you know."

Frances found herself smiling, too. An insult, when given so lightly, could not be taken seriously, even from the sane. And if it tumbled from the lips of Tom o' Bedlam, only an idiot would take offense. The best thing to do was enter into the jaunty spirit of Forman's madness.

"I have many servants," she said.

"Yes, you do," Forman said. "But they have you as well. I prefer liberty to ownership by servants. Physical ease is an illusion, you see. Actually, servants do no work. They cleverly pretend to serve their master, when in fact the opposite is true. The master has no need of the services he receives, though you cannot convince him of it. Though he profits not by these illusory services, without complaint he provides for his servants and their families in all things."

Forman was more than amusing; he made a peculiar kind of sense. Frances could see why he exercised so great an influence on educated people. Many thought him a prophet endowed with "peculiar grace," the kind enjoyed by saints.

When he served up a pot of tea, Frances noted that its aroma was unusually heady.

Forman agreed. "My own concoction," he said. "A mixture of Indian leaf and Phoenician flower: an orient of hospitality in a small English cup."

He poured, and for a time they sat enjoying the tea. If Frances had felt apprehensive about the trip, or about this meeting, her sense of well-being now more than compensated for it. She not only felt relaxed in Forman's company, but it seemed that she was in the presence of an old friend. She was aware that Forman reminded her of her uncle. He had the same sharp glance, the same self-assurance, the same wit. He was more direct than her uncle, far less subtle and not nearly as elegant (he wore no ruffs, no doublet, no jerkin, no wings), yet he instilled trust.

"Are you," she asked, "as I have heard, a witch?"

"Perhaps." He smiled.

"Perhaps? You don't know?"

"Surely I know," he said. "But you jest, which doesn't help you. This foolishness of burning witches, especially in Essex County, has gotten out of hand, thanks partly to our silly King. Most of these sad creatures know nothing of witchcraft. Anne Mortlak of Birdbrook hired a charlatan to cast a spell on her husband, to drive him mad. She wanted his property. When the poor man found out the plot against him, he went wandering the streets of the village, and the fools about said, 'See, he *is* mad.' So they convict Anne Mortlak of witchcraft, and she burns. Another, Mary Hart, they try for bewitching seven pounds of meat belonging to one Robert Smart of Dovercourt. Magnanimously, they clear poor Mary of this charge, but only so that a year later they may burn her for bewitching a sailor who died mysteriously. Whenever a body expires in Essex, an unwed maid must hang as a witch. Yet what do any of them know of witchcraft?"

"But many have confessed and done penance before hanging."

Forman's eyes widened in mock astonishment. "Does this mean that if you say you are a witch, then you are so? I can make you *think* you are a witch, flying through the air. Or a child. Or an ox. Or alive a thousand years ago. Now, I am no witch—to wit, I have no desire to be denounced before the nearest illiterate magistrate. I do not relish being roasted like a pig. I prefer my present status: hounded from court to court by the College of Physicians as one lacking the proper license to heal people. Yet in a way I am a witch, a magician, yes, a sorcerer, or, as I think of it, a scholar, or reasonable man. One who reads books: Albertus Magnus. Roman Lull. Hermes Trismegistus. Forgotten books from Egypt. There is more knowledge in Paracelsus than in all the Church Fathers combined."

Frances laughed good-naturedly, which seemed to disturb Forman.

"You laugh, but you are here," he said. "You came to me. Why?"

"Because I need your help."

"Why?"

"I need your love-philtre."

Now Forman seemed genuinely angry. "Unless I have your respect, I cannot help you. You make a serious mistake here. You imagine I can give you a draught to slip in someone's ale, and then he will love you. What nonsense! Why come so far when it is obvious you could have made a fool of yourself at home? I demand respect. Absolute respect, not because of irrepressible conceit, but because it is the only way I can be of service. To impress you with the importance of this,

I now demand that you present me with your most precious possession."

Frances untied the bag secured beneath her kirtle, and handed it to him. Without looking at it Forman tossed it aside.

"You consider this your most valuable possession? Nobody is that naïve."

"It is much," she said, "all that I could bring without attracting attention."

"You are the envy of men and women of quality, but not because of what is in that bag."

"Dr. Forman, how much do you want? You have not given me the philtre yet. And I assure you there is a substantial fortune in that bag."

"I do not doubt it. But you do not value it. You cast it aside too easily."

Frances began to catch the terrible drift of what he was saying. "But surely," she protested, "all services have a cost, a limit . . ."

"Most perhaps. Not mine."

"You contradict and insult me," Frances said in exasperation, pretending that she had not guessed his meaning.

"You are free to leave," Forman said, smiling. When Frances did not move, he continued: "You must part with what you value most, not to suit me, but to secure your goal. First you want one potion, then another. You want to repel, to attract, and yet you attack me for contradicting you. Do you begin to see? You bring me so many guineas and doubtless some jewelry, and I tell you that money—especially to you—is not a value but a necessity. I accept the token, for to me money is a value. This helps me, but what has it done for you? I am not rich. Now, to help you, I must have from you all that you think so important, the source of these weeks of activity, which has sent so many people in so many different directions. What do you value?"

"Robert Carr, Viscount Rochester."

"You desire your social inferior?"

"Yes."

"You accept this in yourself for all time?"

"Yes."

"You want him entirely to yourself, to own him?"

"Yes. To own him. To have him completely for myself."

"And apparently you are determined."

"Yes."

"At whatever cost?"

"Yes."

"And, if I deliver him wholly to you, you understand how completely you would be in my debt?"

"By the love-philtre?"

"I said nothing of a love-philtre; you insist that I have a potion to attract Viscount Rochester, and I tell you, if you'll but listen, that you shall have this man, but not by any philtre unmatched by your own desire. If a drop or two of mine—yes, I have an interesting concoction that will help you—can hasten your delight, so much the better. But your desire, not the philtre, will provide the key. And you will know that desire when you place it above all else by meeting my single demand: that you part with your most valuable possession—which cannot be Robert Carr, for you came here to obtain him. Do you agree?"

Frances was not quite sure what she had been asked to agree to. She felt strangely light-headed, giddy, yet on the verge of nausea. She thought she heard music, as at a wedding.

"I do," she said, but sensed that her answer was not in the least appropriate.

"You know, of course, what I am talking about is the envy of the King's court: yourself, your body, your virginity. This is what has brought you here. It is the source of all your magnificent, misdirected energy."

Her vision was blurred, and Forman's words seemed to stretch out in time, punctuated by shifting chords played on a church organ.

"I feel a touch ill," she said, and her voice rang with higher chords from the same organ.

"You are not ill," Forman sounded. "It is my tea. Sometimes this happens. It will pass."

She saw that Forman was watching her closely; his face changed color. She had noticed that his hair was partly gray, but now it showed pitch-black, and seemed much thicker, the hair of a young man.

"Don't worry," he was saying in a voice that was now much softer, like an echo, reassuring. "Relax. Take forty winks if you wish, while I . . . while I . . ."

All nausea, all fear vanished. Perhaps she slept, for she thought she was dreaming. The distinction seemed remote and trivial now. She opened her eyes in a dream or not in a dream: warm yellow light flooded the room. Torches rimmed a marvelous blue dome; at its base was a golden band emblazoned with the signs of the Zodiac, which seemed to move slowly.

"A kind of paint," Forman said, "not used in England. It's simple."

Yes, simple it was. The word had never made such sense. Simplicity was important: hadn't someone like a poet said so? She had to remember that. The world was simple, reducible to this one element. There, on the centerpiece of the dome: a great ball of fire, inscribed IGNIS. Simplicity. Glowing: "In the beginning was the Word and the Word was with God and the Word was God," but she had not until now known what that Word was: IGNIS, simplicity, fire. What could be simpler than that?

"It seems to burn," Forman said, "because the paint has a special ingredient. Your mind is specially wary, made so by the tea; so when your eye moves, objects seem to move with it. The paint picks up the light from the torches. See the figures in the firescreen? They'll move, too; they're of the same substance. Just relax and enjoy them."

The truth of it was stunning to her: "They're of the same substance" —sun-Son-God-Word-IGNIS.

"They want you," he said.

And they did. Perfectly gorgeous bodies motioned to her—simple substances attached to beautiful forms, like the statuary on the parterre at Audley End. Only she hadn't thought of them that way.

"Just think," he said. "Just feel."

Hands were caressing her—their simple hands—so many and so smooth, and she had waited (hadn't someone said that, too?), waited so long. Handsome young men: silent, smiling, smooth. Young women with long blond ringlets by the stream in the embrace of young men. All wanting her. Beckoning. Running toward her. Making love, or just before, embracing, lost in the dream of possession, complete possession. They must be making love to her.

The simple, true, solid flame (IGNIS) penetrated Frances to the painful desired depths. She thought this elemental fire must tear her apart, yet welcomed the soft kiss of this nameless blond youth, and yes, welcomed the deep driving pain inside her: arms (smooth), naked skin moving against her skin, blond, broad, smooth as a woman, but with a rippling belly, firm, strong, good inside her (IGNIS), inside her now, loving her fully.

How did the song go? She had to—it was simple!—remember it. It was made of words, simple important words now, there in the golden haze, in the arms of this charming seducer. The song was clever, "Love to Be Enjoyed," and Frances lay smiling as the young girl's voice sang out, lay listening and basking in the radiance of love in the summerhouse.

The story was very simple. Bessy only pretended to sleep; her self-deception was simplicity itself, because Jamy, the young man (*this* blond young man), found her, and she only feigned to stay asleep. Oh Bessy, Francie, Francie (how could the poet so simply have remembered her childhood name?), Francie "By sleep beguiled." The girl's sweet, clear voice mocked all pretense:

> *Robin then began to play,*
> *Francie as one buried lay,*
> *Gladly still through this slight,*
> *Deceived in her own deceit.*
> *And since this trance begoon,*
> *She sleeps every afternoon.*

That was how it went. Francie remembered, and the joke was on Robin Carr, not her. Forman had said she must surrender her self-deceit, and now, by seeing how she had used her own self-deception, she had completely surrendered.

And yet a voice, Forman's voice, remonstrated with her: "Now do you see what brought you here? Look."

It was appalling that anything, much less simplicity or truth, could produce so monstrous an object. Frances drew back, not in horror at her lost virginity (though she had struggled against man and God to preserve it), but at the object Forman held in his hand: a large waxen carving of lovers—Forman and her—copulating.

"I'll have a bronze casting made of it for you," Forman said.

Most humiliating of all, they were no longer alone: a low workman stood beside Forman. Presumably, he had carved the figures during her visit, the length of which now escaped her.

"I shall have the both of you hanged for this!"

Frances thought she had shouted, but Forman asked her to speak louder.

"I could have you hanged for this!"

"Of course you could," Forman said, "but why should you? That would only defeat your purpose. I'll send the casting to you—discreetly. You may trust me."

"I'll have you done in another way," Frances said.

"Don't say such things," Forman said. "I am going to help you as only I can. To do so, you must have your wits about you. And this, too." He held the wax carving in front of her. "This is what brought you here. This is what you brought to me, and what you bring to Carr. You want your social inferior, and you have had him, and shall have him. Now you know that what you want others want also. Forget your station. Forget your virginity. Forget everything but your desire for Carr."

He handed Frances two bottles which appeared filled with the same liquid.

"The philtre will help, too," he continued. "But more important, remember: whenever you see this Carr, you must think of the bronze statuary which I will send you. In this"—he handed her a small envelope sealed with wax—"I have placed pieces of your skin, hair and fingernails. See to it that the envelope is always under Carr's pillow. Keep the statuary in your room—you must hide it, of course —and every night before retiring, place it in front of you. Ponder it seriously, as monks regard their skulls in the *ars moriendi*. Do not let a single night pass without this discipline: caress and ponder it until you feel yourself genuinely moved. Then sleep and dream of love in his arms. When you see Carr, think of this statuary; it does not matter what you say to him, or even if you look at him. But when he looks at you, you must without fail be thinking of this love-statuary. Do you understand?"

As Frances wept quietly, Forman asked the intruder to leave; then he took her tenderly in his arms.

"My child," he said, "I worry about you. You are so willful."

"You have ruined me."

"Rubbish," he said.

"Even if you are not a charlatan, and I have Carr, I'll not have my 'nullity' . . ."

"Rubbish," he said again.

"Which requires virginity."

"A cavil," he said. "A jape. What good did it ever do you?" But when he saw that Frances took no delight in his levity, he spoke gravely. "Remember, my child, that 'nullity' is a public instrument, and therefore responsive to my efforts. It has naught to do with maidenheads nor physical conditions of any sort, but only with the wishes of the men involved, who are, by virtue of their appointments, already corrupt. Prepare your case, lodge it in the courts, and let these fools spend a day or two displaying their ignorance. Deuteronomy this and Numbers that. My God, it's enough to make a man glad of being old and near to death. Don't you see that because you are a Howard the 'nullity' is yours?"

Frances wanted to believe Forman, but could not. She knew now what Ann had meant by urging her not to visit him: Forman was not so much vile as mad.

"These old men at the 'nullity,' " he was saying, "will hold forth on the sacramental nature of marriage, on the Old Testament and the New, on medicine, on horseback riding and its uncertain effects on more robust female riders, on the manifold varieties of physical shapes which God in his infinite wisdom has bestowed upon womankind, and when it is over they will examine you with trepidation, pronouncing you more untouched than the Virgin Mary."

With a chuckle, he took an enormous jade figure of a hideous-looking animal from one of what appeared to be many compartments of his desk.

"Before you go," he said, "I want you to take a look at this."

SIR THOMAS OVERBURY could not claim that his job was physically demanding, but in the weeks that followed the May festival it was surely time-consuming. Bills poured in from every imaginable creditor; petitions for charters seemed to have doubled; members of the Admiralty and Mayors of port cities were uncommonly anxious to meet with the King. Almost everyone wanted money, and those who didn't came to let James know that he could hope to get no more from them.

John Rainolds, under whom Overbury had studied briefly while at Oxford, came to request money for the translators of the Bible; he had hired some twoscore postgraduates to assist the principal translators. Like so many of the King's pet projects, the translation of the Bible, finished two years ago, had become a drain on the Exchequer, and yet many of the project's creditors and most of the professors and students remained unpaid. Even so, Overbury felt obliged to put Rainolds off.

Rainolds, the aging Dean of Corpus Christi College, was one of James's favorites, and the King was unhappy that he had been turned away: "I want to see him," he said. "He is certainly the best Hebrew scholar in England. Give him what he needs. He may be a Puritan, but more than anyone he got the translation going." Since the project's inception following the Hampton Court Conference held the first year of James's reign, the King had taken every opportunity to help with the translation himself. "Don't be stingy with my time in religion," he had said. "This English translation will be the best one yet, and at last they've finished. It would be a pity if Rainolds didn't live to see it paid for."

The Bible scholars. The Royal Navy. The Army. The dressmakers. The tailors. The vintners. The butchers. The acting troupes. There seemed to be no end to the stream of people who, either in person or by post, presented claims on the Crown's already depleted resources.

The King's speech to Parliament had only made matters worse: Commons refused to recognize the new tax rates, and proclaimed that no tax was legal without their consent. A pall descended on St. James Palace. Members of the Commons were now in almost constant session with old Cecil, who looked as if he must soon die beneath the strain. Even so, "the little beagle" promised to put together a compromise, to be tried out during the month of July, before leaving for Bath. James would be guaranteed an annual income, and in return he would renounce the principle of impositions.

Probably Carr's mood contributed much toward making St. James seem gloomy. Nothing seemed to please him: "Thomas," he would say, "when I need your advice I shall ask for it." Or, "What good are you, Thomas, if I must beg and cajole you for advice?" Overbury was alarmed by these symptoms of Carr's independence, the source of which could easily be traced to contact with the Countess of Bedford and her lot. Acquaintance with intellect had infected Carr with an illusion of his own intelligence. Carr resented Overbury, whose air of superiority implied that he, and not Carr, was the Viscount and

Member of the Privy Council and near-owner of Sherborne House. (Parliament had, in outrage, challenged the King's gift of Sir Walter Raleigh's estate to Robert Carr.)

Yet Overbury knew that he was not the true cause of Carr's malaise: Viscount Rochester was jealous of George Villiers, the enviable young man who had attracted James. The more love for Villiers shone in the eyes of King James the more desperately Carr pursued the Countess of Bedford, and the more abrupt became his treatment of Overbury. Overbury suspected that James saw through Carr's truculence, but the King had much on his mind these days, and seemed to revel, regardless of Carr's pique, in Georges Villiers' youthful, uncomplicated good looks.

Carr, in childish reprisal, began to talk wildly of marrying the Countess of Bedford. So far as Overbury knew, this foolishness had not yet gotten a rise out of the King. From Overbury's point of view, the Countess was, at best, a nuisance; at worst, a serious threat to his position at court. Overbury was wise enough to know that, should Carr marry her, he would look no longer to him, but to one of Lucy's minions. In the beginning, the Countess had merely toyed with Carr to the great amusement of her intellectual coterie. Overbury had encouraged this, for it gained him admittance to the routine dinners and conversation at the Mermaid and the Mitre. But the affair soon became more than that.

Sophisticated Lucy, Countess of Bedford, was not content to watch Carr hurl himself at her feet. She took to displays of temper when members of her entourage made him the target of jest. Even the Earl of Northampton saw the danger signs, and it was he who first drew Overbury's attention to her change in attitude. The Countess had taken a fancy to this handsome Scot who showered her with affection in the teeth of scathing insults from the intellectuals whom she patronized. She, like many others before her, had fallen to the lure of Carr's face. Though an older woman, she was still attractive, and Overbury could see what romantic visions had finally filled her otherwise sensible, aristocratic head.

In itself, her infatuation gave no cause for concern, but repercussions soon emerged on several fronts: the Countess let it be known that she might seek annulment of her marriage. When this rumor failed to scare Carr off (on the contrary, it was about that time that he began his own loose talk of marriage), she took to treating Carr more seriously, openly rebuking her poetic clients. "I am fond of my Scottish Robin," she would say, insisting that they treat him with respect.

Too swift of mind by half, John Donne approached Carr about employment, suggesting, it appeared, that he would make a more suitable assistant than Overbury. Obviously, Donne had gathered that one might now have the Countess and the Viscount, too. No, Carr's marriage to the Countess was out of the question.

Beyond the obvious threat to his own position from the Bedford-Jonson axis (he was confident that he could handle that), Overbury had heard rumors of ominous stirrings in the Howard camp. Northampton had approached Overbury at the festival, pointing out the dangers to his position as Carr's secretary should the "nullity" proceed. This in itself showed cause for worry: Northampton seldom approached men openly, and also he made few mistakes. Yet within days he and Suffolk could be seen cultivating George Villiers. They made it their business to push Villiers forward at court, to keep him ever present in the King's sight. In no time at all, James had taken a fancy to the lad, was pleased to kiss, embrace, and pat him on the behind in public, to treat him in all respects as he had his favored Carr. While this did not seem to bother Queen Anne in the least, it obviously distressed Viscount Rochester.

Not only was Villiers younger, but he was considerably more intelligent than Carr, and, if possible, even more beautiful.

"Look at him," Overbury said to Carr. "This is all your doing! The Howards fear they will lose all access to the King, with your inane talk of marriage. Villiers is all your doing."

Carr mumbled, and showed concern; Overbury knew that he had touched a vulnerable spot. Though Carr's perceptions were limited, he had been around court long enough to admire the Howards.

So with reason Overbury looked forward to the stay at Audley End as the means of ending Carr's infatuation with the Countess. She had already departed London for her country estate, and while it was possible for letters to keep love alive, Carr seldom wrote to anybody. And even if Carr felt inclined to write to the Countess, Overbury, who handled his correspondence, had no intention of ruining his own career by any such prose flourishes.

As it happened, Overbury found in the younger Howard girl an unexpected ally to his cause. From the moment they arrived at Audley

End, a week in advance of the King, he saw that Lady Essex was always underfoot, following them about, casting ardent glances Carr's way or (after displaying herself in a fetching pose) pretending not to care that he was nearby. No one else seemed to notice this outrageous behavior, but to Overbury her intentions were ludicrously obvious. He was delighted by what looked to be a windfall in midsummer.

That bitch is in heat, he decided.

After making judicious inquiries, he spoke to his friend: "How did that line go in *Romeo and Juliet*?" he asked, for they had seen Shakespeare's play together. " 'Compare her face with one that I shall show,/And I will make thee think thy swan a crow.' "

Carr had forgotten the line, the scene, and the general point of the play.

"Forget this aging Lucy," Overbury said. "The Howard girl fancies you . . ."

"Me?" Carr asked in amazement. "How can you tell?"

"How can you not tell? She can't take her eyes off you. And she is by consent the most luscious peach in this year's orchard."

"She *is* attractive," Carr allowed, "but she is also married. Like Lucy."

"Yes," Overbury said, "but I've done a bit of checking. You don't see her husband about, do you? He left for London a week ago, looking as out of place as teeth on a twat."

This was all the encouragement Carr needed. From then on, he left Overbury with all the chores of settling with Lady Suffolk on accommodations for the King's party. Within days, he and the Howard girl were inseparable: strolling by the ponds, standing on the stone bridge, gazing into the stream, sitting on the parterre, watching tennis matches, lingering for hours in the Picture Gallery. Every morning, they were up with the milkmaids; Lady Essex was giving Carr much-needed lessons in horseback riding. She was a a fine rider and an uncommonly attentive teacher. It seemed that the more time she spent with him, the more passion she displayed. Her lovely face took on a permanent pink tinge; her eyes shone as if she were in a perpetual ecstasy.

And then the King's Progress reached Audley End.

*   *   *

FORTUNA WITH HER WHEEL was looking kindly on Frances these full and festive days and nights. From early morning, she spent most of her time with Robin; she found him so pleasant, so winning, so delightful that she was tempted to test the potency of Forman's love-philtre at once. She and Robin rode out daily with King James and the others; she stayed close to Robin by giving pointers on how to sit in his saddle. She was happy, but growing restless with the daily following of the horn over walls and hillocks, through the same meadows and groves, when all she wanted was to let the others pass on, leaving her alone with Carr: evenings at Audley End were too well-organized and crowded for privacy.

One night, she sampled Forman's concoction herself, and its effects were such that she sent word to Carr the next morning: she'd be delayed and would he please wait for her at the stable, for she hated to go riding by herself. The windows of her dressing room faced north, toward the stable, so she had no trouble observing the royal party ride out. Moments later, she was with Robin.

"Hurry," he said. "We can still catch them."

Frances smiled as if pleased, but fell to scolding the stableboys: they had cinched the wrong saddle to her mount. "You know I don't like this one!" she said. "It's too firm. Now you've delayed us. Get on with it!"

"Hurry," Carr said.

"Yes, my lord," the older stableboy said (understandably perplexed at having to replace his lady's favorite saddle).

By the time they had fastened the other saddle, Robin was in a fret.

"Come on," Frances said. "Race you to the bridge."

As they made for the stone bridge, she kept her stallion under tight rein.

"This way," he said, still stiff as a captain's boot. "They must have gone this way."

"Oh, Robin," she said, "please, no. Let's ride that way. I want to show you something."

She gave him no choice; as if to tease him, she goaded her mount across the bridge ahead of him and cantered west.

They approached the summerhouse, and the warmth and familiar smell of the place stirred a sense deep within her—pleasant, as if part of memory, but unsettling and new. The moisture between her legs made her undergarment slippery.

"See?" she said. "It was my favorite place. Come, look."

Carr dismounted. Perspiration glistened on his forehead, and as the sun shone in his face, he squinted. Long days in the sun had left his brow and cheeks deeply tanned.

They stepped through the opening in the hedgerow; bees circled drowsily among the blossoms of untended woodbine and rosemary and sweetbrier.

"Let's go inside," Carr said. "It's frightfully hot out here."

It was even warmer inside, and ungodly still. Frances opened all the French doors. She touched her kerchief to her brow, which she suspected looked rather flushed just then. With each heartbeat, her very bones seemed to throb.

"Yes," she said, "it's hot out there, but so nice in here."

Playfully, she touched the kerchief to Robin's forehead. His blue eyes seemed so large and luminous against brown skin; she dabbed at his mustache. The scent of rosemary was in the summerhouse. The bees hovered outside, and a lark sang, yet the summerhouse seemed as still and motionless as a young girl's limbs as she lay behind the hedgerow, listening enthralled to Catherine's rapture in her lover's arms.

Now Frances deliberately traced Robin's lips with the tip of the kerchief. She heard the catch in his breathing, saw the vein in his neck swell, and drew him to her. His arms were strong. His full lips parted hers in their kissing. Twisting ever so slightly, he freed her right breast from its tenuous support in the low-swept bodice of her gown.

With couches all about, and a fourposter in the privy chamber, Robin chose the handier appointments of the floor beneath them. Trembling, he unfastened the kirtle from her waist; the tearing sound informed her she'd have to dispose of her chemise. When she had nothing on but her silver-buckled buskins, silk hose, and green garter tied round her lower thigh, he guided her to rest on the kirtle. She lay with the green light from the glass panes—overgrown with woodbine and eglantine—in her eyes.

Robin slipped from his Venetians and leather doublet, and went after his shoes. Soon he wore only his earring. A man's naked body had never moved her before. There were many statues on the parterre at Audley end, but they were nothing like this: wild blond hair, veined neck, firm shoulders with moist tufts of darker hair beneath, surging breast, muscled belly, skin glistening, a bramble bush of more curly brown hair, and, awesome to behold, his sex swollen not like any statue she had ever seen, as if reaching up for the bud of his navel, its tip mantled pink—swollen, whether by Forman's magic or no, with desire to match her own.

He pressed himself between easy-to-part knees, and then with difficulty (for here was a detail she was determined not to overlook) between the nearly virgin lips designed to receive him.

How wonderful and mysterious—that no one need be tutored to master such art! Robin uttered no word; she clung as silently to him, with a mind fully to receive each kiss, every thrust, every tremor: she had waited so long for this, wanted Robin so much, ere she had ever met him, wanted love, and now, completely, it was hers.

She recalled the feeling in the middle of her when she had hid behind the hedgerow only steps from where she now lay, afraid to see yet helpless to unfasten her gaze as the French tutor made love to her sister: the passion, the rage, the jealousy, the longing (under her petticoat small fingers clutching beneath the thin, soft down of her disappearing childhood). The feeling came back to her now with even greater fury, the searing energy of it descending from her belly to the sensitive low center of her: down, down, more and more intense until she thought she must scream or expire.

"Oh, Robin!" she said.

Their simultaneous cries seemed lost in the drowsy stillness of the summerhouse.

THE COUNTESS OF BEDFORD was no longer a threat to Overbury; she was not even a healthy nuisance.

"Francie is younger and more beautiful," Carr said.

Francie.

"Francie?" Overbury said.

"Her pet name," Carr said. "Her father calls her Fanny, but I like Francie better."

It turned out that they had exchanged pet names in the summerhouse down by the river, a lovely, isolated spot surrounded by trees and brush. The Howard girl, Carr explained, had loved the summerhouse from the time she was a small girl.

"Oh," Overbury sang, paraphrasing a rousing tavern song, "to be swiven in the summerhouse . . ."

Carr laughed. "You should go there," he said. "But now you've found me Frances, find a woman for yourself."

It was not a kind remark. Carr knew that Overbury was having trouble with the Countess of Rutland. Perhaps he had been unwise to propose marriage on so short an acquaintance; the swiftness of her negative reply had stung him. But he had not given up. Should he be able to insinuate himself into noble rank, this gorgeous creature might still be his. He had heard talk of a new rank to be created, with its membership put up for sale. Should this plan be enacted, Overbury had every intention of being the first to buy into the new title, regardless of the price.

So now he laughed and brushed the remark aside.

Lucy, Countess of Bedford, was a thing of the past, which meant that Northampton and the Howards would probably back off from their sponsorship of Villiers. Warm feelings between Carr and Lady Essex could only help Overbury at this juncture.

He had done well; he had taken Salisbury's remarks with the seriousness they deserved.

Overbury had gone to see the Secretary of State about negotiations with the Commons, and had mentioned that he was worried about the Queen's hostility toward him: "I've heard she wishes me discharged."

"You've heard correctly."

"There is a misunderstanding," Overbury protested. "I spoke to Lord Bacon about it . . ."

"Ah." Cecil smiled. "My eminent cousin, who considers me a freak. Why him?"

"He speaks well of you, my lord."

"Except in print."

Everyone knew how deeply Bacon's essay, "Of Deformity," had wounded Cecil, the obvious butt of Bacon's scorn.

"He said you might be able to help me, or at least lend advice . . ."

"I never lend advice lest the borrower feel constrained to pay me back." The little gray fox looked at Overbury with warmth. "You're a talented young man. Trim your sails. That is good advice in stormy weather, which is all we've been having lately, and all I see on the horizon . . ."

Overbury tried to interrupt, but Cecil continued.

"Listen, now! Stay out of sight."

Overbury could hardly believe his ears. "Out of sight?"

"Yes. Queen Anne despises Carr, and adores Villiers. You can't win. Since she despises Carr, she naturally hates you."

"Shouldn't I try to talk to her?"

"No."

"But she misunderstood my conduct. It happened—"

"It doesn't matter what she misunderstood, or where."

"So I should not even try to explain?"

"No."

"What then?"

"Nothing."

"Nothing, my lord?"

Cecil recognized the line from *King Lear* and smiled. "Something *can* come from nothing in politics," he said. "And much sorrow can come from something when nothing is required. Do nothing. But if, as I suspect, you must do something, be nice to Northampton. He can help you if he wants. The Queen trusts him absolutely."

Overbury had, within limits, taken Salisbury's advice: he had responded sympathetically to Northampton's initiative on the Countess of Bedford. And if he had not precisely done nothing, he had certainly been friendly toward the Howards. When the occasion was right (Northampton and he were enjoying sherry and biscuits on the parterre the evening before the King was expected to arrive), he broached the subject of the Queen's attitude toward him. Northampton obliquely recalled the opportunity he had offered Overbury to align himself with Howard interests. "I understand you are a gambler," he said. "Good gamblers never wager more than they can afford to lose."

It occurred to Overbury that gambling had been the underlying metaphor behind Cecil's remark: "You can't win." He felt uneasy. "I demurred only at becoming your spy," he said. "I have never been an adversary of the Howards' interests."

Northampton made a point of slowly sipping his sherry, a gesture which Overbury took to mean: Neither have you made yourself the champion of those interests. Or, more ominously: To date you have not made yourself my adversary—see that you don't in future.

At that moment, Carr and Lady Essex crossed the parterre in the direction of the small stone bridge that arched across the stream almost directly opposite, though a distance from, the majestic main entrance to Audley End.

"We are enjoying our visit here," Overbury said, indicating not only that he was well entrenched with Carr, but also that the two of them were now potential allies of Northampton.

"We are pleased," Northampton said, but added disparagingly, "Lady Suffolk could not have managed without you. As it is, things ought to go along nicely."

Overbury thought later that he might have resigned himself to that. Northampton had effectively ducked the request to intercede with Queen Anne. And yet when would he have a better chance to speak to the one man whom Cecil claimed could help him?

He chose to speak, and to be blunt: "I would be most awfully grateful if you would explain this embarrassing business in the court-yard to the Queen. You see, she quite misunderstood a certain gesture. It was my fault, of course, but I meant no discourtesy. I had not realized it was she till she went by. I wish to apologize, to sort this out . . ."

Northampton observed him coolly. "Did you discuss this with Cecil?"

Overbury said that he had. "He told me you were the only man who could actually help," he added a bit sheepishly. "The Queen trusts you."

"Perhaps," Northampton said. Then, after a pause, "Perhaps we can help each other."

After the King's party arrived, Overbury waited hopefully for a sign from any source, preferably the Queen herself, that he had been restored to her good graces, but as the days passed it became more and more evident that, if anything, the situation had worsened. Though Queen Anne seemed to be in good spirits, her face hardened into a mask of regal distance when Overbury happened about.

Both Suffolk and his wife seemed genuinely pleased to have the King's party at Audley End. The few unfinished details of redecoration were overlooked in the festivities.

"It is a magnificent house," James said, "fit for a king." He smiled. "How much will she cost your beggar-King?"

Suffolk laughed nervously—thinking, perhaps, of Cecil and Theobald's, and how the great house had passed into Crown possession during just such a royal visit. Suffolk said the estate was not for sale.

For the time being, London's troubles seemed far away. James was happily in his cups, riding afield daily with Prince Henry and Villiers, who (at Northampton's suggestion, Overbury learned) had joined the Royal Progress. The nights, too, were full of good food and drink. In the long evenings, the family provided entertainment on the parterre: music on the virginal accompanied by recorders, young people singing and dancing. James was so delighted by the terrain, the estate and the events that he put off all thought of an exact date of departure.

"We're here for good," he said, patting Suffolk on the shoulder, as Northampton looked on with a smile.

Everyone but Overbury was having a good time; he could think of nothing but pleasing the Queen. Cecil's advice ("Do nothing") seemed impractical to him, for it left him the outsider to the court. Beneath the surface of revelry, he perceived the festering of his unspoken offense in the Queen's mind. He thought of her as constantly after James with complaints about him. Cecil had, after all, agreed that Overbury's position was precarious, and now the sense of Queen Anne's hatred was taking its toll on his nerves.

He was actually relieved when Carr drew him aside to instruct him that he must go to Bath on a King's errand: to call on Salisbury.

"Jamie says the old bastard is sinking fast. He can't go himself, of course, and you know my reasons for staying. You don't seem to be enjoying yourself anyway, Tom. You don't like riding like the rest of us. I'm getting quite good at it, you know. Jamie insists that Francie and I go hunting with him tomorrow. He's got several new goshawks."

It would be good to get away from Carr. He was physically attractive, but he could be repulsively smug and insensitive. Truly, Overbury felt relief; he had grown weary of the overeating and overdrinking and going without sleep. The revels gave him diarrhea.

He left the next morning, instructing the coachman to drive easily ("We'll only try for St. Albans today"), and was settled in the Carriage Inn before three: he had a long afternoon and evening to relax. He called for water, towels and soap, as well as a pitcher of beer.

The cool water felt good on his face; the beer was especially satisfying. It was such a pleasure to be alone, to have no one to cater to, no one's eccentricities but his own to consider. He was glad that he had left Gibbs in London to look after the apartment (looting was always a danger during plague summers). When he had drained the pitcher, he called for another.

The chambermaid, he noticed upon her return, had a fetching look: a saucy mouth and quick, sure movements, which she executed while watching Overbury on the periphery of her vision. The skin of her arms was tawny, thrust out of a loose, revealing blouse. Her hands looked so smooth and young that Overbury felt a stirring in his cods.

She set the beer on the dresser, sent an impertinent glance his way, and was gone.

Overbury had almost forgotten this aspect of freedom: the unplanned encounter, the unexpected arms, thighs, bellies. Strange breasts. Mounts of Venus whose heights remained to be discovered. Occasionally he allowed himself the diversion of a young boy—Carr at the age of fifteen—if he were unusually attractive. He preferred women, but found them not so easy of access at St. James, at least not since he became the King's Server. Tonight would be different.

He had not written anything since returning to England, except on demand. He called the girl back.

"When you can manage, I'd like pen and paper," he said, responding to her brazen display of interest with a smile.

She was a clever one, well-developed and aware of her effect on men. Her blouse was open at the top to show incipient but firm cleavage. She was probably fourteen years old.

"What is your name?" he asked.

"Elizabeth."

Most of the girls her age were named Elizabeth; a few Catholics baptized daughters with the Christian name Mary, after the Queen of Scots.

"Do you like your work here?"

"Yes, my lord."

Overbury laughed. "I'm not a nobleman."

"Your carriage," she said. "It has the King's insignia."

"That's only because it belongs to him. I'm a servant, like yourself."

Elizabeth appeared not to believe him, to find the remark amusing. Overbury wondered if she, unaware of Prince Henry's age, thought him the Prince of Wales.

Overbury liked Elizabeth; she had that firm, smooth, thin body that disappears in a year or two with the advent of womanhood. When she returned with pen and paper, he made love to her. And later, when she reappeared with a pitcher of beer though he had placed no order, he made love to her again. He gave her a guinea, many times the amount she likely expected; he planned to stop by on the way back to Audley End.

The next morning he set off early, and by nightfall they had reached Reading. He finished the sketch he had started the night before, "The Chambermaid," and went to work on another—"A Puritan: A Diseased Piece of Apocrypha." He tired quickly and fell asleep.

The last leg of the journey was the longest; when they reached Bath, Overbury proceeded directly to Cecil's lodgings. Mayerne and three other doctors met him with expressions grave enough to confirm what he had expected of Cecil's condition.

"Am I too late?" he asked.

"Nearly," Mayerne said. "He is hemorrhaging badly. The growth in his abdomen is enormous, and still growing."

"The King had heard that he was better . . ."

"I sent word to him that Lord Salisbury had responded to the waters. I fear the gain was temporary."

Overbury listened to the medical report. Then, with Mayerne's permission, he entered Cecil's bedroom.

Looking frightfully pale and thin, Salisbury was propped up in bed; he held a deeply blood-stained kerchief to his mouth, and tried to smile. "They say I am better, Thomas," he said, "but the look in your eyes has more truth in it."

"I've heard the waters can work marvels," Overbury said. "I must come here myself sometime."

"Be in no hurry," Cecil said. "The waters are hot, smell most vile, and taste worse."

It was important, now, to open the interview with care. Decorum and common sense required tact. He bore the King's message, but he might subtly move discussion from King to Royal Family to Queen: hence, to his troubles with her.

"My Lord Secretary," he said, "I need your help."

Cecil dabbed at the corner of his mouth. "I fear I can be of little help to anyone."

"You could write a letter," Overbury said. "You could dictate, and I could write it down . . ."

His callousness appalled even him, but, after all, aid from this quarter would come either now or never.

"To the Queen?" Cecil said slowly.

Overbury nodded; the room fell silent.

"So things are worse?"

Overbury nodded again.

"You refused my advice."

In one sense, Overbury had indeed followed his advice, but he had not—certainly not—stayed out of sight. He gave no answer as Cecil slowly sank back into the pillows, letting the hand with the kerchief fall to his side.

"No, Sir Thomas. I cannot help you. If I could, I would not. It is too late for me to change. In all my life I have helped but two people: Queen Elizabeth and King James. Not myself. Not my own son. Scripture says a man cannot serve two masters; I have been a good servant of the Crown and a poor father. And yet my son is on his way to see me. I told him not to come, but he is on his way. Should I antagonize the Queen, I would jeopardize my William's advancement. Naturally, I hope for him to take my place."

How foolish he had been to suppose that Cecil would spend his fading strength to help him; if anything, Cecil probably considered him, as an associate of Carr's, a possible competitor to his son. He should have known that Cecil, sharp even *in extremis,* would exert himself on interests much closer to home.

"I do appreciate your calling on me," Cecil was saying. He sounded out of breath. "It was kind of His Majesty to send you; he is not fond of farewells."

"My lord," Overbury said, alarmed, "the King sent words not of farewell, but of substance."

"I think I shall sleep," Cecil said. "Pray tell me now before I drop off."

"His Majesty wishes your candid appraisal of this Great Contract."

Cecil lay very still, and for a moment Overbury feared that he had expired.

"Will the July Contract work?" he asked in a loud voice.

"Tell him this," Cecil said, his eyes closed. "I have sent a letter with details, but you may amplify them. I can only guess that the Contract will fail."

Overbury thanked him and prepared to leave.

"Sir Thomas!" Cecil called out in an astonishingly clear voice. "You did not answer my question. I gave you advice. Am I wrong in assuming that you have ignored it?"

Overbury remained silent.

"No one listens," the old man said, not in anger, not even in weariness, but bemusedly. "Nobody learns."

These words rang eerily in Overbury's ears as, without ceremony, he took his leave, ordering the coachman to turn back immediately for Audley End. Salisbury was wrong about him: he did listen, and he learned. With the letter already on its way, Overbury knew that he had been sent on a fool's errand. He urged the coachman to great speed and long hours on the road; it took them only two long days to get back to Audley End.

On his return, Overbury took the proper precautions. He rested, bathed, trimmed his beard. He put on a handsome outfit of waistcoat, trousers, jerkin and cap that he had not worn before. He wanted to join in the festivities tonight, to feel that he belonged.

And yet he was frightened when he saw Carr on the parterre with Northampton. He tried to look jovial. "Where is the lovely Francie?" he asked, feeling somewhat relieved to see Carr's broad, clean smile.

"Thomas," Carr said, embracing him and planting a warm kiss on his lips. "I have the most marvelous news."

Overbury cast an eye at Northampton. "Let me hear it at once," he said.

"Francie has gone to Essex House." Carr beamed.

"Oh," Overbury said. "Surely this is *not* good news."

"She is an honorable woman," Carr answered excitedly, as if Overbury had suggested the contrary. "She will give this marriage of hers one more chance."

Overbury tried to read the answer to this enigmatic statement in the placid face of the Earl of Northampton.

"We're to be married, you see," Carr said. He seemed delighted by the fact that, for once, it was Overbury who was at a disadvantage.

"Married?" Overbury's voice had carried to the far side of the parterre, where heads turned. "That's impossible!"

"Why so?" Northampton put in easily.

Overbury found himself looking into cold, grey eyes. It was a hard question made harder by the person of its propounder. "Just because it is," he said flatly.

"That is no answer, Sir Thomas," Northampton said.

Carr's mood matched itself to Northampton's inflection. "No answer at all," he said. "Why, everybody knows that Essex is impotent."

" 'Oh sacred hunger of ambitious minds/And impotent desire of men to reign,' " Overbury recited.

"Thomas," Carr said, "nobody cares about your poetry, or knows what it means."

"It isn't mine, and it means that all men are alike impotent."

"But not legally," Northampton said.

"Legally," Carr chimed in, "Francie is not bound to remain barren."

"Nor is she likely to," Overbury said.

Northampton showed displeasure. "This 'nullity' issue is an interesting one. You ought to look into it. You know the law is very explicit here. Marriage bestows certain privileges on the husband, but it extends rights to his wife as well. Both are responsible to God and to the Crown. *You* should find the legal ramifications passing curious."

"I do already," Overbury said. "If the Countess of Bedford can seek a divorce, so can the Countess of—"

"Not divorce," Northampton said sharply. " 'Nullity.' The difference is considerable."

"Because the words are so?" Overbury asked.

"I think the law suggests a substantive difference of considerable magnitude."

"You think so," Overbury said angrily, "for obvious reasons."

"Oh? And what are they?"

"It is in your interest."

"Thomas," Carr broke in, "don't be angry. We thought you'd be happy for me. And we don't even know what will happen at Essex House."

"But you said yourself the man is impotent. What can happen?" Carr looked befuddled.

"You fool," Overbury said. "Don't you see how these people are trying to use you?"

"Rash man," Northampton said to no one in particular, as he turned smartly on his heels and sauntered off.

"Now look what you've done," Carr said. "Why must you always insult people?"

"I insulted no one."

"You insulted Francie and her uncle. I thought you liked her. And you called me a fool in front of Northampton. No wonder Jamie wanted you out of here. You ruin everybody's good time."

Overbury felt fear and anger at once. "Would you feel more comfortable if I were to leave?"

"Yes. If you can't be civil, go back to London. Who needs you?"

"You need me, you clod. You haven't got the brains of a Muenster cheese. Can't you see that the Howards only want what you can give them? I apologize for being short with you—and with Northampton, bless him. But you must forget this business of 'nullity.' It is dangerous."

"Oh, no," Carr said. "I'd hoped you'd go along with this, but even if you don't, Jamie does."

His remark—so smug, so coy, so stupid—was infuriating. "I don't give a damn!" Overbury said. "The King is not above the law. And the law on 'nullity' is clear: it requires virginity of a female complainant."

"And what else could she be with a eunuch for a husband?"

"If the eunuch wears the feathers of a bull for his cap, then his wife is no virgin."

With Carr's blue eyes studying him, Overbury wondered if he had said too much. Cecil's words came back to him once more: "No one listens. Nobody learns."

"I'll oppose you," he said. "James, too. In print, if necessary."

He watched as Carr, always an imitator, copied Northampton's swift, sure turn on his heels, and strode off.

V

He'd kept them waiting too long. The sensitive ones were probably worried about the timing of their interviews: this was the first day since Henry died that he'd permitted—ordered—a return to the business of state. Given the circumstances, even worthy men might find it hard to speak, much more to come by decent phrasing.

For weeks, now, grief had rendered him limp and useless. He had spent terrible nights without restful sleep. A painful biliousness of the abdomen added to his woes.

One day he had gone to Morning Prayer in St. George's Chapel at Windsor to hear Daniel Price deliver a commemorative sermon entitled "Lamentations for the Death of the Late Illustrious Prince Henry." He remembered nothing the chaplain said except the text of his sermon, which was from Matthew: "I will smite the shepherd, and the sheep of the flock shall be scattered." Since then he had read the published version, but the point made of the text still curiously eluded him. The mind, he decided, was an unreliable instrument, quick and ingenious at one moment, at another flaccid and dull.

As the weeks passed, funeral elegies sent to him from printers had piled up—over fifty of them, double the number of competent poets in the realm. He took to reading them in the hope of lightening his spirits; with the funeral elegy, a good ear was of more use than a warm heart. William Basse had sent a poem misguidedly entitled "Britain's Son-set, Bewailed by a Shower of Grief." The longest elegy absurdly began with this axiom: "Small woes have words but mighty cares stand mute." Henry Peacham's verses were equally disheartening; he thought the Royal Family would find comfort in a grisly poem recounting the many ways that earlier Princes of Wales had met untimely deaths: by drowning, suicide, poison, stabbing, infanticide, plague—a royal *Danse Macabre*.

Now Carr entered the room. "Jamie," he said, "forgive me for breaking in again, but you asked me to let you know when St. Albans arrived."

Carr was practically the only one about who had shown himself untouched by the shock of recent events. He remained confident, as oblivious to others' feelings as ever.

"Yes," James answered. "I want to see him, but give me a moment."

It would be good to talk to Bacon, good to have him around, now, with Cecil gone.

And it would be good to get back to work withal. He checked the list. Who followed Bacon on the agenda? Scribbled names began to coincide with specific eyes and noses. Then too, the sheaf made a good pointer, and before long he was idly turning the pages of an enormous folio volume, printed but as yet unbound, bearing the immodest title *The History of the World*. He had tried without success to read the book; isolated phrases got through, but not in relation to each other, and soon the fragments themselves were forgotten.

Here was a topic for the Cambridge Orator: Why has so much knowledge of the past been accumulated, and almost none of the human mind? Over two thousand folio pages in this single volume proceeding only as far as the Second Punic War, and the anonymous author promised—"God willing"—two more volumes of at least that length to bring his history up to the present time. (Was history present, with King James, accomplished Latinist, unable to penetrate these paragraphs written in plain English?) He must speak to Bacon about this. Bacon wanted to have a science of everything under the sun, so why not a science of mind?

The Stationers Company had registered the work but delayed distributing it for fear certain passages would offend the King. Anne must have known something beforehand, since without effort she discovered the author's identity in this evidence of a last-minute change:

It was for the service of that inestimable Prince Henry, the successive hope and one of the greatest of the Christian world, that I undertook this work. It pleased him to peruse some part thereof, and to pardon what was amiss. It is now left to the world without a master, from which all that is presented hath received both blows and thanks.

Clearly the words of Sir Walter Raleigh. James had often wondered about Henry's fascination for this enigmatic figure in the Tower. Henry believed Raleigh innocent of the charges under which he'd been convicted. James thought the evidence flimsy himself, but Raleigh was a pest, all in all better off where he was—out of harm's way, and comfortable in quarters once occupied by kings. (At one time a royal palace, the Tower still housed the Mint and the Crown Jewels.) Besides, in the Tower he was not well situated to contest the Crown's claim that his deed to Sherborne was faulty. James had acceded to his request that he be allowed to assemble paraphernalia for his agricultural and medical experiments, and likely he was happy enough, although ever so often he wrote to the Admiralty proclaiming how much he missed his wife.

Henry had been Raleigh's frequent visitor in the Tower, and Raleigh seemed genuinely fond of the Prince. He had dispatched a specially concocted medicine to Audley End with amazing speed, almost as soon as the news of Henry's fever was generally known.

The sequence of events had passed swiftly. Had James noticed the danger signals earlier, perhaps their progress might have been slowed. From early spring, Henry had uncharacteristically hurled himself into physical activities, as if in a mood of exultation. He played court tennis through the midday hours, peeling off garments as the game and the heat wore him down. He swam long distances in the Thames, and later, at Audley End, in the River Lee. In late June, by evening, he appeared at table looking pinched and tired. "Best play your tennis in the cooler hours," James had said. But since he found the tennis exciting to watch, he had let the matter drop.

During July, the frenzy of tennis, riding, swimming and shooting continued, and Henry began to lose weight. Looking back now, the change was almost imperceptible at first. Henry would be keen for play in the morning, but toward evening he would disappear for a rest, or complain of headache. His appetite faltered, yet he still consumed prodigious quantities of beer and water, so James saw no cause for concern.

Anne was more persistent: "With your headaches, you ought to stay indoors. Play trump with Count Palatine and your sister."

Henry laughed. "We play cards at night, Mother. And not trump —a game for dowagers and dolts—but primero! Won ten guineas off Frederick last night. He can't stand trump either. We play cards when it's too dark to play tennis or swim."

Anne responded sharply. "You mustn't swim now! The river is full of dead fish."

Henry kissed her lightly on the cheek. "I promise not to breathe the water," he said, and went on as before.

The headaches intensified and fever set in. Though from childhood he had had a slight tendency to costiveness, he now complained of diarrhea. Then one day—Henry was scheduled to meet Palatine in a match to determine the best player of their series—the fever flared violently. He apologized to his prospective brother-in-law and said that he'd not be able to play. "Not to worry, Frederick," he added. "The fifteen guineas are forfeit."

The Prince's attempt at levity was met by smiles, but his voice quaked with fever. James sent word to Mayerne, who hurried up from London looking not much better than Henry after weeks at his dreary task of coping with the plague. Within two days, Mayerne mentioned receiving Raleigh's medicine; it had been sent to Anne, who wanted him to use it at once. Tactfully, the doctor explained that he and the other attending physicians agreed that Raleigh's medicine should be used only as a last resort. "No one knows what's in it," he said. "Raleigh won't say."

The headaches and fever got steadily worse, and at times Henry was delirious.

A fortnight passed before James felt dread. He had gone to his son's room as usual one morning, and had found doctors bent over the sickbed, their faces grave. Mayerne was methodically scraping the inside of Henry's forearm with a razor. Then, having placed a cupping glass over the wound, he motioned for help. One of the doctors brought a chafing dish, whose flame Mayerne touched to the cupping glass. He motioned again, and the nurse came forward with a small cage holding two white doves.

With stunning swiftness, Mayerne threw back Henry's blankets. The other doctors helped him place a thickly doubled white sheet beneath Henry's feet. The Prince lay motionless: the only sign of life that James could see in his son was the movement of his tongue; he was trying to wet his cracked lips. He seemed to know what they were doing to him, but he offered no resistance.

Mayerne took a dove from the cage and, as it fluttered, sliced it lengthwise. When its blood had drained into the pan held by the nurse, he slipped the dove over Henry's left foot, securing it with a blue ribbon, and repeated the procedure with the remaining dove and the other foot.

They were bleeding Henry, to draw off the noxious vapors in the blood. By this they hoped to return his body to a balanced mixture of humors. These were extreme measures; taken together, they were signs of the most pessimistic medical judgment.

"But he is young," James said without preamble, contentiously, as if to remind them that medical opinion was neither fact nor divine decree. "He can survive the fever if you but give him sufficient water."

"He takes no water," Mayerne said quietly.

The rebuttal, though offered gently, struck James as if accompanied by bell, book and candle: He takes no water. He takes no water.

James was not surprised when, by nightfall, the Archbishop of Canterbury arrived in a flurry of carriages and clergymen. Abbot went immediately to Henry's room, where he read the proper Psalm for that day and administered the Sacraments.

"This is my body which was given for you and for many in remission of sins . . ."

Henry was too weak to participate, so Abbot dipped the bread in the wine and, after breaking off a tiny morsel, pressed it between the Prince's lips. John Davies of Hereford sent an elegy in which he instructed James that grief, being a sign of weakness, was an emotion unfit for a King. Neither then nor now would James have contradicted that wisdom. But when Abbot pressed his thick fingers to Henry's unmoving lips, James wept so loudly that the Archbishop, distracted, lost his place and fumbled with the pages of his Prayer Book. Later, Abbot assured the King that the boy had actually smiled as he received the Sacrament.

In the morning, Mayerne gave in to Anne's hysterical pleas that Raleigh's medicine be tried. The concoction was forced down Henry's throat, but James knew that Mayerne took this measure more for Anne than for his son.

Raleigh had sworn to the Queen that his nostrum would cure Henry of any condition save one: poison.

"He was poisoned!" Anne shrieked when James, accompanied by Mayerne, brought the news she feared most. "Who would want to kill poor Henry?"

Raleigh's proclivity to dramatic overstatement, compounded by Anne's naïve faith in him, did much to stimulate an almost instant cacophony of rumor throughout Britain. Depending on the area or faction, men claimed that Catholics, Puritans, Spaniards, Germans, Scots, Anabaptists or courtiers had poisoned the Prince. Anne suspected Sir Thomas Overbury, which was sufficient comment on her state of mind: Overbury was and had been for several weeks skulking about London with no means and less motive to poison Henry.

One rumor held that James, on orders from the Pope, slipped poison to his own son to assure a Romish successor in Prince Charles; an eyewitness had seen the poison spirited out of the Tower of London and rushed to Audley End.

Henry's death, rumors aside, all but destroyed Queen Anne. Dr. Mayerne kept her sedated, on the edge of sleep, with a recently compounded substance called laudanum; still, he worried about her.

"Take her away from here," he said to the King. "Take her any place but far away from here."

James reminded him that the family had to stay near London for the funeral.

"The Queen cannot go," Mayerne said. "Neither can Princess Elizabeth. And, Your Majesty, I urge you not to go, either. The funeral at Westminster will be an occasion of state. Go to Windsor. I am going with you. You need care now, all of you, except perhaps young Charles."

The King's two bodies: one needed in London, the other at Windsor. So Charles, heir to the throne, went to London by himself.

Raleigh's request to attend the funeral had to be turned down. Now, thanks to a passage from Sir Walter's *History* (the one that most alarmed the Stationers), James knew where he stood in the eyes of that enigmatic man. Recounting the life of a Babylonian queen (Semiramis) whose adventurous ways outstripped her lover's, enabling her to extend the Empire, Raleigh made this woman the obvious counterpart of Queen Elizabeth. Semiramis was succeeded by a king with a vice to match her every virtue:

> Her son, having changed nature with his mother, proved no less feminine than she was masculine. He was so much given over to licentious idleness as to suffer his mother to reign forty-two years, thus witnessing that he preferred ease before honor, and bodily pleasures before greatness.

Always the intrepid critic of pederasty in the Royal Navy, Raleigh had loosed a thinly disguised diatribe against Elizabeth's successor, denouncing James as an appeaser, a coward and a Sodomite.

"Have publication of this tome delayed indefinitely," James said to Carr. "Tell the Stationers we'll not be needing Volumes Two or Three, either. We'll help Sir Walter find more time for his experiments with tobacco. And," he added, "see that all the poets who wrote elegies for Henry receive personal notes."

"Over whose signature?" Carr asked shrewdly.

"Yours, if you wish," James said. "No matter."

"How shall I sign?"

"In your usual manner." James laughed. "With difficulty."

"I mean in what, ah, capacity?"

So it began. Carr wanted to know if he would be appointed to Cecil's post.

"As my Secretary, if it pleases you," James said.

Carr brightened. "Of State?"

"No," James said. "Just Secretary for now. I must give this matter some thought—hear arguments, nominations, and the like."

Carr slouched away as if rebuked: no matter what James did for him, Carr was never satisfied. His ingratitude was all the more ridiculous given the fact that the Commons regarded James's generosity to this Scottish page a scandal. Beyond investing Robin with enormous wealth in money and land, the King had elevated him to Viscount Rochester. And yet only yesterday, in the midst of James's depression, Carr had observed that Essex held a more honored title.

"What does it matter," James had said, "if Francie prefers you?"

"Why should she wed her social inferior?"

"You mean to ask why she might marry a man of lesser rank."

"Precisely."

"You have a point," James had said, for it was obvious that subtleties of language were lost on him.

"She'll not be a true countess. She'll have to surrender her title and be only a viscountess."

Did he imagine she wouldn't marry him? This Howard girl was preternaturally patient to have aroused Carr to such rage on so small a ground for envy.

"We must see to the 'nullity,' " James conceded, "and then we'll look into the matter." Now he remembered Overbury. "Apropos of Francie, I hear that my new Server, whose absence begins to annoy me—your close friend!—holds forth in London against your Lady Essex and the 'nullity.' "

Carr looked crestfallen. Had he proposed to hide from James his falling-out with Overbury?

"Talk to him," James said. "His opposition is embarrassing."

"It will do no good. I have tried, and so has Francie's uncle."

James nodded with feigned weariness at this note: Northampton and Rochester—what a pair! "*You* handle him," he said. "I have other things to think on. Show Palatine in."

So the first business of state since Henry's death was to assure Frederick that his marriage to Elizabeth would go forward as planned. Then it was time for real work: the interview with Francis Bacon.

Viscount St. Albans entered carrying a leather folder; he greeted James and, with his usual air of composure, did what perhaps no other man in England could do effectively and with ease: in a low monotone, he described Henry's funeral without once referring to the fact that of the Royal Family only Charles had been able to attend. Then, without the slightest note of transition, he turned to the King's business.

"You asked for my recommendations to Parliament when it reconvenes in the fall," he said. "If Your Majesty has no objection, I shall suggest, until such time as you name your new Secretary of State—"

"I shall name none soon," James said, "but only a Secretary—Carr."

"Your Majesty," Bacon said. If he was disappointed, he did not show it.

"But if you have a nomination, I shall hear it gladly."

"My cousin may have had his faults, but they were not in his blood. I think young Salisbury might be of good use to the Crown."

"What about Carr?"

James took note of Bacon's silent, evasive nod, and asked him to get on with the proposals for legislation.

"Unaccustomed as I am to this role," Bacon said, "I suggest the following be put to Parliament: an act for repressing of duels."

James sighed. He had no strong feelings on the issue, but the clergy was aroused by the growing number of deaths and serious injuries resulting from the practice. Because of local ordinances, most duels were already fought on foggy mornings in the Netherlands.

"An act," Bacon continued, "for proceeding with the plantation of Ireland, and another for the better plantation of Virginia, with supplies furnished on a regular basis. An act against the abuse of the Sabbath," he said, pausing to observe the King's reaction. "To please your Puritan subjects."

"They will like it," James said.

"An act for naturalizing Count Palatine and otherwise settling the issue of Elizabeth's marriage."

James agreed.

"An act naturalizing Elizabeth Meres."

"Who is she?"

"A rich friend."

James nodded.

"An act forbidding brewers, alehouse-keepers and bawds from becoming magistrates of their own boroughs," Bacon said with a smile. "Seems we have a minor scandal in Hounslow."

James shrugged.

"Lastly, an act for reform of deceit in dyeing silk. Charlatans have found a way to counterfeit true color in silk: the color disappears whilst the fabric is in its first washing."

"This is all?" James asked.

"Unless Your Majesty wishes further legislation, perhaps specifics

171

on the forestry and timber and deer-hunting issues raised in your speech . . ."

"Not just now, Francis," James said. "I want you to proceed as you think your cousin would have. We have more serious matters to discuss. We need money. What would you think of a new rank of the nobility—the baronet?"

"How would investiture be handled?"

"As they are now, by letters of patent and, when convenient, some formal ceremony or other. It is the concept, Francis—how does this new dignity between a knight and a baron strike you?"

"Does my new dignity of office require an answer?" Bacon asked. "I shall draw up the letters. What are the terms?"

"We return to ancient practice here. These baronets will approximate the old rank of Vavasours; their purpose will be to defend and improve the province of Ulster. We will say that they must be prepared to proffer their lives, fortunes and estate to perform this duty, should, for example, any kingdom or province or rowdy papists show themselves ready to attack the Crown. They will contribute the equal of thirty foot soldiers each for three years at eight shillings *per diem* . . ."

"Let's see," Bacon mused, "how much would that be?"

"One thousand ninety-five pounds sterling," James said.

"And with how many baronets?"

"Two hundred."

"A weighty sum, Your Majesty. And how shall these soldiers be billeted?"

"I said nothing of billeting, nor of soldiers, explicitly. We speak of equivalences: eight shillings might, under such-and-such conditions, retain the necessary services, should our need require them . . ."

"Sound," Bacon said.

"Just to make the idea sounder," James continued, "we might limit applicants or nominees to men whose fathers—or grandfathers—bore arms in defense of the Crown, and who have a clear income in land of no less than a thousand pounds per annum."

"This stipulation should diminish irresponsible criticism," Bacon said.

"It was one of your cousin's last bits of ingenuity. He knew that Parliament would challenge the legality of our impositions. So to get money he designated our 'Great Contract,' which leaves me in debt on the first day of the year with its miserly two hundred thousand pounds. Thus he added this novel idea—"

"Excuse me, Your Majesty, but I think you should know that leaders in the Commons will likely rescind the July Contract."

"Indeed? And why?"

"They feel the figure is too large."

"Too large. And?"

"And that control would be not in their hands. They wish to regulate expenditures—"

"Let them regulate the smell of chamberpots in stews!" James said. "Tell them to go hang. I reject their July Contract. Tell them that. Tell them I'll not answer to these scurvy Puritans for every hogshead of sherry or yard of silk that crosses King's Street. I'll have all these twits thrown in the Fleet. We'll have our impositions, as before. And now another potful from our baronets: one thousand pound donation from each, over and above the yearly due."

Bacon thought the idea a mixed blessing: "We shall have a new source of revenue, but we find ourselves infested by a democracy of too much nobility, as in Poland."

"Ah," James said, "but in Poland all the sons of earls are earls. Not here. But enough of this, Francis. We have put off politics long enough. I must know what you've done with those creatures who upset my festival, and with Talbot, Cotton, Peacham, Oliver St. John . . ."

Bacon explained his reluctance to put his explanation in writing: in London, spying had become a major occupation. As it happened, Sir Edward Coke had not only declared his open opposition to the policy on customs, but, having learned of the King's warrant to examine St. John under torture, had moved to quash it. "This old man is too old to survive the manacles," Coke had said. "Even if he were not, under English law such auricular evidence cannot be weighed by the court."

Sir Edward was a formidable man—brilliant, dedicated, honest. But Bacon had stood his ground, first by conceding that direct evidence obtained by torture (confession, for instance) could not legitimately be used against a defendant, then by arguing a further point: "And yet in cases involving possible danger to the Crown the record is clear. As a device of discovery, torture is not only permissible, but convenient and even obligatory. It is one thing to extract a confession by manacling a prisoner, and then convicting him with that statement, but quite another to use the ordeal to unstop the mouth of a stubborn traitor, who would use his silence to frustrate both truth and the Crown. If he knows where the gunpowder kegs are hidden, it is right that he tell us. Only St. John knows where he has hidden the traitorous documents, and he must tell us. The documents will be our evidence, and he need never confess; indeed, we will no more listen to his confession than to his pleas for mercy."

It was brilliant even when retold, and James wished he had been at Lambeth Palace to witness the effect of the speech.

Bacon added that his private differences with Coke (some years ago, the two of them had courted Lady Walsingham, but she had wedded neither) may have marred his handling of the case. And yet given the fact of Coke's intransigence on impositions, he felt that Sir Edward would be better off placed wholly in charge of criminal prosecutions: "He takes the Common Pleas too seriously; he is always distracted by the philosophical claims of suspicious Puritans in the Commons."

Bacon was probably right; James decided to follow his advice. Then, as the Viscount prepared to leave, James asked him to be a good fellow and quiet Overbury.

"You are old friends," he said. "Tell him he displeases me, but that I've a way for him to make amends. We shall move him up, but out of London for a spell. He'll assume duties as my emissary in Muscovy. Surely you know why . . ."

"The 'nullity,' " Bacon said.

James nodded. "Our position is well known. And yet Overbury— my Server—holds forth nightly at the Mermaid, arguing against it. And I'm already beset with Rochester, who thinks his station in the kingdom too humble."

Bacon saw the point; he was a reasonable man, one whom James must consider for even higher office.

"I'll tell him," Bacon said.

WHILE AT ESSEX HOUSE, Frances kept the family posted on her travail as a hopeful wife—nothing too graphic, but enough to pave the way for an early return to Audley End. Even so, there were plenty of questions to field when she arrived home.

Her mother, who was out of patience with the entire episode, dismissed Frances' letters as uselessly vague: "You protested your unhappiness, which could mean anything or nothing," she said.

It was true that Frances had avoided details; she thought everyone would know from events prior to her leaving for Essex House where the difficulty lay. "I thought you'd understand," she said. "How can one write in proper words of such a thing, which is private?"

"With more servants standing about your bedroom than at Britain's Burse?"

Yes, it had been humiliating to have Katherine in the bedroom with Essex, but someone had to be present as a witness. That was the law, which was not of Frances' making. "Ask Katherine," she would say if braced with a query on some detail of the story. But of course nobody would bother the young servant girl, who went about her chores, silent and serene as gold, as if nothing had happened to concern her.

"Katherine will have to bear witness," her mother said.

"Yes," Frances said.

"And be closely questioned by some cross Puritan . . ."

"She need only tell the truth," Frances said. "I was open to my husband, anxious to please him and be a wife, but he was unable."

"Doubtless," her mother said wryly. "Even if anyone believed that, will it suffice? Will dear Katherine testify to your virginity?"

Frances had learned how to bear with Lady Suffolk, of whom she was not fond. "She must only testify to the truth, Mother, as she knows it," Frances said, realizing how irrelevant her answer was, but trying to invest it nonetheless with a touch of piety.

Lady Suffolk would not let the matter go. "The truth," she said with guttural fury, "would hang us all! Don't speak nonsense, as if you were a child. Do you think I am stupid? Or that your examiners at the 'nullity' will be stupid? Have you no ears or eyes?"

That night Frances and her sister took tea in the Great Hall with their parents. Catherine had received a brief but friendly note from her husband, who announced that he would be elevated from Viscount Clapthorne to Earl of Salisbury. The note presaged reconciliation.

"My Lady of Salisbury," her father beamed. "I look forward to congratulating your—our—young William. He is a fine man despite . . ."

"Yes," Catherine said, sparing Suffolk the difficulty of silence after this awkward remark, "he is. He always was. I shall answer, if you

think it well to, with sincere apology. In the past he has refused
. . . would not accept . . ."

"I do not advise apology," her mother said.

"Perhaps just a warm, winning letter," Suffolk said, "as if nothing
has happened.

"Just tell him you love him," Frances said.

"By all means, just tell him you love him," her mother said, mim-
icking her daughter. "Frances, where did you learn such rot?"

"It is late," Frances said, rising as if to excuse herself.

"Why must you torment her?" Suffolk demanded. "Leave her
alone."

"My lord," her mother said, "I cannot do that. She is my daughter,
and this 'nullity' may well ruin us."

"I don't see how," Suffolk said. "I spoke to the King but a day ago.
He was pleased to assure me of William's prospects, and when I
broached the subject of Frances' troubles and the 'nullity,' he foresaw
no let to a favorable outcome."

"Oh, he foresaw no let!" Lady Suffolk said. "Why didn't you tell
us? King James can see no let. But then King James can also see no
interest, either. Why should he care if all the Howards go hang?"

"But he does," Frances said. "He wants Robin and me to be
happy."

"I had overlooked this wonder, too," her mother said. "He knows
you are in love, doesn't he? My, love has proved the obsession of the
Howards—and their downfall. Do you understand the public nature
of this trial? That is what your 'nullity' will be: a public trial. With
public—or should I say pubic?—examination by lecherous doctors,
slatternly midwives, heretic theologians, and God knows who else—
perhaps a stableboy or two. What an opportunity for the enemies of
the Howard family!"

"What *are* you driving at?" Suffolk demanded.

"Are you aware of this Overbury creature? It is obvious that your
daughter hasn't the slightest notion of his villainous blather about
London."

"We'll handle Overbury!"

It was Northampton's voice—and never more welcome it was. He
entered the Great Hall with an easy stride.

"Overbury and others," her mother persisted, unperturbed by
Northampton's intrusion. "Others oppose the 'nullity,' too, many of

them honorable people in Parliament and at court. My friends . . ."

"Your spies," Northampton put in with a smile.

"My friends tell me of obscene tavern songs about my daughter, her frigid Essex, and her cock-Robin . . ."

"Are we to worry about these twits?" Suffolk asked.

"Only Cockneys listen to this filth," Northampton said with a superb blandness.

"*And* Puritans," Lady Suffolk added. "Puritans oppose the 'nullity,' and their influence grows. If it suits the King, he will gladly—"

"James will do as his cock-Robin wishes." Northampton smiled. "You know they sing raw lyrics about His Majesty, too. And about Cecil. Who knows," he added, "there may be a low verse or two about *you* circulating at John Cole's Cock in Liquor Pond Street, or the Gin House in Lincoln's Inn, Back Side."

"Henry," Lady Suffolk said, "it is easy to see why you never married. Your need to laugh at people far outstrips your capacity to . . ."

"Oh," he gasped, "don't say it! Spare me the indignity of your searching and probably accurate appraisal." He kissed her on the mouth, and said, "With you and Thomas and my lovely nieces, I have more than mere good fortune in love. I am happy."

When it came to handling her mother, Frances thought, no one could match her great-uncle.

"Which leaves us where?" Suffolk said, his tone suggesting that his wife retire as victor, with the battle behind.

Frances tried to help out. "Let's go to London," she said. "Who cares about tavern songs and broadsides? Who cares about this upstart Overbury?"

"Be careful," Northampton said. "Your mother is right there. We must not take Overbury lightly. He is a dangerous man, with a rapier wit and many friends."

"But all of them poets and penniless," Suffolk said.

"Unfortunately, not so," Northampton said. "Yes, he trafficks about with Webster and Jonson and that lot at the Mermaid, but he is a close friend of Francis Bacon, who stands to advance rapidly now, with Cecil out of the way."

"What about our young Cecil?" Catherine said. "My husband?"

"We'll be pushing him," Northampton said, "as no doubt Bacon already has. But first he must settle this silliness with you."

"So you think Overbury is well-connected," Suffolk said.

"And dangerous," her mother added.

"Without question," Northampton said. "And bright to a fault."

"How can he hurt us?" Frances asked (but wished she hadn't).

"By talk, my dear. Loose talk. By writing scurrilous diatribes against you, I'm afraid. I've seen a couple of these. He can work on Carr. Having dispatched Essex in your inimitable way, you have brought us willy-nilly into Carr's camp. We need Viscount Rochester now. We had a *modus vivendi* as long as that canny bastard Cecil was in there. He aimed at stability. Who knows what will happen now? We want to take advantage, influence events—control them if possible —but, as always, there are risks and adversaries . . ."

"Overbury," Suffolk said.

"Yes, and our old nemesis, the Countess of Shrewsbury."

"But she's to go on trial herself," Catherine said.

"She'll not likely be convicted. And she has ways to get at us— Villiers, for instance. But I'd add a handful of Puritan fanatics in Parliament, and the Archbishop."

"Abbot?" Suffolk said.

"Yes. He'll oppose us. Has already."

"Is he powerful?" Frances asked.

"Not as devious as Shrewsbury, but powerful enough. He'll be on the Commission to try your case."

"You know this?" Suffolk said.

"It will be at Lambeth Palace."

"When? When will it be?" Frances said.

"I came to get you." Northampton smiled. "We have only a few weeks to prepare ourselves."

As they were dispersing moments later, Frances approached her great-uncle. "This Overbury," she said. "What does he say about me?"

"Just gossip."

"What gossip?"

"I'd rather not say."

She was getting nowhere. "What can you do to him?"

"I don't know. Not much really. Try to deal with him, I suppose. Buy him off if I can."

"But Robin says Overbury doesn't value money as he should."

"Are you in touch with Carr?"

He seemed displeased when she said that she was. "But I love him," she added. "I adore him . . . I've written dozens of letters, and he answers . . . he *does* answer some of them . . ."

"Warmly?"

"Oh, yes! He loves me."

"Good. We need him."

"Do you think Robin is right? About Overbury not caring for money?"

"Up to a point. I've heard the same rumor about him. I've had some dealings with him, nothing definitive. He is an odd duck, hard to deal with."

"So?"

"So we deal with him."

"How?"

"Any suggestions?"

"He mustn't go on saying these things to Robin."

"What things?"

"The same things you won't tell me Overbury says."

"I see. To Carr?"

"Yes."

"And Carr has written you to this effect?"

"Yes."

"This is not good."

"How can we stop him? What if he convinces Robin?"

"Convinces him of what?"

Frances understood his meaning; the question was not whether Overbury could persuade Robin of any particular fact, but whether he could erode the bond between the two lovers. Robin knew that Frances was no virgin, for he (she hoped) believed that he had taken her maidenhead that first of many afternoons in the summerhouse at Audley End.

"We do have a problem," Northampton said, "but I've not yet decided the best way to handle it. The solution will come to me."

Frances was far from convinced of that. She knew that Northampton would try; she and her sister and the Howard family were very important to him. But he had many things on his mind, and she must be, as she had been, ready to act on her own. It stood to reason that if Overbury was as clever as they said, regardless of his lack of interest in money, he would listen to reason. For as Aristotle or someone had said, intelligence and reason were the same thing. And if he would not listen to reason, well, he might respond helpfully to threats.

Now Frances stood before her mirror in the candlelight, admiring herself, noticing how the down of her arm caught the light. What a relief! To have the explanations behind her, to be on her way to London, within sight of shedding her husband, soon to be with Robin again, soon to feel him warm inside her.

She did have this nuisance of the virginity test to face, but then she had a way to look after it. She planned to revisit Dr. Forman, who had turned out to be a considerate person: she had written him numerous letters and received prompt and friendly replies every time. He had promised to help her with the medical aspects of the "nullity" —aspects which, if her mother's suspicions were an indication, could not be taken for granted.

Though a man of sinister reputation, Dr. Forman had helped her thus far. Frances opened the drawer, withdrew the bronze sculpture he had sent her, and placed it on the tabletop. As Forman had instructed, she sat with her gaze fixed on the figurine. The bronze was more attractive than the wax original; its smooth exterior shone, and yet its texture of almost invisibly small pits on the surface gave the lovers a lifelike appearance.

Given her polite upbringing, Frances at first found it hard to respond to the sculpture as directed. She had to sit for a long time, stroke the lovers, imagine them moving; if that failed, she would recall Forman's firescreen or the summerhouse.

She had learned the method, but with unforeseen help. Since Robin had responded to her so quickly, she had much love-philtre left over, which, to make perfection of Forman's discipline easier, she regularly took herself. Soon she required only moments with the bronze lovers; indeed, at times she had to fetch the figurine quickly, lest the discipline succeed whilst the lovers were still in their drawer.

She thought of Robin, of that first time in the summerhouse, of his smile, his voice, and of the good, faint, leathery scent of his clothing. She imagined him as she had known him—naked, except for the diamond earring, whose flash of light so well matched the sparkle of his blue eyes. It took scarcely no time at all.

*   *   *

OVERBURY LEFT Bacon's house near the Strand and went straight to his apartment, where, with a bottle of sherry and a silver goblet, he repaired to his study to read and think. Bacon, not given to overstatement, had issued a warning that upset him: "Don't be foolish, Thomas," he had said, echoing Cecil's words. "Trim your sails."

Overbury had smiled inanely. "What have I done?"

"Too much, and not enough," Bacon said. "But in his kindness James would rescue you from yourself. He offers you the post vacated by Sir John Edwards."

"*That* post"—Overbury spat—"is in Muscovy!"

"His Majesty wishes to rescue you all the way to Muscovy."

Overbury, feeling slightly uneasy, rejected the offer at once: "Tell King James I'll not be able to go to Muscovy. Health. Rheum. Whatever."

Bacon shook his head. "Not wise," he said. "Not wise, Thomas."

So events were moving too swiftly, and Overbury was worried. Bacon was right: it wasn't wise to reject, nor even lengthily to ponder, a royal offer, which was more properly called an assignment. It was one thing to have Queen Anne upset with him; he had known the dangers of her jealousy from the start. That calculated risk had been worth taking so long as he could be sure of Robin's support, and of at least the neutrality of James. He had never considered the possibility of a break with both James and Robin. Such miscalculations had led good men like the Duke of Norfolk and Essex to the block, and might soon do Raleigh in as well.

Suppose this "nullity" issue went against him? To whom could he turn for protection? The Queen despised him, laying the blame for Robin's preferment at his door. (And where would Robin be were it not for Overbury's political ventriloquism?) Many would be happy to see Sir Thomas Overbury out of the way.

The tricky die is cast, he thought, pacing the floor. The agony of political choice lay in the fact that it eliminated all other possibilities. He wanted to get drunk. When the sherry was almost gone, he still felt no relief. He was aware that in this, the most important competition of his career, perhaps of his life, he stood a good chance of losing. And to a woman not yet twenty.

He had been wrong to think of the Howard girl in purely political terms. One could deal with political men—the Northamptons, the Cecils, the Bacons—even with the Queen's Spanish phalanx at court.

But he could not get at Frances Howard without directly opposing the "nullity," which meant opposing Robin, who had been his only support. And now James had openly backed the "nullity."

Suppose Overbury dropped his opposition. That would quiet James, and make Robin feel better for the time being. But then his future at court would rest solely in the hands of Robin's wife, who would in due course undermine him in Robin's eyes, with Northampton and his papist entourage applauding her at every turn. No, to shift positions now—to "trim," as Cecil and Bacon urged—meant political and economic suicide. His only hope lay in going forward. The fact was that Overbury had to win in order to stay even.

This meant that he must endure for a time great peril: he must continue to press his views against the public policy of James, and against the expressed wishes of Carr. His last hope lay in the desperate course of a complete break with Robin.

Overbury felt a wave of nausea, and blamed it on the fact that he had missed high tea. He called for a plate of biscuits, a pot of tea, and another carafe of wine. Feeling better after he had vomited and finished the warm tea, he dozed and was not disturbed until Gibbs tried to undress him for bed. He shrugged his valet off, insisting that he had important work to do.

For the next two hours, he scoured the books in his library for authoritative views on the female sex. He went from Scripture to the Church Fathers to medical and philosophical giants, ancient and modern, scribbling down quotations and mumbling to himself. When he had worked furiously well into the night, he dozed again, only to awaken at first light.

Throughout the next day, he remained in his study, writing a poem. He had wafers, tea, oranges and sherry brought to him. He wrote, and he revised, pausing at intervals to laugh and shout lines from his poem.

He had found the way to reach Lady Essex, a way so obvious and so devastating that he was surprised he had not thought of it before. Though devastating and public, this attack would not overtly touch the technical issue of the "nullity." Best of all, publication of his poem, which he ironically titled "The Wife," would sway Robin from his present course and advance his dependence on Overbury at the same time. He need only return to his earlier role as tutor, spiritual guide and confidant to Viscount Rochester—Server to King James I.

Ignoring particulars of the "nullity," from the dispassionate pedestal of the scholar he would insinuate truths of a more abstract and important order.

For issues of morality were not the only ones here: Robin's downfall would be the downfall of every man who placed himself at the disposal of an arrogant woman. The infuriating truth was that Lady Essex was a woman who had not learned her proper place. She ignored man's superior station in the scheme of things. So Overbury ended his poem with his most telling and philosophical couplet: "When by marriage both in one concur,/woman converts to man, not man to her."

Perfect. Even Robin had complained about his lover's obstinate ways; this poem would be the instrument of humbling her: cosmic order and matrimony. Relieved from his anxieties, Overbury polished off another bottle of good Spanish sherry, and sank into a profound and pleasant sleep from which his man refused to wake him.

It was past ten o'clock at night when he stirred at the sound of a carriage arriving, and then of someone working the large brass knocker at his front door. He was vaguely startled by the sound of a strange and resonant voice asking after him. Slipping from the couch, he glanced through the open doorway to the vestibule. A tall, slim man, slightly stooped of shoulder, stood just out of reach of the light. Gibbs was already on his way to the study.

"Pardon, sir," he said (for others were about), "but my Lady Frances Howard, Countess of Essex, requests the privilege of a brief visit."

Gibbs's eyebrows only slightly hinted at the impropriety of the visit. Overbury stared at him, aware that for the moment his own breathing had ceased.

A more perfect example of what he had been thinking and writing could hardly be imagined. She, whom he regarded as his mortal enemy, she, who had no business calling on any bachelor, unescorted, simply appeared, announced her wish to see him, and, presumably, expected to be invited into his private study.

"I understand," Gibbs was saying, "that the master of the house is unable to entertain visitors . . ."

"No, Gibbs," he said suddenly. "Please welcome my Lady Frances, and bring us brandy."

In what seemed the briefest of intervals, Gibbs had presented Lady Essex and disappeared, leaving Overbury alone with his guest.

Seldom had Overbury's background at Oxford and the Inner Temple failed him. He was by almost any civilized standard a man of the world. But in the circumstances of this meeting he had no experience on which to fall back.

It was Frances Howard who spoke first: "I trust, Sir Thomas, that you will pardon this intrusion."

She made the statement as a fact!

"My lady, you are welcome," Overbury said (for lack of anything else that came to mind).

Again, Frances Howard spoke to break the silence: "Sir Thomas, I understand that you are not feeling well, and I am quite aware that my untimely call would be unusual in any case. But certain facts have been brought to my attention which make an interview between the two of us necessary."

Overbury tried to hide his amazement. How beautiful she was, standing there in the candlelight, her long blond hair laced with touches of amber, her lovely child's face flushed with emotion, her marvelous breasts heaving from her now-famous décolletage. Was it possible that such a lovely creature could be his deadly enemy? For a moment, Overbury felt that everything that had happened in the past few months had been a mistake; he felt shame. He hated this woman whom he hardly knew. He feared a young lady of considerable background who had harmed him in no way.

As quickly, shame turned to rage at her arrogance.

"I can imagine," he said, "no more pleasant prospect than a visit from my lady on what otherwise promised to be a cold and overly damp evening. But," he added coolly, "I am not informed on any matter that might render that pleasure a necessity."

"Sir Thomas," she answered, "I came here to help us both. I shall not try to measure wits with you."

Her words were at once confident and sharp. Her dark blue eyes glittered as she returned his own steady gaze.

"Madam," he said, "you are welcome here whatever your purpose."

He caught the trace of a smile from her, and was a touch disappointed with himself for having again drawn attention to her presence, unchaperoned, in his apartment. This repetition seemed to give her the initiative.

"Sir Thomas Overbury," she said, and the hint of a smile was gone.

"I have come to see if the conflict about to befall us might be avoided. I am more than aware that custom—the tyrant of tiny minds—forbids my presence here under any circumstances. But when the matter is sufficiently urgent, custom—even for a woman—*must* give way."

This remark irritated him. Especially the *must*.

"Custom," he said, "seems perilously near giving way on all sides. One is scarcely certain one day to the next whether sufficient custom survives to admit of further giving way."

"We shall," she said firmly, "have done with this word-game of tennis. I concede your victory."

Now she was openly sarcastic; she was saying that the important victory was already in her hands. But this made no sense. For if the issue were not still in doubt, why had she come?

"You are here," he said, "at the behest of your great-uncle—"

"Decidedly not," she interrupted. "My great-uncle has urged me to ignore your indecent efforts to degrade my name. You have sought to destroy Robin's love for me. You have assaulted my reputation—without cause—from the beginning of our slim acquaintance. All of which puzzles and disturbs Robin. I am humiliated and afraid and angry. And I have no notion of why you wish to destroy me."

"Destroy, my lady?"

"Yes, destroy! I am here because I am desperate to hear that you have told my Robin that I, Frances Howard, am a whore."

Overbury raised his hand to object.

"It is useless to deny this, sir, for Robin has told me it himself. He has told me that you tax him daily with terrible things about me, and press him to surrender all feeling for me. And I who have never so much as wished ill of you."

"My lady . . ."

"Please tell me what I have done to deserve this vile treatment."

"My lady," he said, "if you will allow me, I assume that you are speaking of the 'nullity' suit?"

"Yes, and well you know it, too. And of your singular opinions on this matter, which should be of no concern to you, and of my virtue . . ."

"Virtue?" Overbury said, suddenly angry. "Virtue, did you say? I have neither publicly nor in private remarked upon your virtue. Nor have I ever heard it cogently argued that you possess any."

"Such wit," she said scornfully, "is for schoolboys and fools. I have

done with it and with you. I shall but warn you, Sir Thomas. Do not
—*do not*—speak to Robin of my marriage. Do not prey upon his
imagination with suspicions. Do not sully my name with 'whore' and
'harlot.' Beware, sir, beware. I will be free of this ninny Essex. I will
have Robin, and you shall interfere no longer."

"My lady," he said firmly, "you must believe that what I do I do
only in Robin's interest—yes, in his best interest. I have known and
loved him for years. We have lived and worked together, shared all
we have. I have been his tutor and guide in all things. As for what
I said of you, I have no fear of saying the same to you now. You are
married in the sight of God to the Earl of Essex, whose name you bear.
But married or not, you are no maid, as your suit of 'nullity' absurdly
proclaims."

"Rumor. You would destroy me by rumor."

"No," he said. "I do not bandy rumor, nor do I listen to it. Rumor
is recreation for the old and indolent. I do not speak of your French
tutor, or of your fond stableboys, but of your own acknowledged
connection with Robin. You know well you are no virgin."

"Why should this matter to you? Why do scholars and priests
worry about what so little concerns them?"

"My lady, without such worries there can be no law, no decency.
Civilization itself is but the stuff of someone's worry. You think of
morality and religion as a cavil, the split of a hair, the nagging of a
busybody. And I tell you that where the smoke rises a flame burns."

"So, I am to be undone by a rumor-monger."

"You endow me with powers I had begun to doubt I had."

"Your powers, sir, are all in my Robin's honest love for you."

"You imply that my love is less than honest."

"Unlike you, I lend no credence to rumor. Robin has told about
you, about this Edinburgh episode of which you make so great a fuss."

This came as a surprise.

"The rumors about you," she said, "which I have not repeated until
this moment, are all true."

She had reduced him to silence again.

"Sir Thomas, you are a pederast and a seducer of young boys. And
it may be that you are other things as well. As for Robin, he was
briefly your lover, not your minion. And you refuse to release him
from that youthful fancy. My love—and his love for me—is no threat

to you! He had hoped you would love me, too, but you have sought to ruin his love for me instead."

Now there was a long pause; Overbury sipped his brandy, then finally spoke. "I acknowledge it."

"But why?" she cried out. "Why would you not accept my friendship, too? I bear you no ill-will for Edinburgh. Why will you turn Robin away from me? He trusts you, admires you, believes you."

Overbury tried to answer, but she prevented him.

"Don't you know how desperately I love him?"

"You do not love Robin," he said. "You have little if any capacity to feel love."

Her large eyes widened.

"Love," he said, "is a capacity of the soul, not of the body. I have watched you; you love Robin's beauty, because you see it as the reflection of your own."

"So you would deprive me even of my own desperate feelings?"

"No," he said, "the body feels as well as the soul. Most of humanity spend their lives on the sensate level of beasts, feeling, eating, seeing to their bodily functions, buying, selling, so they may survive and do the same another day."

"Do you think Robin is like this?"

"Yes and no," he said, realizing that he had followed an unpromising line of thought.

Lady Essex cocked her head scornfully.

"Yes," he said, "in that he is young. The young are the most sensual, the most intense. Intensity is the opposite of love, which is based on truth, and therefore requires intellect and distance."

"Such as your admirable passion for the Countess of Rutland? Love, sir, is not only for philosophers. I love Robin, and—"

"Perhaps, and in a perverse way, he desires you. But desire also is the opposite of love."

"I hate riddles," she said. "Nor did I come to Quadragesimals. I do love Robin, and—"

"And I love him, too, in a different way, which is beside the point of your 'nullity.' "

"So," she said impatiently. "Agreed! We both love Robin in our ways. Can we not both have him in our ways?"

Overbury did not answer.

"How can you say you love him," she pleaded, "if you torment him with doubts about me?"

"Because—"

"Because you are jealous."

"No."

"You call me a whore because you are jealous. And because I love Robin, I now beg you to abstain from further accusations about me. We can begin our friendship from this moment, forgetting all that has been said these past weeks."

"Again," he said, "you imply that I accuse you falsely . . ."

Just then Gibbs entered with brandy and wafers; Overbury knew that he must have heard most of their conversation, for he had been fetching the brandy for some time. Frances refused the glass he offered by ignoring it. He took a gulp himself, and then they were looking hard at each other. He was much taller than she, and he found, gazing down at her curiously luminous eyes, that there was something faintly comic about the interview. He smiled, and at that moment her mood appeared to change utterly.

"Have you made the mistake," she said, "of supposing the end of my hopes to be a jest?"

Her voice was strangely sinister, and yet Overbury knew that, now, despite himself, he was grinning, and, then, laughing outright. Lady Essex looked grave.

"Forgive me, my lady," he said, "but—"

"But to you my agony is a jape."

She turned to leave, and he tried to stop her.

"Lay no hand on me," she said, swirling about.

Just as suddenly he caught a look, deep in her eyes—a hint of something primitive, something wolflike and wild. She stood there regarding him and—yes, that was it—regarding him quietly with a low, chilling, passionless curiosity. Was it possible that hatred, like love, was also detached, calm, devoid of intensity? Here was a creature to fear—perhaps to hate, but surely to fear.

"The die is cast," he said, watching her eyes closely.

She would not speak.

"You have lost him!"

And still the eyes observed him. Perhaps it was the brandy, or his fatigue, or the two in tandem, but suddenly he took the manuscript of his poem from the desk and waved it in front of her.

" 'The Wife' will see you no wife!" he shouted.

Lady Essex strode toward him and, before he thought to withhold it, took the manuscript from him; she began to read, slowly at first, then, with finality, flipping the pages swiftly.

"So," she said at last, almost in a whisper, "you think you can call me a whore with all England as your audience?"

"I will spare my Robin from this disastrous connection," he said.

For a moment he thought that she would tear the manuscript to shreds; curiously, he realized that he wanted her to tear it, to give some sign that she feared him as he feared her. Instead, she let the manuscript fall from her hand, turned, and walked swiftly to the door, pausing only to say:

"It is presumptuous of you, Sir Thomas, to speak of Robin as if you own him."

Then she was gone.

Overbury went to the window to watch as a man held a lantern for Lady Essex; she stepped into the coach, and Overbury wondered whose hand it was outstretched to meet hers. Northampton's? Probably not. And Robin would not likely allow her to enter his apartment alone. The carriage did not move.

He poured another brandy; he would have to get very drunk, now, to be able to sleep. He sat for a while, rereading "The Wife." His head reeled and again he felt nausea—whether from his poor diet of late, or from the enormity of what he had done, he did not know. In politics, sins of omission were seldom fatal: it was the act, the public sin of commission that did one in.

Having shown the poem to Lady Frances, he had no compunction now from placing it on sale. What was said could not be unsaid; the meeting with Frances Howard had settled his course of action once and for all.

He lay down on the couch again, grateful for the drowsiness enveloping him. But before he could drop off to sleep, he felt someone's presence.

"What is it?" he said in words he knew to be slurred.

Gibbs looked at him, picked up the tray and said nothing.

"Something is wrong," Overbury said, sitting up. "You disapprove of me tonight."

"It is not for me to approve or disapprove," Gibbs said. "I do wonder about your condition."

"You are afraid for me," Overbury said. "You think I have bungled things."

"It would be presumptuous of me," Gibbs said quietly, "and I am not the sort."

"Gibbs, you are a clever man—a diplomat. And a good friend."

Gibbs set the tray on the desk, where he gathered up bits of biscuit that had fallen. "Thomas," he said, "one does hear talk in the New Exchange . . . men in service . . ."

Overbury was awake now and interested: "Yes?"

"Such men may well know less than they tell," Gibbs allowed, already backing off.

"And," Overbury said, "they may tell less than they know."

That tack seemed to work; Gibbs spoke slowly and deliberately, and what he said did not differ substantially from Bacon's remarks.

"You make it sound ominous, old friend," Overbury said.

Gibbs gathered up the tray and left the room.

Overbury felt tense, alert; his stomach churned so vilely he could taste it. He had never felt physical fear before, but he suspected that these were its symptoms. He had thought of his peril in political terms only, with a loss sending him back to the financial straits into which he debarked on his return from the Continent. He was beginning to suspect otherwise.

He could not afford to sleep now; like everything else, time was against him. He had to act before dawn, obtain an audience with James, the only man with sufficient power to help him. Such a gambit was dangerous, but Overbury knew with a terrible certainty that he had to try it, and that he must succeed. He would publish his poem, but only after laying his case directly before the king.

Taking no heed of the hour, he summoned Gibbs, told him of his plan, and ordered him to fetch a coach. Gibbs was astonished and, at first, refused to cooperate; he insisted that King James would not condescend to see even the Queen, unannounced, in the middle of the night, and that a hackney at that hour would cost him the earth.

"You must be mad, Thomas!" he said. "You need sleep. You are exhausted; anyone can see it. You know one must lay plans for any meeting with the King."

God's nails! Gibbs had a point, especially in view of the offer from James for the post in Muscovy. Overbury knew he had erred: "Not wise. Not wise, Thomas," Bacon had said. But if he moved fast perhaps he could reach James with his acceptance before Bacon got there with his rebuff.

Overbury saw the problem: the "nullity" had absorbed all his energies for many weeks. Because of it he had rejected a direct request from the King, one meant to extricate him from his difficulties to boot. To James, whom he had insulted by his opposition, Overbury now offered a more serious offense.

Tomorrow might be too late. By then, Lady Essex could maneuver either Carr or Northampton or both into making hostile representations to the King, who, with Queen Anne's calumnies fresh in his mind, sat with Overbury's refusal to serve in his pocket.

He had freshened and changed clothes by the time Gibbs succeeded with his errand. Rather than lose more time arguing, Overbury let him ride along.

The streets were very dark, and the coach rocked along slowly; a light rain had started, scenting the cool air with freshness. Overbury's head cleared.

When the coach stopped on the road, and the driver exchanged words with someone, Overbury paid little heed but fumbled for money. Highwaymen were common, especially at night. Ordinarily, one merely passed the coachman his loose change and a bauble or two and was seen on his way again. Most highwaymen were content to leave the carriage doors unopened; they were neither fussy nor looking for serious trouble.

So Overbury was justifiably surprised when both doors of the coach were flung wide and he found himself hurled by the roughest of hands into space. He landed painfully, his left shoulder taking the worst of the fall. There were sounds of fighting, and as he had been taught at Eton his first move was a quick roll; he heard a blade strike the cobblestone.

He leaped up and drew his own blade in one graceful movement. He was an excellent swordsman, and in France he had indulged himself in the one extravagance of his long trip: he had obtained a blade which was, by consent, fashioned to be the strongest, thinnest, sharpest and deadliest in the world. Placing his back against the wall of a building, he avoided the second awkward thrust before he easily dispatched his assailant.

"Gibbs!" he shouted. "Gibbs!"

" 'E ain't likely t'ansah ye, matey. Can't 'ear nuffing."

There were three of them left; the coachman had driven off.

Overbury could make out the outlines of the men as they grouped to attack. Two had swords, and the other seemed to be carrying a long knife. The two with swords advanced in front, the other behind them. Overbury lunged, and both swords came at him at once; he felt the heavy blade tear into his arm, just below the shoulder that already felt broken. He ducked under the other blade, and ran.

The men chased him, and, as he expected, one was faster than the other two. He stopped short, and almost laughed when he realized that the swift-footed one was carrying the knife. The man almost fell upon Overbury's sword. Did he die with a look of astonishment on his face? It was too dark to tell, and the two men were on him again, swinging and swearing.

Overbury wanted to run, to try the same trick again, but he was tiring. He fell and rolled, and took one of his unskilled opponents by surprise; the man stabbed into the cobblestone, and stumbled into Overbury's cunning steel.

Now Overbury stood and watched the large shadow before him; hunched, it was holding a sword that should have been an ax. The shadow was breathing loudly.

"Come on," Overbury said. "Come on."

The shadow turned slowly, and then Overbury could hear the footsteps rushing away.

He went to Gibbs, knowing that he was much too late. Had they pulled them both from the same side of the coach, Gibbs, who had no sword, might have had a chance.

Gently, Overbury dragged the body into a doorway: he had no choice but to leave it for a spell. He must get to St. James; this incident left no doubt that his life was in danger. He would send the King's Guard back for Gibbs; that was all he could do for him now.

He set off running—past the Strand toward the Haymarket and beyond, all the way to St. James Palace.

The guards would not let him on the grounds, appearing unimpressed by his claim of being the King's Server.

"Off with you," one said. "There isn't such a title. Think we're sods?"

The Captain of the Guard came, and though he recognized Overbury he gave no instructions that they release him. He disappeared, Overbury was certain, to carry out the Server's orders, which was all that was required. He would see James, beg his forgiveness, and be off to Muscovy within a day or so.

The Captain was not gone long. He ordered his men to take Overbury—to carry him if necessary—to the docks, where they were to load him for transport to the Tower.

"But why?" Overbury shouted. "Didn't you tell the King I'm here?"

"His Majesty knows," the Captain said.

"But what did he say?"

The Captain would not answer.

"Is this too much to ask?"

"Not to worry," the Captain said. "They'd not likely hang the King's Server, now would they?"

ANN REOPENED the shop in mid-August. The chains closing the Bridge were down; for weeks, people had been drifting back to Southwark. The taverns and Bear Garden were in business again; the court was assembling and Master Jones had work for her to do. Since his return from Holland, Sir Ralph was more attentive than ever. She dismissed the promised summer in the Lake Country as one of life's small disappointments: what of the many who had died in agony—their groins distended—of the plague?

Her son Davy was happier than she had ever seen him. Master Jones had entered him in St. Paul's School, and if he did well he might earn admission to Brasenose, a college at Oxford set up for boys like Davy.

Ann still had to cope with Franklin; her efforts to break off with him had failed, hindered by the impediment of Lady Frances' "nullity." She had hoped that after obtaining the love-philtre for her friend, she would be free to drop Franklin and Forman for good. But Franklin had been right about one thing: it was Frances who took the lead in continuing the acquaintance with Forman. Communications never varied, with letters passing from Frances to Ann to Franklin to Forman and back the other way.

Ann could not imagine what kept Frances in such a fret; her friend was always after her for letters, and doted on every detail when she received them. And yet they seemed to infuriate her.

"The fool sends letters to everyone in England," Frances said one day after her return to London. "We must stop him."

"The magician?" Ann inquired.

"No," Frances said. "Never mind. Oh, what matter! Overbury!" She explained that the culprit of these letters was named Overbury, who himself wrote letters, causing much stir and delay of the "nullity." "They have changed the Commission," she complained, "larding it with Puritans. Mr. Attorney required delay because of this creature."

Thoroughly mystified, Ann nodded sympathetically. "Who is Overbury?" she asked.

"A man. A nobody in the Tower."

"Shall I ask after him?"

Frances asked how she could do that.

"Why, through Sir Ralph," Ann said. "I have spoken of him."

This distressed Frances all the more; she extracted from Ann a promise not to mention her name in Sir Ralph's presence.

"But he likes you," Ann said. "You have met him, have you not?"

Frances said she had, but this connection seemed merely to increase her agitation. Ann claimed to understand (she didn't), and made no further mention of Sir Ralph. She had learned to make allowances for great ladies, who were often possessed of strange notions. Frances, a beautiful lady of place and power, honestly feared this man whom no one had ever heard of, though he was powerless to help himself much less to hurt Lady Frances.

Few commoners would fear a man rotting away in prison, not if he wrote a dozen letters to everyone in England who could read. And if he wrote to King James, as this Overbury did, why, they'd take no heed, seeing that, if King James liked his letters, he'd not be keeping him in the Tower. Great ladies were short on common sense.

"If the King believes Overbury," Ann said, "why'd he put him in the Tower?"

Annoyed, Frances said the King had imprisoned Overbury just to get him out of sight until after the "nullity."

"But what can Overbury say that could harm *you?*"

"That I was . . . not pure."

Imagine! Her friend thought a King had time to worry about such things; Ann did her best to show concern.

"You understand," Frances said, "it isn't James, but Robin I worry about."

Understand! As if the whole idea made sense! Now, why should Frances worry lest Rochester find her no virgin, when he had been her lover these many months?

"What if he finds out about Forman?" Frances added.

"But, Frances . . ."

What could she say? It was foolish to think Overbury would put news of her relationship with Forman in the letters. If he knew of it, then Forman must have told him, which, with the two of them such friends and correspondents, made no sense.

So the madness of epistles grew more mysterious every day. Frances would arrive early in the morning, returning often late in the afternoon, vexed when no letter greeted her, furious with its contents when one did. The packets themselves grew thicker: Forman's price, presumably, was going up, but for what services Ann could not tell. She waited for the right moment to query Franklin.

"What is it?" she asked one night as they lay abed. "What's all the fuss? What do the letters say?"

Franklin dismissed her lightly. He claimed that the wax seal on the letters could not be counterfeited, but she figured he knew their story well enough. Since he was in good spirits lately, enjoying all his old privileges (yet mindful in his goings and comings to avoid collision with Sir Ralph), Ann persisted, much to Franklin's amusement.

"Your good friend," he said, "has she not told you?"

"Not in so many words," she said, kissing him coyly.

"She means to kill this chap Overbury," Franklin said, laughing. "I thought you knew."

Although until then Ann had given little thought to Franklin's character, her realization that he could talk matter-of-factly about murder came as no surprise: he was a vicious, greedy man. But the Countess of Essex? Who could believe it?

And yet Franklin related details too precise, too complicated, too enormous not to be believed. Frances' letters were stuffed with money, part of it used to bribe a jailer named Gervase Elwes, who, in return, got himself assigned to Overbury's cell to carry out a murder plot involving fruit tarts (delivered daily, supposedly from an anonymous friend) laced with mercury something. Fiendish clysters administered by Franklin were to weaken Overbury's resistance to the poison.

"A friendly token, Elwes told him," Franklin said of the pastries. "The ignorant sod looks forward to them, gorges them down at once.

Thinks they're from the King, or some earl!"

"Will this mercury sumblate really kill him?" Ann asked.

"Mercury sublimate," he said. "Likely he'd be dead already, but we mustn't hit him full dose. It would turn him quite blue. Puts out blisters big as plague whelps. Somebody'd get wind of it, sure. So steady's the word: slow, a bit each day, with my clysters sapping him. He'll die slow and no one'll catch a whiff of it."

She had to convince Franklin that he was in great danger. Although this took the rest of the night, she was certain she had finally assured him that he could find more profit, with no risk of hanging, if he but limited the dose even more than at present. Let Overbury be sick, let the word spread so that Lady Essex would know they were at work. She'd continue paying in the hope that each packet would be the last. Then, when the "nullity" was over, she'd be pleased to learn that Overbury had survived, unharmed, and that she was therefore in no danger.

In the morning, as she watched Franklin slope off east on Southwark, she despised him, knowing that for the foreseeable future she was tied to him. Even at the risk of losing Sir Ralph, she had now to spend as much time with Franklin as possible, for only then could she hope to control events in the Tower.

That day, she told Frances what she had learned.

Her friend was angry. "It's more dangerous, with you knowing," she said.

Reluctantly, Frances related the complete story, which not even King James knew: Overbury hated the Howard family because he hated all Catholics. He hated Frances because he was a pederast and cared for Rochester as a lover. Also, Overbury knew that Carr thought ill of Sodomites, found Overbury tiresome and jealous, and would soon bring John Donne into service as his secretary. Donne was Catholic in sympathy; all his friends and his mother were Catholics, which was why Overbury had Donne thrown in jail for getting married. Her uncle's spies were witnesses to all this; besides which, Overbury had caused the torture and martyrdom of Catholic priests, Father Gerard for one. He was a spiteful, hateful, disgusting heretic.

"Oh, Ann," Frances said, "please believe me. I couldn't bear it if you thought less of me."

Ann embraced her, but for some reason she thinking not of Frances, but of Davy, wondering what it was like at St. Paul's School.

"It will turn out well," she said, knowing that now her future—and Davy's—rested in Franklin's hands, as the apothecary measured out the mercury for the prisoner's tarts.

FRANCES LEFT Ann's shop to keep a midday appointment with her attorney, Mr. Everard. The briefings bored her: the nine articles of the "nullity" all sounded alike. She suspected that these legal niceties mattered far less than did Ann's knowledge of the plot, which secured the only link in a chain leading from Frances to Overbury's cell.

Her first impulse had been to call Forman off. Not that she thought he would implicate her; but for some reason Forman had told Franklin, who had told Ann, on whose innocence of the plot Frances could no longer depend for safety.

Unfortunately, to follow this impulse removed her from one danger by hurling her in the path of another: "The Wife." Frances dreaded publication of this diatribe. The scurrilous poem would be a greater embarrassment than Catherine's indiscretion. Overbury's arch tone would be on everybody's lips. The "nullity" might be denied; or, if granted, her marriage plans could go awry. Robin might take up where he left off with the Countess of Bedford.

No, having taken charge of her own destiny, Frances was constrained to consider all possibilities. She realized that, like Sir Walter Raleigh, Overbury might remain in the Tower for years. And here was the issue more plainly than Mr. Everard's whereases and notwithstandings: imprisonment guaranteed Overbury's silence no more surely than it had Raleigh's. As her great-uncle had said, Overbury possessed important friends, and the smallest bribe could deliver pen and paper to the lowest dungeon in England. So it would have been pointless to destroy the manuscript that night in Overbury's study. He'd only write another, wherever he was. Frances understood her dilemma very well: if Overbury lived, then she must live with "The Wife" and—worse—with his insolence toward her. She loved Robin, but he was weak and impressionable. Sooner or later, fashion would drift, however briefly, to Overbury's snide opinion, and Robin would follow along . . .

"My lady," Mr. Everard was saying. "Do you understand this last consideration?" He was cross with her; she'd not been listening. "Your demeanor in court is all-important. You must keep your head down." He gently tilted her head as if his obvious meaning might escape her. When she gave witness, she was to speak softly: "Do not affect boldness. Appear diffident. Be nothing loud, or seeming sure of the proceedings. Speak thus—a touch above a whisper—that they will know your apprehension of them. I shall instruct you to speak louder, lest they have not noticed your hushed tones. Will you remember?"

It was so simple. Why did he fret so?

"Do not behold the King's Commissioners abruptly, with a stare," he said. "You may look at them, but keep your eyes askance . . ."

Only one of small wit would do otherwise. At last, Mr. Everard, who loved the sound of his own voice, bid her goodbye till the morrow.

Luckily, Lambeth Palace was to the west on the South Bank, so Frances had no trouble posting another packet at Ann's shop on her way to court the next day. She had penned her boldest letter to Forman, insisting that he settle the business between them at once. Acknowledging that difficulties may have arisen through Ann's timidity and Franklin's greed, she was constrained to lay down several requests which Forman must regard as urgent.

Lest Franklin prolong their design in the hope of greater gain by diluting the poison, Forman must increase the original potency or compound it with a second more deadly substance. To meet the possibility of complete subversion through that source, he must find a second route for the poison. She reminded him of her own success with this multiple approach to conditioning Essex' food and drink.

Furthermore, he had to act swiftly, for as things were developing Overbury promised to live longer than Methuselah. And she reminded him, too, that she knew precious little at dear cost of his promise to help her with the virginity test, which could occur at any moment. She was worried and pleaded for reassurance.

The trial had been set for Lambeth Palace in the hope of avoiding the riot of Puritans and dissenters on the embankment side, but the street near the palace was thronging with malcontents. They were a rowdy pack, shouting, preaching and praying with a brave show of indignation, as if the "nullity" were their concern, not hers.

By the time Frances made her way through the crowd and into the palace, formalities of the trial had begun. She took her assigned place between Mr. Everard and Katherine Fine. As the Court Recorder stood, her great-uncle entered with her mother on his arm; as agreed, her father would remain at Audley End.

The Recorder read the King's charge to the Commission, then dozens of witnesses, from both sides, entered depositions under oath recounting family histories and circumstances surrounding the contested marriage. Essex gave sworn testimony that, except for smallpox when he was a child, he had suffered no disease that might hinder carnal copulation with a woman. In fact, he had proved able to copulate with other women.

"But by a perpetual and natural impediment," he said, "I am unable to have carnal copulation with the Lady Frances."

Here was the fact that must have bedeviled him: the impediment was real, but could she say that it was natural? As Frances watched him (against her lawyer's advice), an unfamiliar emotion moved her. She assumed it to be pity.

He had married, Essex was saying, at fourteen, when no one could expect him to appear the full man. In the years that had passed, he had tried many times to consummate his marriage, returning from the Continent determined to do so.

"Sometimes my wife seemed willing," he said, "and sometimes no. But on occasion she did refuse me, barring the door and keeping her ladies about. Mr. Attorney says that I must admit that I have not carnally known my wife, nor penetrated her womb, nor taken the true pleasure inside her. As for this perpetual and natural impediment put forward against me in Article Six, I know not what it means. What must I do to protest the truth? I have oftentimes felt motions and provocations of the flesh tending toward carnal copulation, even toward my wife—but toward her in fancy only, when I was in France or in Holland, not when I am close in bed with her. I cannot sign these undertakings, but say what Mr. Attorney instructs me to say."

Mr. Everard glanced her way: a reminder that she appear subdued. Now she ignored him to observe her husband. As Essex turned from the Commissioners their eyes met, and Frances knew, in spite of all that he had suffered at her hands, that he loved her and would gladly take her back.

The Commission questioned Katherine Fine, who said that from a few weeks after Midsummer to All-hallow tide Essex and Lady Frances had lived together at Audley End, at Leicester House in

Warwickshire, and then at Essex House in Stratfordshire.

"I did see them in naked bed together as man and wife," she said. "They were together for diverse nights—once at Midsummer's Eve, and many times at Audley End. Often my Lord Essex chided me for tardiness when he cried out for warm brandy in the midst of night. He would bid me light a candle; then I must find it, chaff it and fetch it, and he often vexed by my delay, and naked, too, as I saw when he reached for the brandy. I slept in the chamber next them. They talked for most of the night and I was sore fatigued in the morning."

Her other women, Eleanor Ray and Sylvia Britten, gave similar statements. Then, in a voice little above a whisper, Frances gave her deposition, expecting, as rehearsed, that Mr. Everard would ask her to speak louder, which he failed to do. Soon Katherine was helping her to her seat.

At the recess, Mr. Everard said the trial was going well, and that Katherine Fine had proved an especially effective witness, seeming at once poised and disinterested.

When court reconvened, Mr. Everard argued that, since Essex had in effect stipulated to the truth of his wife's claim, the Commission ought without further inquiry to find in favor of the "nullity," as it was in the best interests of all parties, and of justice.

"My Lady Frances wishes no public scorn visited upon my Lord Essex," he said. "She hopes that he might find marriage to another possible. Our suit touches only these two. We affirm, sires, impotence in relation to this one woman, as laid out in our brief: *propter maleficium versus hanc* (because of the evil against this one). We claim, as Scripture in many places avows, it is every woman's right—nay, her bounden duty—to bear children."

Her lawyer had finished, and for a moment Frances thought the trial was over, and that, by dashing off an angry letter to Dr. Forman, she had fretted herself unnecessarily.

"Is it over?" she whispered as Mr. Everard returned to her side.

"Certainly not," he said angrily.

And yet her husband's attorney made no move.

Then Frances knew the trial was far from over. Very deliberately, Archbishop Abbot stood. He strode across the platform, and back again; as he stopped and turned, she could see him smile wryly.

"We must ask," he said in a low voice, "that my Lord Essex by inspected by physicians, if only to learn the wonders of this rare impediment."

Here was a snide remark! And then this vile clergyman turned toward Frances, his brow and mouth frounced with abundant show of sarcasm.

"This Commission must know beyond doubt that no carnal copulation ever took place—awake or sleeping, drunk or sober, ague or none, remembered or forgotten, brief or prolonged, warm or cold, in bed or out, welcome or endured, pleasurable or no, in all that long time of seven years of marriage, months of cohabitation, with so many longings and motions and provocations of young flesh."

No wonder her great-uncle feared this man.

"Sires," he continued, "the Church will be no party to divorce at will. These undertakings must be proved or we can have none of it. And even if they be so proved—that in all these years, with Lady Frances testifying to her lying about, 'naked and alone,' with so great a desire to be made a mother, and with no reluctance anywhere to deny that desire—with all these promptings and motions and provocations, my lords, I say this: What if these undertakings be true?

"What follows from any truth that lays low the holiness of Scripture, the sanctity of marriage, the honor of English law? Tell me what 'impediment' bars this robust couple, notwithstanding their previous cohabitation, from cohabiting again for further trial of their God-given rights and duties?"

Mr. Everard had made no mention of this low rhetoric. She expected someone, probably Abbot, to stand up, quote a few scriptures and vote against the "nullity," but the Archbishop was suggesting a line of thought which neither her lawyer nor her family had considered. It took no lawyer or scholar to understand Abbot's drift: he believed that, even had Essex signed *for* the "nullity," which he most assuredly had not done, the two were married, and must try again, and again, with no end to it.

The Archbishop was more vexing by half than Overbury had ever been.

"My lords," he said, "inasmuch as Scripture directly or by consequence contains matter sufficient to decide all controversies, especially in things appertaining to the Church—and among Christians is marriage not one?—I would be delighted to know by what text in the Old

Testament or the New a man has warrant to make a 'nullity' of a marriage by this *propter maleficium versus hanc.* As if a magic spell —an evil eye!—obtains against but one person or connection."

Frances glanced at Everard; this *maleficium* approach was his idea.

"I put my question this way," Abbot said, "because I do find warrant in Scripture to make a 'nullity' *propter frigiditatem* (Matthew 19:12): 'For there are some chaste (or eunuchs) which were so borne from their mother's womb,' and so on. But I would like to know what Church Father has ever mentioned this reason of *maleficium versus hanc.*

"I *demand* to know!"

Suddenly Abbot's tone had changed, and Frances was not the only one present who was startled.

"In what council, local or ecumenical, important or inconsequential, in what major or minor commentator upon Scripture do we find ever mentioned this *maleficium versus hanc?* Sires, believe me, the gospel has set us free of this particular *maleficium,* and from *maleficia* in general. Have no fear, especially since amongst the million men in our age not one has been found in England who complains of the same affliction. But if anyone should ever seem molested by this *maleficium,* we have remedies at hand: one temporal (medicine), the other eternal. And yet I have heard precious little here today of prayer and fasting, the remedies preferred by our Savior."

Frances was worried. Not only was Mr. Everard following Abbot's every move with unconcealed admiration, but against her wishes she was being swept along by Abbot's wit and intensity. Was it possible, Frances inquired of her lawyer, to interrupt Abbot's speech by some legal device?

"When you speak," Everard told her, "they can see that you ask questions. One asks questions only to express uncertainty. You have brought this suit. Therefore, what is the cause of your uncertainty? Be quiet."

The situation was alarming; Frances could see that every member of the panel was enthralled.

"Is divorce," Abbot asked, "a recognized medical remedy? If one's spouse suffers a broken bone, will divorce mend it? Has a devil ever been cast out by the exorcism of divorce? If we grant this 'nullity,' will this *maleficium* make swift exit? Suppose this *maleficium* is no more than ordinary disease—no *maleficium* at all, much less *maleficium versus hanc.* I ask you, then, what alms have been given, what fastings undertaken, what prayers poured forth, what physic procured, what clysters poured, what medicines applied over these months of lying about naked in front of so many faithful witnesses?

"None. Not one. No, instead on first herald of this case we must declare a 'nullity,' of whose declaration you may know the beginning, but no man's wit can foresee the end."

With a sweeping gesture of his clerical robe, the Archbishop removed his mitre and, as he stalked from the room, dismissed the delegates. The clergymen on the panel followed him; the others looked after them and whispered among themselves, but remained seated.

"Is it over?" Frances said.

Everard did not answer; he moved to leave.

"Do we come back?" she persisted.

"I most fervently hope so," he answered sotto voce. "If we do not, the suit may be over before our cause is won. We must hope otherwise —that the Archbishop's histrionics will pass like the dumb show in a tragedy, a pleasant diversion with no weight on the outcome."

Frances regarded Everard warily. "This *maleficium* business was your idea," she said. "You were sure it would suffice."

"Abbot will move for a peremptory close of the trial," Everard said, ignoring her challenge. "He may have already."

Obviously, her every plan was in jeopardy. Frances managed to attract her great-uncle's attention, and he came to her with a peck on the cheek and his usually reassuring smile. But Frances was in no mood for levity.

"*Do* something!" she said. "Do *something* besides talk!"

VI

Inigo Jones wanted to refurbish the Banqueting House, to rebuild its façade in the Palladian manner. To improve the interior, he planned to do the panels of the coffered ceiling in murals recounting, as had Henry's armor, the history of the House of Stuarts. The centerpiece would be a massive allegory: "The Apotheosis of James I."

Politics had dominated discussion of the artist to receive the lucrative commission. James listened bemusedly as Northampton followed the lead of the Spanish Ambassador: Velásquez would be good; Murillo, better.

"Carr is keen for Sir Nicholas," James said.

Naturally, Carr knew no more about art than he did about casuistry, but James was nettled by the unerring organization of the Spanish party. He would have been happier to support them if, occasionally, they were wrong, or at least unprepared.

"Carr said *that* prior to the break with Overbury," Northampton said too quickly; now he seemed to sense that James was toying with him.

Though Sir Nicholas Bacon was England's greatest living painter, in the Commons he was about as popular as boils. He painted barons and earls and cookmaids (with large, exposed breasts, seated by tables heaped with deer and pheasant: tokens of aristocratic pleasures, all). In the Lower House, Bacon's name kindled fiery speeches taxing the court for its luxury, decrying expense such as that sustained by the May festival. In connection with the festival, commoners had come by accounts ledgers for the event and now demanded explanation of

Suffolk, who held forth in silence at Audley End as if he had never heard of Parliament. The subject of expense led the Commons, willy-nilly, to Carr and favoritism for their theme. As they insisted on control of the King's expenses, they so demanded say in his appointments.

"What about Rubens?" James asked without preamble.

After a moment of embarrassed silence, Northampton spoke, his tone unusually strident.

"The attempt to govern England by commissions will not work. Religion is its own faction. Meddlers and harpies oppress Crown and subject alike!"

"The 'nullity'?" James said.

"I have sources," Northampton answered, as if unaware of the King's deft thrust, "close to members of the panel, who fear the outcome. Today Abbot moved for a peremptory decision, and as things stand now the panel will concede, with only three physicians, and Bishop Andrewes, declaring for continuance."

So, James was right: this "nullity" was inescapable. For weeks now, it had absorbed much of his time. Opposition in Parliament was surprisingly vigorous; more zealous dissenters inveighed against what they called "the issue behind the divorce," by which they meant episcopacy itself. Thus the issue which James thought resolved by the Assembly at Hampton Court a decade ago was loose again in Parliament. Perhaps it would be best to lose the "nullity" and have done with it.

And yet that issue was transforming doctrine into politics; hence, acquiescence was not a promising course of action.

Nowadays the area outside Parliament was an assembly to itself: low rabble listening to or making speeches against the King and all ecclesiastical authority. The Puritans were getting out of hand, and should James appear to temporize, they would only wax bolder.

Most of these madmen were harmless, wandering the streets of Westminster (some without clothes), proclaiming James to be the Anti-Christ. They saw in the summer plague the fourth horse of the Apocalypse, and demanded restoration of their "prophesying" groups, congregations known to speak in strange tongues and to prognosticate the end of the world and the downfall of the monarchy. Taking Christ's words to the Pharisees ("What therefore God hath joined together, let not man put asunder") with the proximate fancy of an ox, another outlandish sect calling itself the Family of Love opposed the "nullity," official marriage, and the keeping of records. Presumably, all Englishmen should be born alike, without surnames. And since these stalwarts also opposed Infant Baptism, Englishmen would have to make do without Christian names as well. "I grow weary of these Anabaptist Toms o' Bedlam," James had said. "I've a mind to hang the lot. I'll set Raleigh loose from the Tower. He can take these lunatics to Virginia. Let them set up their New Jerusalem in that bog." Northampton liked the idea, but then he would.

James returned to the subject. "The 'nullity' is over, then?"

Northampton answered evasively, allowing that Abbot had probably won.

"But," James observed, "if the Commission has decided, why should you press the matter with me today?"

"Your Majesty," Northampton said, "like you, I opposed this childish romance. I opposed this divorce, as the Puritans call it. But the Howards are now, perforce, committed to it. If the Commission decides against us, it will seem that you, who appointed it, decide against us. The loss of influence will go far beyond upsetting my niece's fancied marital arrangements. Howard interests will be vulnerable on all fronts."

Northampton's mission was to assure that this misunderstanding did not become widespread. James was curious to know how one localized the effects of a public trial.

"One possibility did occur to me," Northampton said. "Logically, the Archbishop has refuted the ground on which the Crown established the Commission. As a scholar, you require no instructions on the legal implications of so rash a move. Politically, Abbot aims beyond the Howards by attacking a cause to which Your Majesty most graciously offered support . . . and," he added after a studied pause, "his notable erudition."

James pursed his lips; his eyebrows wrinkled, and soon the two of them joined in hearty laughter.

"Henry," James said, "I can't decide who's the cleverer: my court fool, Archie, or you. So you'd have me play at theologian, ay? Beat old Abbot at his own game?"

"That might do it," Northampton said.

Only Northampton could induce him to fly with all speed to Lambeth Palace, there to interfere in a private matter—one that, moreover, had become a political liability. The truth was that James had taken the wrong side; at the time, he had no reason to expect the "nullity" to cause such an uproar.

Northampton was shrewd, but he was overlooking one important fact: James was not a Howard. What good would come from his arguing one rather than the other side of an issue which he had appointed a commission to decide? Why should James quarrel with the Archbishop?

Because, as Northampton was quick to point out, the Crown no less than the Howards would suffer by the suit's denial. Having involved himself, rightly or wrongly, in the dispute, James could not afford to lose. Nor could he tolerate his own Commission overruling him in public. He had no choice but to meet these Puritans, head-on.

"When do I go?" James said.

"If you could send word asking delay . . ." Northampton said.

He was observing James keenly, as if dispatching orders to the King came naturally. Pretending not to notice the affront, James wondered if Northampton detected anything in his eyes resembling the remoteness, the reserve, he felt at that moment. For all Northampton's cleverness and cynicism, he had betrayed in that unguarded instant —in the casual air of his remark, the light toss of his head—an arrogance that made him more vulnerable than James had thought.

The "nullity" had become as vexing to James as the Puritan resistance to it. He blamed himself for most of his misery; in the face of Carr's ingratitude, he had tried too hard to please him. Even so, the Howards had played a devious hand in the episode, and they must lose something in the long run. For now, Northampton need not know how deeply James resented them for thrusting the "nullity" upon him, need not suspect that James acted (as he would act now) not out of loyalty to the Howards, but in response to the unspoken challenge of his pesky Archbishop of Canterbury. James could not permit him to dissolve the Commission, lest, urged on by his Puritan admirers, Abbot fancy his mitre a crown.

"What of Overbury?" Northampton asked abruptly. "What will you do with him?"

"Release him, I expect," James said.

The question seemed curious.

Overbury had all but slipped from his mind until, a few days ago, Francis Bacon inquired about the charges against him. James said there were no charges, to which St. Albans had replied that Overbury was not a bad sort. Like Sir Edward Coke, actually, prickly but bright. James agreed, and was in fact ready to release him when suddenly the Commons rallied to his cause, perceiving in his fate the sinister influence of Rome.

Now, James explained, he was waiting for the clamor to die down; he would release Overbury when he could do so without seeming to appease the Commons.

"I understand that he will go to Muscovy," Northampton said.

"I have heard the same rumor," James said.

"They say he's been ill," Northampton said uneasily, for now he knew that James was tweaking him.

Overbury did not fit the King's notion of a convalescent; he looked too tall, too healthy, too self-assured to bow to common infirmities. "Everyone within the Tower walls is ill these days," James said, "Arabella included. I'll have Mayerne look in on Overbury. He's attending my cousin, and will be there today. Mayerne will cheer him up."

OVERBURY LAY very still on the stone floor, listening intently: apparently a visitor was on his way. It hadn't taken long to learn that the acoustics in Salt Tower permitted one to hear his jailers talking, even when they were gathered stories below. All he had to do was lie with his ear to the opening beneath the door.

In the early days of his captivity, the jailers were expecting Overbury's stay to be short, so the eavesdropping sessions left him much relieved. But as the weeks wore on, it was clear the jailers were misinformed; it wasn't Overbury who left Salt Tower, but his burly attendant, replaced by a more talkative fellow named Gervase Elwes.

Overbury wondered what day this was; it was hard to tell. The circular stone enclosure had only one small aperture some fifteen feet above the floor, so unless candles were burning the cell was dark. Beyond that, he had fallen into bad sleeping habits, dropping off for naps whose intervals were hard to judge, especially since Elwes liked to tease him about sleeping whole days away.

He thought it was about a month ago that a Dr. Forman had come to see him. The doctor had cleansed and bandaged his wounded arm, and admonished him to take care of himself for he had signs of fever.

"You require the best diet and thorough purgation," he had said, his brusque, bushy face suggesting that Overbury take heed. He recommended the services of an apothecary renowned for the effectiveness of his clysters. "Eat much fruit," he had added. "And take care to eat only the freshest breads and pastries."

The advice had struck Overbury as preposterous. At the time, he'd been confident of release. But several more weeks passed, with his fever rising. He grew restless.

"What will the charges against me be?" he said one day as the pain gnawed away at his patience.

"Disrespect to 'Is Majesty's the word," Elwes said.

"When shall I be tried?"

"Oh," came the answer, "likely never. 'Is Majesty'll turn you loose, I expect. Cheer up, now. We've a bright spot for you."

And so he did: Elwes passed Overbury a tray heaped with pastries. "Di'n't the doctor say t'would do ye good?"

The crusts were crisp and golden, with butter glistening on top, and sugar and cinnamon melted together most appetizingly; fruit filling welled through the crusts.

"Currant." Overbury beamed. "I do fancy currant tarts."

Elwes watched happily as Overbury devoured the pastries. "It's a friend who's sent 'em," he said, "and who'll send 'em each day, knowin' you're keen for 'em."

"A friend? What friend?"

"Oh," Elwes said, "I canno' say, not knowin', though likely 'e's a great one, per'aps 'Is Majesty 'imself wantin' to cheer ye up whilst things turn better for ye. Canno' say nuffing now, as your friend's amonylous."

Anonymous? What rot! The tarts came from Carr and no one else. Surely not from James. No, Carr had sent them sure enough, and they were a welcome gesture, given the fact that Overbury's letters to his family and friends had gone unanswered. He had begun to feel abandoned. Now he could look forward every day to these home-baked delicacies, and also to their heartening significance: Carr had not forgotten him, and was in fact merely biding his time before intervening at the most propitious moment.

The next few weeks were bearable, though the fever failed to abate and in fact grew steadily worse. Overbury was finding it hard to breathe; the fever throbbed no longer just in his arm but throughout his body. A doctor somewhere had recently written that the blood circulated within the body, which Overbury now believed to be true. He worried about the mounting episodes of delirium; he let no day pass without asking for an account of his symptoms. He had heard that many men set out on their journey to the block by talking in their sleep.

"Gervase, be a good fellow," he would say. "What I said whilst in my fever—was it funny?" . . . "Gervase, you rascal! You reported my fevered calumnies on the King to Weston. What did you tell him?" . . . "Gervase, you cunning bastard, I need more money to bribe you. Help me fetch money from my house."

Elwes cooperated with this last request, and after the pouchful arrived better food and occasional laundry were available. Neither did much good: Overbury was soiling his clothes because he could no longer hold food down.

The place stank most vilely, and even more so after he purchased the services of that apothecary, whose clyster loosed a spectacular and irrepressible torrent from his bowels. Even Elwes, whose senses were less keen than his prisoner's, lost his zeal for their conversations. And on top of all else, Overbury broke out in strange, large, excruciating blisters.

"Sir Thomas," Elwes said, wrinkling his nose, "you've got syphilis. 'Ow'd you get it in 'ere?"

"Gervase, you base cur," Overbury wheezed beneath the door. "Where'd you find that lunatic physician, in the pesthouse at Smithfield?"

He could see that he was losing ground. Carr had to help him now; perhaps Carr was the visitor whom the jailers were expecting.

Overbury had written a letter to Carr describing his condition, explaining that the family had not responded to note of his arrest. And, though it embarrassed him to think of it, he had written to James, begging forgiveness and promising to serve with distinction in Muscovy. Several days passed without word.

"Elwes," he rasped, "when will this damned 'nullity' be over?"

"Why, it *is* over, isn't it?"

Over? How could it be over, and him not released? "And yet no news at all?" he asked.

"Why, yes, Sir Thomas. We *do* 'ave news: my Lady Arabella Stuart, God rest 'er, 'as died this day."

"I mean of *me,* you sod!"

"Yes, sir," he went on, "died in 'er sleep, she did. Cold as a Norseman's cod . . ."

Cold. Of course. How had he failed to notice? Winter had descended through the tiny window without his knowing it. And he had lost much weight. Too much, which explained why he quaked perpetually, even when lying still on the floor. Ah, the visitor: Carr was arriving. Best not to appear too desperate or thin! He hefted himself to the darkest corner of the cell, where he stood, leaning with an air of insouciance, out of reach of the light as the door swung open.

" 'Ere's the King's physician 'imself," Elwes said with his typically insensitive inflection as he ushered in a group of men.

Carr was not among them.

"My name is Mayerne," one man said. "We met once. Do you recall? In Bath."

But of course: Bath, Carr, James, Cecil, Lady Arabella.

"I've been asked to examine you. By His Majesty."

The physicians wanted Overbury to lie down; he did not have the strength to protest vigorously.

"I take it you've just examined Lady Arabella," he croaked with an ironic smile.

Mayerne appeared to nod, but the faces were blurred.

Overbury must have fallen asleep; he awoke startled, as if he had forgotten an engagement of surpassing importance. He begged Elwes for as much light as possible, by which he wrote furiously, pausing only when his strength failed. He penned letters to Carr, Bacon, James, Queen Anne, the Archbishop and—yes, he was that desperate —Lady Frances Howard Devereux. He begged forgiveness and help from all, and issued promises of altered ways on his part.

"Gervase!" he called out. "Gervase, here! Here's a guinea—no, two guineas—just for delivering these few letters. That's a goodly sum, you villain. Take it, but please . . . please! I need help. Deliver these. I know you've been too busy, or forgotten some of the others. Make sure with these. It's important."

The grey half-light of morning came, of what day Overbury had no idea. He knew only that he had to hold on a little longer, to trust Elwes, to trust Carr, who, though he had not answered his letters, had only yesterday added a venison pasty to his gift of currant tarts. Just to hold on, despite the fever, the hunger, the blisters, the thirst, the appalling stench around him.

Just to hold on: was this beyond his endurance? Carr! Robin, now!

He was so young and incredibly beautiful when they met. It had taken much courage to touch him that first time. Overbury was giving the lad his archery lesson; they were in the upper courtyard of Edinburgh Castle. The morning light of a clear day brightened Robin's already uncanny eyes, and his shock of blond hair. Far below in the distance, the Firth of Forth lay clear in its shoreline, and the land between was well defined: like a dream, he had thought, before—as if to answer the uncertain yet trusting expression on the boy's face— he kissed him, and then took him there in the open of the Royal Palace at Edinburgh in the dazzling sun of a morning he would never forget. And yet the sloe-eyed Lady Frances did not understand: he felt no jealousy.

"No!" he shouted now. "You don't understand!"

Overbury began to fear madness.

Fevers could bring on madness, one sign of which was random reminiscence. He had to resist the flight of his fancy, to nail his thoughts to the world of second causes, the world that Francis Bacon and he believed in: the real world.

Since the inscriptions on the wall were real, Overbury saw fit to study them. Thieves, Jesuits, martyrs had occupied this cell, and had left tokens of their ordeals—prayers, dates, insignia, sad tales cut in stone. Where were they now? What word of them or of himself could penetrate these thick walls? Perhaps they had all been dragged to Bedlam from this place. He would write another letter introducing himself to the warden of Bedlam as a poet, student of law and connoisseur of wines.

No. Escape was a better idea. He could see that earlier prisoners had tried the same, and their efforts would guide him: certain bricks were loose and easy to remove; the holes they left formed a ladder.

He felt weary. It seemed that his every sinew was torn in the crucible of the greatest endurable pain. And yet he started his climb, removing the loose bricks as he went.

He climbed, slipped back, climbed, rested, fell, and climbed again. He struggled upward, scraping, tugging at the bricks. Since his efforts were unfitted to stealth, it was not long before Elwes heard him.

"Sirrah!" he called to him. "Sir Thomas! I told ye it ain't no use, sir. The windows is all grated 'ere."

Now it was warm; the breath of winter had suddenly stilled, and the next time Overbury fell he shed his clothing. This would cool him off and make climbing easier. He ascended with renewed vigor, urged on by Elwes, who, joined by his fellow jailers of Salt Tower, was becoming boisterous in his derision.

Overbury remembered a Sunday afternoon when he and Gibbs had gone out to watch the inmates at Bedlam.

He was near the top of the ladder. With a lunge, he caught a firm grip on the grating and pushed. The metal plate moved; it was definitely loose.

With every last bit of energy he could muster, he pulled himself up, straining upward from the purchase of his right foot. He perched himself with his elbows wedged between the narrow casements of the aperture.

He was met by a splendid panorama: the once-familiar river, the South Bank, the Bridge far in the distance. Sunlight glittered on the Thames, and the air was fresh from a cool autumn rain. The river was so deep, so brimming with such wonders of life, so self-sufficient and serene, that for the first time in many, many weeks Overbury felt at peace—grateful and secure.

"Oh, Lord," he cried out, "how manifold are thy works! In wisdom hast thou made them all; the earth is full of thy riches."

Elwes and the others found these words from the Psalter wonderfully amusing; though they did not know it, Overbury had guessed why. He had no need now to grapple with that grate, loose or otherwise. He was back with Gibbs and the other Londoners, enjoying an afternoon's distraction at Bedlam; he understood—shared in—the amusement.

But the fingers were tiring; Overbury breathed deeply, trying to restrain his laughter as, slowly at first, then more hurriedly (for he could sense the flood of hilarity from within), he descended.

"Oh God, Gervase," he pleaded a moment before his fingers lost their grip, "don't make me laugh."

Then his weary sides quaked with the laughter he had struggled too long to contain: all strength in his fingers disappeared as quickly and completely as water through a sieve.

VII

Mayerne's report was shocking: first Cecil, then poor Henry, and now Arabella. James dreaded having to tell Anne, who would doubtless blame him; she had begged his forbearance from the moment Arabella's hopeless escapade became known. And now another Royal Stuart was dead—like the Queen of Scots, the victim of Love's mortal shaft. It was pitiful that James had to deal with her so mercilously; she had erred only by giving way to feelings admired in others. Pitiful, yes, but James could not be blamed for her descent into madness and death. Elizabeth had been wise enough to see that, while her signature sent Mary Stuart to the block, her cousin had pursued that destiny from the moment she impetuously crossed into England.

James had treated Arabella as best he could, short of surrendering the claim of his heirs to the throne. Her motives were innocent, he knew that, but had she burgeoned with a child of that love for William Seymour her good intentions would have been no help to Charles. The heads of those high but not highest claimants to the throne had not rested easy on their shoulders since the Wars of the Roses.

The primary agent of Arabella's grief was the Countess of Shrewsbury. It was she, and not James, who planned that mad adventure, arranged for Arabella's disguise, provided the means of their secret marriage and escape, set the meeting place for the newlyweds on the far side of the Channel. And yet Arabella, safe in France but fearing for her husband, who had missed the appointed hour and place of rendezvous, turned back to Calais to look for him. From that moment, though William eluded capture, she was doomed as surely as Lot's wife.

She was lovely, naïve and vulnerable. James should have visited her, or answered her pathetic letters. He had intended to. Though he could not accept blame for her death, he knew he would grieve for her with an intensity equal to Anne's.

Now James sifted for the last time through the letters Arabella had sent him from the Tower: a passel of complaints, confessions, regrets, apologies and pleas for mercy from a distracted mind:

"I would never have matched with any man but my husband, and must have lived all my days as a harlot, with Your Majesty's condemnation . . ."

"I am the most penitent and sorrowful creature that breathes . . ."

"I can get neither clothes nor my mulled wine nor anything but the most common diet . . ."

"I am sick even unto death, and yet no word from Your Majesty . . ."

James retied the letters and put them away; he was dallying to avoid the unpleasantness of seeing the Queen. It would be better to call on her and have done with it.

But before that, he had to speak to Carr about Overbury. Mayerne had found him gravely ill, though neither he nor his colleague, Dr. Edwards, was very clear on what was wrong with him.

"He's delirious," Mayerne said. "Hardly recognized me, though not long ago we spoke together at length. At Bath, it was."

"He imagines everyone to be his enemy," Edwards said, "as if all his friends wish him dead."

"What friends?"

"He raved about many. My Lord Rochester, Northampton and . . ."

"Yes?"

"He did protest that Your Majesty despised him . . ."

James inquired into Overbury's other symptoms, but learned little more. Edwards said that Overbury was emaciated.

"He had a multitude of blisters about him," Mayerne observed.

When James asked what the blisters indicated, the doctors were evasive: they had not made a thorough examination, the lighting was poor, the King had asked only that they look in on Overbury, many interpretations were possible . . .

"Then what is your inconclusive judgment?" James asked.

"He is dying," Mayerne said.

"But of no particular malady?"

Either they did not know or would not say.

James related the news of Overbury to Rochester, explaining that, while he wanted to release him immediately, the Commons was still protesting his imprisonment. Overbury must wait a while longer.

"Visit him," James said. "Take Bacon with you. Tell him we'll have him out in another week or so. See he's moved to good quarters, and look after his diet."

To James' astonishment, Carr refused to go. "Let him rot in the Tower," he said.

"But, Robin," James said, "it was I whom he raised from a rum-soaked sleep in the midst of night. It was I whom he insulted by refusing the appointment to Muscovy. Why is it you are the angry one?"

"Let him stay in the Tower until he shows himself more humble," Carr said.

This was a side of Robin that James had not seen before; the handsome face was twisted in rage.

"But the man is dying," James said. "Surely that is sufficient humility for any man."

"Let him die. He has written a poem calling my Francie a whore."

James opened his eyes in feigned outrage. "Have you not heard the vile ballads they sing about me?"

Carr would not be put off.

"Then Overbury must write another poem," James said, "extolling Francie's virtue—a companion piece. Or better still, an epithalamion for your wedding. Don't you see, now that the 'nullity' is over, his opinion is a trifle."

Carr was adamant. Here was an odd distemper of the times: ordinary men were inordinately sensitive to words, perceiving insult in the mildest rebuff. One could not deal with men in the common way. Religious fanatics seemed to have turned the commonwealth upside down, to have infected it with melancholy. James must see to it that his schools of medicine raised up a modern Galen to look after this London malady. Nowadays, if one averred a wrong opinion, he was not merely drunk or disagreeable, but a heretic or fool. Put him in chains. Off with his head.

Sometimes extreme measures were necessary. But only a king was above constraints of passion and self-interest, and so able to judge fairly. When one subject dismissed the physical person of another—and him an old friend—simply because of an untoward remark, why then a wise monarch must beware. Melancholy had seeped into the vital organs of the court.

"I had thought you summoned me on more weighty matter," Carr said "What of my request for Cranfield's appointment? Do you support his new Book of Rates? I had thought that, with the failure of the July Contract, we might look to your needs with new devices . . ."

This was Northampton talking; all Carr lacked was the gold snuffbox and the air of complacency.

Lionel Cranfield was Northampton's creature, a promising man with a shrewd understanding of commerce. A commoner, he had amassed a fortune in only a few years by securing the King's charter for alum, salt and pepper, the price of which items had since tripled. With the profits, Cranfield—along with the Howards, who had recently taken him into service in the Exchequer—had entered into several land purchases.

Cranfield had an uncanny sense of timing. When it was obvious to all that Cecil had no hope of survival, he sent forward an attack on the little beagle's impositions policy. It was a devastating document, daring (after all, Cecil's policy was also the King's) yet poised with facts, dates, figures and alternatives. Parliament angrily rejected the customs policy on constitutional grounds. Cranfield went the Commons one better by claiming the impositions were neither favorable to English merchants nor sufficiently lucrative to the Crown. The man had a genius for politics and making money.

"Have you studied Cranfield's accounts?" Carr asked.

"Casually," James said. "What do they mean? Or should I ask Northampton?"

Naturally, Carr missed the point; encouraged, he launched into a political analysis of the report. "The old Book of Rates makes foreigners our equals," he said. "We must make our laws more fair to Englishmen, and less so to merchant strangers, especially the Dutch, but the French as well. I . . . we propose a three-quid duty on shipments from abroad, which will bring in more money than our impositions. For the Dutch take more money out of England than we get back. Besides which, if you consider that we shall soon have revenue from the sale of titles to our new baronets . . ."

For all that, it was one of Carr's most lucid presentations, though now he appeared to have forgotten his next point, pausing to check his notes. Carr wanted James to patent a new post for Mr. Cranfield: Surveyor General of Customs. For his £200 stipend, Cranfield would produce—Carr consulted his notes again—no less than £21,150.

"You're sure of the figure?" James said.

"Precisely," Carr said.

James was not so sure, though he had no objection to providing Cranfield with an income. He decided to discuss the appointment with other members of the Privy Council. Northampton was waiting about, and James pretended interest in his opinion of the new office. Predictably, the wily Earl reserved judgment, but allowed that Cranfield was worthy of the highest esteem.

"He purchased a new carriage for me," Northampton said. "Persuaded the maker to furnish it with elegant Moorish upholstery and curtains at no surcharge. His ideas on import duties are interesting, in that Parliament is hostile to the present policy."

It was well into evening when James finally went to Anne's suite. She had already heard about Arabella. She had been weeping, but now she looked at James angrily.

"What are you going to do?" she said.

James tried to embrace her, but Anne turned from him ever so gracefully.

"What about Seymour?" she demanded. "Will you allow him to attend the funeral?"

Her question was without preamble, and too direct. James knew the answer, but he knew also that Anne was unprepared to listen to it. She had suffered enough for one day.

As for William Seymour, James would write to him (or, more likely, have Carr do it); he'd be told that he need no longer fear reprisal from James. But he could not expect to return to England. To the Countess of Shrewsbury he would say nothing; she had played her trump card and posed no further threat. Given her defiance of the Privy Council, James could not actually set her free, but now he could let her roam at large within the Tower walls and provide her with all the amenities due her rank.

Anne complained that Arabella's death resulted from James's mistreatment, which reflected his cruel hatred of Catholics. "And I am one," she cried. "And Arabella, too, but she was more frail. You could not expect her to survive with such treatment, and no friends."

Just then, James felt very tired. He strode to the open window, breathed deeply, and let the rain touch his face. "Is there Scots malt liquor within reach?" he said.

His request caused Anne to cease her railing; she sent one of her ladies to fetch the King a drink. James quaffed several long, warm draughts, swallowing the liquor slowly, letting it burn his tongue and the back of his throat.

The English practice of shortening words had produced many vulgarities, of which "whisky" was by far the worst. The Scots word for this marvelous substance—*uisgebeatha*—was much more expressive: the water of life. Scots malt liquor warmed the weariest man to the bone marrow; its aftertaste was as welcome and as lingering as morning mists on highland lochs and moors.

James turned from the window. The Queen stood by the fireplace, tall and willowly and beautiful as ever.

"Anne," he said, "let's take a stroll in the rain in Green Park—pretend Arthur's Seat is just there in the darkness."

She responded at once, quietly but firmly. "I want to know what you intend to do about Arabella."

He had come to answer just that question, but now he knew that tonight, tomorrow and the day after that would be too soon. She and Henry had loved Arabella. Now, with Henry dead and Elizabeth married and gone, Anne had focused all her griefs and disappointments and loneliness into this one agony.

James would say nothing of the orders that he had passed to Francis Bacon, orders which were perhaps even now being discharged. "Let her be carried," he had said, "when it is dark up the river to Westminster Abbey. Deposit her in the vault beneath my mother, next to Prince Henry. I forbid all ceremony. Her innocence of malice matters not, for my subjects know that she died outside of royal favor. Let them read the burial service quietly. Afterwards, send news to her parents, the Earl and Countess of Hereford. Let no marker be engraved."

Greedy for even the briefest of comforts, James took a long swallow of malt liquor and stared out into the cold, black rain. Cecil, Henry, Arabella: with such a summer and autumn behind, what could winter have in store?

He decided not to take a walk in the rain after all.

ANN LEFT the door ajar to let the fresh smell of the rain and the river mix with the scent of burning wood. Sir Ralph had for once agreed to stay for supper, and Ann was busily preparing the first course.

"Would you care for another buttered rum whilst I stir the soup?" she asked.

"I like spiced rum on such cool nights," he said.

So she filled his cup.

"Interesting developments in Whitehall these days," he mused.

"Yes." She smiled, proud of the aroma exuding from the kettle: beef broth and sherry, fresh potatoes, onions, salt, pepper, rosemary, sugar, and her special addition: five fat leeks, tops and all.

"King's ready to take a few heads," Sir Ralph said. He was already pleasantly drunk, having stopped by the Mitre for a pint or two on the way over.

"And why not?" Ann said. "Most of the heads there seem to rattle anyway."

He hadn't heard, but it didn't matter; Ann was pleased to see him relax tonight—to see him tippling—like a normal man about the house. What mattered was that he was there and not in a big rush to go somewhere else. She served the soup and sat down.

"Bacon's the one to watch," he said. "Say, where's the lad tonight?"

"At a friend's," Ann said happily.

"A friend's? When will he be home?"

"Tomorrow. Eat your soup before it gets cold. It's a special one."

"But what friend? Where's Davy? I wanted him to be here."

"Eat your soup. He's with Inigo Jones."

"Really?"

"Yes."

"Why is that?"

He tasted the soup, and she could see that he liked it. He fell to eating.

"Inigo Jones, ay?"

"Yes. He wants to teach Davy how to draft plans for buildings. Thinks the lad's clever."

"He is clever," Sir Ralph said loudly. "But he's a bit young for architecture and that lot, I'd say."

"Mr. Jones thinks one must start early. He's put the boy in school."

"School? Which one?"

"St. Paul's."

"When?"

"Oh, a month or so ago."

Ann ladled more soup into his bowl, poured another cupful of hot rum, and returned both to the table. Sir Ralph was more talkative than she had ever seen him, which she found slightly annoying.

"The soup has leeks in it," she said, "and sherry."

"Excellent," he said, "but you've more important talents. Like Davy, I mean. You know, you're quite famous in your own way. Women talk about you at court. Say you won't accept all requests for service; some think it means that if you'll do a gown for them, they must be beautiful . . ."

Ann smiled.

"Is it so?" he asked.

"No." She laughed.

"So you will work for anyone, then?"

"But I can't. There are too many. I can't promise to design for new ones when I'm behind in my work for the ladies who were with me first! Can I?"

"So. You are lovely. A superb cook. Good mother. And loyal to your clients . . ."

"Yes. And now you must taste my excellent cottage pie, and these bottles of wine."

Ann placed three bottles on the table; one was made of glass, the other two of stone. "We must drink them in their proper order. Canary first," she said, pointing to the glass bottle, "then the Paris wine."

"Hmmm," he said, cradling the cool, stone bottle in his hands. "Yes, Paris. Excellent. Probably Mont Valérien."

"I don't know," she said, "but after with the cheese and biscuits we have the 'sillery' wine, which I've not tasted before."

"It's marvelous. We haven't had much shipped into England. How'd you come by it? It's very dear, you know."

"I got it from a friend. Who got it from a friend."

"If a man, I am jealous. If a woman, she is either very rich or very silly. One doesn't part with so rare a wine to no purpose."

Ann laughed.

"Well," he said, and it was hard to tell how serious he was, "which is it?"

"I'm not going to tell you," she said. "I want you to be jealous. But it came from a man I don't know—very rich—Cranfield, I think, a friend of Mr. Jones. No need to be jealous, as Mr. Jones was just being nice to me."

"Cranfield, ay? That would explain it."

"Explain what?"

"Oh, the wine, and why I've no need to be jealous of your generous friend. For some men, generosity is impossible; a rare wine is but a pittance to Cranfield. That man is the craftiest, busiest thief in England. He steals from everybody, and always with the magistrate's approval behind him. He maneuvered to obtain the license to import wine at the same time that he was buying up the wine-producing farms in England and Ireland left by Salisbury."

"Then you don't like him?"

"Why should I not like him? If King James likes him, who am I not to like him? He's one of the new men ascending with Bacon to power, mark me . . ."

The conversation was definitely lagging; Ann handed Sir Ralph the glass bottle of sherry, and for a time they sat with the wine and the soup. When Ann noted that it was getting colder, Sir Ralph put a log on the fire; as he stoked the embers, a blaze roared up. The mood of the evening was perfect.

"You know," Sir Ralph said. "I am a touch jealous."

"You needn't be," Ann said.

"Yes, I do," he said. "I have reason."

"Oh," she said, "please, let's not be sad or serious tonight. Have more of this rare wine . . ."

But he had finished with it and was already gone to fetch another cupful of hot rum from the kitchen.

"You've forgotten," she said, "we have the Paris wine to go with the cottage pie."

"In a moment," he said. "When you serve the pie."

He was ruining the mood that she had worked so hard to make just right.

"Please don't be moody," she said.

"Very well," he said, "not tonight. We'll not talk tonight. But I'd like a word with you soon, Ann, about you and Davy."

Ann waited for him to finish the thought: *and me!* But moments passed; he drank in silence.

"Ann," he said finally, "do you ever wonder what will become of Davy?"

"Oh, please," she said. "Yes. I try not to worry, but I wonder and worry about him. He's such a sweet thing, but . . . you said we'd not . . ."

Sir Ralph rose from the table again and drew her up into his arms. "Oh, Ann," he said.

She searched his eyes for the meaning of this sudden intensity. She felt alarm deep inside.

"I do love you," he said.

The words made her dizzy; she had not asked for his love—dreamt of it, yes, but she had tried not to burden him with her feelings.

He seemed so troubled by what he had said.

She kissed him earnestly, trying not to betray emotion.

"Don't you love me?" he said.

"Of course I do," she said.

Thinking she had caught his mood, Ann started to undress.

"That's not quite what I meant," he said, but he was after her soon enough, kissing her hard with a fervency unlike him.

She tugged at his waistcoat to remind him to undress, but he was coaxing her toward the fireplace.

She lay with the heat from the hearth on her face. He was trying to penetrate her, and though she offered no resistance—tried to help him, in fact—he faltered nervously.

"Oh, Ann," he said. "I love you."

"Your waistcoat," she whispered.

"Your lips are the most expressive, incredible . . ."

"Are not all lips alike?"

"Not at all. Most women have lips of only half the volume but twice the pressure of yours. I can't describe the marvel of them . . ."

Imagine. Her lips. What of his? She kissed him, pushing herself slowly from the floor. What an extraordinary thing for such a gentleman to say: "I can't describe the marvel of them . . ." And then she made sure that he couldn't, that he'd hush in the face of this marvel.

She'd not made love this way to him before—been frightened to, with him a gentleman and so reserved. But now she took his drooping splitter between the lips he had praised with such extravagance, and made love to him.

"I adore you, Ann," he said afterwards.

His eyes were fastened on her as if he had never seen her before. Somehow, she could not shake the feeling that he was sad.

"I really must go," he said. "I've got work to do."

"I thought you'd spend the night," she said, "with Davy gone. I'll make you a bowl of chocolate in the morning."

"Mmm, sounds marvelous," he said. "But I mustn't."

"What's wrong?" she said. "It's late now. You can work tomorrow . . ."

Now she felt cold. She slipped into her nightgown. She dreaded what he might say next, but it was not her way to deceive herself: she had felt uneasy from the moment he protested his love for her.

"Ann," he said. "I *must* go, but I *am* a touch disappointed that Davy wasn't here tonight. I had something to say to both of you. About Davy."

"Only Davy?"

"No. You, too. You know that Davy needs a more stable . . . background . . ."

"How more stable? He's in school now. I take good care of him."

"Of course you do. But he needs a real family."

It pained Ann to think that someone she cared for could think that Davy had no family. And yet a hint in what he said made her heart beat faster. Was Sir Ralph suggesting . . . proposing . . . that he . . . ?

"Think about it," he said. "Think about it."

As if, despite the legal question of her present marital state, Ann had given marriage no thought. With proper support, "nullity" was not impossible. And did she not now have that support with Master

Jones and the Howards—and Sir Ralph himself? Yes, but for now she said nothing.

"We'll talk about it soon," Sir Ralph said.

He left, and, as it happened, not a moment too soon. Franklin knocked loudly at the door as she was readying herself for bed.

Ann was reluctant to let him in; he was drunk, and evidence that she had entertained a male visitor was all around: half-empty cups and goblets, the aroma from Sir Ralph's pipe.

"It's late," she said. "Come back tomorrow night."

"No." He pushed his way in. "I've come to see you. Got to know the name of that great lady friend of yours."

"What lady friend?"

"You know, you wench!" he shouted. "The one that's had us kill Overbury."

"Overbury's not dead."

"He's dead and damned as well. Died earlier on this evening."

"But you promised . . ."

"I promised nothing," he said, cuffing her on the side of the face. "She paid and she got her due, and now I want to know who she is. She's that silver-haired Lady Rutland, isn't she?"

"No!"

"That's it. He was forever tormenting her. She's the one, I'll warrant!"

"No," Ann insisted. "I'll not tell you."

"You'll tell me," he said, "and now."

As he came at her, Ann let her nightgown fall away. Franklin paused, took the situation in, and leered.

"Oh, so it's that you're ready for," he said.

The stupid sod was too far gone to detect the signs of recent love-making. She finished him off ere he came astride her: one embrace, her knowing hand where men used to wear codpieces, his fool's notion of what women desired, and the ignoramus had filled his trousers. Ann was more disgusted with him than frightened; she'd handled the likes of him before. In no time at all, she'd rushed him, happy, out of doors.

As for the news he brought, that was something else again. And what of his errand's intent? He'd not learn the identity of Ann's friend from her. No, but she would not get off lightly: he would require a reason for her silence. She needed time to think. She could cope with Franklin if she but had sufficient time to think.

And that was only part of it. She could protect Frances, but what about herself? And Davy? Sir Ralph was right about one thing: Davy needed the love and steady surroundings of a family.

It was so hard to believe. Overbury, whom she had never met, was dead, done in, and partly because of her. How dreadful! How needless and stupid! Just when Sir Ralph, full of love and tenderness, seemed on the verge of proposing marriage.

BY THIS TIME, Frances had come to think that Forman owed his success to bribery. How else could he have brought off the virginity test so smoothly? That ordeal—with regiments of doctors and mid-wives poking about while heretic priests offered caveats from the liturgy and Scripture—was intended to embarrass her. Which it did. They let her wear a heavy veil over her face, but this proved no hindrance to their view, and in fact presented but another chance to calumninate the Howard name. A wicked rumor was bruited about court that the masked virgin examined by the Commission's experts was not Lady Frances at all, but a maid from Saffron Walden whom family henchmen had slipped in for the test.

Since this wasn't true, and since Frances was no virgin, she concluded that Forman had suborned the witnesses appointed to examine her. Means aside, the happy verdict was near unanimous, though one churlish midwife from Uxbridge abstained from judgment on grounds which she refused to put in writing.

The outcome of the trial was all the more fortuitous given the fact that, at the time, Frances was with child.

Clever Katherine Fine was the first to notice—only days after the Commission had declared for the "nullity"!—that Lady Frances persistently complained of ills that oft assail expectant mothers. Once Frances considered this possibility, she was besieged by symptoms forsooth to indicate the wisdom of an early date for the wedding.

"Robin," she said one day as a bleak November morning shrouded the land where it sloped to the River Lee and then upward to the hills beyond, "remember those days and nights in the summerhouse?"

Robin smiled broadly before kissing her; he remembered.

"My darling," she said, "we must hurry because of it. We must marry soon."

"We shall," he said. "In late spring. It's to be the grand event of the season. I've already discussed it with Jamie."

"It must be sooner. Next month."

"But nobody will be in London!" Robin cried.

"If we wait on the season," Frances said, "I fear we shall be parents ere we are man and wife."

She tried to make these words sound casual, with no hint of anxiety on her part, but Robin was obviously startled. Frances despaired at the doubts coursing through his mind, doubts nurtured by Sir Thomas Overbury (who would trouble her no longer).

"Oh, Robin," she said, embracing him, "I gave my love to you, and you returned it as if 'twere money lent by a usurer, and I greedy for that gain. Oh, we'll be happy, I promise! But we *must* marry in December. We can say that we desire our Savior's Nativity as the holiest, best time for the blessed sacrament of marriage."

"Marriage is no sacrament," Robin said. "Jamie says that only heathen think it so. Christ's sacraments are—"

"Sacrament or none," she put in, "we don't want our wedding and the child's baptism the same day, now, do we?"

"Are you sure you are with child?"

This remark was disheartening.

"Women know, my darling," she said. "I have to urge the early date on the family. Please don't make it difficult for me. Speak to Father. Or at least to Uncle Henry."

"Your great-uncle would be better," Robin said thoughtfully. "He seems to have a high opinion of me."

"Oh, he does!" she said. "And you must talk to Jamie again. I don't want to be a viscountess, since I'm already a countess. You are virtually Lord Chancellor and Secretary of State, with Cecil gone and Ellesmere ailing. Uncle said so. You must be an earl."

"Northampton said that?"

"Indeed."

"It is true. Except for St. Albans, I believe that James considers my advice without equal. I concede that Francis Bacon is intelligent, but he is not as firm as I . . ."

"But James panders after Villiers. We must not forget him; his way is made easy by the Pembrokes and the Queen. Now that Overbury no longer weighs you down with his insolence, you must be elevated to your rightful place as my equal."

Robin nodded thoughtfully. He seemed agreeable but apprehensive. "Villiers is a menace," he said. "Always the flatterer, hanging about . . ."

"He's a crafty one. Ambitious. He uses James. And we must deal with him. But *now* we must settle on a date, and you must persuade the King to elevate you. Talk to Uncle Henry. He knows how to manage these things. And remember, Christmas Day. That will appeal to James."

Robin consulted with Northampton, but she didn't know just how much that helped him with James. As the week fled by, she hardly cared. Only results mattered, and soon her hopes for Robin's elevation were realized when, in the ceremony of investiture, James handed him his own sword and buckler, naming him Earl of Somerset.

"And he promised he'd attend the wedding, with a handsome gift for you," Robin said.

"Only attend?" Frances said. "What of the Queen?"

"She's to remain at St. James, or journey to Greenwich with Prince Charles."

"Oh? And you accept this?"

Robin was too naïve, too generous and good, to perceive the insult.

"Sweet Robin," she said. "Do you not see how Overbury has damaged you in the Queen's eyes? Your love for James blinds you to her affront. If Queen Anne will not attend the wedding, who will?"

"But Jamie said she has not been feeling well. And Audley End is a fair distance away."

"Dear Robin, talk to James again. I know the Queen isn't fond of you, but she admires Uncle and will give in. Oh, do. I'll talk to Uncle. Tell James that we must have the wedding in London so the Queen may attend. The private chapel where I was married before is an agreeable place. And if James extends the invitations, we can expect a huge success . . ."

"I daresay," he said, and went off to see James.

Frances had work of her own to do: she must get her great-uncle to help with Queen Anne. That afternoon, she detained him for a private word after high tea. Without emphasizing details, she explained her wish for a December wedding, and told of her hopes for an unforgettable occasion. She admitted of one let to these hopes:

"For such a grand event, the Queen must be on hand. If she stays home, I shall be insulted. It will appear that the 'nullity' is . . . that she doesn't approve, affecting the friendship—as she does—of the Archbishop, whose religion is not like hers . . ."

She kissed him and stroked his beard. He held her face to kiss her in return, but his response was subdued.

"I don't know," he said. "It might be wiser to have a quiet wedding at Audley End, with those who wish to come—friends, family. Keep the air of celebration muted . . ."

"No!" She pouted. "Why, if the 'nullity' is not infirm, may I not marry in proper? I shall, for the Commission—"

"But, my lovely," he put in, "the Commission has placed no obligation on Queen Anne. Is it wise to . . . harry her?"

"Yes," Frances said. "If not wise, at least necessary. Tell her we love her, and look for her, and pray for her good wishes—whatever you must tell her—but please, dear Uncle Henry, without her we cannot have the grandest wedding anyone in England ever had."

He would do it. He did not actually promise, but he would appeal to Queen Anne. With the presence at court of Count Gondomar under the Queen's protection, Frances was sure that Northampton's direct approach could not fail. For the moment, the Crown's conflict with Parliament over customs and the wealth bestowed on Robin had overshadowed the return of the Spanish Emissary. But Frances knew that he, with Queen Anne's support, would press for marriage between Prince Charles and the Spanish Infanta, Henrietta Maria. Without the Howards' active help, this connection was unthinkable. Therefore, regardless of the Queen's feelings about Robin (and Frances could change these in time!), she could not afford to alienate the Earl of Northampton and the Earl of Suffolk.

Frances was pleased with herself. She knew that, were Sir Thomas Overbury even distantly in the picture, Queen Anne would stand fast against Robin, regardless of the risk to her influence with the Howards. That man had proved a threat to Frances at every turn. Had. Overbury was no threat to anyone now.

Dear Ann was of a different opinion about that; she was desolate after hearing of Overbury's death. As Frances suspected, Ann had hoped the poisoning would go on indefinitely.

"In doing him in, we've done ourselves in," she said. "They'll find us out, sure."

Ann worried about the conduit, this apothecary, Franklin. From what Frances gathered, he could do her no harm, since he knew nothing of her nor of the motive for the crime. True, he could implicate Ann, who might inform on Frances. But Frances placed her trust in Ann.

"Talk to Dr. Forman," she said. "He'll handle the apothecary, all right. And I'll send letters along, with plenty of money for him; I want to keep in touch with Dr. Forman, anyway. He's promised to cast my horoscope."

The deed was done, she said; there was money for all of them, and that was the fair end of it. Overbury and the "nullity" were behind them now, and if the past months had been trying, then the months ahead would be all the more welcome.

For Frances, all things were falling into place.

Almost all things.

Not that she had trouble persuading her mother to help with the hasty wedding: "December?" Lady Suffolk had said without hesitation. "Why, excellent. I had feared the Commission might announce the banns for the second marriage before their judgment of 'nullity' in the first." And, when asked about the proper site for the occasion: "Audley End? Yes. Or Cambridge, for my husband, your father, is Chancellor of the University, so we have a wide choice of altars, choir lofts and inns for the guests. Saffron Walden would serve as well. The Bear Garden. Location is a matter indifferent."

Her father, less accommodating, was aggrieved by his daughter's insistence on the December date: "I've not yet cleared the balance owing on repairs and redecorations at Audley End," he said. "You might as well know that I owe above twenty thousand pounds on the arrangements for the King's Progress last summer. And I owe Cranfield at least twice that sum . . ."

"Indeed?" Lady Suffolk said. "And why is that? I had supposed that he might owe you, since he's taken over most of your farmlands."

"It isn't that I owe Cranfield, personally, but him and . . . many associates who . . ."

"It only makes sense," said Lady Suffolk, "that you should be in

Cranfield's debt, since you brought him into service, and he works for you."

Suffolk ignored his wife's sarcasm, and turned to Frances. "Why not marry in the spring, like everyone else?"

Lady Suffolk sputtered outright, though the question was not at all amusing. "England's Lord Chamberlain cannot see his hand before his face," she said.

Soberly, her father studied first his wife, then his daughter. "I see," he said after a pause. "Our Howard lasses make it a custom, do they?"

Frances protested at this unkind remark. "I love him, Father," she said. "I couldn't help myself."

"Naturally not," her mother said.

"Ah, well," her father said. "I am—*we* are—in some measure to blame. I did not like your going to London whilst your husband—"

"So this scandal redounds on me, does it?" Lady Suffolk said.

"I said *we* are in some measure to blame. The Howards have too often used the beauty of their women for—"

At just that moment Lady Suffolk bowed, and moved swiftly as if to depart. "I have heard this sophomoric disputation before. I shall not subject myself again."

Her husband tried to detain her, but Lady Suffolk fled up the stairs. Frances felt sorry for her father, who looked very tired and sad. For a time, he sat regarding her, not in anger, but in cold silence.

"You are certain of this?" he asked finally.

Frances nodded.

"And it must be a grand occasion, I assume?"

"Oh, please, Father," she said. "It will make things right again. We can forget this awful year, with Prince Henry dying on our hands, and Catherine's folly, and Essex and the 'nullity,' and now me. Let's be gay. With Robin, we'll be the happiest, most powerful family at court."

Suffolk smiled—warmly—and nodded his concession. "Perhaps we shall," he said. "We'll surely be the most sought-after. With but half of our worried creditors alone, we could fill Westminster Abbey."

This parting note of self-pity did not bother Frances. If all went well, her future was now bright indeed. And if that were so, then the Howard family would fare well, too. Given the King's wonted generosity, she thought it fair to assume that Robin's ascension to earl would soon be embellished by gifts of land, charters, jewels, money. Since Robin was not one to forget those who had raised him to eminence, the Howards would be able to cultivate him slowly, deftly, surely. They'd bring him inevitably into the Queen's camp, and to the cause of the Spanish Alliance.

With Overbury out of the way, only opportunity lay ahead; neither Frances nor her parents nor any Howard had cause for worry . . .

Preparations for the wedding occupied most of a cold and wet December. When Yuletide was upon them the weather cleared a bit, and now even Lady Suffolk expected the wedding to be successful. Celebrations would last the entire twelve days of Christmas, beginning with Bishop Andrewes' Nativity Sermon Christmas morning, with the wedding itself on the twenty-sixth (James had frowned on Frances' idea of Nativity nuptials). Feasts and revels, with as much ale and wine and rum and wassail as ever anyone had seen, would start before noon and end with a new masque by a different poet for every evening until Twelfth-night.

Much to the relief of her father, James, after prodding from Carr, insisted that the wedding be in Whitehall, and that he be permitted both to bear all expenses of the occasion and to give away the bride. Frances knew that once Inigo Jones was involved in the masques the design alone would cost the earth, and there would be food and drink and entertainers to pay for, too. "And we must have a sea fight on the Thames," James had said one day whilst in his cups. With the Royal Navy participating, her father said, they had best look after the Crown Jewels, for the costs would truly soar.

James had also sent invitations printed with his own seal; as a result, such an influx of respondents had befallen the Howards that it was doubtful now that the guests could all be squeezed into Westminster Chapel.

"Everyone in England will be here," Robin crowed one night at Suffolk House, where the Howards were gathering for the occasion.

"So it appears," Northampton said. "And a few from Spain as well. And Count Gondomar is known for his generosity."

This pleased Robin. "Jamie has sold more Crown land to add to our coffers," he said. "And we've got Sherborne, and now Somerset House . . ."

Northampton smiled. "You'll be needing an indigent uncle as a house guest. Perhaps I'll bring James along, and we'll go a-hunting."

"No," Frances said. "Robin can't hunt until he learns to ride better. Remember what happened to old Bedford . . ."

They enjoyed that remark. It was a warm time, with carolers about; even the cold air was welcome. Frances had always loved the Christmas season: the movement of people, the badinage, even the drinking. This year it seemed more a blessing than before, with the friendly smell and sound of festive preparations in the air.

The day Frances became the Countess of Essex, she had worn her mother's wedding gown; now Lady Suffolk held that the same gown ought not be worn again so soon by the same party.

"Find another," she said to Frances, "perhaps one less frayed by overuse . . ."

Ann Turner was delighted when Frances asked her to design the wedding gown. Since the wedding was an affair of state, at Inigo Jones' direction Ann was again installed at St. James Palace, the center of activity. They spent many lazy afternoons in the Palace basement, with Ann taking and retaking Frances' measurements (which, God wot, she must have learned by heart months ago).

"Oh, Frances," Ann said. "I'm just so happy for you."

Frances planted a fervent kiss on her friend's full mouth. "Dear Ann," she said. "I love you. I hope that soon you'll find someone, too."

Ann smiled. "Perhaps I have," she said.

"You have? Who?"

"Why, Sir Ralph," Ann said, as if the answer were obvious.

"Winwood?"

"Yes."

"Oh," Frances said. "Him."

"What's wrong?" Ann said. "Don't you like him?"

"I like him," Frances said.

How could she not? Only yesterday the man had offered her the use of four of his fine horses. It seemed that with all their wealth the Howards could not find four horses among them presentable enough to draw Northampton's stunning new carriage, in which Frances would ride the short distance from Suffolk House to Westminster Chapel. And there was now no time to repair to the stables at Audley End. Winwood, overhearing their conversation and anxious to be of help to any Howard, had offered his string of carriage horses, which was, after the King's (and nobody wanted to trouble him for such a trivial matter), admired as the best in London. "They are most awfully fine animals," Sir Ralph had said, "and I'd be in your debt if you'd let them draw your carriage. I fear I've ignored them lately, poor creatures. They love to get out. So, if you'll do me this kindness . . ."

Northampton had accepted the offer at once. "Winwood's a comer," he said.

"I don't like him," Suffolk said.

"But we need his horses," Frances said.

"He's well connected," Northampton observed. "We must deal with him. We ought to be ready, should James give him a major post . . ."

"What major post?" Suffolk blustered.

Northampton didn't know. "Best to accept his generosity in any event," he said. "Once he's wedded the Countess of Rutland, he'll be the one to reckon with in London, wait and see . . ."

"He's to wed?" Frances asked. "Her?"

"So I have heard," Northampton said.

And yet here was sweet Ann, baring her hopes of marriage to the same man.

"Something *is* wrong," Ann was saying. "Please tell me. Have you an ill opinion of him?"

"Not at all," Frances said. "I quite like him, actually. It's . . . I . . . only, what of his feelings for you?"

"You are concerned for me," Ann said. "How like you!" Her startled expression melted into one of her most radiant smiles. "He has mentioned marriage," she said, "not in proper, but words round-about. Oh, Frances, I am just waiting. He said we'd talk soon about the three of us. What else could it mean?" Now she made to strut and talk like Sir Ralph. "He said, 'I love you, I adore you!' *Me!* Ann. Oh, be happy for me, Frances. I do so care for him."

Sir Ralph Winwood: what a despicable man! Frances smiled reassuringly, but could not think of a word to say. She wondered what cruelty in a man could unleash itself on such a lovely, helpless thing as Ann Turner. Tears of rage welled up when, at last, Frances escaped from that basement retreat. Sir Ralph Winwood: to think that his horses would draw the carriage with Frances in it to the event that Ann had done so much to make possible!

But what could she do? How could she tell Ann? And yet how

could she, after the love and loyalty that Ann had given without stint, not tell her? Worst of it was, had Ann refused to help Frances, and had Sir Thomas Overbury lived, perhaps Sir Ralph would not be making plans to marry the Countess of Rutland.

For had he not said that he loved Ann? Would Ann lie about that? If he did love her, why would he marry another? Were not men the same as women? Could ambition make men thrust love aside? Why had Sir Ralph so cruelly raised her to the highest pinnacle of hope?

ANN ENJOYED the weeks of work on the wedding gown. She had pushed most of the other pieces off on the helpers. Five of the basement apartments had been turned over to Inigo Jones, and he had brought in a dozen seamstresses and tailors. Ann was determined to finish this gown by herself: the sketches, the purchase of fabrics, braid, jewels—all of it. She gave no thought to the cost; her aim was to make the gown the most beautiful ever worn by a bride.

It was white: the whitest, palest, brightest that a medley of white taffeta, sarcenet, crisp and tiffany could be. She had layered the white fabrics to produce an illusion of whiteness rather than the mere color itself. The thin fabrics were more space than thread, but the spaces were designed, by the layering of these similar and yet different fabrics, to let light show through, to give the impression of stunning brilliance, as if light were coming from within the very thread.

The train flared from a braid of pearls held fast by a frieze of pennystone, then fell in ever more delicate splays of taffeta, sarcenet and tiffany, trailing into rivelets of fragile white which seemed to grow smaller by degrees, so imperceptible as to appear endlessly receding up the aisle of the church, under the lintel, and beyond. It would take twelve little girls on each side to keep the veil from touching the floor.

A string of pearls to match the headpiece, set in a bolder frieze, also of pennystone, would lift the famous Howard bosom in two graceful half-orbs of silk, the bodice almost transparent. The kirtle was absolutely without ornament; it was like a sheath of white taffeta, designed to provide for the bride's movement while clinging to her legs, leaving the impression of a solid white body against the dazzling white fragments of the veil.

Frances would wear her hair down over her shoulders; Ann was determined on this point, though she had had to argue with Frances about it. Gossipy dowagers would object to the loose hair (a sign of virginity) as in bad taste, with the "nullity" so recently over and all. But the effect that Ann was after required it: a once-in-a-lifetime, brief moment of unstained beauty not meant for this world.

Now, as Ann made one more check of every seam and fastening in the gown, she was startled by a voice that came from behind her.

"Thought I'd find you here," Sir Ralph said.

Ann was overjoyed; she had not seen him since that rainy night weeks ago in Southwark. She was busy these days, often away from the shop, and she assumed that he'd been busy, too. She ran to him, fair hurling herself into his arms. Despite herself, she wept.

"Oh, Ralph, I'm so glad you're here. I've missed you so."

He smiled. He had a nice smile: shy, yet manly. "Hmmm," he said, and she kissed him.

"See?" she said. "I *do* love you. Is there any doubt?"

"Then why so glum?" he teased.

It was early afternoon, and workers drifted in and out of the room, but Ann drew Sir Ralph to her with an intention that was unmistakable. They made love quickly and ravenously. It was the sheerest rapture of Ann's life, and yet she had not even removed her clothes!

"Where's Davy?" he said afterwards.

"At school," she said.

"Who will care for him when he comes home?"

"I've made arrangements . . ."

"With whom?"

"Well," she said, "one rich friend and a silly one . . ."

"Ann," he said reproachfully, "I'm serious."

She had no idea why he was so fussy: many of the boys boarded at school. She had arranged for Davy to spend a week there prior to Christmas; she was to pick him up betimes Christmas Eve, and they were to spend the holiday together. But for now she thought it best to let Sir Ralph do the talking.

"Ann, I'm worried about Davy," he said. "You know how fond I am of him. He needs a home, a true family. You understand?"

"Yes, I understand," she said, holding off tears of joy.

"Truthfully," he went on, "I've been thinking of marriage."

"My," she said, "what a coincidence!"

He continued without noticing her jest. "If I marry, as I believe I shall, I want to take Davy with me . . ."

Ann coughed: the breath had gone out of her, as if she had fallen, or a heavy object had struck her in the belly. "What do you mean, take?" she asked, dreading, hating, knowing for certain what his response would be.

"Perhaps," he said, "as you implied, you will marry, too. But even so, can you provide Davy with as . . . as . . ."

"Good a home?" she said.

"Yes. With as many opportunities . . ."

Silence. How could she answer that question? Was even her love for her own son now an offense? Was it unfair to keep him with her?

"Well, truthfully?" Sir Ralph demanded.

"No, Sir Ralph, I cannot offer him such prospects. Not even if I marry."

"Don't you see? I love you!"

"I can see that."

"I want him because I love you. I want a part of you always with me."

If only he'd not said that. It was not her way, not her way at all, but now it was impossible to restrain the inner swirl of loneliness and defeat. "And what part of you shall I have always with me?" she asked through bitter tears.

He waited for her to stop crying. "Nothing needs to change between us," he said softly.

Though such connections were common enough, Ann felt his remark unworthy and undeserved.

"Marriage will benefit my career," he said. "I think James will make me Secretary of State. You understand."

"Yes," she said, adding after a pause, "but St. Albans isn't married. Neither is Lord Northampton."

"I know," he conceded.

"Queen Elizabeth wasn't, either," she said.

"No, she wasn't," he said, "but it will be good for me—and for Davy—to get on with a proper family."

"You'll marry for Davy's sake?"

"Ann," he cried, "you're being most awfully uncharitable! No! Not only for Davy, but he'll be a beneficiary . . ."

"That's when a man dies, and you're not that old."

"I mean now," he said, "he'll have a home. Will you agree to it?"

"Agree?"

"This is what I came to find out. What I've wanted to discuss with you for some time. You've not been in for weeks . . ."

He sounded petulant; Ann wept again, but more in grief than bitterness. It was over between them. The end seemed even more incredible than the start of it. They'd not been together often, and yet in the months that had passed her whole world—the shop, her work, the ladies, Davy—revolved around him.

She had no regrets; there was nothing to regret. She was too numb to be angry, and he had given her more than she had ever had before. He had loved her, she knew that, so there was no need for anger or regret. But she would grieve for this loss.

Sir Ralph would marry a great lady: she should have guessed. He was an ambitious man, and no harm there. As for his wish to take Davy, and his keenness to have nothing change between them, Ann would see to it that no harm came there, either.

"Think it over," he said. "Take as long as you like. I'll pop in *de temps en temps.*"

"You will?"

"Often. As often as ever, if you like. So there's no rush. We'll not likely wed until spring . . ."

"When exactly?"

"May, actually . . ."

"May what?"

"First," he answered sheepishly.

"King of May, is it?"

Sir Ralph brightened when he saw Ann smile.

"Who is she, or is that a secret?" she asked.

"Not at all," he said, "everybody knows. She's one of your clients, in fact. Says you're the best designer in all London."

Ann nodded.

"Her name is Diana . . ."

"The Countess of Rutland."

"A widow, you know . . ."

"Yes."

"Fine person. Thinks the world of you. I've mentioned Davy to her."

"She knows about us?"

"In a manner of speaking. I've not been crude about it. But I assume she has guessed the nature of our . . . knows I'd not want Davy if I didn't care for you."

"And she doesn't mind?"

"Should she?"

An odd question: Ann would have minded, were the situation reversed. Why shouldn't they have children of their own? Make love of their own? Or was the beautiful Countess merely saying that Sir Ralph was cleverer than those aristocrats who frequent stews? Why shouldn't the Countess mind? Ann was a person, and Sir Ralph loved her, or said he did. Why should the two of them covet Ann's son? Why must she feel guilty in the mere possession of him for now? He'd be gone soon enough.

"She's beautiful," Ann said.

"Yes," he said, "and intelligent. Plays the virginal, you know. Sings like a bird."

Ann saw him to the door.

"About Davy," he said. "You will consider our offer?"

"Yes," she said lightly. "I'll consider it."

VIII

With Robin's wedding and New Year's festivities out of the way, the court returned to its usual infighting, divided now on the issue of calling Parliament back into session. If anything, the cleavage between ranks was more pronounced than ever, with the Howard forces going one way and everyone else the other. Having cultivated Diego Sarmiento de Acuña, Count Gondomar (a clever chap and a fair Latinist), the Howards openly urged relaxation of ties with France, more favorable trade agreements with Spain, the status quo in the broadcloth and alum industries, and Crown governance without recourse to Parliament.

"A session now means serious trouble," Northampton argued. "The Puritans will attempt to put limits on the Crown. Why do you suppose they've sabotaged our Great Contract?"

Apparently, no one but James remembered Northampton's opposition to Salisbury's July Contract. Northampton's self-confidence made subtle shifts of position all but unnoticeable; sometimes he could reverse himself completely without losing his composure. He had effectively defended the view that James could survive without Parliament, but perhaps not with it. He pointed to the sale of the peerage and of government offices, to the £6,000 rent due annually on the royal alum works in Yorkshire, to Cranfield's new tariffs, and to Bacon's clever plan to lease rather than sell unused tracts of Crown land.

The fortunate Howards now had a powerful ally in Robin, whom James had appointed Lord Treasurer of Scotland (a sinecure, inasmuch as the Exchequer in Edinburgh was flatter than the Salisbury Plain) and Lord High Chamberlain of England.

The Howards had thought that with the Countess of Shrewsbury in prison serious competition at court would wane if not disappear. In fact, opposition to Suffolk and Northampton was stronger than before Shrewsbury's fiasco with Arabella. The Earls of Pembroke and Southampton, Lord Ellesmere (he had escaped from his deathbed, though he had to ask relief from his duties as Lord Chamberlain) and their clever protégé, Sir Ralph Winwood, were formidable opponents.

"Your Majesty," Winwood said one day shortly after Twelfthnight, "we believe the situation in the Exchequer has deteriorated. Assets appear to have been diverted to private use. Above eighty thousand pounds cannot be accounted for at all. Debts roll up and no way is made to credit them. Your Majesty, seventy-five thousand people are out of work in the clothmaking industry . . ."

"Why so many?" James wanted to know.

"Continental tradesmen think our tariffs and restrictions offensive; they have stopped importing our cloth."

"Why? We make the best cloth."

"We once did, and could again, but the color of English cloth, they claim, does not hold fast and damages the fabric. Yet our new law forbids the export of undyed cloth, which used to be our mainstay. Now our textile industry depends entirely on proper dyes. Unfortunately, when the Crown purchased the alum works it absorbed Mr. Ingram's debts, while affording him an absolute charter. We must buy whatever he sells regardless of quality, which affects the quality of our dyes and thus the whole of our largest market."

"What is wrong with royal alum?" James inquired.

He was piqued by constant criticism of the plan to nationalize the alum works, which he had sponsored himself. Cranfield's old partner, Sir Arthur Ingram, the original owner of the works, was left in charge. True, he was guaranteed sales, but he faced penalties for underproduction.

"I admit I am no merchant," Sir Ralph said, "but I most respectfully put it to you that we have all been misled in this alum business. We urge you to raise the issue again . . ."

"Where?"

"In Parliament, perhaps. Or the Privy Council."

"Then you and your patrons think I should summon Parliament?"

"To see to Your Majesty's Exchequer."

"What do these churls care for my needs?"

"We are concerned about fanatics who drum up support in the counties," Sir Ralph said evenly. "But they succeed because Parliament is not in session, which fact is their pretext for treasonous attacks on Your Majesty, which we contemn . . ."

Winwood was skilled and well-prepared. He'd require a sufficient post in the government bye and bye: Secretary of State, but that would take time.

"Your Majesty," he said, "the Earl of Southampton, the Earl of Pembroke and my Lord Ellesmere wish me to inform you that, should you call a meeting of the Privy Council, they will enter evidence of gross improprieties and irregularities in the Exchequer, the alum works and the Port of London Customs."

All three enterprises were under Howard control, the latter two being run by Ingram. It appeared that rivalries at court were taking their toll on the old and lucrative fraternity of Cranfield and Ingram.

"Who would make the report?" James asked.

"With your permission," Sir Ralph said, "Lionel Cranfield, who asked me to extend greetings and to thank you again for making him a knight."

The Howards had brought Cranfield into government service, but now he was poised with a knife at their throats. James wondered why he would take so daring a risk; he was not one to act impulsively.

It was said that Cranfield had acquired most of his wealth by paying a seller of land one-half of his asking price. Then, after taking possession of the property, he would have his lawyers come forward with some real or imagined fault in the title deed. The harried seller, rather than face years dragging himself through Chancery courts while profits from the land went to his adversary, would settle for a small part of what was owed.

So the Howards had Carr, but they had problems, too. There was good reason why Winwood and the Pembroke faction were moving confidently these days: they had brought to court the most beautiful lad in Christendom. Even the Howards fell silent in awe when George Villiers passed their way.

Georgie was thinner, more ethereal than Carr, and more intelligent (though Carr's intellectual deficiencies had done nothing to mar his charm). Villiers' beauty was more like that of a woman: he had long, lithe limbs, smooth, slender fingers, pouting lips, large, misty brown eyes. His voice was slightly aspirate, and his face and demeanor made one know the torment of Narcissus: one must not be deprived of full possession when such beauty is near. The lad's presence produced instant perturbations of the flesh in James, who began showering Villiers with love and expensive gifts almost the day they met.

It was James's good fortune that Villiers, though born to a great and ancient family name, was virtually penniless. His appearance at court was made possible by a large loan from Ingram and Cranfield, who may have felt guilty for their treatment of Villiers' parents while wanting also to curry favor with the Pembroke faction, which had been looking for a lad with merits to match Carr's.

Having entered into several complicated negotiations with the combine of Ingram and Cranfield, the Villiers family found itself heavily mortgaged with many debts and no way to pay them. Within an astonishingly short time, they were left with nothing but a small rocky hillside on the west coast of Anglesey and a great name whose honor was now upheld only in the face and charm of a beautiful child whom they had sent to France a decade earlier.

Robin was jealous of Villiers from the start; he hadn't wanted Villiers at court at all, but he was livid when the King invited him to spend a few weeks at St. James following his appointment as Cupbearer and Master of the King's Horse. After a quarrel, James went further, making Villiers a viscount and Gentleman of the Bedchamber.

"It isn't right for a viscount to act as Gentleman of the Bedchamber," Carr said.

"You did," James said, "and besides he's not acting. He's a proper viscount, and performs with utmost fidelity."

Robin found this jape in poor taste.

"Laddie," James said, kissing him, "don't fret! You are an earl and Lord High Chamberlain and far richer than my Georgie . . ."

"You gave him land worth ninety thousand pounds!" Carr protested.

"Yours is worth more."

"But you dote on this English Albiciades."

"Alcibiades," James said. "Yes, I dote on him, but love you above any man."

Yet James's protestations of love were never enough for Robin; the more James fondled and kissed his Alcibiades in public, the more desperately Carr needed like treatment in private.

"Robin, he's only a lad," James explained over and over, to no avail. "I love him as a lad, a beautiful child."

"He's no child," Carr shot back. "He wears Venetian trunk-hose tight across the cods. When he walks, from behind, he looks like a pair of tongs."

James laughed. "He speaks well of you."

"Nails!" Robin spat.

"He's got nice legs, too," James said.

"God's nails, Jamie!" Robin shouted. "I didn't say he didn't. I meant how tight he wears his Venetians. You can see his splitter hanging there as plain as a pot."

It stood to reason that marriage would calm Robin down. The Countess of Somerset was acknowledged, even by women who were no friends of the Howards, to be the most beautiful woman in England. And James had more reason than they to agree.

The night after the wedding, despite Frances' objections, James conducted the newlyweds to their bridal suite at Somerset House, followed by a train of drunken courtiers singing lyrics and epithalamia appropriate to love-making. Campion (than which no modern poet could be filthier with taste) was there with his lute. When Robin had slammed the door on the revelers, James helped Frances off with her headpiece and curious veil.

Robin, well in his cups by then, appeared unconcerned by James's company. "Not to worry, Francie," he drooled. "He's the King, and we're his subjects, and he's given the wedding."

Lady Frances was reluctant to undress. James had given them much plate, Somerset House, £50,000 outright, and the twelve days of masques and revels, but she wanted him to leave. "Sing from outside," she said, and then to Robin: "Let him sing outside, and he can come in later."

"No," James said. "That wouldn't satisfy a court. We must have an authoritative witness, lest another Commission be called for 'nullity.' "

James had saved the most expensive gift for last: a necklace whose value London jewelers had declined to assay.

"It is rare," one had said. "Rare. The size of the diamonds! Their shape and perfection! The emeralds themselves, and the settings! I could not possibly say. It would be . . ."

"Fifty thousand guineas?"

"Easily," the man had said. "If the owner would part with it. The man who had this made—Your Majesty, I know no words to describe such wealth."

The necklace was the finest piece taken from the *Pearl,* a Portuguese ship under private sail which had foundered near Land's End and, under the salvage rights of the sea, been towed into the pool of London, where it now sat. Under the purview of Sir Arthur Ingram, the ship belonged to James, who had permitted Somerset and Northampton to conduct the sale of salvage for the usual fee of 10 percent.

Forgetting her state of undress, Frances took the necklace and held it up to the candlelight. "Oh, thank you," she cooed. "It's so heavy. Look, Robin. Have you ever seen gems so large?"

"He brought me the necklace," James said.

"Give Jamie a kiss," Robin said, and though Frances appeared suddenly shy just then, she complied.

"Now, on with it," James said, taking a pull from the tankard that for hours had been like an extension of his arm. "I'll be the witness no man may confute. Here's to no *maleficium,* no *frigiditatem,* no *impotens.*"

Never much of a drinker, Robin was now thrashing his way out of his jerkin and calling on Frances to obey James. She resisted by half measures while her husband, whose clothes were in an unsightly heap on the floor, tore at her undergarment in his effort to speed things along.

Frances was magnificently molded; for a moment, she stood naked for her King. James was drunk, too, but not too drunk to feel the lump in his throat. He had made love to many women, and Queen Anne was a fetching woman herself. But here was beauty—a strange luminosity of attraction, a physical perfection that set the brain on fire and left one short of breath.

And still it was Robin, and not James, who was jealous, forever taxing James for his dalliance with Villiers.

"Go on," James said, "make me a proper witness now," and as they giggled like coy children he left them to rejoin the revelers, sure that his problems with Carr were over—so sure that he had it in mind, in some degree, to control the Howards through Carr.

He proved mistaken. Robin grew more restless than ever, more greedy, more jealous, more demanding. He was furious that James appointed Villiers to the Privy Council.

"This minion only uses you," he said the day before the Council was to meet on questions posed by Sir Ralph Winwood.

"Robin, Robin," James pleaded. "What do you want from me that I've not given? I have pillaged the kingdom so that you might have nice clothes, fine food, excellent wine, elegant houses, horses, land, buildings, companies, ships, riches beyond your poor Scot's imagination. Parliament sets her teeth against me because of you, but I give more. Would you rob me as well as England of all I have? What do you want?"

"Your happiness, Jamie. I hate to see him use you."

James asked advice of Bacon, who, himself hoping for appointment to the Privy Council, was struggling to retain support of both court factions. "Carr's half mad with jealousy," he said. "Did you see Shakespeare's *Othello*?"

"I was in Twickenham at the time," Bacon said, "but I liked the tale when first I read it in Giraldi . . ."

"Robin is possessed by Othello's 'green-eyed monster,' and I his Desdemona. This makes poor Georgie his Iago—though a lovelier villain is beyond fancy."

"He *is* an attractive young man," Bacon said.

"How does one convince another of his love for him?" James asked, as if thinking aloud.

"Impossible," Bacon said. "One persuades by rhetorical devices, but conviction lies in the hearer."

"Hmmm, you are right."

"Some techniques are more persuasive than others. Boiling in oil almost never fails."

"It would ruin Robin's complexion."

"You've tried bribery . . ."

"Yes, and pandered for him, intruding on the 'nullity,' and the wedding, too."

"Perhaps you must try another tack, Your Majesty. You might be more rather than less severe, more demanding and formidable. Give

Villiers more, not less: make him an earl. Love him more joyfully in public more often."

James leered. "Ah!" he said. "You *are* shifting to Pembroke and Ellesmere."

"Not at all," Bacon said.

"You'd best take care," James said. "Pembroke is in tandem with your old nemesis, Coke."

"I admire Coke," Bacon said blandly. "Occasionally, I disagree with him. Don't you feel he's doing better, now that he's on the King's Bench?"

"He's in my hair less often," James agreed, "but you've not answered my question. What do I do about Carr?"

"Your Majesty," Bacon said, "love is a disease that no physician will treat, much less cure. I am your most humble servant, but must stand mute."

"You won't help me," James said. "You won't budge off center."

Bacon took this rebuke in stride, answering quietly. "I suspect that you will know what to do about the Earl of Somerset when you decide what to do about the Howards."

"Then you must think this meeting of the Privy Council important . . ."

"Very. It is a shame that no one, myself especially, will be able to understand the issue."

"Evidence, you mean," James said. "The issue is simple honesty."

"Perhaps. But the ledgers are frightfully complex . . ."

"You have examined them?"

"Rather tried."

"And . . . ?"

"Difficult. A mess, really. Someone's made off with eighty thousand pounds or more. Discrepancies all round. The Puritans will see the rise of Anti-Christ. Simple greed or incompetence, I suppose . . ."

"And yet you favor a new session of Parliament?"

He did.

"You're in touch with them," James protested. "You know them. They'll want to hang me."

"Not even Coke would argue that they have such power. They'll settle for a strict accounting and household reforms."

"I'll have no Puritan scabs snooping about in the pantry."

247

Bacon smiled easily; he had won his point. Immediate improvement of the situation with either Parliament or the Exchequer was unlikely.

"You're moving into Pembroke's camp," James said.

"If Your Majesty wishes," Bacon said.

"What if I appoint Winwood Secretary of State. Will that satisfy you?"

"It will satisfy many. The Howards might object, and I favor my nephew, Salisbury."

"A Howard?"

"Inasmuch as one Howard is a .Cecil."

"How about you? Will you accept Winwood, though the Howards object?"

"Yes."

"Yes, what?"

"I infer from conversations that the Howards would view his appointment as an affront."

"To whom?"

"They prefer young Cecil, or Carr himself. The Spanish Emissary believes Winwood too rabid a Protestant."

"Well, he is not. The Spaniards think my son-in-law is too rabid a Protestant, too. They think all Protestants are too rabid; we may be fighting another war to stay Protestants, rabid or no. Winwood is not rabid."

"But so Count Gondomar deems him."

"And so the Queen never ceases to inform me. But I asked you. Will *you* accept the appointment—that is, gladly—as if 'twere wisdom incarnate?"

"I will, since experience has taught that your wishes are at least as wise as the man who conforms to them. And Winwood is an intelligent man."

Knowing the interview to be at an end, Bacon bowed and started out of the room.

"You are with the Pembrokes now, and no denying it!" James called after him.

The Council meeting was one of the stormiest in history. Cranfield made his report, which Suffolk promptly dismissed as calumnious: "Sir Arthur Ingram has done an admirable job as Comptroller of Customs in the Port of London." he said, as if oblivious to the fact that the attack on Ingram was aimed at him. "He has increased the rate of duties on every article crossing the dock."

Lord Ellesmere dragged himself to his feet. "The rate has gone up assuredly on every article, but what a pitiful few articles seem to cross the docks from those teeming decks we see in the harbor. Everywhere porters stumble over each other in their haste to dispatch their booty. Materials invoiced on ships disappear ere they slide from the deck. One thinks it is the moisture in our air, perhaps. Except that I daresay I have myself purchased this day in Piccadilly a tun of Rhenish wine which matches the description logged on the *Pearl,* but was never received in—"

"Liar!" Carr shouted, leaping to his feet. "Base liar! The law provides a fee to His Majesty's servants who handle his boo . . . ships salvaged under the law of the sea!"

"So I was told forty years ago," Ellesmere began, but Villiers had already interrupted him.

"Indeed, sir," he said to Carr, "but the percentage applies to the whole of His Majesty's shipment, to the gross debarked, receipts of His Majesty's supposed . . . *servants* . . . notwithstanding."

Robin was not the most sensitive of men, but he caught Villiers' acid tone, and began moving toward him. During his ten years in France, Villiers had become the total master of his rapier; Carr was no better with a blade than he was with a horse. Apparently sensing that Carr was on the verge of issuing a challenge, Northampton took the floor.

"My lord," he said to Villiers, "have you perchance documents showing such anomalies?"

The Earl of Pembroke, his voice shaking with rage, begged leave to speak. "Persons and privilege aside," he said, "a serious deficit exists. Every Tom o' Bedlam knows we've had problems with imports and exports. And now a scandalous condition in the broadcloth industry has put tens of thousands of good Englishmen out of work.

"Many of you here know that I admired Lord Salisbury. Didn't always agree with him, but I remained silent as he led us toward these impositions. But now, with new men and new rates and new charters and the sale of new titles, Crown land, seafights on the Thames, masques, revels, gifts, weddings, divorces—the kingdom is simply on her knees! We sell nothing, make nothing, yet purchase or give away all! It is not possible to borrow forever, or to ignore our poor creditors forever.

"Yes, it grieves me to say we do have evidence. It grieves me even more to show it . . ."

Pembroke waved, and three men trundled in with their arms full of ledgers, packets, sheets and boxes.

"Whose accounts are these?" Suffolk stormed.

"Yours," Ellesmere boomed. "Cranfield's."

Suffolk and Northampton exchanged glances; Cranfield looked decidedly uneasy.

Slowly, Northampton rose again to speak. "I would be grateful if someone would tell me who is charged with keeping the Commissioners informed of deficits, however small."

The immediate target was Cranfield, but neither he nor anyone else responded.

"Your Majesty," Northampton went on. "I've not looked at these documents, but I am constrained to inquire how my knowledge of them would help me vote on this question of summoning Parliament. If the babe is slightly singed, do we hurl him into the flames? What support will Parliament give us before suggesting that we part with our heads? The Puritans are in a nasty mood—intemperate fanatics! To call them into session now will not improve one piece of English broadcloth, nor make one sale abroad. No, but the counties will elect vile Puritans, to everyone's—most especially England's—woe."

Effective: he argued against the Puritans, whom few Councillors loved, allowing the question of £80,000 belonging to James to slip from sight.

Archbishop Abbot and the Earl of Pembroke remonstrated with Northampton, but one could see from their faces that they knew their cause was lost, at least for the present. When defeat loomed up in the form of the final vote, Villiers lashed out angrily. "At the very least we must have a thorough inquiry into these charges. I beg Your Majesty to appoint a commission of undisputed fairness . . ."

The idea bore the stamp of Pembroke and Ellesmere, and had likely been laid out as their most effective response to an unfavorable vote. Northampton and Suffolk were furious; the opposition, far from retreat, was opting for a state of siege.

James cheerfully agreed with Villiers: his wife protested that her wardrobe required immediate attention, and the £80,000, after all, belonged to him. "Have you someone in mind to head the Commission?" he asked innocently.

Villiers trumpeted his response as if announcing the results of the investigation before the panel had even been named: "Sir Edward Coke!"

Who in the kingdom would publicly argue against *him*? James had to wrestle with the muscles in his face to keep from grinning like an idiot. The commission was soon appointed and charged; even Northampton had to go along.

Dusk had fallen by the time the meeting ended. James decided to wait for the members to disperse before asking that his carriage be readied. Archie, the court jester, was underfoot, making faces of pained abandonment; he had heard of the planned festivities and wanted to go along.

"Did you eavesdrop on the meeting?" James asked as the royal carriage dipped from the courtyard.

"I attended disguised as a fool, and went unnoticed," Archie boasted.

"Clever," James said.

"Yes, for the other fools went disguised as people."

James smiled, but he wasn't in the mood for Archie's knavery.

The trip from Westminster was short but cold and windy. By the time they reached Cockayne's house, it appeared that everyone else had arrived.

Cockayne was an unattractive fellow, wide of girth, who perspired too much whether the season was warm or cold. Now he scurried forth, greeting James with a fawning, gap-toothed smile, and ushered him into his comfortable old half-timber house, where members of the Privy Council met the King with bows. They looked to be in good spirits.

James had lingered at the Palace hoping that the tension of the meeting would dissipate in the gaiety of the first few tankards of dark beer. Now the Lord Mayor led him to a huge tun of wine that had been rolled out.

"Try this," Cockayne said. "It's called 'sillery.' "

James tasted the wine, looked at it in surprise, then finished the cup. This drink was almost as pale in color as German wine, but it was infused by a myriad of tiny bubbles, which greatly enhanced the pleasure of partaking.

"Can one mix it with ale?" James asked as the Lord Mayor promptly refilled his cup.

"Your Majesty may," said Cockayne, "but no one else would dare."

Cockayne was obviously relieved that his reception was moving along well, that most members of the divided Council had shown up, and that King James himself had come.

While the Lord Mayor was not precisely one of Northampton's spies (at least not so far as James's spies were able to discover), he was a close friend of Ingram, and his house was elegantly furnished by gifts from the Howards. He had invited the Privy Council to a feast hoping for a favorable outcome of the meeting. Had Ingram and the Howards fared worse, he might well have required a scrivener's loan to pay the reckoning for a wake: a dynasty done in.

But the gathering was festive. Even Pembroke and Southampton were enjoying themselves. Perhaps they meant their assault as a warning to the Howards, and were secretly pleased to have avoided an irremedial breach in the court.

James was enjoying himself, too. "Sillery" wine made one giddy, pleasantly so, and the King decided it must never be mixed with ale or any foreign substance.

Villiers appeared, and James leaned forward for a kiss.

"How nice of you to provide the wine," Villiers said to him, rather obviously ignoring the Lord Mayor, who tactfully glided away.

"It's not my gift," James said. "I'd not tried this wine before. It's from the Mayor."

"Is there a difference?" Villiers said. "Most of the wine now in London came off the *Pearl,* did it not? And doesn't it therefore belong to you?"

"Georgie!" James said, giving him a juicy kiss on the lips. "Be nice. You were superb today. So assertive! So . . ."

"Cunning." Carr had stepped up to finish the King's remark.

"Well-informed," James said, annoyed.

"He's not well-informed at all," Robin said. "He merely affects what Pembroke tells him."

"Listen to this Tom-cony," Villiers said, "who parrots—not at all well—the worthy Corinthian that last he talked to . . ."

"Talked to, did you say? Your aim is not so high," Robin said. "If you'll bend over, I'll try that product you're at such pains to fob off."

The exchange had been hearty, but before anyone—before even James, who was standing next to them—had time to grasp what was happening, much less to intervene in any way, Villiers struck Robin hard with his open hand full across the face.

Robin stood, his mouth open in surprise rather than pain; the stroke was heavy, as one could see from the long red marks which now were slowly disappearing in the flush of his anger and embarrassment.

The room fell silent. Only Northampton moved, hurrying from the entrance to the orangery at the far corner of the room.

Villiers stood tall and lean, ready for the challenge that everyone expected, to be followed by the departure of the two parties betimes the next morning for the Netherlands. James had no intention of permitting the two of them to fight a duel, and yet he was too fascinated to interfere at the moment.

"Sire," Villiers coaxed, when the sounds of restlessness in the company were heard.

"My lord," came the riposte, "you know the law, I presume . . ."

Now it was Villiers' face that reddened, but his voice did not weaken. "Honor requires but one course."

"And the law but one," Carr said, turning to James. "Any man who strikes another in the King's presence shall have the offending hand stricken from him . . ."

This was so; Coke, who was standing close by, smiled and nodded his head ever so slightly in the affirmative.

Villiers glanced at James in alarm, but to his credit stood firm and silent.

"Is it not so?" Carr demanded.

"Hmmm," James said.

"It is the law," Carr said.

Here was a piece of chicanery: Northampton had taken up study of the grain in the floor timbers. Bacon, Ellesmere—no one to help his King.

"Sir Edward?" James said.

"The Earl of Somerset is correct," Coke said. "Either the offended gives way or the offending hand must go."

"There, you see," James said. "The law is flexible."

"I am not," Robin said.

"But, Robin, you aren't hurt!" James chided.

"The law speaks not of pain but only of offense and withdrawal. I shan't withdraw."

"It's over, Robin," James said, calling for a tankard of ale. "Enjoy yourself. Here, I excuse you both."

"You can't. He's attacked my honor—called me a thief, in effect." Robin trembled in deadly earnest.

"You'd have his hand chopped off for a cuff on the cheek?"

"The law will have it, and I, too," Robin snapped.

"Like Shylock of Venice, you'll have your pound of flesh, is it?" James said, alluding to a play he'd not seen.

"Yes," Robin said.

At last Villiers spoke. "You are a coward," he said. "The course of honor is still open to you."

And then Villiers hit him again.

"Georgie!" James cried. "Whatever . . . ?"

Now Sir Edward and the others were laughing loudly: Villiers had struck out without warning, but awkwardly and without effect, with his left hand. Nearly missing his adversary, Villiers spun himself around in a full circle. In the midst of the confusion, Archie hurled himself high in the air in repeated but unsuccessful attempts to match Villiers' pirouette, pretending chagrin and desperate fatigue as his leaps slowly lost energy.

Carr looked first at James and then at Northampton; he seemed to be trying to read Northampton's thoughts. James had the strange picture in his mind of Villiers, like the unfortunate lass in Shakespeare's bloody *Titus Andronicus* (he *had* seen that one), spending his life with two stumps where his hands used to be. But now it appeared that this idea was too preposterous even for Carr, whose silent colloquy with Northampton's eyes had ended his brief infatuation with the law.

Robin sent a swift hard fist into Villiers' face, which was awash with blood ere he landed on the floor.

"You see?" Robin said, grinning down at him. "There's more than one course open to gentlemen and Christians."

Perhaps the Councillors laughed in surprise, for, God wot, Robin was not a witty man. Or they may have wanted to signal an end to the nasty exchange, which could have led to ugliness enveloping them all. The sudden gaiety seemed to satisfy Robin, who, taking it to be at Villiers' expense, was smiling brightly, with white teeth, blue eyes and earring a-twinkle.

Villiers' friends helped him from the room.

"Too much 'sillery'!" James said. "Our Mayor's hospitality's too blame."

That would do for now. Well and good. But James was concerned: about Robin's response to accusations on his handling of the *Pearl,* about his jealousy, about Robin himself. Now James remembered Carr's ruthless dismissal of Overbury in the Tower: "Let him rot there!" he had said. He had reason; there was always a reason. But those callous words rang true to Robin's sudden attraction to the law's letter: "The law will have it, and I, too." Chop off any hand that offends me. Make that two.

Was it possible that he had miscalculated Robin's character? Perhaps there was more to him than the slightly stupid, innocent, beautiful Scot plaything that he had loved and loved still. Perhaps, like his friend Northampton, Robin was a man to fear and watch.

AT LAST, Frances had what she always wanted: a husband to match her own worth. She and Robin were the brightest stars in the courtly firmament, invited to every important banquet, every auspicious gathering, every state function of any consequence. Often they received more than one invitation for the same evening. Robin was happy; though from time to time he grumbled about some minor tempest between himself and James, he was getting along well with her family, especially her great-uncle, and seemed to have their affairs in hand. Frances liked to have leisure to dally and shop at Britain's Burse, where she had learned to spend huge sums of their new fortune. Because of the awful summer London had been through, almost no one left the city that winter, and she was all the happier to be enjoying Somerset House in the center of activity.

It took her weeks to write notes of appreciation to those who had remembered the newlyweds with gifts. Good treatment was customary for such as she, but the generosity of the guests was awesome. Northampton said that not even Princess Elizabeth and Frederick had been so handsomely endowed.

London's Lord Mayor sent many articles of plate, and so did Gondomar. The East India Company, the Virginia Company, the Merchant Adventurers, the Farmers of the Customs, the Association of London Merchants, the Stationers Company, the Merchants of the "New Exchange" (with which title the shopkeepers wanted to replace Britain's Burse)—people Frances had never met socially sent extravagant gifts of silver and gold plate. Sir Ralph Winwood gave them a basin and ewer of remarkable beauty; Sir Thomas Lake brought six heavy candlesticks worth at least £1,000. Sir Robert Carey and Sir Robert Mansell gave a clever set of fire-shovel, tongs and bellows, with chimney set and grate of solid silver to match. Sir Fulke Greville sent a drinking cup of solid gold. There were warming pans, basins, ewers, pots, vessels, gloves, rings, tapestries, lockets, seals of the most extraordinary heaviness and quality, many set with precious stones. The Lord Privy Seal (her great-uncle) presented a single plate assayed at £1,500, then added a sword for Robin with a hilt of curiously wrought gold interlaced with silver; Robin said the work alone must have cost the earth, and the precious metal was wonderfully heavy.

Catherine and her husband sent them the most admired of the tapestries that the first Earl had collected for Hatfield House; its edges were of spun gold. Even Archbishop Abbot came to the wedding with a copy of the Book of Common Prayer in a jeweled binding of Moroccan leather, and though he may have meant this token, presented to Catholics, as an insult, that didn't change its value; King James, who had long coveted the volume for its curious binding, offered Robin £500 to have it for himself. Her father gave Robin four riding horses, a medal struck from solid gold bearing the Earl of Somerset's coat of arms, and £100,000 sterling: "Now all I need," he mused, "is to borrow it back to pay the interest on the money Carr's already lent me."

The newlyweds were well situated; and one mustn't forget the generosity of King James himself, which exceeded even her father's. Before their marriage, they'd been well off; now they were wealthy, the richest young couple in England.

And the wedding celebrations themselves were greatly admired, with old rivalries melting away in the warmth of Christmas carols, decorations, masques and wassail bowls.

Not that the twelve days went off without worry and embarrassment, as when James elbowed his way into the bridal suite and refused to leave, and Robin pretending the while to think his intrusion good fun. Old Bishop Andrewes had caused uneasiness, too. She had thought him a friend of the family, and was pleased to learn that he'd deliver the Christmas sermon at Westminster Chapel, the day before she and Robin were to marry. Since Bishop Andrewes was famous for his witty sermons, it was possible that Frances imagined his words more clever than he meant them to be. Yet he was on the "Nullity" Commission, so it seemed passing strange that of all the texts in the Old and New Testaments he should take for his sermon this one in special from Isaiah: "Behold, a virgin shall conceive, and bear a son . . ." And it seemed strange, too, that he should fix his sharp eyes on her when he said, "The Jews see no virgin here, for Isaiah's word means only a young woman," as if intending a veiled conceit of that maid from Saffron Walden. But in designing the wedding gown, dear Ann had done her best to dispatch ungenerous rumors that often accompanied hasty marriages. The shift that Frances wore the next day was curiously stitched and gossamer-thin so to display the bride's slender midriff. It would have been impossible to guess the truth. When she knelt beside Robin, and Bishop Andrewes solemnized the marriage, she knew her suspicions to be mere fancy. The Bishop beamed innocuously as he pronounced them wed, and Frances left the imagined insult at that.

She gave herself to the pleasures of freedom, wealth and true love. She forgot about Essex and the "nullity," forgot about Overbury, spent money, enjoyed city life, met poets and artists and architects and emissaries, and doted on her husband to excess.

Hopeful of the future, she visited Dr. Forman with as much information about Robin as she could gather without arousing his curiosity. Dr. Forman was glad to see her—thankful, he said, for her loyal correspondence (she saw no reason to deprive him of a share in the Somerset windfalls). He cast their horoscopes, giving a full account of the effects of heavenly bodies on their lives. Judicial astrology was a vexing science, full of lore and antiquated words. Patiently, Dr. Forman put the truth of the stars in such language as Frances could understand. She learned that her marriage to Robin would last forever! They'd not suffer as others had through war or ruin or long separation; nor would they go childless (truth to tell, this last judgment was less weighty than the first, for her pregnancy was by now no hardship to perceive). She had not thought to let nettlesome questions intrude on their friendly interview, but when Forman ventured this last opinion the reply was on her tongue ere she had time to think: "Will Robin be the father?"

"Assuredly," Forman said.

"I am with child," she said.

He beamed. "I am delighted!"

"Truly, it could be yours," she said.

"Sweet child," he said, "take solace from my word. It is my misfortune not possibly—*ever!*—to be a father."

Her surprise must have shown in her face, for, appearing amused, he explained that his condition in no wise lessened the value he placed on the beauty and pleasure of women. She believed him sincere, and wanting no intrusion on her perfect sense of the future with Robin, soon departed, leaving as a token of her trust in his sincerity £20 and a gold ring set with a large ruby.

Hoping to share her good feelings with Ann, who had been in frightfully dismal spirits lately, she asked the coachman to cross the Bridge to Southwark. The soft rain on the carriage top made her drowsy; she tucked her head against the leather backrest and thought of her new baby: just five more months. She should have asked Dr. Forman if it would be a boy or (as she hoped) a girl. It would be better for the second child to be a boy, when Robin was riding better. Now Frances wanted a girl-child to fuss over, to mold, to teach how to dress and how to be a fine young lady.

The cold weather had broken; even the wind had lost its bite. Frances sensed spring in the air. This season in London would be the best ever; she and Robin would see to that. They'd invite everyone, even those who pestered the Howards at every turn. Even Ann would come round to her old self.

Frances assumed that news of Sir Ralph's betrothal had reached her friend, for she'd looked wan and distracted for weeks. She'd taken on new clients as well, which surprised and disappointed Frances. The shop was crowded these days, with mercers, ladies, seamstresses and porters pushing about in close quarters. The more frenzied activity became, the more Ann seemed to like it. She fell ever more silent and serene; often her great blue eyes seemed to drift off to ponder some reassuring article or scene.

"Pardon, mum," one of the helpers would say, "the stitching in this gown, should it be thus or so?"

"Sorry to bother you again, mum . . ."

Though Ann was never sharp with them, she went no further than to answer each question singly before she turned away as if recalling some forgotten task.

It was past time for Frances to speak to her, to tell her that she needed a good friend, and that Frances intended to be as loyal to her as she had been to Frances.

For a while, now, the carriage had not moved.

"What is it now?" Frances called out.

"We're in Southwark, my lady. Nobody's about."

Frances peered from the carriage window. This was strange.

"Perhaps Davy's sick," she mused half aloud. She'd return in a day or so.

That afternoon, Northampton visited Somerset House to talk to Robin about their marketing of the cargo from the *Pearl*. People were murmuring that Robin and her uncle were fetching too great a profit from handling the cargo. Ordinarily, such conversations were too dreary to be borne; Frances never ceased to be grateful that men busied just themselves with such loathsome burdens.

Ordinarily. On this occasion, Frances caught a few words that not only fascinated but strangely disturbed her.

The men had been discussing that endless investigation of the Port of London. Since Commissions could not exist without store of charges and denials (equally indignant), she would have thought this investigation, like all the others, routine. But it appeared this wasn't so. For some reason, Robin and Northampton were incensed by Sir Ralph Winwood's appointment as Secretary of State, which would not have been strange in itself. Since Sir Ralph was frantically Protestant, everyone expected the Howards to oppose him.

It was not the sense alone but the tone of Northampton's remark that was singular—and not merely singular, but unsettling. Ominous.

And yet it was more a fragment of thought than a remark. Nor did what she hear bear her great-uncle's special emphasis. On the contrary, its matter-of-factness seemed intended solely to calm Robin, who had been railing ferociously against Winwood. So exercised was he that Frances, who but weeks ago had sent a note thanking Sir Ralph for his expensive wedding gift, thought Robin unkind. As her thoughts drifted, Northampton's voice was suddenly arresting: ". . . serious, his hands full with this Tower affair."

No more than that. Someone, presumably Winwood, had his hands full. The Tower meant but one place: the Tower of London. But what affair? Why was it serious? Why should Winwood be in any way connected with the Tower? What possible connection could they see between Winwood and the Tower? Or between the Port of London inquiry and the Tower?

Frances could construe the overtones of the word "serious" without knowing precisely what Northampton had in mind. Had he merely meant that the investigation under Winwood might have serious repercussions for Howard interests, she would have thought no more about it. It was the sense of an understood connection between the Port of London Customs and the appointment of Sir Ralph Winwood on the one hand, and the Tower of London on the other, that filled her with foreboding. The Howards were unhappy to have Winwood and his lot ransacking their records and ledgers, as well they should be. But Robin and Northampton assumed that Winwood's investigation seriously extended elsewhere.

The elements fused in her mind, congealed like the colors in stained glass when they were melted together: Winwood, Ann, Forman, the Tower, *Overbury*. It was possible that Winwood's investigation—this Tower affair—involved Frances Howard Carr, the Countess of Somerset.

She could think of no immediate way to test Northampton's meaning. She could not shout across the library: Pardon, Uncle, what was this about Sir Ralph and the Tower affair? Sorry, Uncle, but would you kindly repeat, as I was artless in my eavesdropping? On the contrary, she perforce must hide all semblance of interest in the *Pearl*, in Sir Ralph, in the Tower, and in all three taken together.

And yet how would she manage that? For to her these elements— and a fourth, now, Ann's deserted shop—were suddenly the most important in the world.

She knew that this danger, like that lurking in Bishop Andrewes' Nativity sermon, might be no more than a phantasm of her mind. The Tower was full of people: prisoners, wardens, officers, turnkeys, workers of all kinds. Perhaps Sir Ralph had gotten wind of another plot laid by the Countess of Shrewsbury. Perhaps someone was stealing money from the mint.

Except that she sensed these explanations were no more than desperate hopes. She wasn't at all surprised by the news she heard the next day.

Arriving at Britain's Burse to have tea with Catherine, she found her sister excited, her cheeks flushed, and looking more attractive than she had in a long time.

"Fanny," she said, "why didn't you tell me?"

"Tell you what?" Frances said.

"Surely you know?"

"Know what?"

"Everyone at St. James is talking about it."

"I've not been to court for days . . ."

"Of course you haven't. Silly of me. Then you've not heard. Oh, I hate being the one to tell you. I was worried about you. I knew how much she meant to you . . ."

"Catherine! Who?"

"Why, your little seamstress. Mrs . . . ?"

"Ann? Mrs. Turner?"

"Yes."

Silence. Fear. Was it possible to ask even one question, when its answer was so dazzlingly, hopelessly clear?"

"Oh, my dear," Catherine was saying, "she's been taken. Arrested. Everyone's talking about it. The Countess of Rutland is in a fret. She left her best gown at Mrs. Turner's for repair . . ."

Frances tried to listen; she knew this news was important. And yet she mustn't show undue alarm, nor seem stonily unconcerned. Gossip. Here was the appropriate tone.

"How fascinating," Frances said. Then, "I mean, how singular."

Ann. Taken. The Overbury skein was beginning to come undone.

"Frances, don't you care? Don't you want to know what happened, what it's about?"

"Yes. Yes."

"Murder, Frances. Can you believe it? That seeming angel. They say she killed Sir Thomas Overbury."

"Who says that?"

"Why, everyone. The Countess of Rutland. The Countess of Denbigh. Everyone."

"Oh." No, more interest: even gossips would show more interest than "Oh." "Yes," Frances said, "but why would she want to kill him? I was just in the shop the other—"

"This is the strangest part of it. Some people say she had never met him."

"How perfectly silly. Why would a dressmaker—Ann Turner, of all harmless people—want to kill someone she'd never met?"

"For money. They say she must have been paid handsomely."

"I don't believe it."

"Neither do I. She was your friend! But she *could* have been paid an extravagant sum. And people do strange things for money."

"I don't believe it for a minute," Frances said.

That night, while Robin was sipping sack and complaining about the Customs scandal, it was all Frances could do to keep from crying out: Tell me! I must know! What is this Tower affair? Why is it serious? Why is Sir Ralph involved? Do you know of Ann Turner's arrest? Are the cases related? Robin, have you heard anything—anything at all in this connection—about me?

When she finally did speak, she constrained herself to muted tones. "Will it all affect us?" she said.

"In what way?" he said.

"Will we lose money?"

"Certainly not!" he said, as if offended.

The next morning, Frances readied herself to visit the shops at Britain's Burse. Taking Katherine Fine with her, she gave the coachman directions to the Strand. There she slipped Katherine a crown and instructed her to amble through the shops while she herself attended to an errand.

"This will be our secret," she said. "No one must know I've left the arcade."

Katherine took the coin and smiled saucily. "Yes, my lady. No one shall, not even I."

Frances strolled through the arcade and back again, taking care that no one noticed her when she hired a hackney coach.

"You must hurry," she said. "I've little time. Toward Blackfriar's, please. Then I've a second stop."

The driver was an insolent Cockney, with a foul-looking mouth full of tobacco juice and not many teeth. But he knew how to handle horses. Frances thought the carriage would shiver to pieces as they hurtled toward the Bridge. She took fast hold of her seat. People flung curses after them as they raced by. Within moments, they were in front of Forman's tenement, the horses stamping and Frances trying to catch her breath, not because of their plunge through London's streets, but because deep inside her a shapeless dread was swelling: the danger that had befallen Ann might even now be threatening her.

"Mum?" the driver called out.

The churl had not so much as climbed down from his rickety perch. "We can sit 'ere all day if you'd like, mum," he sneered. "I've nuffing else to do, you see. But if you'd like to go some'ere else, you'd best tell me where."

"No," she said, "I must call on someone here."

She was grateful to find Dr. Forman at home, but when she moved to pass beyond the vestibule, he blocked her path.

"Dear Frances," he said, "you must get away this moment. Don't ever come here again!"

Frances was surprised and humiliated to find herself attempting to push her way into the house. "I must see you," she said. "I'm desolate with worry."

He let her step into the hallway but no further. "I know," he said, taking her in his arms. "I was trying to find a safe way to contact you . . ."

"Safe?"

"You're not safe here any more. You must go now. The authorities are watching me . . ."

"They always watch you," she said, hoping that the meaning she perceived was not the one he intended, giving him a chance to refashion it if it were. He was a perpetual offender of medical statutes.

"Dear Frances," he said, "this has naught to do with my medical practice. Surely you are here because you know the danger. You know about Ann?"

"No," Frances lied. "I know she's been arrested. I'm worried, and . . ."

"And?"

"There's Overbury."

"Yes."

"Then it's true."

"Yes. She's likely in Newgate by now."

"That awful place! Poor Ann. What can we do?"

"Very little, I fear. *You* can get away, for now. Stay away from me. Try to save yourself. I'll do what I can."

"What will happen?"

"You mean what can they find out."

"Yes. That, too."

"They'll question them, try to break them down. They've got Franklin, too, you know. He's the one they'll work on last. They'll have all they can get from the others, which they'll use against him. Weakness cries out from him. Poor wretch! He's the one deserves our pity. He's nothing. Less than nothing."

"How did they find out?"

Dr. Forman seemed startled by her question. Her eyes had grown used to the darkness, and she could see his eyebrows flicker.

"I don't know," he said. "It was only a matter of time before they did. Likely someone's silliness did us in."

"You knew they'd find us out and yet did it?"

"Why, yes," he said, again as if the question had surprised him.

"But why?"

"You asked for my help. Did you only do what you did because you thought you'd not be discovered? I warned you to make sure you'd surrender all to have your desire. I could have told you, had you asked, how temporary are these stratagems. They are most satisfyingly effective, and their goals are delightful, but temporary. And what is not?"

It was no good answering him. It was too late for that: because she had not asked him! Still, mad as he was, he was trying to comfort her.

"You're not implicated yet," he said. "Fly from this place. Enjoy what you have gained now. Pray to the eternal brothers, as I've taught you, to prolong your pleasures as long as possible."

"I've forgotten their names," she said.

"They will not mind," he said. "Go now. I'll find means to contact you. You'll know what to do when the time comes. Don't come here again until I tell you it's safe. And do not go near Ann Turner."

He opened the door to the vestibule and peeked out. "Who is your most trusted servant?"

"Katherine," she said. "Katherine Fine."

"The younger one, yes. Now hurry. Hurry." As the carriage rocked down Fleet Street toward the Strand, Frances wept. She had time; he had promised her that. How much time no one knew, not even he. This depended, not on Forman, not on the stars, not on the eternal brothers, but on the slim frame of Ann Turner, whom Frances must now abandon.

Perhaps by now the authorities knew everything. But had not Forman promised her long life, accompanied by Robin, the two of them together, unhindered? And that she would bear children?

She could talk to Robin. She could hold out for a day or a week or a fortnight, perhaps even longer, but if she didn't hear from Forman within a few weeks she'd be compelled to talk to someone. And who was left whom she could trust, and who could help her?

Who but the man for whose love she had risked everything that she possessed, and more?

IX

He was glad to see winter pass.

February had been merciless, so cold the chamberpots were emptied with insufficient regularity to suit him; nobody wanted to go outside. The cold, damp Palace stank. He strayed from the fireplace in his suite only seldom and reluctantly. Anne was in a foul temper most of the time. As the weeks wore on with bitter winds, freezing rains and, finally, a foot of snow, he settled in for the duration, comforted with Robin, Georgie, plenty of ale and sack, an English translation of Boccaccio's *Decameron,* and the more scurrilous poems of Campion and Donne.

Bacon had kept him abreast of sentiments among the likely leaders of Parliament, should the King decide for a new session. Had it not been for an improbable sequence of events in the far-off Tower of London, the winter might have passed in quiet reflection disturbed only by the gnawing sense that the Crown was—baronets, rented land, alum works, the *Pearl,* all of it—£3,000,000 in debt, and still spending far more than it was taking in. He needed help from Parliament; Bacon, Winwood, Cranfield, Ellesmere and the Pembroke entourage were growing restless with his delay.

Until this odd bit of intelligence demanded everyone's attention.

An insignificant turnkey in the Tower had been caught taking a bribe, which usually meant only that he had refused to share the proceeds of his craft with his superiors. Ordinarily, such incidents wouldn't come to Sir Edward Coke's attention, and never to the King's. In the prisons half-hearted discipline was the rule. Since jailers were not well paid (when they were paid at all), their lapses were understandable and overlooked. If they became too flagrant, offenders might be punished by temporary inconvenience—a fine or reprimand, nothing permanent, never the loss of a job. For who would replace them?

So the attention to this case was singular from the start.

Sir Ralph Winwood brought James the first report: someone along the line had grown suspicious. An offense had occurred which had more to it than the customary extortion of a prisoner's money. This happened only if the person in charge feared withholding the evidence more than its disclosure. By risking a minor charge of collusion, the official informed his superior, thus to assure himself against indictment on the more serious charge.

In an effort to elude punishment, a jailer had sought to turn his examiner's gaze to another part of the prison, to a well-known man who had died in Salt Tower many months ago: Sir Thomas Overbury. " 'E was done in, 'e was, an' it's everyone knows it, too," the man said to the Lord Keeper. If he had been left in the lockup himself for weeks after that, it was not because the charge against him was serious (for, in fact, his plan to avoid all punishment worked), but because, amid the charges and inquiry that followed, he slipped from mind.

"What do you think?" James asked Sir Ralph.

"I urge you to insist upon the fullest inquiry," he said.

Winwood was proving effective as Secretary of State, and James liked him.

"Another investigation?"

"I fear so, Your Majesty. But it could be handled as a criminal case, by ordinary means."

This being so, it was Bacon's job, as Attorney General, to handle the investigation. Predictably, Bacon was not satisfied with the ordinary course laid out for such cases; he tried to shift responsibility to Coke, whom James, at Bacon's behest, had just appointed Lord Chief Justice of the King's Bench.

Bacon and Coke had never gotten on well. They had been candidates (two unlikely ones at that) for the Lord Chancellorship at the time James appointed Thomas Egerton, Lord Ellesmere, to that post. Now Ellesmere was in poor health, so James was not surprised to see their competition stir again. Bacon's earlier strategy was to maneuver behind the scenes, reminding James of Coke's persistent attacks on the

Crown's prerogative. Bacon was persistent himself in avoiding entanglement with controversial cases. James took an interest in this case the moment it became clear that Bacon wanted Coke put in charge.

Coke had made his reputation taking cases nobody else wanted, and then arguing them persuasively even when few precedents supported his cause. He could berate the bench with arguments based on Common Law until courts handed down entirely unwarranted opinions, which he promptly invoked as precedents in other cases pending.

From his early days in practice, Coke enjoyed easy success. While this was not his major concern, he did like money, which he lavished on books and manuscripts touching the history, theory and practice of law. It was said that he forgot nothing once he had read it, but if precedent favored the opposition he coldly turned from the lawbooks to the oratund phrases of the Magna Carta and the Common Law.

Coke was to law what the Puritans were to religion: a purist, a stickler. He had found himself by discovering this supreme value beyond himself. Even in the King's presence, he seemed perfectly at ease. Though he never spoke of this to James, gossip held that Sir Edward was of no opinion in religion, attending church only because the law required it. It was a law seldom enforced, but that didn't matter to him. He saw no difference between kinds of prayer, it was said, whether from the Prayer Book or, as advocated by the Puritans, as the spirit moved. Except for this one, unalterable, all-important detail: one bore the impress of law while the other did not. Since he was uncertain of an afterlife, so the gossip went, beyond law Coke could imagine no reasonable existence. Thus, if the law required him to declare belief in an afterlife (as it did by mandating the Apostle's Creed), then that law compelled him to the action of declaring (as distinct from holding) that belief.

These days, his love for the law was greater than ever; only recently, he experienced the great misfortune of outliving his wife, Bridgett, a handsome, intelligent woman whom James remembered with admiration. Coke said that he still awoke at night, ready to hear her breathing, to awaken her, to tell her a novel line of argument. His children were slender comfort to him. One was dead, two were in the King's service, another off to America employed by the Virginia Company. Only his daughter remained with him. Named for the Queen who had pushed her father upward by appointing him Attorney General,

Elizabeth, a fetching beauty, would probably soon marry and leave him, too.

He seemed to indulge himself in only one strong personal feeling, a professional one: he despised Francis Bacon.

Coke was convinced that Bacon's was the inferior legal mind, and that Bacon was a moral and intellectual coward. He saw Bacon as one who used his intellect on trivial matters of self-interest, never serving the law, nor tradition, nor England, nor the Crown. Thus, as Coke once pointed out to James, not one of Bacon's briefs had ever borne the slightest impact on the practice of law in the kingdom. "By his *Advancement of Learning,*" he added, "St. Albans means the vaulting of himself. His epistle dedicatory to Your Majesty is an insulting flattery, transparent in its moribund intentions."

They had been rivals at Lincoln's Inn, where both studied law, and so they had remained through the years of Elizabeth's reign. Coke won the contest for Attorney General, and he made his victory the more oppressive when he refused to recommend Bacon for Solicitor General. From that time on, theirs were the two names always considered together for high legal appointments and honors. James was not the least surprised when Bacon sought to transfer the case to the King's Bench: letting Coke lose the Lord Chancellorship would be as good as Bacon winning it.

Still, it was Bacon's job to prepare the outline for prosecution. When invited in, Coke offered no argument but leapt at the chance. Bacon wanted out, and soon Coke was all but pushing him out. It was Coke who decided to shift the sequence in which witnesses would be examined. "Bring me this turnkey, Gervase Elwes," he said. "We'll consider the cell itself."

Little progress had been made before Elwes was brought in; investigation had centered on the running of the prison, corruption of officials, and Overbury's family. According to Bacon, who apprised the King of the inquiry's progress, Coke knew many ways to prey on a suspect's mind with fancies of doom. He used his reputation as a prosecutor to demoralize them.

Elwes was nervous, but then many judges showed signs of discomfort when Coke was around. Coke tried to calm him, or pretended to; he spent time asking about the turnkey's family and boyhood. As the inquiry wore on, hour upon hour, into the second day, and then the third, the poor man began to weaken. He altered his story, restated it, begged for release, proclaimed his innocence of wrongdoing.

The sight of Elwes' fading energies was all the encouragement Coke needed (if ever he required such). He bore down on him with a barrage of questions, scarcely leaving time to answer: Why, he asked, did Elwes wish to know the name of the turnkey in another Tower? Was he calling this man a liar? How, if he himself were innocent, could he be sure that Overbury was not murdered? Could he not have been murdered without his knowing it? Was he a doctor? Did he know how Overbury died? Was he God, hence omniscient?

"One of your fellows has said that Overbury was murdered, is that right?"

"Yes."

"Yes, what?"

"That Sir Thomas was done in."

"Is that so?"

"Yes."

"You're sure now?"

"Yes, my lord."

"I'm not a lord, but a commoner like you."

"Yes, sir."

"You're sure."

"Yes."

"That he was murdered?"

"Yes, but I was not in on it."

Now Coke was like a demon from hell: Had not the doctors agreed that Overbury died of natural causes? If Overbury had been murdered, why had Elwes not come forward earlier? How did he know it was murder if he was not implicated? He must know how he was murdered, if not by whom. How? Poison? Impossible.

"It was poison, truly," Elwes swore. "Poison tarts."

But he could not rid himself of Coke. Since he was Overbury's jailer, was he not responsible for every morsel of food, every drop of liquid that entered Overbury's cell? Was he not in fact accusing himself of a capital offense against the Crown?

On and on until, hoping to save his life (a hope carefully nurtured by Coke), Elwes confessed that he delivered poisoned tarts, knowing their contents, to Overbury.

Then, according to Bacon, Coke had borne down even more vigorously. He had done so, had he? And where in London—at what bakery—does one purchase fruit tarts filled with poison? Or had Elwes baked the tarts himself? If he had not poisoned the tarts, how did he know they were poisoned? Yes, His Majesty's servants knew that Elwes knew, or thought he knew, that the tarts were poisoned, but by what *means*—how?—did he know? He must have talked to somebody, trusted somebody.

Elwes had no reason to wish Overbury dead. Excellent. That made sense. Hadn't Overbury, from time to time, given him money? A great deal of money? One didn't bribe his jailer to cashier him, did he? Overbury tried to contact friends, didn't he? He had mentioned a woman, hadn't he? A woman of quality—*he* remembered. He told the Lord Keeper this weeks, ages ago. If not him, then someone else. Did he deny it? Did he know this woman of quality?

What was her name? Was she a Londoner? A relative of Over-bury's? *What was her name?* Coke was growing impatient, did Elwes realize that? Hell was his reward should he tax him further. What woman of quality? Was she old? Young? Married? How did he know it was a woman involved? Had he seen her? If not, how could he be sure it was a woman and not a man dressed like a woman, or a woman of the ordinary sort dressed like one of quality?

Did Elwes know what a rack was? How it worked? Was he able to distinguish an ordinary rack from a rack of quality?

Elwes was now more fearful than any man Bacon had ever seen: he knew nothing, no one, but was merely paid to deliver the tarts. But on whose orders? Who paid him? Alas, his superior, Jack Weston. The three-day ordeal led to this second unfortunate, a Lieutenant of the Tower. With scrupulosity, patience and not the slightest hint of mercy, Coke pressed Elwes and, two days later, Weston, to sign confessions. Weston implicated an apothecary named Franklin who had informed on a dressmaker of some renown, a sometime occupant, it seemed, of the basement of no other place than St. James Palace.

Ann Turner, Bacon said, was a beautiful woman. When Coke confronted her, he'd gone into a rage of indignation. "Am I to believe, after all these days of labor and suspense, that we have fallen upon our woman of quality?" he shouted. "You, madam, are a low slut, a papist and a sorcerer. You arranged for the transfer of money from a woman whose name you have steadfastly withheld from the authorities, but which you will tell me now, before I have your miserable body pressed into the stony floor until you beg, until you pray to God Almighty, to be dispatched.

"You brought this money to the apothecary, Franklin. You instructed this simple man to murder the helpless prisoner, Sir Thomas Overbury, who lay sick in the Tower, awaiting His Majesty's justice and mercy. You solicited the murder of this man, and yet I have found to my satisfaction that you did not so much as know him. Perhaps you would not have recognized him, had he been so fortunate as to have escaped your fiendish clutches.

"You, madam, are the filthiest human being I have ever known, and I have prosecuted witches and violators of their own children. You are so low that I will have this interview over soon or I must expire of my own revulsion at your wretchedness. You will tell us immediately who solicited this despicable murder. If you do not, I shall instruct the executioner to lift your skin from your body in slits and have them burnt before your eyes, which themselves already burn with the fires of hell. I shall have your entrails pulled from inside you and put before your eyes whilst you live, before Derrick mercifully sees you drawn and quartered."

"You should have witnessed it," Bacon told the King. "It was quite amusing. Coke could hardly believe this woman, blandly fixing him with huge vacant eyes, as if she'd not heard him. All that spark and cinder, and she'd not so much as tremble."

"Hmmm," James said. "And pretty, you say?"

So this Overbury business proved vexing even to the intrepid Coke. The Lord Chief Justice had taken ledgers from the dressmaker's shop. They were scribbled in a childlike hand. A few days later, he admitted that he'd not been able to make much of them except to show that Ann Turner had for clients most of the women of quality in England.

"From her ignorant hieroglyphics," he said, "I have gleaned the misspelled names of the finest women, for whom this low seamstress presumably designed and altered clothes. Every one of the Queen's ladies-in-waiting must have stood in line to have Ann Turner mend their kirtles. Queen Anne herself was a client as well."

Nothing conclusive there.

However, once in Newgate, the apothecary had implicated the notorious charlatan, Simon Forman, in the plot. (That Dr. Whiting certainly had a marvelous record of dealing with condemned prisoners.)

James was inwardly pleased to hear of Forman's complicity, for it introduced a new dimension to the scandal. He offered Coke a copy of *Demonology*, his own treatise on witchcraft, to use as a guide in examining the magician.

"Proceed cautiously," he warned. "That gull is slyer than a Yorkshire fox."

Coke reminded James that he had crossed paths with Forman when the College of Physicians had pressed charges against him for practicing physic without a license. Coke had infuriated the College by claiming the charge spurious.

"I had only recently argued the successful brief in the case of the Ipswich tailors," Coke explained. "That judgment established that no guild may prescribe the nature of services extended by practitioners who are not members. Forman had the right, under Common Law, to cozen people, just as under the same law they had the right to be cozened."

It appeared that, so long as Forman did not claim to be a physician certified by the College of Physicians, he could practice as he wished. From that time on, the College of Physicians, while keeping an eye on Forman, avoided bringing him before the bench; Forman's first contact with Coke had proved fortuitous.

Now, however, with sheriffs and constables, Coke descended on Forman's residence near the waterfront. Forman refused to let them in.

"To enter," Forman said, "you must give me all that you possess."

Coke served the summons to the King's Bench. "You must be present on Thursday week," he said.

Forman was unimpressed. "At what o'clock?"

"Two in the afternoon . . ."

"Then," Forman answered lightly, "I shall be dead by one."

James asked Coke where the inquiry was headed. "You've examined these men; they've confessed. Likewise, the woman. Two men have gone to the Executioner; the apothecary and the dressmaker must be on their way by now. What does it come to? They had no motive."

Coke answered evasively, which, for him, was uncharacteristic indeed. "I don't quite know yet," he said. "But nobody kills without a strong motive, except he be mad."

"And these?"

"They were well paid."

"By whom?"

"I don't know. When I know why, and I'm beginning to have some ideas about that, then I ought to know who. Someone wanted to kill Overbury very badly, to go to such lengths, to involve so many people . . ."

Seeing that he would get no more out of the Lord Chief Justice, James decided to work on Bacon; if Coke was being secretive, it probably meant that his suspicions involved—more than a woman of rank—someone with power.

"Who has Coke in mind?" James asked Bacon.

"I'd prefer he answer that question himself," Bacon said.

"But you do know?"

"I've a suspicion . . ."

"So have I," James said. "I must hear yours."

"Someone very high, Your Majesty. Very high."

"High enough," James said, "to shake the throne . . . ?"

"Perhaps," Bacon said.

"The poor fool doesn't suspect dear Anne, does he?" James said. "No one hated Overbury as much as she, unless it might be Gondomar, who thought him a surly enemy to Spain."

"The thought may have crossed his mind," Bacon said, "and might help explain why everyone confesses all save the one name. I doubt that he's considering either seriously. And yet all four of those convicted were Roman Catholics."

"So," James said. "Shrewsbury, as usual?"

Bacon gave an amused nod. "Here's a woman of certain quality," he said. "But other names do come to mind."

James laughed. "Such as Catesby and Guy Fawkes, I suppose."

"Yes," Bacon said. "Droll. Guy Fawkes. Yes."

So Bacon was being cautious as usual; it didn't matter. James knew what was going on. The whole scandal had come about in response to the investigation of the Howard crew. It was beginning to look as if he might be able to topple them soon. One thing he'd insist upon from Coke, though, and he'd be unstinting in this one demand: Coke must have the facts. He'd have to *have* the bastards; absolutely nothing must seem contrived.

*   *   *

THE WAITING had become unbearable, and yet no more than a week had passed. Frances had to keep informed; she listened for rumors of the Overbury scandal. Meanwhile, she worried lest her interest betray her. News of Coke's investigation was becoming, to her, alarum: he was an invisible force working night and day to destroy her.

Elwes and Weston, Overbury's jailers, were executed on the tenth of March.

"They died well," Robin said that night.

"Were you there?" Frances asked.

"No," he said, "but several of our lads were. The vermin. Derrick should have used a saw, not an ax, on their miserable necks."

They had been hanged, of course, not axed to death, but what bothered Frances was his manner of speaking. Her father used to make such statements, but she was surprised to hear Robin talk like that. She decided that he was merely emulating James, who was forever making wildly vindictive threats against the Puritans.

"But you didn't like Overbury," she said. "Why should you care?"

"Who said I didn't like Overbury? I thought he was a touch ungrateful, but I didn't dislike him. I rather liked him, actually."

Best to drop the subject.

Another week passed, and still Frances was not approached by Coke; the men must have died ignorant of her part in the conspiracy. That left only Ann Turner and the apothecary.

"What about the other man?" she asked Robin.

"What other man?"

"The apothecary," she said, "in the Overbury murder."

Robin shook his head. "Don't know of an apothecary," he said. "Another man's to die soon, but I've not heard he's an apothecary."

That night, Frances prayed that Ann and the apothecary (should he have learned her name) would hold out against Coke until the end. If lovely Ann held silent, Frances would find a way to help her boy —through an anonymous donor. It was no good establishing a direct link for others to see. Davy couldn't afford to lose his benefactress. If Ann collapsed in the end, and incriminated Frances, she would ruin all of Davy's hopes for advancement.

Frances yearned for evidence (she would have settled for an informed opinion) that Coke was not invincible. She approached her great-uncle with an air of disinterested curiosity.

"Why does everyone praise Sir Edward Coke?" she said. "Is he not a commoner?"

"A commoner, yes," Northampton said, "but far from common. No adversary in this world is more fearful than Coke."

"Why is that?"

"His voice alone would make the hellhounds tremble."

So! Only that. A loud voice was not so dreadful.

"Others must speak as well," she said.

"Ah, they speak far better. Coke is not eloquent. He is savage. Quick. Merciless. He has the instinct of a viper that knows just when to strike but is endowed with infinite patience. He is without fear or ambition. Except for the law, he has nothing, cares for nothing. I have tried to deal with him. He is impossible."

"You said the same of Sir Thomas Overbury," Frances reminded him, wondering if she had said too much.

"So I did. And there is an odd resemblance. Most men are in some measure corruptible, which is only to say that they are human. Good men aren't corruptible until manipulated through fear or age. Coke is different. He is incorruptible. If men conspired to kill Overbury, why, then he will root them out. If he must harrow hell to get them, he'll do it gladly, and without thinking it out of the ordinary."

Frances found little comfort in these words. Far from it, Northampton had convinced her that as long as Ann Turner lived so did the mortal danger of Coke's finding her out.

She could no longer bear this anxiety alone. She needed comfort, help, someone to talk to. Forman would know how to deal with Coke, if not by bribery, then by some other means. What difference did *that* make now?

Forman was not happy to see her.

"You have done the most dangerous thing possible," he said. "Don't you see? I told you to contact me only indirectly, by note or trusted messenger!"

"But I have no friends left."

"Find one. Preferably a man who cannot read, is desperate for money, has a large family, and very little time on his hands. Time stokes the imagination; we don't want that just now."

"I'm so afraid," she said, throwing herself into Forman's unready arms.

"This is so," he said, pushing her away, and glancing at the hackney-coach that had brought her. "But you must understand your situation lest you lead them to you."

As he ushered her inside, she thought how wise and how powerful he was.

"Help me," she said.

"You feel guilty," he said. "Guilt has driven you here. That is your deadliest enemy now; it marks you. The finger pointing to accuse you is your own." He touched her own right index finger to her forehead.

"My dear, you must go. Truly! They mustn't find you here . . ."

"But I must talk to you, lay plans . . ."

"My dear child," he said, leading her to the couch in his study, "you act *without* plan. Are you aware of the danger you are in? I tried to tell you: Franklin is taken, which indicates that our dear Ann may soon reach the limit of her capacity to resist. You have not met her friend Franklin, but he is now to you the most powerful man in the world. And to me as well . . ."

"But he doesn't know me," Frances said.

"Regrettably," Forman said, as if he'd not heard her, "he isn't strong, like Ann, who must annoy old Coke with her indifference." Forman seemed to enjoy his vision of Ann's endurance, but soon his expression darkened. "Unfortunately," he said, "Franklin lacks the imagination, the moral stamina, to withstand Coke. When the gallows loom up, he'll tell Coke whatever he knows."

"You seem to dote on this loathsome Coke," Frances said.

"I do. Not personally, you understand. I've not met him, you see. Coke once intervened in a case concerning our interests. A matter of legal theory, it was, a subject which, from time to time, I have explored, but of which Coke is the true master. He has said intelligent things respecting an Englishman's rights as a commercial agent, which limit the charter of the College of Physicians. Kept me out of the lockup, he did. Coke is the only worthy person in the whole of James's government, which explains why the two of them don't get along."

"But he rags the Howards, torments us, who do nothing against him! And has he not plundered your own household? Why defend him?"

"Ah," Forman said with a smile, "but you see he requires no defense. So he did a bit of digging about here—nothing personal! The wife let him in. He acts out of a disembodied love of law. He is, though he does not know it, a devotee of Astaroth and Ashmodeus, the eternal brothers. He pursues the two of us—you and me—with irrevocable even-handedness. Equal relentlessness. And he did this even before he knew who we were."

"But he has no notion of who *I* am!"

"Ah, well," Forman said with a bare suggestion of a shrug, "you aren't listening. Frances, you are determined to destroy yourself; I fear there is nothing I can do to help. You don't understand my point here: Coke would as soon hang you as me. You must understand that with no mistake."

"Do you find this cause to admire him?"

"Yes."

Frances stood quietly, observing Forman, wondering what she had missed in her acquaintance with him, why everything that he had said seemed either cruel or mad. She had no doubt that he cared for her; he was trying to warn her—to warn *her*—as if any warning now would not be tardy by months. But he was laughing at her, too.

"You see, you don't see," he said. "You are blind to the advantage you give Coke by holding your life more valuable than mine. To me, it makes no difference; your life is no less valuable than my own. Why, my child, should Coke hold one life more valuable than another? How would that serve his God of Law?"

It was a trick question; Frances chose not to answer. So many questions were like that lately. Scorn and contempt: nowadays, they were the watchwords. The name Howard was nothing but a name; no standard of judgment stood, no respect, no privilege. Here was the agony of England: no strength, no nobility, no greatness remained. James made aristocrats of stableboys, so what was the sense of arguing with Forman or Coke or anybody?

What mattered was to survive, to succeed, to dispatch these meddlers and assailants before they dispatched you. Forman wasn't as loathsome as the others; she liked him—loved him, in fact—even when he was being perverse, as he was now, yes, even when he found the terrible, true, near danger to her life a source of amusement.

"You actually believe," he was saying, "in this folly of your own privilege, which insists that God made other men solely for the service of your person. It is one thing to enjoy privilege, should it happen your way, but quite another to think it reasonable. Why should God trouble himself creating legions of souls whose only purpose is to endure

all manner of pain and degradation in order that one creature—*you!*
—should dwell in perpetual comfort?

"Was Carr of noble blood when he was a page? Was it God made
him a peer? Let him be, I say. I am no enemy of privilege. Most of
my patrons are of rank. I merely observe how passing silly it is to
suppose that Carr's good fortune thus far, and the catastrophe awaiting him, are alike decreed—*'In nomine patri et filli.'* "

Forman feigned to bless her with the Sign of the Cross.

"From everlasting to everlasting," he said, his voice reverberating
with a bitterness she'd neither seen in him before nor witnessed in any
man, including her majestically jaded uncle.

She had no heart to argue. It astonished her to see that Forman,
except for this flash of temper, was as unhurried, as happy, as serene
as always.

"Aren't you afraid?" she said, aware that her question was unre-
sponsive to his own.

He paused, strode to her, held her by both arms with his strong
hands. She found herself looking into brown eyes, shining fiercely
beneath large, ragged brows. They were the eyes of a man far younger
than Forman's years, not those of an old man bent in the shadow of
the executioner's block. He was the most fascinating man she'd ever
known.

"Child," he said. "I need fear nothing, for I shall be dead betimes
noon Thursday."

Because the words were said without emotion, Frances studied the
magician's face for some sign of how she might respond. She fought
mightily against an almost irresistible urge to smile. Could it be that
Forman was promising to make things easier for her by dispatching
himself? Perhaps by a poisoned pot of tea for Thursday breakfast?

Not likely. He loved life too much for that. He was saying that,
through his network of spies, he had learned that the constables would
come for him on Thursday with orders to kill instead of capture. He
knew too many secrets that Coke might force from him. Some tortures
never failed, even with a man like Forman.

That was it. And though Frances loved him, she couldn't help being
pleased, for she would enjoy the unacknowledged benefit of their
treachery. With Forman out of the way, assuming that the apothecary
had never learned her identity, she need worry only about Ann
Turner. Clouds of suspicion notwithstanding, only Forman would

remain to connect her with Overbury's murder.

"I understand," she said.

"I don't think you do," Forman said, taking her face in his hands. "Perhaps you do."

Frances kissed him earnestly.

NOTHING COULD be worse, she thought, than for the clamor to go on as it had since they had brought her there. She had been to Newgate once a long time ago, but only to visit a friend taken for a thief. She remembered the noise, but it hadn't seemed so awful then, perhaps because she knew she'd be going home bye and bye.

The screams and wails and curses never ceased. Nobody slept. The women were herded together in their ward like farmyard creatures, with no place to lie but on the stone floor. The unluckiest, and she was one, were nearest the corners, where the women stooped to relieve themselves; many of the women were sick, vomiting, and running for the corners of the ward as if Franklin had spent his time in Newgate plying them with clysters. All the smells mixed together, making every breath as unbearable as the ceaseless noise of the place.

Because she had money they let her visit the taproom during its open hours. Though the smell was slightly better there, she had to put up with the men. They had found means to see into the women's ward, and were forever hooting and jeering at the ones in the corners. But they could only get at her in the tap room. In the ward, the women spat and cursed back at them, but here the men had their way.

Not that it mattered where or how or with whom. It was no time to protest or make trouble. Men were only men to her now, as once they had been. She paid them no mind. It was no use swearing at them; they meant no real harm. It was easiest to satisfy their foolish wishes, not just to quiet them and push them away, but as relief from the awful noise and stench of the ward.

She had found a few moments of peace here, to sip brandy and remember more pleasant times.

Ann had no regrets. The magistrates had abused her far more than these sad creatures in Newgate. Coke was the worst of them; he had threatened harm to Davy.

"We all depend upon God and King for our sustenance," he had said. "You, I, everyone. Who will care for your lad, without His Majesty's kind wishes?"

She was not well-educated, but she understood his meaning. He wanted her to trade assurances about her son for damaging witness against her dearest friend, Frances. Still, education or no, she knew that once she was gone, no words from Coke would help Davy. She had to do the least hurt possible, now that the great damage was done: she must remain silent.

Coke was furious with her; she had heard what a frightening figure of a man he was, but she met his guarded threat against her son.

"He's not done anything," she said. "He's only a lad, and knows nothing."

"He knows nothing," Coke answered, "but you know everything. And if you care for your son at all, you will tell me this moment the precise name of this lady of quality."

She said nothing. She let them rail at her, follow every of their wishes in abusing her, knowing that soon both she and they would be out of time.

This ordinary, for instance, Dr. Whiting. He had come to see her, he said, to help ease her burden of conscience. Disgusted by the noise in the ward, he had Ann taken to the chapel, where they might be alone.

She wasn't to be taken in by him, though. He was the ordinary of the prison, so when he appeared to be distressed by the foul conditions in which he found her, she knew it to be a ruse. All the women were as naked as she was; they were all equally cold, equally uncomfortable.

And yet, since he seemed interested, she slipped out of her torn shift and embraced him. He was old, but he smelled clean and looked friendly—the sort of man she'd seen kneeling among roses behind walled gardens in Chelsea.

"No, my child," he said, retrieving her shift and offering it to her. "Put this on, now. I didn't come here for . . . What do they do to you poor women here, that you should think . . ."

Ann wrapped the shift about herself.

"Aren't you cold?" he said.

Ann smiled.

"I have come to hear your confession," he said.

"Why should I confess to you," she said, trying to be polite. "You can't absolve me."

"No man can do that," he answered.

"A true priest can," she said. "Will you bring me a priest?"

"I am an ordained priest."

Ann smiled again, trying to be friendly.

"I *am,*" he said. "This is no disguise."

"You were sent here by the court," she said.

"Yes, but as the ordinary of this prison, to minister to all of you who must leave us shortly. I am concerned for your soul. Our Lord has given his word through Paul the Apostle that in your confession is your salvation: 'For with the heart man believeth unto righteousness; and with the mouth confession is made unto salvation.' It is now up to you: 'The word is nigh thee, even in thy mouth, and in thy heart . . .' Do you believe this?"

"Yes," she said. "You have priests here, prisoners waiting like me. Please bring one. It will hurt no one, as we are all doomed together. I want to make my confession."

"Then confess now to me, and I'll pray for you . . ."

Pulling the shift as far over her head as she could without completely uncovering herself, Ann knelt in the nearest pew.

"We all have to die," Dr. Whiting said. "It is God's will that you pass from this life tomorrow, having transgressed man's law as well as God's. But man only takes your life; God offers restoration through our Lord Jesus Christ."

"Yes."

"God's law is just. Man's law is not always so. You had no quarrel with Sir Thomas Overbury, but were only used by powerful people who escape the King's justice. His Majesty is concerned lest his justice seem less than even-handed. I am prepared, for your sake, to pray for you and with you, and if you wish, to stay through the night with you. But I beg you, *beg you,* make your peace with God and with King James. 'The word is nigh thee, even in thy mouth, and in thy heart . . . in your confession is your salvation . . .' Please. Will you now join with me in making a full confession of your conspiracy with others? Will you tell your King, who waits to see that you do not suffer unjustly and alone, who led you into destruction?"

Ann took in the quietness of the chapel, grateful for the warm smoothness of the wooden pew. No, she'd not inform on her friend in this life, and there'd be no need to do so in the next. Dr. Whiting was a patient man, but she had known his errand from the start.

When he saw that she was firm in her resolve of silence, the ordinary gave her instructions on what to say from the gallows. It was important, he said, to repeat the words exactly; he made her say them over and over, and to promise she'd not stray at the last moment.

She promised. The speech would make it sound as if she'd informed on her noble accomplice, but she knew the words would make no difference: Frances trusted her.

She let Dr. Whiting pray and read from the Psalter as long as he wanted. She found it pleasant to hear his comforting words before having to return to the tumult and stench of the ward.

Somehow, she managed to sleep that night. Now that it would do her no good, she'd grown used to the stone floor. She awoke to the sound of a tolling bell.

"St. Sepulcre's, dearie," said the heavy woman they called Princess (of Ram Alley, she had discovered).

"Can I 'ave the shift?" another asked before Ann had quite opened her eyes. "They'll be givin' you a warm cloak of sacking . . ."

When the soldiers came for her, the women hooted and cursed. Several of them helped her into the course plunket gown, which hung about her loosely. She noticed how thin her arms had gotten.

The men saw her now and put up a hideous clamor.

"Save 'er gulley for me!"

"I'll 'ave 'er corse before they nail 'er in!"

"A thruppence for 'er eel-skinner, mates."

"Bring that stinking cunt back 'ere, you bloody turnkey bastards."

Just this side of the gate they were met by the Lord Keeper, who had admitted her only a week ago. An angry mob awaited them, he said; he warned the soldiers to move carefully. The mob had been drinking for some time and could make trouble. The Lord Keeper turned, she thought to give instructions to the gatekeeper, but for a moment no one seemed to move.

And then Sir Ralph stepped from behind the gatehouse.

"Ann," he said, embracing her. Her own arms were now tied at the elbows.

He looked different; he had lost weight, too. She saw tears in his eyes.

"I know I shouldn't have come here, but I couldn't bear to have you go without knowing the truth. If I'd known . . . I did love you. I still love you. If I'd any idea . . . any . . . I would never have participated. You must believe . . ."

He seemed to expect her to say something, but she was too weary to think much less speak. She hadn't prepared herself to see him, only to die. She needed all her strength to remember Dr. Whiting's speech. But now she felt a draining wave of self-pity go over her. Looking up at his handsome face, the carefully trimmed beard she loved so much, she wanted to live.

"It wouldn't have made any difference," he said. "They'd have found out. But we might have fled to America."

"No," she said. "No."

He covered his face with his hands; his shoulders shook.

"Is Davy with you?" she asked as they lifted her into the cart.

She could see him shaking his head.

"Where is he?" she said.

"I don't know," he cried. "I've betrayed you completely. My wife refused . . ."

Ann smiled at him and turned away. So. His wife was more like her than she had thought; she *did* want children of her own.

Who was left to care for Davy?

The gate swung open now, and the soldiers pressed their way into the unruly crowd, guiding the mule-drawn cart.

Inigo Jones liked Davy, probably had him with him now, in fact. And if no one else could be trusted, surely Frances could; she liked Davy.

People waved and jeered, but made no show to block the soldiers. Ann managed well to keep her feet when the cart swung a sharp turn toward Holborn; Dr. Whiting had jumped aboard as they left the yard, and now he lost his balance and fell against her. His lips were moving, but she couldn't hear him.

Slowly, they rumbled in the direction of the tolling bell.

THE TURNPIKE leading from the city was jammed, and the carriage hardly moved. The shops were closed, deserted by the men who now packed the taverns along the way. Nor was hers the only fine carriage moving with the flow of traffic.

She gave Eleanor and Katherine a friendly smile; having them along made it easier. And she was glad, too, that she'd announced her carriage ride into the country to no one's noticeable surprise.

The morning air was clear and bracing. Her ladies were delighted to get away, and Robin, distracted by work, seemed glad to be rid of them for a while. Her luck had held in another way as well: the shops were closed for the very reason she felt it safe, when the coachman inquired as to their destination, to affect indifference.

"Which way shall we go?" she asked. "I've no preference today."

"Out the turnpike," Eleanor said.

"To the junction," Katherine agreed. "Everyone will be there."

"Very well," Frances said.

The coachman displayed no visible distress. Perhaps he was keen to go there too; from his perch he'd have a perfect view.

So off they went early Monday morning only to find themselves caught in a mad crush of people as traffic edged slowly up the road toward St. Albans. Men, women, children of every age and class; horses, oxen, mules, dogs: she'd seen smaller crowds turn out to greet the King.

Several young men took a fancy to Eleanor and Katherine, who enjoyed their obvious glances. One drunken Cockney put his smelly head right into the coach and offered the young ladies a draught from his tankard. Frances let them enjoy themselves.

Had it not been for the church bell endlessly tolling in the distance, one might have thought it a holiday.

Bye and bye, the carriage passed the old city gates and the milestone at the boundary of Hyde Park; the crowd spread out near the junction. The coachman, seeming to know that his passengers were in no rush, pulled over to one side.

Viewers had already filled the grandstands. Orange-girls were everywhere; Eleanor bought an orange and shared it with Katherine. Both girls pretended not to notice the young men who were offering brazen signs of interest from but a few steps away. Frances wondered what it would be like to be Eleanor or Katherine for one day, to give herself to such a man—broad-shouldered and shaggy, one who made his living by the brute strength she could see rippling beneath the leather jerkins.

"They're coming!" a voice cried.

"Which one is it?" Katherine called out.

"The whore's first," a ruffian said as the crowd slammed him against the carriage door.

"There's the cart," Katherine whispered excitedly.

Frances had no trouble hearing her above the clamor.

She had taken her normal breakfast (two eggs and a bowl of chocolate), light on the stomach, and yet now it sat most precariously. She could not afford to feel ill. She had come to this place—the last spot on earth that common sense would send her—and now she mustn't leave it without a sign that Ann had held firm to the last. But how could she apprehend that sign? She was too frightened to look.

Except that she had no choice: Eleanor and Katherine had leaned to opposite sides, leaving their mistress the best view through the center of the window. The carriage seat placed them high above the crowd; Frances could see everything.

Ann stood in the cart beneath the outside stave of the Triple Tree. an awful-looking thing made of three sturdy pilings about eight feet high, supporting three staves joined to form a triangle. It was built so as to permit several felons to hang at once.

Ann was fettered; she looked very thin. They had dressed her— Ann, who had designed the Queen's most festive gowns—in a coarse robe of grey sackcloth.

A priest stood beside her in the cart, reading from what looked like a missal but was probably just the heretics' Prayer Book.

Around the cart, soldiers good-naturedly restrained the surging crowd.

Merciful Mother! Frances was grateful that Ann had come there only to hang. In recent weeks, she had much pondered the means of execution. She regarded it admirable that England was more civilized than in ancient days, when they tied the ankles of the doomed to the tail of the Executioner's horse and dragged them up the high street from Newgate Prison to Tyburn House. Ann came by cart, and along the way at every tavern her passage from this world was no doubt made easier by beaker upon beaker of brandy given her by publicans and good-hearted folk. The rope would strangle her, but she'd probably not feel a thing!

It was a comfort knowing that, should the worst happen and Frances herself be taken in Coke's investigation, she'd not be convicted as a traitor: the worst punishment by far was drawing-and-quartering, when Derrick let the doomed hang only for a moment, then cut them down, sliced off their privy members and methodically slit them with his cunning knife from groin to breastbone; he tore out the entrails—the heart, too!—and burned them and the privy parts before the villain's eyes as he perished in agony.

Frances caught her breath, tried to breathe evenly, but could manage no more than short gasps: Tyburn was a place of terror. And yet pressing was slower, and losing one's head was bloodier and more agonizing to think on. So hanging wasn't the most horrible end. If one were fortunate, friends came forward to attach their weight to one's legs, thus to hasten merciful death by sundering the neckbone. Frances prayed that Ann possessed such a friend. Were the place not full of witnesses, she herself would have rushed from the carriage to fasten her body to Ann's frail weight.

Now the priest motioned to the crowd.

Frances fought the urge to cry out: I am the Countess of Somerset! I demand you stop at once! Ann Turner has done nothing! Nothing except stay loyal to a friend. Out of love. Yes, only that!

And yet Frances knew that, had she the power to intercede, she'd not use it. However loyal Ann might try to be—had tried to be—the body had its limits. Betrayal by treachery or accident was possible so long as Ann lived. Which would not be much longer. And Franklin was only hours behind, perhaps already making his way with guards and cart through traffic, on the road to Tyburn.

Dr. Forman, as he had predicted, had suddenly fallen dead only four days ago, on Thursday.

Ann's voice, a hoarse whisper, came to her; the mob had quieted suddenly to hear her last words.

"What have I not been that, in the world, is evil? What is in me that I dare call good? My youth was licentious. My age was wicked. All my days are offensive and odious to man and God. Yet notwithstanding . . ."

Ann appeared to forget—it was obvious that she'd been taught these words by rote—and turned toward the priest. He must have forgotten, too, for he searched about in his book, and then in his cassock, finally withdrawing a paper which he unfolded. He leaned close to Ann, who returned her face to the crowd. With the priest's lips close to her ear, she continued.

"Notwithstanding, Heavenly Father, my repentant soul comes crying to thee for mercy, as before my sins cried to Heaven for vengeance. Bend to me thine ear. Dry up my ocean of sorrows with thy beams of Grace."

A murmur went up from the people as Derrick twirled the hangman's noose; he was showing a young man, whom Frances took to be his son, the technique that need be mastered by only one man in the realm at a time. Ann took the opportunity of this diversion to kneel, which appeared to distress the priest; reluctantly, he knelt beside her to read the prayer.

"Let not my name be blotted out of the Book of Life," Ann said, "but set thy seal on my forehead that you may know me as thine own."

Now she stood and her back appeared to arch; it seemed that she pushed the priest away by leaning a shoulder into him. No longer trembling, she observed the mob, which, except for some elbowing beside the cart, was very still. The priest moved aside as Derrick put the rope about her neck and stepped back.

"I desire not to live in this world, which, with its great ones to mislead us, is as weary of me as I of it . . ."

Frances was alert: "great ones to mislead us." Was this the sign that she needed—or, more likely, the one she feared most? She strained to discern every tremor of a possible inflection in Ann's voice.

If Ann held firm, why, then Frances would find a way to look after Davy. Through an anonymous donor, that was it! It was no good publicly declaring the connection; Davy couldn't afford to lose his benefactress to the clutches of Sir Edward Coke. If Ann faltered, the blame for Davy's dashed hopes would rest with her.

"I long to exchange my troubles here for rest," Ann said, "and I pray for myself, as a burden to you and to my own child, who . . ."

Ann's head fell forward; she lurched sideways. She was sobbing now. Derrick, who had finished with his instructions to his apprentice, looked to the priest: Ann's suffering was not yet over.

"Oh, God," Ann cried out, "I shan't see my boy again . . ."

The priest raised his hand; this last was not rehearsed. Derrick moved with incredible speed. Almost before Frances was aware that he'd moved at all, he had covered Ann's eyes with a black scarf. Then, with help from no one (for the law gave only one man the right and duty to kill), he lifted Ann from the cart.

Now only Ann's upper body was visible; soldiers fought to keep the mob away from her. She swayed ever so slightly to and fro, then appeared to jerk or tread the measures, whilst the cheers from everyone went up.

Frances, who could bear no more, motioned for Eleanor to get the coach moving, and was prepared to rest comfortably with the country breeze in her face, when, without preamble—before they had yet moved—the door of the carriage flew open.

Feeling panic, Frances sensed that the insane mob had now decided to assault her.

In the next instant, she saw a uniformed man, who must have worked the door latch of the carriage; then, almost immediately, he was eclipsed by another—a tall, handsome man, with a slightly greying beard. Without the slightest doubt of his welcome, though in the absence of an invitation, he stepped up into the carriage and took the seat opposite Frances, pausing only long enough to let Eleanor avoid his sitting on her lap.

The uproar outside the coach seemed of no concern to this intruder; his demeanor was one of propriety and composure.

"Good morning, my lady," he said, smiling and bowing slightly from his seated position. "I cannot tell you how trying this day has been for me, nor how pleasantly surprised I am to catch sight of you!"

"But, sir," Frances began.

"Permit me," he said. "We know each other only indirectly. I am Sir Edward Coke, His Majesty's Lord Chief Justice, and I have had the good fortune of working closely on several cases with your esteemed great-uncle, my Lord Henry Howard."

He went on speaking, but Frances made little sense out of the words following "Sir Edward Coke." The noise around them seemed suddenly to be baffled. She heard voices as if from afar, as, when a child, she could hear the jubilance of the inner court at Audley End carried to her northwest corner dressing room. And now she couldn't see well, either. Sir Edward's distant insolent face moved dizzily in front of her.

Perhaps she fainted; she didn't know, but she felt hands now holding her. Katherine's hands. And Eleanor wanted to know if her lady required assistance.

Sir Edward was still talking amiably.

"Apparently you were caught in the same madness as I. I came this way only partly out of curiosity, having had an interest in the outcome of a case. Got separated from my coachman, actually, back quite a ways. Dropped off for a pint since we weren't moving. My coachman, the scoundrel, wasn't about when I returned. Decided to walk. Discouragingly impolite crowd out there, you know . . ."

Frances could see him more clearly now: he wasn't smiling at all. She must have thought so because of the trim of his mustache and beard. Rather, he was regarding her steadily while he talked, appearing to give no thought to his own words.

"It is really my good fortune to have stumbled upon you. Did you observe the festivities firsthand? It's always awkward to hang a woman, unless she's convicted as a witch. This one went fairly well, I thought."

She couldn't tell whether "this one" referred to Ann or to the hanging.

"Would you find it awfully inconvenient if I and my man were, well, to squeeze in? Actually, I could leave him here, if you'd prefer. He seems to be enjoying himself anyway."

She opened her mouth to protest, but he went on without seeming to care.

"It will be a slow ride back, I fear. Another poor soul—Franklin, by name—will be on his way in the other direction. We'll be moving against traffic all the way. Streets won't clear for hours. To be perfectly frank, my lady, I had hoped for the opportunity—at your convenience—of an interview. And what time would be more convenient than now? Perhaps, since we are both captives of the same calm, shall we say, we might sail on slowly together?"

Frances could think of no useful response.

Of all people, of all places, she had picked the worst. She had proved, as Dr. Forman said, her own most dangerous enemy.

Sir Edward knew; had Ann told him? ". . . great ones to mislead us," she had said. And yet Dr. Forman, who had proved true to her trust in him, considered Ann strong enough to withstand Coke.

It must have been Franklin. Perhaps Ann had told him more than she intended.

Did it matter now? If Coke had doubts before, wasn't her presence here like a confession? Still, almost everyone in London was here at this junction: her presence was not convincing proof of guilt; it wasn't evidence at all. She had to fight for control of this difficult circumstance—fight, as she had before, to survive. She knew that now was not the time to talk to Coke. Instinct cried out for retreat; she must appeal to her condition. Had she not fainted? The reason was obvious: she was pregnant. She couldn't talk to him now, and, while she regretted the inconvenience, she was constrained also to tell him that he must seek other means of conveyance back to London.

"You *are* going back to the city, are you not?" Coke asked pointedly.

At that moment, she heard a single, loud rap at the carriage door opposite the one Sir Edward had entered. The door opened almost simultaneously with the peremptory knock, and there stood the Earl of Northampton.

"No," he said firmly. "I am sorry, my friend, but my niece and I have other plans. We were on our way, having both overlooked the inconvenience of the occasion, for a trip to St. Albans. A day's outing, you see."

"Ah," Sir Edward said, bowing curtly, "then the two of you came together from your gracious lodgings in London?"

Northampton, now seated in the carriage, looked straight at Coke, nodding slowly. "Yes," he said. "I stepped out a ways back for a short stroll into the park. Uncomfortable things, these carriages. Hard on the posterior. I told Niece Frances to wait here at the junction. Had no idea they'd hang a woman right in front of her! She doesn't . . . you can see, she's very upset . . ."

"Of course," Coke said. He turned to Frances before taking his leave. "I hope you'll permit me the pleasure of a brief chat . . . soon."

The carriage door closed, and Frances slumped against the cool leather of the couch. She was afraid to look at her great-uncle.

Northampton asked Katherine and Eleanor to fetch a pitcher of water for their mistress, then took her hands firmly in his. "My sweet, sweet Frances," he said. "What on earth have you done to draw the attention of Sir Edward Coke? In this place?"

"Nothing," she whispered, aware that he couldn't possibly believe her. "He lost his coachman, and wanted—"

"My child," he interrupted, "if you are involved in this bloody business here today . . . I fear . . . that I must pity you."

She would have felt no worse had he been the court, with "God have mercy on your soul." She wept. His arm was firmly round her, but she felt no comfort. He knew.

And Coke knew. It was now only a matter of time. Northampton's lie had offered her a week of freedom, perhaps two. She'd not spend these days, as Forman urged, in trivial enjoyments. No, she'd fight, as she always had, but with this difference: at last she'd seek the comfort of Robin's support. Perforce, she must tell him the truth.

Northampton's words resounded with a low, metallic ring: "Does Coke have weight of evidence against you?"

Apparently her silence was sufficient witness to her distress. Northampton went to arrange her ladies' return to the city by hackney-coach.

"We have no choice," he said, climbing back into the carriage, "but to sort this out. Time presses. A feckless memory can be dangerous. You may think you have poisoned Overbury. But do you *know* he was poisoned? If poisoned, did he die as a result of the poison and nothing else? No ague or noisom airs? No festering of wounds? No distempers whatsoever in that closet of them?"

The carriage pitched from side to side; she could think of no appropriate response. Through tears, the crowded road to London seemed a blur of bodies attached to excited, grinning faces.

Her great-uncle's voice lowered now, as if he wished to measure not his words, but her reaction to them:

"Overbury was wounded in a street fight shortly before his arrest. Didn't you know?"

Someone may have remarked on the incident at the time, but she could not recall attributing it any importance.

"Silly child," he said. "This may have been the cause of his unfortunately protracted death. Since attending physicians say naught for certain of it, why will you—to our misery—proclaim an odious demise? The mishap of that indecisive duel in the night near the Strand confirms only this principle: nieces but slenderly attend the wisdom of aging uncles . . ."

At first the undertone ("his unfortunately protracted death") had been too tenuous to grasp with confidence, more a curiously braided turn of phrase than a definite meaning. But this last utterance, though subtle even for him, was nothing shy of confession.

"I told you to let *me* handle Overbury," he said.

"You," she said, "were responsible . . . for . . ."

"For the attempted assassination of Overbury? Are you mad? Would I tell you if I were? In directness lies vulnerability. Learn this now or embrace despair: if Coke has evidence against you—here is the question and you must answer it!—no Howard will survive the scandal. A murder trial, outcome aside, would make the 'nullity' seem like rites of canonization."

"Can't we . . . you . . . pay Coke sufficiently to . . ."

"Then he *does* have evidence?"

"I don't know . . ."

"Who? Who could give evidence against you?"

"No one. They're all dead."

"What then?"

"Nothing."

"Then Coke will have suspicion, and no harm there. You are certain, I presume, that you put nothing of your contact with these people in writing?"

"Writing?"

"Surely you didn't pen letters to these villains! A recipe for mercury tarts!"

They rode as far as the Strand before he spoke again, and then his voice was barely audible above the clatter and creak of hooves and carriage wheels on the cobblestone:

"I earnestly hope you understand with what . . . tact . . . we must prepare Robin."

Here was some relief, though small.

"Then you'll tell him with me?"

He nodded. "He's the clog, you see, not Coke."

"Oh, Uncle," she said, "I adore you for not hating me. But you malign sweet Robin. Can we not hope for his love? He *is* loyal, withal."

"We must tell him in any case," he said. "His loyalty, now, if tempered by stern judgment, will match your worth in love and mine in gratitude."

James felt awful. His body trembled when he breathed; the inside of his head seemed painfully too large for his skull. He had vomited last night many times, and once this morning, too, but his belly was unrelieved. No need to fetch Mayerne; it wasn't ague. This sparkling "sillery" wine, harmless enough in small portions, was venomous if many bottles were consumed with quantities of malt liquor and brandy.

"Beer," he whispered, but his ribs felt full of wind, and he lay back dizzily.

Bye and bye, Georgie brought a brimming beaker of sturdy March beer: heady of scent, with a deep, muddy-brown mist in it. He drank gratefully.

"What's all the noise?" he said, trying to speak without moving his jaws. He'd heard strident voices as Villiers had passed through the antechamber.

"It's Somerset, Your Majesty," Villiers said. "He wants to speak to you."

Hmmm. He swallowed uncertainly. Carr was the last man James wanted to see just then, but procrastination would solve nothing. Coke had made a mess of things. Poor Robin.

On the other hand, if Coke's suspicions held up, poor Overbury.

"Admit him," James said.

Carr sauntered in and stood with his lower lip curled; James waited in vain for him to bow.

"Don't I handle your appointments?" Carr said. "Here's Villiers in *my* place telling *me* you can't be disturbed."

"I do feel rotten, laddie," James said. "Too much 'sillery' and malt. I—"

"You replaced me!" Robin said.

James sighed. The back of his eyes throbbed miserably. "Alas, Robin," he said. "I'd no other choice. 'Twill be but temporary . . ."

"But why?"

Incredible. Quietly, James explained that Sir Edward Coke had made rather serious charges against him.

"Innuendoes!" Robin said. "That bastard refuses to talk to me or to bring true charges. Which is why I've come to see you. I want this maniac put in the Tower."

When he was angry, he reverted to a thick Scottish burr. Villiers was laughing at him.

"Get out of here!" Robin shouted. "Jamie, make him leave. This is private. He's gulled Coke. I don't want him here."

Reluctantly, James signaled for Villiers to go. Now he'd have to field Carr's questions on Coke's report: decidedly unpleasant, and James was flatulent at both ends.

"Have you read it?" Robin asked.

James nodded. He'd read the report—with interest. "Mmmhhmm. It's a touch vague," he said, "but you understand it wouldn't do for me to have you handling appointments until the issue's . . . clarified . . ."

"But I'm innocent," Robin said.

"Hardly," James mused. "We are all born in sin and persist in wickedness. Happily, the law requires mere compliance . . ."

"I killed no one," Robin persisted.

"Nor hired the deed done?"

"You . . ." Robin appeared shocked. "You don't believe I did him in?"

How typical this was of Robin's intellectual deficiencies: asking a question which was, under the circumstances, either unanswerable or irrelevant, most often both. What difference did it make what James believed? Coke claimed to think that Overbury was murdered, which fact mattered. Coke suspected Carr; that mattered, too.

The problem, Robin explained, lay in Coke's prejudice against the Howards. He had no right to conduct the investigation, being spiteful toward himself and toward all Catholics.

"But you're no papist," James reminded him.

Robin conceded the point, but held that others considered the Howards so, and that he had married Francie, which made him a Catholic in everyone's eyes.

"You're sure of this . . ." James said.

"Indeed!"

"And it's as you wish it?"

"Precisely!" Robin said, insisting in the same breath that James remove Coke. "The man's vicious, and a lackey of Anabaptists, antinomists, socinians, and all sectaries. Often has tea with them. And he's an atheist himself."

"But he's effective," James said. "Men fear him."

He was sorry he'd said that; it was sheer pique. And Coke *had* acted irresponsibly in the Overbury case, as he had, for that matter, in prosecuting Raleigh. Coke was brilliant—his adversaries agreed on that—but stubborn and not always fair in his treatment of suspects. He had announced his suspicions of Carr in a confidential report to the King's Commission on the Port of London Customs. A clear offense in iself, Coke had compounded it by promptly imparting his secret intelligence to several of the most undisciplined gossips at court.

Still, one note of Robin's innocent refrain vibrated a minor discord. He could not have known about the report until he arrived at St. James. And yet he had shown no surprise when the matter came up. Had he already learned of the report? It was possible; Howard spies were everywhere these days.

"Now, now," James said, extruding his tongue as a quantity of stout rose in his throat. "He's not indicted you . . ."

"But I have no influence as Lord Treasurer of Scotland to stop his irresponsible and illegal slander."

Northampton's words: Howard notions infested the court as thickly as did their spies.

"You have influence," James said. "But it is a serious charge."

"Coke's the pawn of Villiers," Robin said.

"Rubbish," James said.

He doubted that the two had ever met. In fact, Villiers had held himself aloof from the criminal aspects of recent investigations. He had pressed for the original inquiry into customs, but he'd scrupulously avoided involvement in the later stages. He knew that any effort on his part to denigrate the Howards and Carr would help rather than hinder them.

"I know what you want," James said, "but Bacon won't take the job."

"Please," Robin said. "Francie asked me to beg, if necessary. I *am* begging. Make him take it."

Somehow, even that affirmation of obeisance could not disguise Carr's arrogance. When James refused to answer, he returned to raillery against Coke, who, he said, had molested his wife in her own carriage.

"Yesterday, it was, ere he vilified me today. Caused her to faint, he did. And Francie pregnant with a lad we're to name for you, Jamie."

Appalling.

"Give dear Francie our love," James said. "And now I must chastise my Chief Justice for his indecency . . ."

Robin's back literally arched. "Am I dismissed?" he snapped.

James chided him with an embrace; he would merely carry out Robin's wishes and deal with Coke, whom he had, in fact, already summoned.

"If you'll tell Villiers to show him in now, I'll deal with him."

Robin colored; he didn't move.

"You don't wish to be present when I talk to him?"

"I do."

"But only moments ago you protested Villiers' presence!" Carr could be tiresome. "I want to see Coke alone."

"Jamie!"

"No. I'll speak to him alone."

Robin's thick, well-molded lower lip trembled; his eyes moistened. He was still attractive, but his eyes were puffy, perhaps from lack of sleep, and he was gaining weight. (Or was it only the constant contrast between Robin and thin, lithe Georgie?)

"You see, I've conned this cannily penned diatribe, and before you came in, I was preparing to reprimand Coke for his slovenliness . . ."

Looking pinched and uncertain, Robin withdrew.

From the moment Coke strode in—with his stiff, almost imperceptible bow, his self-assured carriage, his winning air of composure—

James felt at a disadvantage. He asked about Coke's family, and they talked about the weather. After a while, a prolonged silence signaled that amenities were at an end.

"You knew my wishes," James said. "You were to do nothing without evidence."

Coke said that, lacking evidence, he'd done nothing.

"Sir Edward!" James said. "You have slandered Lord Somerset in a report which is neither public nor confidential. Worse, you have declined to bring charges against which Somerset might defend himself." He let Coke know that he refused to allow such calumny in the name of the King's service: "Carr is, after all, a peer, and Lord Treasurer of Scotland."

"I have heard that he's Scottish," Coke said.

James chose to ignore the diversion. "*And* a valued member of my Privy Council."

"I deny him neither title nor due privilege," Coke said. "He has the right to trial by the House of Lords."

"If I choose to have him charged! Be careful, Sir Edward. You have denied him—and your King—due respect . . ."

"I humbly beg Your Majesty's pardon," Coke said calmly. "Due respect is always due."

"You must either retract your charge against Somerset—"

"I've made no—"

"Sir Edward Coke!" James intoned.

Coke bowed.

"You must either retract your . . . implied . . . accusation or indict Somerset."

"As Your Majesty wishes."

"Nor may you exceed warrant of your evidence. You must present that evidence to me ere you move against Somerset."

Coke received this news coolly. "Overbury was murdered," he said. "The law requires punishment."

"The Crown insists upon it."

"The law," Coke repeated, "requires me to file charges—save Your Majesty's request for my withdrawal from his service—when my inquiry so indicates."

This remark was nothing short of a threat. The Puritans would regard Coke's removal in the present circumstances as evidence that

---

298

James would not permit the law to take its course when the life of a favorite was at stake.

The King's Bench, James reminded Coke, was still the King's. And if he wished to jettison the prosecution, the Lord Chief Justice must give way.

"On this island," Coke replied, "the law has always been supreme. It is as much the bulwark of the sovereign's power as of his subjects' rights."

James emptied his tankard and fastened a hard gaze on the Chief Justice. This zealot would rest the King's sovereignty solely in the laying of it down.

"You will arrest Somerset only upon my word," he said.

Now Coke bowed with an exaggerated show of supplication. "Your Majesty," he said, "I most respectfully submit that the Crown may sooner possess itself of my successor than of my willing compliance in subverting the law."

Though spoken mildly, this was open defiance: blunt, unremitting.

"I could have you hanged for that statement," James said.

Sir Edward bowed again quietly, without rejoinder. He agreed.

James commanded Coke to leave his presence, and to take care to follow his instructions: "As if they were chiseled in stone on Mount Sinai."

He had been as direct as he knew how with this courtly lover whose coy mistress was the law.

All in all, Coke was useful at the moment. This probe of James's affections—here was the distinct sense of the preposterous investigation of Carr—had its salutary aspects. Carr had grown arrogant from basking too long in the sunny opulence of the King's love. For a time, James had channeled that arrogance, used it as a scourge to fashion the court's consent to the Spanish Alliance. He needed money, and the dowry from Spain when Charles took the Infanta for his spouse would be the largest sum of its kind in history.

Unfortunately, now Gondomar, mindful of James's deteriorating posture in Germany (his losing regiments there were still unpaid), was much given lately to evasive rhetoric. Not more than a week ago he mused, as if talking to himself (well in the presence of St. Albans) that fickle Philip was presently entranced by the notion of marrying his daughter to an Austrian. "The attractions of St. Peter's as against St.

Paul's," he had breathed, dismissing the thought with one grand, ironic flourish of a richly jeweled hand. So Carr's helpfulness had its limits there.

And his jealousy was an open embarrassment.

James was of the opinion that Coke's investigation, which would come to nothing with respect to Carr, might nonetheless help tame the wilder expressions of his ingratitude. If it frightened him enough, Carr might surrender his carping jealousy of Villiers and seek means to mask his belief that he, and not James, was England's rightful sovereign.

The charges, the insinuations, the whole procedure into which Coke had been drawn was no more than a clever design by Pembroke and the others to counter the Howard hegemony at court, which the Somerset connection had all but assured. James had decided to play along for a while, to let Robin suffer. He had his own ideas about Overbury: the man died of natural causes; in prison, that was easy to do.

Designs against him may have been launched, perhaps by one of Gondomar's more stupid agents (who braced a dressmaker with "I've a need for a yard of pennistone and—oh, yes—a quantity of mercury sublimate"), but common sense argued against a man taking six weeks to die on a diet of that substance. Furthermore, Spaniards dispatched their enemies at court with a poignard in the ribs (else why would his courtiers suffer with those double-leather jerkins?).

No, Carr hadn't killed anyone, certainly not Sir Thomas. But he did require discipline; a touch of fear might teach him manners. James would let him squirm for a while.

SHE LAY curled with the blankets pulled round her, leaving only space enough to breathe and see. The French doors were ajar, and a soft breeze off the water coaxed her to rise. Slipping her bedgown over her night clothing, she stepped out to the terrace of Somerset House, which faced the river.

Far out on the water, fishermen's boats drifted downstream, silently, with the morning sun streaking their wakes—sailing, as it seemed, dreamily toward Greenwich, the estuary, and the peace that she imagined went with honest labor fetching the stuff of life in nets from the river and the sea.

She could easily have slept till noon; Robin was up early, gruff and in a hurry, cursing Northampton under his breath.

Last night's harsh words would not soon be forgotten. Her great-uncle, who thought it best to settle in at Somerset House for a spell, returned from the first day's errands in a fret with Robin, who proved equally distressed by his reproach.

"My friend," Northampton said, "you were to deal with James, not to dally with the dice at the Serpentine."

Robin said he'd gone to St. James, but tried in vain to sway the King against Coke. " 'Twas no use. He'd put that quean popinjay, Villiers, in my place."

Northampton listened without sympathy. "So you vacated the field?"

"By dicing at the Serpentine he did seem unworried," Frances ventured.

"Oh?" Northampton said to Robin. "Did *Coke* find you unworried?"

He hadn't told her that Coke had followed him there.

" 'Twas but to annoy me," Robin insisted. Coke had merely inquired about his relationship to Overbury at the time of his arrest. "He seemed to think I assaulted Tom with a rapier the very night he was sent to the Tower." He laughed: "The idiot! Tom could carve his initials on anybody's spine with a blade. In my hands, either end of the weapon serves as well."

Northampton refused to respond to Robin's levity; he held the sojourn to Knightsbridge to be a serious error. "We've given Coke the initiative," he said. "Conceded the King's ear to our adversaries." Worse still, Robin had let Coke put him off his guard. "This pretended suspicion of you as Overbury's assailant—'tis no more than the drag betimes the fox hunt. Do you suppose him ignorant of Overbury's reputation as a swordsman?"

Undaunted, Robin seemed to swell with pleasure at his own cleverness. "You think he gulled me. You suppose my visit to the Serpentine mere dalliance. Time will have the truth of it out. I came near settling this entire matter today."

Now Northampton betrayed signs of alarm: "I am too fearful to inquire about your occupation there. I do but pray you lost only your money, for then your loss would still be gain."

Robin's eyes gleamed with mysterious knowledge. "Coke's the one bedeviled," he said. "He thinks he has lulled me to sleep, but I'm awake."

"I feared as much," Northampton said, and then wounding words flowed on both sides.

Robin accused Northampton of using and patronizing him by turns. Northampton answered that Robin had jeopardized the family by a feckless disregard of dangers which a man of even less than moderate perception should see at once.

"I told you to let *me* look to the letters," Northampton said. "You blundered after them, didn't you?"

It seemed like long moments before Robin answered. "You'll soon see who's right or wrong here."

Immediately afterwards, Northampton retired, and Robin sulked with a bottle of brandy.

"You said your great-uncle admired me, but he holds me in contempt."

More than the truth of Robin's remark, the mood of despair hanging over him seemed the immediate threat. When they themselves had retired, Frances made overtures (lengthy sighs, languorous stretches, exaggerated wakefulness) to comfort her husband. Robin caught her meaning. In virtually identical moments, he had mounted and dismounted her, with neither words of endearment nor signs of satisfaction. Though with child, this trying night Frances herself longed for true company and comfort, and its absence left her restlessly chagrined.

So this morning she was specially glad of the sun, the open air, the river, breakfast now in front of her; she was hopeful, too, that by evening the men would return in better spirits—with happier news.

She took the one letter from the salver and broke the wax seal: the coat of arms of the Earl of Salisbury.

Her sister wanted to come visit her, to spend a few weeks shopping together before the season opened. Would her presence be too great an inconvenience? Dear, sweet Catherine: how Frances longed to answer, Yes, come at once, by Wednesday week. Spring is dawning with majestic speed, perfect for the finest purposes of love and celebration and shopping. We'll visit every good shop, refurbish our wardrobes, have tea every day, and talk without surcease!

But one may truly idle away only innocent hours. She knew what her answer to Catherine must be.

How she envied her sister, whose sins once had loomed so awesome in her imagination, but which now seemed like surpassing innocence: no wonder that, at last, Robert had forgiven her. Catherine had to suffer loneliness and humiliation, but her husband and her friends had gathered round her once that travail had reached its natural limits. But were there limits to the indignation which *her* sins had roused? Would Robin ever forgive *her*? And what if her mother and father, and Catherine, and the court discovered her? Would the world's adulation—for that is what she now enjoyed—ever be restored to her?

She was surprised when her great-uncle joined her on the terrace for breakfast. He, too, was getting a late start. Having braced Robin the night before with the many tasks that lay undone, he seemed unjustly tardy to her; she was nettled.

"Slug-a-bed," she muttered. "Robin was off hours ago."

He seemed disheartened by her partisan show of feeling, and she tried to make amends.

"Catherine wants to come to Somerset," she said.

He pursed his lips: the visit would be untimely. "We've too much to sort out just now," he said.

"Will you write to her for me?"

"It would be better if you wrote. Tell her you're not feeling well—with child, and the like . . ."

Yes, that would do it; Northampton was at his best when solving family problems.

Frances was ready to see him off to do the bidding their situation demanded when the butler announced the presence in waiting of His Honor, Lord Chief Justice of England, Sir Edward Coke.

Northampton observed her with thin-eyed interest. "Are you up to it?"

"I don't know," she said.

"It would be better if you were. I *can* tell him you're unwell . . ."

She agreed to see him, and shortly he was ushered to the terrace. She caught what looked like a trace of disappointment in his glance at Northampton.

"Excellent view," he said, strolling to the balustrade.

Her great-uncle refused this invitation to idle chatter. "Awfully sorry, Sir Edward, but Lady Somerset is feeling a touch ill this morning. May we be of assistance?"

For a time the two men parried with each other. Finally, Coke got round to asking her opinion of the precise relationship, insofar as she could recall it, of her husband with Sir Thomas Overbury at the time of the latter's arrest.

"I'd be most grateful for any help," he said.

Northampton shrugged, looking vacantly her way. "It couldn't have been very good," he said. "As I recall, about that time Somerset was looking to replace him."

"I was particularly curious to hear Lady Somerset's opinion," Coke said.

"Indeed!" she said, proud of her sudden courage. "I had thought King James's displeasure—and the Queen's—were the stuff of *commoners'* gossip." She glanced at Northampton, whose impassive expression offered no clue to the propriety of that assault.

"Yes," Coke said. "The Royal Family wasn't fond of him . . ."

"He'd rejected the King's appointment abroad, as I recall," Northampton put in.

"Had he?" Coke said. "Formally, I mean. I've heard the King doesn't regard it so."

Northampton grinned, which Frances took to be his cue for her to call for tea.

"I'd prefer coffee, if I may," Coke said. Even here, he seemed to gain the upper hand. "In point of fact, I'm not so interested in the Royal Family's vexatious dealings with Overbury, nor with Sir Thomas' standing at court, generally. Appears almost nobody liked him. Except for Lord Somerset. Their friendship, I gather, was singular. Is that right? Knew each other for well over a decade? Worked together? Lived together?"

Nobody answered. Now it was Coke's turn to smile: he'd been caught out. Rather than asking questions he was imparting answers.

"Is that, in sum, correct?" he said.

"Does it matter?" Northampton said.

Frances thought—she hoped—the initiative was changing hands.

"Was it a *close* friendship?" Coke persisted.

"Ask Somerset," Northampton said.

"From your point of view, Lady Somerset?"

"Yes," she said, thinking that she had already said too much. "I suppose it was, at one time, Lord Somerset was very busy. He depended on Sir Thomas a great deal. They often—"

"I mean earlier on," Coke interrupted. "Before Lord Somerset was an earl, or even a lord . . ."

"Your point?" Northampton said. "I really must ask you to get on with it. My niece is—"

"Yes, unwell. Yes, get on with it," Coke said. "I want to know why these close, close friends—David and Jonathan, so to speak—fell out. Was there animosity? A dispute over money?"

"Will that be all?" Northampton said.

Coke indicated his readiness to leave and in fact apologized for bursting in on them, considering Frances' condition. It was hard to tell if he referred to her pregnancy, or to the fact that, though modestly covered, she was nonetheless still in her bedgown. He had turned to go when, as if orchestrated, her own butler bustled across the terrace and presented him with a leather portfolio.

"I wonder if I might trouble you for a moment longer," Coke said.

Northampton rose to object, but Coke had already seated himself and was thumbing through what looked like two office ledgers, which he had taken from the portfolio.

"Fascinating, really," he said. "See if you agree with me here, my lady."

One ledger was in a hand familiar to her, the other in barely legible script belonging, if not to a child, then to someone hardly literate.

"Ignore the figures," Coke said. "Do you notice anything?"

Both she and her great-uncle leaned over the ledgers.

"No," Northampton said.

Frances agreed.

"Not surprising," Coke said. "Took *me* a while." He turned the pages for them, pointing here and there, turning again. "Had to check and recheck. Only two names—initials in one case, see?—appear in both ledgers."

Northampton laughed, and Coke chuckled in amusement, too.

"Fascinating," Coke said, "as I said, only one. Yours, my lady. In both ledgers. This one belonged to a dressmaker—egregiously deficient in numbers. One Ann Turner. You *did* know her?"

"Slightly."

"Only slightly? It seems that you—though Mrs. Turner couldn't decide how to spell your name—were one of her best customers."

"I understand Queen Anne was her faithful client as well," Northampton said.

"But not *as* faithful, I think," Coke said lightly. "In any case, her name doesn't appear in our other ledger."

"But this one has no names at all," Northampton protested.

"No," Coke conceded, "Forman seems to have thought that by using initials, and by also reversing them, he could guarantee his clients' secrecy . . ."

"Initials? In reverse?" Northampton said. "What drivel!"

Coke smiled. "Look here. It's fascinating. I didn't catch on myself at first. The dressmaker convinced me. Look."

Frances followed his finger as if entranced: "La. Francis . . . La. Essex . . . Audlee end . . . Fr. How. Dev. . . . La. Essex . . ." Again, pages later: "La. Fr. . . . Fr. How. Car. . . . La. Som. . . ."

"How clever of you," Frances said. "Two married names."

"But look here," Coke said, switching ledgers and repeating the process: "DHF. £10. . . . DHF. £10. . . . CHF. £50. . . . CHF. £50. . . . CHF. £100 . . . Didn't tumble to it myself—he'd reversed the initials. Don't you see?" He was watching her very closely now. "And," he went on, "I checked very carefully. Once CHF appears, the other initial never reappears, but the payments increase substantially . . ."

"This means nothing," Northampton said.

"But it's fascinating in one respect," Coke said. "I took pains carefully to eliminate all names and all possible initials one might extrapolate from all names which do not appear in both ledgers. I was left with only three entries which, I submit, designate one and only one person. You, Lady Somerset, Lady Essex, Frances Howard Devereux, Frances Howard Carr. Frances Howard."

His voice produced a roaring sound in her ears; she felt nausea. Her great-uncle insisted that Coke leave, now. Afterward, he talked about her going back to Audley End. They needed as much time—any delay would help—as possible: to rally strength, to gather intelligence, to talk to Mr. Everard.

Frances was confused and angry. Hadn't Northampton said the initials were meaningless? Many names—Feltham, Fuller, Fox— would fit as well. How could one prove the initials had been reversed? Did the initials prove her contact with Forman?

"No," her great-uncle said, "but Coke knows you were there. Your face was a rosy map of confessional. Besides, he has other evidence. This is how he works. He merely unsettles his victims with the least weighty evidence against them. He'll be back. Soon, I'm afraid."

As usual, Northampton's judgment was unnervingly sound: the servants were readying luggage for her departure, and she was in the midst of her letter to Catherine, when Coke's men came with the warrant for her arrest. They told her she could finish the letter in the Tower, where a comfortable apartment—once occupied by Arabella Stuart—had been prepared for her.

XI

James had nodded off, and was startled when Queen Anne stormed into his bedchamber. She had been in a frightfully unpleasant temper lately, but the wrath now wrinkling her once lovelier but still lovely brow was more than usually menacing.

"Dear Anne," he said, "how delightful to see you betimes midday."

The tone of her voice more than matched her taut expression. "I am mortified to hear that you have arrested one of my few remaining friends . . ."

"Who?" he said.

"Lady Somerset."

"*Lady* Somerset?"

"Do not dissemble," she said. "I've suffered sufficient humiliation at your hands."

Truly, James was astonished, which but infuriated Anne, who thought his incredulity pretended, and therefore an insult.

"You are determined to destroy all Catholics in England, and to leave me desolate!"

With Gondomar breathing down his neck, he'd not likely succeed in that venture! Naturally, he denied Anne's interpretation out of hand, urging her to remain until he could fetch the Chief Justice. Though this offer seemed to attenuate her rage, Anne refused to wait, leaving James with a warning that, should Lady Frances be harmed or treated unjustly, she would be forced to consider either return to Denmark or exile in Spain.

James regarded her threat seriously; he had taken Anne too much for granted. Restoring his marriage was ascending in his scale of values requiring attention.

It took a while for the King's Guard to find Coke. It turned out that he had, for days, been conducting the virtual demolition of Simon Forman's house. Coke left the project reluctantly.

"We're on the verge," he said. "Forman was a proud man. He destroyed nothing."

"On the verge? When you've already arrested Lady Somerset?"

Coke reminded James that he'd said nothing about consulting him before a move against the Countess; besides, the evidence against her was overwhelming.

"My men have disassembled Forman's great desk," he said. "It had a false back. Full of interesting intelligence, including most rhapsodic letters in Lady Somerset's hand, conveniently signed with her own name."

"Rhapsodic?"

"And voluminously incriminating. She handled the payments. We had it wrong, you see. Somerset was in it, but the motive . . . Your Majesty . . . periphrasis will not do. It was simply insane."

"Not money?"

"Love."

"Love?"

Surprise compounded upon astonishment!

"And pride of reputation."

So. Love. And pride of reputation.

Coke proceeded to unfold the strangest tale from life or art that James had ever heard. The rendition held that beautiful, luscious Frances Howard was possessed of instincts fit to bring the blush to Lucifer's cheek.

"Utterly without conscience," Coke said.

"And Robin?"

"You told me not to arrest him without your express instructions."

"It's fortunate I did," James said. "You've no evidence against him. Lady Frances knew the magician, and had hired him, long ere she knew Robin . . ."

Coke admitted as much, but the sound of the Forman house being torn down had produced in the magician's wife an unexpected willingness to witness against others besides Lady Somerset.

"I fear your men dragged me away in the midst of it," he said.

"Mrs. Forman met someone: a man. She didn't know or wouldn't tell his name. The man wanted to buy letters from her. Forman must have run out of secret compartments; she'd found several letters stuffed into some of the tomes lying about. The man offered her fifty quid for all the letters in her possession. She sold him three, keeping two more to bargain with later."

They were interrupted as the door to the bedchamber opened and Villiers stepped triumphantly forward: Sir Edward's presence was urgently required without.

Coke came back with news that Bacon, who had proceeded with the interview of Mrs. Forman, had induced her full cooperation: the man's name was Ordway. He'd not be hard to find; the word was that he worked for the Howards, and had, most recently, been attached to Somerset.

"Where's Somerset now?" James asked.

"If my information is correct, Your Majesty, he's on his way here to call on you."

James shook his head. The whole episode—Carr's effrontery, his stupidity, his wife's callousness—defied belief. Only his fool, Archie, could make sense out of it.

James had wanted merely to cut the Howard crew down a bit, but this calamity, entirely unforeseen, was also without precedent. Win or lose in court, what could Robin salvage of his life now? And what about the Howards themselves? Frances, Suffolk, Lady Suffolk, Lady Catherine—and young Cecil? What about Cranfield, and . . .

"Northampton," he said. "What about Northampton?"

"Nothing," Coke said. "He's a clever man. I didn't expect we'd find anything against him."

"Still," James said, "it would seem odd that the one man whose hand is always in the fire is the only one never to get burned."

"He's cunning," Coke agreed, "perhaps unscrupulous. Even dangerous. But he's too intelligent to break the law."

James doubted that, himself. Still, it was a tantalizing thought. Perhaps when accused of paying court to Mary Stuart, escaping the block only by shifting blame to his older brother, he'd learned his limits well. But perhaps not.

"Or too clever to leave himself open," he countered.

Coke smiled.

"You don't think that's possible, do you?" James said.

"I don't," Coke said. "I couldn't. The law evens things out. Justice and virtue, though related, don't seem to me inseparable." Now he bowed gracefully. "But as a theologian, I am pleased to defer to Your Majesty."

That remark, though double-edged, was warm.

"About Somerset, Your Majesty. Shall we proceed? Is the evidence sufficient?"

"Take him," James said. "To hell with him. I never want to see his face again."

What else could he say? Coke seemed to have the evidence. And yet James wondered when, if ever, he *would* see Robin again: those twinkling blue eyes, that stunning, boyish smile.

"Oh, by the bye," Coke said, "come with me. I want you to see something."

In the antechamber, on a table, he indicated many pieces of statuary, all of them delightfully obscene.

"We found these, mostly at Forman's place. But look here." He held up two identical pieces for him to see. "One of these we found in Lady Somerset's closet."

James took one of the figurines—lovers copulating—and, turning it about, examined it closely.

"Fascinating, isn't it?" Coke said.

It was no more than expected when Carr proclaimed his innocence, but they knew he'd resist the inevitable regardless of means when he threatened to have Coke beheaded. From the time of the Somersets' arrest, Sir Edward and Francis Bacon worked in tandem; James let them know his need for confessions, without which he had little hope of quieting Anne, even less of settling the stirring passions of England's Catholic minority.

Coke thought it best to separate the Somersets until the trial. Carr protested, but by then they had grown accustomed to his spleen. He'd protested (besides the general outrage of innocence taken in false charges) his quarters, the food, the service, the wine and the chamber-pots.

"What about Gondomar?" he said to Coke. "He hated Overbury. He's got regiments of spies. I want to talk to James!"

By the time a fortnight had passed, Robin was almost demented with rage. "I'll not stand for this trial," he told Bacon. "You tell Jamie I'll not stay silent. Tell him the entire business will come out—the

Pearl, the whole of it—if he leaves me here. I know how he managed the whole affair. About Prince Henry, too. It was that bloody Mayerne. He's the one. Do you think I'm ignorant? He's the common agent in both affairs! Hanging on the doomed men's breasts: Prince Henry, Tom."

Bacon tried to calm him. "My lord, I caution you. Loose tongues respecting kings wag hard enough to shake off heads."

"You tell Jamie," Carr said, "that if I stand accused before the Lords, then Mayerne and His Majesty go with me to the dock!"

Unfortunately, it wasn't a threat James could treat lightly. What if Robin held forth in the House of Lords with mad accusations? James wanted to reassemble a friendly Parliament. The Howards were working strenuously (using their usual arsenal of persuasion, bribery and coercion) on two fronts: with the Lords on the Somerset case, and with the King's Commission on Port Customs. In the latter case, they had won a two-month delay at just the time a very negative outcome seemed assured; James now feared a complete turnabout, in which the Howards would storm back more arrogant and powerful than ever.

Villiers had come forward with a good suggestion. Why not use Sir James Hay as an intermediary? He was Carr's original sponsor, with whom he had sojourned in France. Carr and he had remained on good terms, and if Hay did well, he could be made a viscount, perhaps.

Hay, a decent man with very expensive tastes, agreed to the mission. After telling Carr that James was a forbearing, generous friend, he returned with the news that Carr had responded with a threat.

"You told him I'd see no harm came to him?" James said.

"Yes, Your Majesty."

"And his reply?"

"He fretted himself more. He said that Your Majesty must prohibit this trial lest he reveal such facts as will require Your Majesty's summons before the Peers as well."

Hay was an honorable man; James had always admired him, but never more than at that moment, carrying this ridiculous message, carrying it without cowardice despite the danger its possession might mean to him.

"He said this in words round about or in these exactly?" James asked.

Hay was a few years older than James, but he stood very handsome and tall; he looked younger than the King.

"He made roundabout a good measure," Hay said, "but this was the substance . . ."

James strode about the room; he tried a door of the cabinet near the window, which stuck at first but then flew open with a clatter of silver. He poured himself a large draught of brandy and swallowed a good bit of it before speaking.

"That ignorant, outlandish cur," he said, biting off the syllables slowly. "I gave him love and wealth and power to my own detriment. Loved him above any man . . ."

He poured again, then thought to offer Sir James a drop. Now, drinking as he traversed the room, he spoke in part to Hay, but mostly to himself, his voice rising steadily.

"Then I, after elevating this base creature from a stupidly grinning page, for whom it was great pain merely to sit a horse, to an earl, must be threatened by him? I, King of England, Scotland and Ireland, must prohibit the House of Lords from reaching its own judgment? Or be tried myself?"

Hay looked grave.

"For what?" James almost shouted.

"Your Majesty, my Lord Somerset was grievously agitated. He spoke rashly."

After weeks of alarums, shocks, charges, suspicions, indictments, it was nonetheless difficult for James to digest—to believe—Hay's report. If true, then Robin had gone mad. Like Arabella Stuart, fallen melancholy, demented.

Insanity gnawed at the edges of his court these days, had ever since the Powder Plot. But this Somerset affair was surely the maddest of all. How could self-deception have been so great as to give the Somersets hope of success? A complete break with James meant that Robin's life was forfeit. Surely he knew that?

No, in his stupid, Scots way, Carr was following the promise of a frail hope: he might create a stir among the Lords, who hated James even more than they hated him.

James had no way of knowing what Carr might reveal, but he had confided in him virtually all of the confidential workings of his government. One might ask: Who would believe Somerset when, in an effort to save his own life, he shifted focus to the sins of others? Who would listen to accusations of King James from this source?

The grim answer was too apparent: Why, those who wished to

believe Somerset, those to whom that belief gave advantage.

One could always depend on that sodden lot of thick-headed Puritans to believe anything. "Credulity" was the proper Christian name of that dull crew. No matter what the accusation, somebody would believe Carr; James would be in for more unpleasantness.

Statecraft was an uncertain art; its rules guided rather than guaranteed power. When someone in a high and favored place like Robin turned his coat, he was as dangerous to a sovereign as was the plague to a congested city. His insinuations were like the unraveling of a knitted garment: once it started, it could continue until nothing of the useful form remained.

"And," James said, "of precisely what offense will I be charged?"

Hay was showing signs of stress. In merely bearing the message, he was a party, in some degree, to this idea of James's complicity—in what? How much did Hay know? How much had Robin told him? Now Hay flushed; perspiration dotted his forehead. His usually fluent speech came haltingly. He knew that no matter what he did or said the question would now remain: Did Carr say anything that might incriminate the King? How much of what Carr actually said would Hay admit to James?

Though a loyal subject, and a competent ambassador, in this instance Sir James had not proved a very lucky one.

"If memory serves, Your Majesty," he said, "these were his words: 'James will regret it.' He mentioned Your Majesty's trial, with himself as witness . . ."

"*For* the Crown?" James said.

Hay bowed. "A paradox," he said, "which he perceived not. I repeated your instructions thus: 'My Lord Somerset, I am not here as audience to seditious lies, nor to advise you in anything other than the King's good wishes for you. He urges you to plead guilty before the Lords, and to put your trust in his love and mercy.' "

His words had the clarion ring of truth in them. Though smooth government was impossible without Machiavellis like Northampton, no king could survive, much less flourish, lacking the helpful hands of honest men like Hay about, especially where money changes hands.

Suffolk's failure had proved that.

However, even honest men will give pause at entangling themselves in dangerous matters of no immediate concern to their families. It was unfortunate that James had so entangled Hay, yet it was also too late not further to entangle him.

No matter what Robin had said or might say on a second meeting, James had to send Hay back. He deserved better treatment, but better two than three people should know more than was good for them.

Hay knew the dangers of his position very well: what if Somerset survived his present circumstances, and returned to favor?

By now, Hay was aware that James depended on Robin's silence, but he was too loyal to repeat what Robin might have said.

"Sir James," the King said, making his voice as firm as possible, "I must ask another favor of you. I see that you are tired, but you must return to the Tower with this further word from me. Tell Somerset to beware lest he exhaust the love and patience of a sovereign who has been generous to him above all reason, at much pain often to himself and to the Queen. Tell him to beware lest all mercy fly from me and turn to rage against him and his wife. Tell him that my anger can be as awful as my love was warm. I will not be threatened. If he persists, I shall let Coke loose against him with a charge of treason. Coke will see his skin hung in strips on pikes before his eyes, and his intestines set afire in front of him."

He watched Hay for his reactions: the man looked suddenly older than he had moments ago.

"Is that all, Your Majesty?" he said.

"No. Tell him this also: that if he is to expect any indulgence of the King's mercy, he must itemize precisely those offenses of which he fancies me dragged before my own Lords."

Hay flushed and returned James's gaze with beseeching eyes. Here was a man wise enough to avoid confidences, especially those of such substance as this.

"You would have him tell me this by word, Your Majesty? I beg you ask it in a letter which I may convey to you under seal."

James caught just the faintest suggestion of a sob in his voice, but if he was feeling pity for himself he showed no other sign of it. He was moved by Hay's request; it was a filthy piece of work he was asking.

"I'm afraid not," he said. "Let him put nothing in writing; if he has pen and paper, see they are taken from him. Tell him his vagrant pen would but inscribe 'Jacobus Regis' to his death warrant."

---

*   *   *

THEY TOLD her it was May 24, 1614, the day they led her forth through Traitor's Gate to the pier, and thence by barge upstream to Westminster. The date meant nothing to her. For weeks, the days and nights had melted together into indistinguishable episodes of vomiting and weeping.

Nobody, not even her great-uncle, had come to see her.

Her counsel, Mr. Everard, had insisted on this regime as part of his tactics. She was not to give any appearance of subterfuge. It must seem that she rested wholly in her trust of James's mercy.

"Your life depends upon it!" he said at frequent intervals. He had tried to convince her to plead guilty: "This is our best tactic. Your life depends upon it. Lay your trust in God and your King."

The Assembly House in Westminster was surrounded by an angry mob. She thought she caught sight of young men of the Howard clan; they were fighting with soldiers and heretics, as if they would free the prisoner. She got only a glance at them, and their cause was hopeless.

She listened wearily as the indictment was read out against her, and the names of its signators were called: Thomas Ellesmere, Chancellor of England, Earl of Worcester; Sir Ralph Winwood; Fulke Greville, Lord Brooke. Then the names of the lords themselves resonated in the large chamber: Worcester (again), Pembroke, Sussex, Montgomery, Hereford, Surrey, Norfolk—on and on, but not a single friend. Even the Earl of Bedford had found means to attend. He'd be enjoying himself: how he despised the Howards. The only face present in which she could discern the least sign of sympathy was that of the Attorney General, Sir Francis Bacon.

The Sergeant-at-Arms delivered the patent to the Lord High Steward, who placed it on his knee; he kissed it, then passed it to Mr. Fenshawe, its original holder. The process, Mr. Everard had said, was meant to be slow; she must resist the tendency to fret or to feel despair at the ceremony.

Nobody was looking her way, and yet it seemed that all eyes were upon her. She was dressed in a black tammel, a cypress chaperon and a cobweb lawn ruff and cuffs. She had brought her black fan (that also was Mr. Everard's idea); she moved the fan across her face as one "Oyez!" after another echoed through the chamber.

Mr. Everard coaxed her to her feet; as they had rehearsed, she made three low bows to the court.

Mr. Fenshawe, Clerk of the Crown, stood up. "Frances, Countess of Somerset, hold up thy hand!"

Now he repeated the indictment, the greater part of it based on evidence linking her, as the woman of quality, to the confessions of Weston and Gervase. Apparently Franklin had never learned her name, after all.

She hadn't meant to, but she trembled, and tears scorched their way down her cheeks. She covered her face with the fan and struggled for composure.

Just then, a stir passed through the assembly. Sir Edward Coke strode toward the platform carrying the brass figurine that Forman had given her—and another just like it.

"You see?" Everard was whispering to her. "And he must have the letters, too."

"Frances, Countess of Somerset!" Mr. Fenshawe cried. "What sayest thou? Art thou guilty of this felony of murder, or not guilty?"

"Remember," Everard said.

Frances bowed to the Lord High Steward.

"Guilty," Everard whispered (but with such resonance that all must have heard him).

She could not take her eyes from the statues, which Coke had put on full display on the platform. She could not bear to hear that insolent man read her letters to Forman in that place, with all the great lords of England present.

"Guilty," she said, and she saw Coke smile directly at her.

Now Mr. Everard went forward. "My Lord High Steward," he said, "may it please Your Grace, I am glad to hear my lady's so free acknowledgment, for confession is noble. Those who have formerly been indicted, at their arraignment, persisted in denial, as Weston, Elwes, Franklin and Turner. And yet some here say to you that since the crime was the same, the punishment must be so, too. But now you see Lady Somerset's humility and repentance. Certainly she is worthy of some commiseration, if you consider her sex, and the gift of life— of God—in her, for she is with child. Or if you consider her honorable parentage. I beg you recall that the Mercy-seat is in the innermost part of the Temple. I pray you record this confession, and arrive at merciful judgment. Since the peers are met, for honor's sake, I beg you recall that no noble blood has yet been spilled since His Majesty's reign. My lords, I pray you declare for the King's justice, but also for the King's mercy . . ."

He went on to rehearse the history of the murder, pointing out that she had suborned the silence of others at such length that she began to wonder if he were not, in his love of rhetoric, undercutting his client's claim to mercy. When he finally sat, the King's instructions resounded in the chamber: James wanted two questions answered. Did the Somersets kill Overbury? If not, who had cast aspersions upon them?

Sir Edward Coke proclaimed that no jot of His Majesty's instructions had been overlooked. "Rumor aside," he said, looking at Everard, "regardless of the whisperings pertinent to Weston's death, we have the record to the hour of his death. He *did* confess, previous efforts of counsel to obscure this fact notwithstanding. He confessed and died penitent, which is all we ask here: the King's justice is firm in being even-handed. If we need him to prove this point, Weston's confessor is here with us, namely, Dr. Whiting, who can wondrously testify to these things . . ."

"May it please Your Grace," Mr. Everard said, "whereas Lady Somerset has been indicted as an accessory before the fact, of the willful poisoning of Sir Thomas Overbury, whereas she had been indicted and arraigned and upon her arraignment pleaded guilty, I ask only that her confession be recorded, and that your judgment be given now against the prisoner."

The lords fell silent.

"Frances, Countess of Somerset, hold up thy hand."

Placing her fan in her left hand, but still trying to cover her face, Frances obeyed.

"Whereas," Fenshawe said, "you have been indicted, arraigned, and pleaded guilty, as accessory before the fact to the willful poisoning and murder of Sir Thomas Overbury, what canst thou now say for thyself why judgment of death ought not to be pronounced against thee?"

Frances swallowed and gasped for breath. "I can much aggravate," she said, "but nothing extenuate my fault. I desire mercy, and that the lords will intercede for me with the King."

Lord Ellesmere indicated that he'd not heard her, and asked that

318

she repeat the statement; Everard repeated it for her. Then Sir Richard Coningsby, who had remained seated before the Lord High Steward throughout, rose, and from his knee lifted a long white staff.

Ellesmere spoke in tones which seemed to reverberate while seeming subdued: "Frances, Countess of Somerset, whereas thou hast been indicted, arraigned, pleaded guilty, and since thou canst say nothing for thyself, it is now my part to pronounce judgment. Only I must say this before. Since my lords have heard with what humility and repentance you have confessed, I have no doubt that they will signify as much to the King, and pray for his grace toward you. But in the meantime, according to law the sentence shall be this: that thou shalt be returned to the Tower, and from thence to the Place of Execution, where you are to be hanged by the neck till you be dead, and the Lord have mercy upon your soul."

Hanged by the neck.

Hanged by the neck till you be dead.

Now the chamber was still. Someone coughed; it was she. Her legs refused to hold fast beneath her. It was terrible: the picture in her mind of being hanged by the neck until, like Ann Turner, she was dead—it was more than she could bear. She needed her friends. Where was her family? Her mother? Her great-uncle? (To be hanged by the neck!) For this sentence she had humbled herself, trusted Everard, trusted the lords. And yet her sentence was no different from Ann Turner's.

Now she trembled violently; Mr. Everard helped her from the chamber, out into the air, for which she opened her mouth hungrily.

The wind was blowing, she was grateful for that. She longed to stay out of doors, and not to be hanged by the neck until she was dead. She longed to breathe the air, even, yes, even to be a commoner, playing in the marsh where the land sloped from the Great House at Audley End to the river. She longed to be young again, truly young, with all of it to do over again. She'd be less sure of herself, less greedy, less of a Howard. How was it, she wondered, that others avoided this fate—to be hanged by the neck? Was she so different?

To have the rope placed about her neck, where no mother, no father, no great-uncle could remove it. They would cover her head with a cowl, a black cowl, and hang her by the neck. Lead her to Tyburn Tree, guide her because (she knew) she'd be weeping. She would plead with them, beg, pray, but they'd take no heed. She had seen the marvelous efficiency at executions when Ann suffered, how Derrick, unmindful of the tumult around him, went about his business as if he were a groom currying a stallion, or a tinker mending a leaky pot. To be hanged by the neck!

She thought Ann Turner had let go a kick when they hanged her, but nobody could have known for sure; the crowd had pushed very close, and there was fighting. When one hanged, death came from the moment the rope went about the neck. No life was possible from that instant. No one had ever been spared, once in the cart. And yet the doomed ones stood there, making speeches, as if words had magic power to match the strength of hemp, of hanging by the neck. But she, Frances Howard, was not stupid: it made no sense to struggle in that extremity.

The lords held out the possibility of the King's mercy; this had been the aim of Everard's "tactics" all along. Her freedom would come in the end, he believed, when it was timely for James to give mercy. Mercy, grace: she was doubtful of receiving any portion of it. And if not, since they would bring her no priest, she must die in mortal sin.

Her agony seemed without limit. Her mind raced, examining minute details of every possible horror: And the Lord have mercy upon your soul. Ellesmere had breathed that prayer, but he'd not provide her with a priest. Then it seemed that Frances would never in this world know another moment of peace.

She longed for sleep. And yet (to be hanged by the neck) it seemed that rest would never return to her.

She could see the waters of the Thames. They were aboard the barge; the watermen were heading back to the Tower.

Everard held her hand. "You'll be permitted your own servants now," he said.

"Oh," she said. "All of them?"

"Several, surely," he said. "Yes. I'll look into it. Which ones do you prefer I have sent at once?"

It didn't matter. She had no preference; she had no one. She'd received no word from Robin. If only a priest were by to hear her confession: May God have mercy upon your soul.

"You know," Everard said, "after Lord Somerset's trial tomorrow, they'll let Robin join you. You'll be together."

"Oh?"

Her sins grieved her, and yet the King had extinguished from the world her only means of penance and absolution. She longed to pray, to sleep, to escape. She tried to give her thoughts to Audley End, to the only thing in her life that had ever afforded pleasures for which she had not been asked to pay with her life.

If only she had a rosary. If only time weren't such a tyrant. If only one event could be dislodged from his mindless dominion: Overbury's death. If the past could be altered by only that single, minuscule moment, when his body gave way. If only she needn't hang by the neck.

Why were men so cruel? Hadn't she suffered enough? She'd not live so see her son grow up to be an earl. Never ride the meadows (Christ have mercy) with her sturdy mare surging beneath her, never see (Lord have mercy) Audley End again.

Now Frances exerted all the pent-up energy of weeks with little movement in an effort to hurtle the barge railing. She braced herself against the rude grasp of the men's gnarled hands, which she knew would never let her go. She felt instead the vertigo of one falling into space.

And then the cold waters of the Thames took her.

She was so grateful she'd not learned to swim, always resisted the taunts of Catherine and her great-uncle.

The angry currents of the river turned her over, and drew her down, down.

Somewhere, she could hear a young girl's voice, marvelously clear, marvelously innocent, and it made her glad: "Hail Mary, full of Grace, blessed art thou among women, and blessed is the fruit of thy womb, Jesus. Holy Mary, Mother of God, Pray for us sinners now and at the hour of our . . ."

Death was Robin's sentence, too. He had pleaded innocent, but to no avail.

They brought him to the Tower apartment late the following afternoon. Frances was still rocky from her brush with death by drowning, from which the watermen (with, according to them, no time at all to spare) had rescued her.

"Hanging!" he cried. "*Me!* This is all your doing."

"I, too, Robin," she said. "I'm to hang as well."

"But you killed him," he said. "I didn't."

"I told them that," she said. Talking hurt her head. "Mr. Everard said you were tried as an accessory after, as well as before, the fact. You'd get the same sentence in either case."

"The sentence of hanging for merely marrying someone."

"They'll not hang you. I'll not let them."

"You'll not? Do you think they'll listen to you? You and your child will get clemency, but not me."

"*My* child?"

"You don't suppose I'll claim the little demon, do you? With the coals of hell burning in his eyes?"

"The child will be yours. Oh, Robin, everything I did—don't you understand?—I did for you. For the love of you. Only that. I couldn't live without your love."

"You fool!" he cried, slapping her in the face with the flat of his hand. "So I can't live because of it."

Frances felt at that moment as if she were made of stone or wood, devoid of either fear or grief or hate or love; she couldn't weep, and when she spoke it was without a trace of self-pity or reproach.

"The child will be yours."

"I'll not have it," he said. "I refuse to be its father. I hope they hang you ere its born. You are a despicable . . . whore! Just as Tom, the only true friend I ever had, said of you. He warned me. But I'd not listen. I was too foolish to know the truth when it was told me."

"You wish me dead? You wish the child dead?"

Now, though she felt weak and light-headed, she tried to focus on the meaning in Robin's eyes, in the lines about his tightly closed mouth, the deep trenches of hysteria etched on his brow and splaying from the furrows of his eyes.

Was it all for this? Had she separated herself from her family, the King, from all that was good in her life—and from God—for this sallow, bloated, cringing wretch?

"Yes," she said. "Sir Thomas was an intelligent, discerning man. He thought you insufferably weak. Hopelessly stupid. Ridiculously dependent. And silly. He said your looks were your fortune. He was a witty man. What a riotous laugh it would give him if he could see you thus!"

XII

Now James had the initiative, and he aimed to make the most of it.

The first order of business was to see Gondomar; James served notice on Philip III that either the marriage contract between Charles and the Infanta Maria be settled soon or England must look elsewhere, perhaps in France, for a suitable match. He wrote to Frederick with greetings to Elizabeth and a stern warning to his son-in-law against further delay in suppressing religious opposition in Bohemia. He signed the death warrants of two fiery dissenters who refused to accede to the Oath of Allegiance or repeat the Lord's Prayer. To make the issue even clearer, he set about writing a tractate on the virtues of Church government and the simple beauty of the Lord's Prayer, which his subjects were to regard as the model of devotion. He finished the manuscript, dedicated it to his son, and before day's end instructed Villiers to take it to the printer.

He slept well that night.

Early the next morning, he set out betimes for a stroll in Green Park. The swans were gliding on the smooth surface of the pond; birdsong filled the trees. It would be a fine day for a boat ride.

At first, the transport of his thoughts shut out the insistent cries of excitement, but now he could see the smoke. He moved toward it: the Banqueting House was on fire.

Men were trying to put the blaze out, but it looked hopeless. The fire was spectacular; it drove the men back to where they could only stand watching as the Banqueting House roared to destruction . . .

When James arrived at the state room, Villiers looked nervous. The

French Ambassador, Gondomar, Bacon, Ellesmere and—most important—Northampton were waiting to see him.

"Anyone else?" James said.

"John Donne has been about for days," Villiers said.

"Send Northampton in," James said.

In consideration of their past intimacy (friendship wasn't quite the right word), the King began amiably.

"Too bad about Rainolds."

"Yes, Your Majesty. I heard."

"John Rainolds," James said. "Dean of Corpus Christi. Did you know him?"

"Not actually . . ."

"He'll be remembered for his great work. Have you studied the new translation of the Bible?"

He handed the folio to Northampton.

Northampton smiled. "The Archbishop sent me a copy," he said.

"We needed it," James went on. "It's no good having thirty-seven versions of God's Word floating about. Angers people! Causes trouble. What think you of the new translation?"

"I've not had a chance to look at it, Your Majesty."

"Naturally not," James said. "I mean what do you think of the idea?"

"Of uniformity . . . ?"

James answered only half in jest. "Yes. Of an end to anarchy, dissent, arrogance."

"You know my feelings," Northampton said. "I'd be happier with the Douai. Save the expense."

Here was an understated, flat statement of allegiance to Rome.

"Hmmm," James said. "I prefer an English translation authorized in England, done in England for Englishmen: the same text, the same good sense, the same loyalty in every parish on this island."

Northampton nodded. "Politically, I can see value in it," he said. "But ten years of work by thirty or more men and ten thousand pounds is a cost very dear for a token conformity."

"The cost, yes," James said. "I'm glad you mentioned money. I have in my possession the final report of my Commission on the Port of London."

As he'd expected, Northampton was surprised: James had taken steps to have the report completed by a sequestered panel the day before.

"I have already replaced Suffolk at the Exchequer, and his minion, Ingram, at the wharves. A commoner, whose talents you first brought to my attention, will take over the Treasury . . ."

"Cranfield," Northampton said.

James smiled. "Furthermore," he said, "I have asked your brother kindly to look after his own estates with greater propriety than he has mine. As one evidence of his good wishes toward us he shall agree— I know that you will help see that he agrees—to look after the care of his daughter, whom I shall release from the Tower, and from the sentence of hanging, so long as she never returns to London, so long as she remains in a certain cottage of my choice, and so long as she makes no effort to contact anyone outside her immediate family: Suffolk, her sister, you . . ."

Northampton listened quietly to what he knew was the death sentence to his own aspirations and to the prestige of the Howard family.

"Lady Frances and her husband have spurned the love I have poured out on them," James said. "They threaten me. They murder my subjects. They suborn witnesses. They traffic with devils. They break all laws of God and of man. Yet certain lords desire that noble blood not be spilled. I accede to their wishes. And you know, as Somerset appears not yet to know, that I had no intention either of them should pay with their lives for their misdeeds. However, lest anyone—even you—misunderstand this mercy you must hear me now and well. For you are not guiltless in this. Much suspicion hangs over you—and has hung over you since the Powder Treason. I take note of this only to remind you that nothing is forgotten. Nothing. No king can afford to forget a suspicion of treason, especially when it involves one in a powerful position. The Howard family has offered great services through the years, and we are grateful for them. But it is time for the Howards to be . . . less in evidence."

Northampton nodded his consent, but looked very grave indeed. Slowly, he withdrew his snuffbox.

"Times are changing," James said. "It may interest you to know that I am appointing Sir Francis Bacon as my new Lord Chancellor. Sir Ralph Winwood will continue. Sir Edward Coke will go on as Lord Chief Justice, and I shall use him as an adviser on my relations with Parliament. I shall recall Parliament. Does this surprise you? The times. Coke may be no friend to my views, but to Parliament he's a hero—their hero. Therefore, I acknowledge his manifold accomplishments. Though not from one of our great families, if the need occurs he can be made an earl, like Villiers here, whom I shall name the Duke of Buckingham. A king can make favorites, as I have, but he can give no assurances of what befalls them afterward. I wish it were not so. You are a man who wears well on the tastes of a jaded monarch. But kings must bend before the swelling storm of popular discontent."

"So the Puritans win," Northampton said. "New Bible and the lot."

"No. I shall deal with them, too. But let us deal with the Howards first. It grieves me to say that, like your brother, you must answer for the sins of others. History is unkind to bystanders. On the other hand, you could be held to answer for certain discrepancies with the *Pearl* cargo. I prefer to forget that. If—and only if—you agree to find immediate retreat from the trivial distractions of my court."

"Your Majesty," he said.

"A way of life is coming to an end in this country," James said. "The Crown must survive this clamor from the papists and the Puritans, and the Howards will provide the Crown with one last service by being instruments of that survival. The ultimate expression of their love shall be a quiet exile from the prominence which so well suited the family's history and breeding. Goodbye, Henry."

It was the first time James had ever called Northampton by his Christian name; he intended it would be the last time they would meet.

"I'll have time, perhaps," Northampton said, "to have a surgeon look at that ulcer in my leg."

"Ah," James said. "Is it painful?"

"Rather. Either it grows more painful, or my years have added impatience to my faults. Farewell, Your Majesty."

"May I send Mayerne?"

"No. No. I have old Clark in mind. He's an—"

"Incompetent butcher!"

"But an old friend."

James noticed that Northampton limped lightly as he withdrew . . .

Obviously, Suffolk's idea was to ride out the storm at Audley End. But he answered the King's summons, arriving late the following day. James told him much the same thing he'd told Northampton (knowing that probably Suffolk had heard it all the night before). Suffolk took the news gracefully; James had the impression that Suffolk was relieved to have all responsibility off his shoulders.

"You understand," James said, "that my exile of your daughter depends on the Somersets' remaining on the grounds of a small cottage in Westmoreland. Once belonged to Cecil. The family must support them; all their properties have been confiscated. They are not to leave the cottage grounds; they, who claimed to desire nothing in this world (including honor) besides each other, will have nothing more. You may visit them once a year: at Christmas."

"When will they leave the Tower?" Suffolk said.

"The moment Somerset admits his guilt."

"And if he persists in claiming innocence?"

"He won't," James said. "If he does, then the Somersets will cleave to each other's bosom in the Tower rather than in the country air of Westmoreland. The family will undertake their support in either case."

He understood.

"There is the matter of one million five hundred thousand pounds."

Suffolk had read the report.

"Your Majesty's Commission did concede the figure approximate."

"We shall be flexible: approximately one million five hundred thousand pounds . . . of Crown revenue . . ."

"Your Majesty," Suffolk said, "I believe it was wise to replace me. The responsibility outweighed my limited skill . . ."

"Not at all," James said. "You did splendidly. Had you not hired Cranfield, probably nobody would have found you out. His practice with numbers deserves praise. He replaces you, as you may know. Which leaves us with the . . . embarrassment of the one million five hundred thousand pounds . . ."

"I could sign articles of debenture," Suffolk said.

"I think not," James said. "If you outlived Methuselah, you'd not find means to make them good. The Crown needs money, goods, not promises."

"Am I to infer that I, too, will be hearing from Coke?"

"No," James said. "You'll hear from *me*. Now. Given present conditions, Parliament would not have permitted me to construct so elegant a palace as Audley End. You have perfected a royal estate. Here is the means of your repayment."

"But Your Majesty, Audley End is worth many times the amount . . ."

"I know it."

"I spent more than the million and a half redecorating, and adding the new wing!"

"Then you agree," James said. "It's unseemly to split hairs, or cavil over small coins. The felonious spending of our funds was—as you admit—approximately one million five hundred thousand pounds, give or take a decade in the Tower, with your friend Shrewsbury, and a fine of . . . how much did you say Audley End is worth?"

"I shall have our weary Mr. Everard prepare the deed," Suffolk said.

"Ah, yes. Lawyers," James said. "Remember you what Shakespeare's rabble clamor for in Jack Cade's rebellion?"

He did not.

" 'The first thing we do,' " James reminded him, " 'let's kill all the lawyers.' Overbury was a lawyer, and look what happened to him. Imaginative. Lawyers can't have imagination. John Donne's out there waiting for me to tell him that he can go into the Virginia Company, or into my service, as a practicing lawyer. I'll make him a clergyman instead. He's got too much imagination. Imaginative attorneys are a peril to themselves and others. Lawyers have to be hard-headed and stubborn like Coke, or elusive, like Bacon, or canny, like . . . your brother. Everard is right to stay with ordinary practice—out of politics. Had Northampton done so, perhaps . . . Craft and guile are mixed blessings, except when characteristics of a monarch."

"Yes, Everard is wise . . ."

"I, in turn, shall instruct Coke that the approximate amount of the discrepancy has been restored," James said, "with proper interest . . . amicably."

Suffolk was gazing at the floor as if transfixed, unable gracefully to withdraw.

"Sad about the Banqueting House," he mused irrelevantly.

"Quite a blaze," James said. "But if it hadn't burned down or fallen down, Inigo James would soon have set a torch to it. He never liked it. Wanted to rebuild it after the Palladian manner of his Italian masters. We'll let him do it, I think. Let him build it with coffered ceilings fit for murals. We'll invite the world's greatest painter to London to discharge the commission!"

"Ah," Suffolk said. "Michelangelo Caravaggio!"

"Do you like Rubens?" James said, hoping to end the interview on a less formidable note.

"Yes . . ." Suffolk said uncertainly.

"Excellent," James said. "Then it's decided."

He felt a jaunty spring in his stride when, that evening, he went to Anne's suite. He had settled the Howard matter with great aplomb; he was proud of himself. And he'd sent word to the Queen that they might have dinner served for just the two of them. Since he'd received no open rebuff, he was not surprised to find his visit, if not precisely welcome, at least expected.

The supper boded well, beginning as it did with his favorite appetizer: whitebait. Guessing that Anne was trying (with no sacrifice of poise) to provide an opening for him, he plunged ahead:

"I'm sorry, actually, about the Somersets, I mean," he said.

"What have you done with them?"

"I gave them mercy. They'll not die. But I can't release them until Robin confesses. His lawyer will persuade him, or Suffolk."

She seemed resigned to it.

"Anne," he said, "I want to talk about us. I want you to be happy again. Forget the Howards. Forget these ideas that I wish to destroy your friends, or the handful of papists about you. Move into Somerset House. It's yours."

She didn't speak, but the lines in her face softened.

"You can hold court there more comfortably," he said. "Get Inigo Jones over there to redecorate. Let Ben Jonson open the season there, with a masque on the terrace, and a good seafight, with fireworks on the river."

Now she was pleased; he took the occasion to kiss her on the cheek. She offered no resistance.

"And what say you to another good idea? Let's go to Audley End again this summer."

She looked startled.

"You liked it there, didn't you?" he said.

"Yes, but I have terrible memories of it as well."

"Of Henry?" he said. "Charles will go with us. He'll ride out with me every morning . . ."

"But what of the Howards? You said we'd forget them."

"We shall. I have already. Audley End is now a royal palace—a preserve, so to speak, for a selfish royal family, seeking privacy. We freed old Suffolk; you'll like that. Let him off the hook. He settled the debt by surrendering what was never his."

He offered her an embrace, and coaxed a smile from her.

"I'm glad of Suffolk's release," she said. "I do like that area near Cambridge. I love Somerset House. But what of Villiers? What will you give him?"

"Less."

"Than Robin?"

"Much less than I gave him."

"Not Sherborne?"

"Sherborne belongs to Sir Walter Raleigh, does it not?"

Now she beamed.

"Raleigh has the curious notion that in parts of America he can dig up gold only a foot under the ground. I've a mind to let him try. It will give us more room in the Tower, and it's apt to make you more . . . tractable."

"Charles and I would like to spend more time with you . . ."

"*Charles* and you?"

"I . . . would," she said.

"And you shall," he said.

IN THE SUMMER the Tower of London was hot; gnats swarmed off the river, and it seemed that, unless she moved about with Anne in her arms, the baby squealed without surcease, much to Robin's chagrin. Robin had expected a son—born with horns no doubt!—and a portion of his resentment waned when little Anne was born. Still, he had said little to her during the months of waiting under the death sentence, whose execution the lords delayed until after the child's birth. Then James sent word of mercy to Frances.

Weeks more of waiting followed; Mr. Everard said the King wanted only Robin's public confession, which Robin stubbornly refused to give, saying that he was innocent and therefore had nothing to confess.

But the enervating heat and the insects wore him down, and by the time Anne was a month old he signed the confession.

Frances was glad to be quit the Tower, but she hated the prospect of leaving London forever. It would be good to live in the country air, but she wondered if life could be borne without the excitement of the city.

Accompanied by two lieutenants of the Tower, they left London by carriage. As they rolled through London's narrow streets, Frances drank in every sight: people scurrying, shops teeming, fruitmongers bent over their barrows, St. Paul's. The trip took five days; Robin fretted every evening, for the guards insisted that he dine with her in their room. Frances was exhausted when they finally arrived.

She hadn't expected quarters comparable to Audley End or Somerset House, but the cottage, unbelievably small, was made to look even smaller by the high stone wall surrounding it, overgrown as it was with roses and eglantine.

Robin was horrified. "It's a clownish gamekeeper's cottage," he said.

The lieutenant nodded: "This is it, my lord."

"You mustn't pass beyond that gate," the other man said.

"But there's scarce room to turn about in here," Robin said.

The men from the Tower went about unloading baggage from atop the carriage; the coachman watched them, yawning obscenely.

"It may not be so bad," Frances said. "We can at least breathe. We can cut back these vines, and grow things. Work in the dooryard."

"For forty or fifty years!" he cried. "With you? And that squalling twit in there? It's hell. Hell. I should have stayed in the Tower, or let them hang me."

"Not so loud, please," she said. "You're frightening the baby."

"Don't shout orders at me," he said. "You're not the King's warden here, but a prisoner, just like me."

"Sshhhh," she said, "the baby's crying . . ."

"To hell with the baby!" he said. "To hell with you. To hell with this miserable hermit's cell."

Frances placed the child in the carefully groomed crib that had been prepared, and went to the kitchen.

"There's plenty of good food here," she said.

"To the devil with it."

"Aren't you hungry?"

Robin didn't answer, so she knew he must be. There were many kinds of fruit in the larder: apples, oranges, grapes, currants, blackberries. She bit into a large, firm, tangy apple.

"Would you like some fruit?" she said.

"If you want to know," he said, "I'd like a venison pasty. I'm famished. All the way from London I've been watching that little monster guzzling at your paps. Now I'd like a pasty."

Frances stood uncertainly.

"Well?" he said.

"The oranges look good . . ."

"I want something with meat in it, and a crust," he said. "A pasty."

"How does one make them?"

"Wouldn't you know it?" he said. "In Scotland every girl learns how to bake a pasty ere she's old enough to have her bottom pinched!"

"I'm not Scottish," she said.

"You slovenly Englishwomen never learn anything."

"Be quiet. You'll wake Anne."

"God's nails! I'll have to teach this whore how to cook."

"I'll not let you teach me. I'll teach myself."

The taller of the two lieutenants bent over as he stepped through the doorway.

"We're leaving now," he said. "I was told to warn you that, if you violate conditions of the King's mercy, you are subject to imprisonment or to the original sentence. Do you understand."

They did.

"God save the King!"

"Sard," Robin said. "I'm so hungry. I'd fancy a pasty or a great, sizzling slab of gammon, and a half-dozen crisp blueberry tarts."

"We have pears," Frances said. "Tomorrow I'll try to cook a pheasant, if you'll help me get the feathers off. There's a pheasant hanging out there. Do you like pheasant?"

"It's good with orange sauce, but I'm famished now."

"There's a loaf of bread out there. Shall I see if they left cheese?"

He seemed agreeable to that. Frances went to the kitchen to sort out supplies. She was feeling peckish, too. If she could find a brick of cheese to go with the bread, they'd be satisfied until morning. She could start learning then.

"Stupid cock-chafer," Robin muttered from the next room. "Doesn't even know how to bake a venison pasty."

"Ignorant sod," she responded, "probably knows no more about getting feathers off a bird than putting the handle to my broom."

She heard him coming, and now he stood in the doorway, menacingly.

"Just what do you mean by that . . . *vile* remark?"

"You should know," she said. "It's a Scottish expression. Learned it from you. You always talk like that. Besides, we mustn't quarrel now. The baby's asleep."

"Let the scurvy little whorecop go hang," he said.

Frances observed him coldly.

"And you, too," he added.

"I gather we shall both miss hanging if we remain on the premises," she said.

"With an ignorant sod?"

"With a whore? A cock-chafer?"

"Don't talk like that! And what did you mean . . ."

"What a churl," she said. "Trifle with his . . . manhood, and let the demons loose!"

"How would you know whether the handle was put to your broom well or ill?"

Oh, excellent! She smiled wryly. "How would any woman?"

"So," he said, "the 'nullity' was so much rubbish."

No response.

"Who was he?"

Nothing.

"Or were there several?"

She found his growing rage, which her silence but increased, most gratifying. This would work better than . . .

She felt the pain of the blow, it seemed, bare moments after the shock of surprise; then the back of his hand caught her on the other cheek. He was waiting for some response; hot tears coursed down her face, but she neither cried aloud nor uttered a word.

"You'll tell me," he said, and now his doubled fist crashed into her cheekbone.

Frances went back against the table. Her hand fell on the mixing spoon, which she brandished at him. He hit her with his fist again.

"So, I'm no man, is it?"

She brought the large wooden spoon down on Robin's head. He wrenched the spoon from her and threw it hard through the window glass next to the larder.

"Robin, stop it," Frances said, trying to duck the next blow, which landed on the side of her head. "Please!"

But now he was after her.

"Ram Alley whore!" he shouted.

He thrust his fingers in at the top of her chemise, and tore it away.

"Oh, no," she said.

"No man, is it?" he said, ripping the kirtle from her waist.

She tried pushing him away, but, holding her fast with one hand, he took the bottom of her shift and pulled upward, flailing until it came off in strips. He drew the leather belt from his Venetians; it stung as it lashed about her hip.

"No!" she cried.

"You'll tell me or add stripes!"

The belt left a cunning smart on the hips, buttocks, legs.

"You sod!" she cried, and the belt bit round her thighs. "I'll kill you!"

"You'll kill no one," he said. Dispensing with his belt, he fondled her breasts. "Stop your whimpering. I don't like it."

Gingerly, she made to push his hand away.

"Don't you dare," he said. "Don't you dare to do that! I'm your husband."

"But . . . you couldn't . . . now . . ."

"Yes," he said, "now."

While the baby screamed with mounting shrillness, Robin methodically doffed his clothes. It was obvious that the whipping had excited him. He took her hand, fair hurling her to the floor.

"Not here," she said, "please."

"Here," he said.

"But the floor's hard. My buttocks . . . the stripes . . . can't we use the bed?"

Too late: he was already inside her.

"No man, is it?" he mumbled, thrusting with blind fury, until (this

334

was the deepest humiliation of all!) she felt a twinge, a definite squirm on her part, an involuntary counterthrust.

"No man, is it?"

The seedy floor would leave slivers in her back, but Robin was astride her angrily, and the stripes on her legs and hips, the swelling on her cheeks melted together, and the single pain mixed with its opposite. Still, she resisted.

"Forman," she said. "Forman was the man."

Robin's thrusts only intensified, as if he had set the lash aside only to take up the rod—as if, having flailed away at her exterior, he would now give stripes to her inside.

"He was the first," she said more loudly.

Robin drummed at her with a persistence born of rage.

"And the best, no doubt," he said.

She should have kept her silence. Here was the best response to Robin's fist. Having told him, she had lessened her power to retaliate.

On and on he went until long after she had—reluctantly, and more than once—felt ecstasy.

"Yes," she said, for if rage were the fuel of this strange love-making, she would be the master of its duration. "He was a better lover."

"More passionate," Robin said between gasps.

"Yes," she said.

"And you loved him?"

"Yes," she wept. Oh, would it be like this forever? With hatred and love forever meanly fused? "I loved him, but not as I loved you, Robin. I used him. I killed for you."

He wasn't finished.

"I love you, Robin," she said.

Still more; the floor was working its way in slivers into her flesh.

"Robin! Won't you please stop?"

"Did you tell *him* to stop?"

"Oh, Robin," she moaned. "Must we . . . please stop. My back . . . the floor . . ."

"Was his floor so much better?"

"No."

Mercifully, the rhythm of his thrusts had slowed.

"May we stop?" she said.

Slowed, but with a rocking motion, nonetheless, he continued.

"At least go to the bed? I'm getting slivers."

"You are?"

Robin paused, leaned backward on his palms, and observed her with feigned concern.

"Even Forman's floor was better!" he said.

And returned to his love-making.

The floor. Her back. The stripes. She felt them all keenly now. If only he would finish; she longed for sleep.

At last, with a mindless, ugly, prolonged squeal, Robin rolled from the top of her.

They lay naked on the seedy timbers of the cottage floor.

About the Author

Born in Minneapolis, Minnesota, STANLEY STEWART moved with his family to California, where he worked his way through Los Angeles City College and UCLA as a produce clerk. While a student, he wrote and published several short stories, and saw two of his one-act plays produced by small companies, one at LACC. In 1961 he became an acting instructor at the University of California, Riverside, where he is at present a professor of English specializing in the seventeenth century. He taught briefly at Columbia University in New York City, and during the year 1971–72, as a recipient of a Senior Fellowship from the John Simon Guggenheim Foundation, he studied in England and on the Continent. He is married and has two sons, aged sixteen and eight.